Art of the Genre represents a huge shared world called *The Nameless Realms*, a place that spans thirteen extraordinary Ages of Man. Each category of fiction in this fantastic world has its own specialized medallion that is 'active' in the upper right corner of each book, thus allowing you to easily tell what specific genre you're purchasing. In the case of ***A Knight in the Silk Purse***, you're about to enter the 5th age of Man, and the shared anthology city of Taux, so the medallion you see above is the symbol for all books in that field.

A KNIGHT
IN THE
SILK PURSE

Edited by
SCOTT TAYLOR

Illustrated by
JEFF LAUBENSTEIN
JANET AULISIO
TODD LOCKWOOD

ART of the genre

Printed and bound in the United States of America 9 8 7 6 5 4 3 2 1

ISBN: 978-1-940528-18-2

This is a work of fiction. All characters, places and events portrayed in this publication are either fictitious or used fictitiously.

Editor: Scott Taylor
Cover: Todd Lockwood
Interior Illustrations: Jeff Laubenstein, Janet Aulisio, Todd Lockwood
Copy Editor Extreme: Art of the Genre Team
Map: Alyssa Faden
Graphic Design: Jeff Laubenstein
Book Design: John Woolley
Writing Instructor: J.R.R. Tolkien
Sounding Board: John O'Neill

Art of the Genre
217 Palos Verdes Blvd,
CA 90277

artofthegenre.myshopify.com

Ordering Information:
For details, contact the publisher at the address above.

As I stated in the first volume of this series, **Tales of the Emerald Serpent**, it seems odd and unfortunate for an editor to provide a dedication since so many talented people came together to make it, and yet it does fall to me.

Since that is the case, I'm going to dedicate this book to the authors who made it happen, especially those who stuck this out a second time around and are already on board for a third volume. So, to Mike, Juliet, Julie, Todd, Rob, Martha, and Lynn as well as our rookies Dave, Dan, Howard, and Elaine, this one goes out to you!

I'd also like to post a special dedication to our artists who made so much magic happen with these characters. To Janet Aulisio for always being ready to spring into action, to Todd Lockwood for his magical covers and interiors, and to Jeff Laubenstein for not only providing so many memorable interiors but for also designing all the graphics and cover design for our Art of the Genre projects.

Last, but certainly never least, to ALL our wonderful backers from the Kickstarter campaign who stuck with us even as delay after delay happened along our path. In the end, we did it, and that is all because of you!

Sincerely,
Scott Taylor
Art of the Genre

CONTENTS

FOREWORD

Recently, I reread my foreword from *Tales of the Emerald Serpent* and couldn't believe it was dated June 2012. As I currently write these words, the date stands at May 2014, with a probable June or July release date for *A Knight in the Silk Purse.*

It has been a long two years, one of which was spent almost exclusively piecing this volume together through both the art and the stories. What started as a cool concept with some roughly linked stories set in the same city in *Tales of the Emerald Serpent* evolved into a much deeper weave this time around.

The experience both myself as the editor, and the bulk of our writers, gained in *Tales* helped us find a way to work even closer together, base all our stories around a single event, and in turn share things I'm pretty sure have never been shared in the realm of fantasy anthologies. If that is the case, then all those involved in *A Knight in the Silk Purse* have done something unique to the industry as late as 2014, which in itself is a feat considering the tenure of fantasy literature in the West.

If our work has indeed been laid out correctly, then perhaps this book will gain the same positive response from fans as the first, and as creators that is all one can ask. So, without going into any further detail I would like to introduce you to the Second Volume of *Tales of the Emerald Serpent: A Knight in the Silk Purse.*

You now stand on the threshold of the Festival of a Thousand Blossoms, a week-long celebration in the cursed City of Taux. If you are brave enough, then turn the page and join the adventure and intrigue that awaits our twelve protagonists. I promise you won't be disappointed, and as always, long live the shared world anthology!

Scott Taylor
May 2014

ACKNOWLEDGEMENTS

T M Reed, Martin Beier, Chris McLaren, Steve Drew , Daetrin, Neil Ferrin, John Beattie, Vernon Ray Jackson, Jennifer Bailey, How-Hing Pau, Ryan Donahue, Kimberly M. Lowe, Keith Thomson, Violette Malan, James Corder, Dave Seeley, Hristijan Stojkovski, Risa, Laochailan Maghouin, Remy 'rule-of-three' Hoffmann, Maryann Cook, Simon Varley, Kent Rice, Ray Powell, Joshua Palmatier, Marcus James Adams, Chris Thompson, Paul van Oven, Scott Mullock, Kyle Pinches, Todd Lockwood, Ruth Stuart, Mikael Olofsson, Wolf, Michael Mock

Todd Alan Gamble, Conductor Bailey Baker, David Chamberlain, Marissa Barter-Waters, Rhel, Daniel Hessels, Wendy Elrick

Benjamin Widmer, Andrew Findlay, The Shadow of Canberra, Andy Ellis, Joshua Villines, Christoph Wolf, Sarah Gruetze, Ingrid Emilsson

Benjamin Bryant, John A. Aiken, Jr., Kristie Tousignant, Mr. Phillips, Nathan Morris, Jay Kominek.

THE INFAMOUS BLACK GATE DISTRICT

A L Y S S A   F A D E N

THE CITY OF TAUX

INTRODUCTION

THE FESTIVAL
OF A THOUSAND BLOSSOMS

During the late spring of every year, the city of Taux participates in a weeklong celebration revolving around rebirth and renewal. This is known as The Festival of a Thousand Blossoms and each one of its seven days is dedicated to a certain common practice by the population. The festival culminates with the crowning of the city's overall 'Queen of Blossoms', as each district elects their own Queen of Blossoms to represent them before the final choice is made for the city as a whole. The names of the days are as follows:

Day One: **LOVERS DAY:** Flowers are put out en mass throughout the city and deliveries are prevalent as lovers show their affection for mates both known and unknown.

Day Two: **DANCE OF SERPENTS:** This day culminates with each district having a large public dance in a common square or prevalent street where local blocks create a feathered serpent [think Chinese dragon dancers] and go about the throngs of revelers giving out feathers and flowers to those with the finest blossoms and masks.

Day Three: **NIGHT OF SECRETS:** The most entertaining night of the festival, it is the 'free night' when men and women alike slip away from their obligations and release their life-toil in all manner of illicit activity. Often, old grudges are also settled on this night and many unsanctioned duels take place. This is the night most citizens go masked. It culminates with a citywide party that runs till 2 AM, at the full height of the Blood Moon, when a mass of fireworks is then released in the Raised Market of the Black Gate.

Day Four: **DAY OF REFLECTION:** After the titanic social events of the previous day, the bulk of the city returns to its normal life and spends time with family and friends. This is the day of reflection and one known to heal many old wounds.

Day Five: **SAINTS DAY:** Huge celebrations take place around the city at the temples of the various Saints, and most marriages for the year take place on this day.

Day Six: **ELEMENTAL DAY:** This is a big day for the populous as it pits the elemental talents of each district's races in feats of power. This covers a wide range of abilities, from Eldaryn throwing fireballs into the harbor, to Kin wrestling, and even air-born Aspara minstrels becoming a one person band.

Day Seven: **THE EIGHT QUEENS:** Each District's choice of one young woman to represent them as the Queen of Flowers is taken before the Red Pillar Council. Once a decision on the overall city Queen is made, she rides her district's flower barge down the canals into the harbor and releases the flowers [which represent wishes] of all her people for the year to come into the bay.

A KNIGHT
IN THE
SILK PURSE

Illustration by Jeff Laubenstein

BLOODCOIN

Howard Tayler

Fourth Day: The Day of Reflection

The knock on the ancient door resonated with power, anger, fear, and murder. In that knock Jonthrel Collish could feel the essences required for the night's work.

"Come in, Master Vash," he said.

The door opened and Folotl Vash strode through, still wearing the costume and mask that had disguised him among the festival revelers on Ruby lane. The man pulled off his mask and looked about as if appraising the place.

"Tome Mage," he said with a nod. "You've claimed interesting quarters for yourself. Is there a reason you're living below your means?"

"Here in the Black Gate I'm off the usual thoroughfares, and the locals don't like the chills they get. It's perfect for my work."

"Well, I have gone to no small effort to procure the material you require. I trust you are ready?"

Such an interesting word, 'trust.' Jonthrel didn't trust this Vash any more than the rest of the clan, and Folotl Vash certainly wouldn't trust him more than was required of service.

"I am quite ready, Master Vash," Jonthrel said with a nod. "Show me the coins, please."

"Prepared per your instructions," said Folotl, frowning deeply as he withdrew a purse from his cloak.

"I'm sorry if you found the preparations distasteful, but you are, after all, asking me to kill a man."

"Yes, but only one man. I had to arrange three unfortunate endings and a burglary to prepare these. I realize that your time in the Black Gate might lead you to think that such things are so commonplace as to be easily accomplished, but it was a significant undertaking."

Jonthrel held up his hand. "Don't tell me about it. Not yet. That telling must wait until everything else is in place. Now, let's have a look at these coins."

The purse jingled again as it changed hands, and in that sound Jonthrel could hear the thick, wet overtones of bloodcoin, spent twice again for blood.

Yes, these had been properly prepared. This city, Taux, was positively dripping with essences that could be imbued into focus items. Miserable weather and politics aside, Jonthrel was thrilled to have brought his research here, and to have found a patron.

Even better, he had found a patron with whom he shared an enemy, even if Folotl Vash didn't know it.

Osment Two-Quills stoppered the eighth and final ink-pot on his writing table. Few appreciated the range of inks his work required. He did not just smith words. He painted them. Blue-black inks had a stark look suitable for public proclamations. Ruddy browns supplied the subtlety required for epistles to distant dignitaries. And certain secret edicts had a slightly crimson irridescence to them, though not so obviously scarlet as to paint death between the glistening black-red lines.

The variety of inks paled in comparison to the huge range of parchments. Every sheet was unique in texture, color, absorption, sheen, and shape, and Osment insisted on doing the final trimming himself, a keen knife always close at hand.

But for all the art that went into the selection of his materials, it was the words traced thereon that made his services so valuable. A mere scribe could never hope to rise to true fame, but Osment Two-Quills enjoyed a blend of renown and obscurity unique to those whose skills were currency in the halls of power. From Zimbolay his prose had secured a throne, ended one war, and started at least two others. And now he was an ocean away, plying his trade for the Dharn Household, rivals to the powerful Vash here in Taux. He was living at least as richly as he had in his former employ, and far more safely. The Dharn had long been loyal friends, and Timar, the new head of the Dharn clan, had granted Osment quarters within Dharn's walls, a bit of additional distance between him and the enemies he'd left on the far side of the Shining Sea.

Loyalty…Timar Dharn's wife had taken to handling business during the man's frequent absences, and her addenda to her husband's notes often ran counter the Dharn's plans, plans Osment was party to. At first this had looked like well-meaning ignorance, but Osment knew words well enough to read what lay between them, especially when the writer was a rank amateur. So Osment loyally returned Timar Dharn's intent to any decree or correspondence that passed under his quill, and was likely making an enemy of the woman.

So be it. He'd seen quite a sampling of the writs that moved back and forth here in Taux. He didn't know who wrote for the Vash, or to whom the various guilds went for these sorts of services, but Taux's native scribes were ham-fisted tradesmen with no sense for the deeper subtleties of this art. Osment Two-Quills was a lion among kittens. The Dharn clan might be struggling, with enemies at all sides, but the right words, smithed and honed with exactness, were both weapon and shield.

Jonthrel Collish reached into the bag and stirred the silver coatls within, concentrating on the essences emanating from them. He felt the amulet at his breast warm, a sensation that spread to his fingers. His weak affinity to fire afforded him no command over metals, but fire-forged or poured metals still spoke, and with the amulet's help he could hear all that they said.

These coins said people had died. People who had handled them. People who had accepted them, exchanged them, stolen them as a price for spilt blood. Jonthrel heard no words, but the signs were there in his mind's eye, echoes across the Afterglow Sea. This was bloodcoin, fresh and powerful.

"Most people look at them to count them," said Folotl.

"It isn't about the counting."

Folotl stepped back. "Do you have what you need?"

"Oh, my, yes." Jonthrel emptied the bag onto a gouged and pitted table. He spread them out, with both hands, splaying his fingers across the coins and the table both. The table's own essences were beyond his sensing, just out of reach, but some focus items could be identified through more mundane means.

"That," said Folotl, "looks more like an old butcher's block than proper furniture."

"Very astute, Master Vash. That is precisely what it is, and that is precisely why I'm using it." He began arranging the coins in a circle. "Just as these coins have acquired essences and echoes, becoming focus items, this table has acquired a measure of power that, to one with the right skills, can be tapped."

"True Wizards don't require these sorts of trappings."

"And true Wizards don't deign to offer you their services. Tome magic is all you have access to, and even that is limited and unpredictable. You depend on focus items you cannot create, and whose effects change depending upon whose hands they are in." Jonthrel continued to arrange the silver coatls on the table. "This need not be the case. Especially not here."

"Well, I'll leave you to it then."

"No." Jonthrel looked up from the table. "The story from your lips is as much a part of this as the bloodcoin itself."

Folotl Vash's eyes widened only slightly, but Jonthrel saw the clan heir's fear as clearly as if the young noble unhooded a lantern.

"Don't worry, Master Vash. Your role here is simple. When this coin circle is complete, you'll tell me how you came by the money. I shall manage the rest." Jonthrel continued laying the coins edge-to-edge, forming a circle on the table.

"This would have been much simpler if I could have simply paid you."

"You're not paying me. You're providing me with powerful foci, and one of those foci is the story you must tell."

"Your death-magic requires blood-money and sordid tales?"

"The echoes of death emanate from coin spent thrice for blood. Those echoes, given story by the lips of the one who spent them, will enable me to beckon a shade to us, and then imbue it with the attributes we require."

"When first we spoke, you gave me the impression that this was a bit more straightforward."

"Loosing an arrow from a bow is straightforward, Master Vash. And yet prior to that release there was the shaping and curing of wood, the stretching, drying, and twisting of gut, the forging of an arrowhead. More than that. I don't know. I'm no archer, but I've seen enough to know that the preparations are quite complex. Beckoning and shaping a shade, milling it from the sundered essences of the ghosts of Taux, and sending it to complete a task is, by comparison, very straightforward."

Folotl Vash sighed in exasperation.

"Straightforward would be having a Kin Sire hurl an anvil into the air over Osment Two-Quills' bed and simply end him."

"You are here because getting a Kin Sire or anybody else into the Dharn compound is far less straightforward than entreating with me. This," he held up a coin before laying it down to complete the circle he'd laid, "will prove to be simpler and safer than the alternatives."

The coins now defined a perfect circle in forty-nine points, seven-sevens spent for blood. Jonthrel unwrapped a small cloth bundle from which a scrap of parchment fluttered to the table. With the cloth wrapped about his hand he slid the parchment to the center of the circle.

It never so much as brushed his skin.

"Two-Quills got his name because he was so prolific everyone assumed he held a quill in each hand and wrote with both simultaneously. Did you know that?" Jonthrel asked.

"I had heard that, yes."

He laid a fiftieth coin atop the scrap, again taking care not to touch the parchment itself. He lit a small candle and dribbled some wax across the coin, the scrap, and the table, then stuck the candle to the table in the puddle of wax.

The flame reddened, and unnaturally black smoke flowed into the air above it. Whatever dark magic had undone the Tolimic Empire here in Taux centuries before, it had left the city positively rich with essences that could be beckoned, bent, and shaped. So rich they could be seen in a candle flame.

"Well, he only writes with a single quill, just like any other scribe, but I have heard that he uses an entire calf's worth of parchment in less than a week. I had little trouble acquiring a piece of material written and trimmed under his hand. There is identity in such a thing. There is substance."

It would not do to explain to Folotl Vash that this scrap of parchment came from Zimbolay, carried here by Jonthrel himself in the angry hope of laying it on just such a table. He had taken great care to never touch the scrap, and to keep it wrapped in a bit of cloth freshly woven and newly purchased, lest he accidentally imbue within it a shadow of himself.

He waved a hand through the black smoke, and his amulet felt like ice against his chest. Oh, yes, there was a shade here, with power like he'd only rarely felt, and never with only three points of focus. Poor Taux, what lies under you?

The smoke began to wind itself about his wrist.

"Gods and jaguars, that looks just like a snake," Folotl exclaimed.

Jonthrel mouthed "Osment" so softly he couldn't hear his own voice, then leaned forward and with the same breath blew the smoke from his wrist. The deep, red flame guttered, and the shade-tainted smoke twisted and writhed, as if momentarily uncertain. Jonthrel held his breath.

The smoke spun about itself, twisting and fattening as the flame waned to little more than a spark, nothing like smoke now. It was a long, thick, undulating cable of darkness.

The candle flared up again, and with the faintest of whispers the beckoned shade shot under the door, thinning as if stretching. Jonthrel reached out and carefully passed his hand through the blackness as it flowed from the candle and raced out into the night. It knew where it was going.

Jonthrel exhaled.

"The shade we have beckoned now knows Osment Two Quills of Zimbolay, Escril Prime to Timar Dharn, and reaches out to call upon him."

Osment Two-Quills sorted and stacked the inscribed parchments on the large table before him. It had taken eight men to haul the table into these chambers, and they had complained that the great block of oak still had them outnumbered. He had never owned a steadier writing surface, and its expanse was perfect for reviewing the day's writing.

The festival revelry outside was less than perfect, even heard from behind the Dharn clan's walls. Osment had been able to ignore most of the noise, but on two occasions a shriek of glee had sounded enough like a scream that he tensed up, and had to spend precious work time forcing himself to relax again.

"Steward," he called.

"Master Scribe?" The aged steward arrived at Osment's door immediately. He looked dour. Ah. Osment had worked quite a bit later than usual. But leaving anything unfinished would only invite Timar's curiously meddlesome wife to try her hand at things.

Osment held up the stack of correspondence.

"Timar may wish to review these, but it would not be appropriate for anyone else to." He slid the stack into a satchel, then fastened the clasp and sealed it with a drop of wax and his ring. "Should he remain occupied with his work in the Black Gate, see to their delivery personally."

"At your bidding, Master Scribe," the steward said, and with a nod and a look of determination he strode from the room, pulling the door closed on his way out.

The old man was loyal to Timar, and quite literate. Osment was sure the steward appreciated the power of the scribe's words, and knew they were used only in Timar's service.

Such service, though. Timar Dharn had not been raised to control the clan, and had learned the healing arts rather than any measure of oratory. Getting a proper speech from the man was beyond difficult. Scripted by Osment Two-Quills, however, Timar's announcements and public addresses were passable, and were improving. Breaches were already being healed, though Osment had to admit this clan would heal significantly faster if Timar spent less time tending to the sick in the Black Gate.

Osment looked across the chambers to his bed. It had gotten quite late indeed, and the broad, empty bed looked quite inviting. His beds had not always been empty, but passion and circumstance had long ago brought him here with no regrets. Language was ever his lover, held far closer to his bosom than any woman. His bed might be empty, but the darkness would fill with tumbling words, consonance conspiring with assonance and alliteration as Osment's subconscious began drafting for the morrow.

Osment lifted the lamp from his desk and carried it to his bedside. The shadows shifted as the light moved through the room, their familiar shapes—

Not familiar.

Osment stared at a pool of darkness on the far side of his bed. The bed's shadow had crept predictably as Osment and the lamp approached, but the darkness in that corner remained un-illumined.

"Hello?" Osment held the lamp before him, as if to banish the errant shade. It only made everything harder to see, so he swung the lamp to the left.

All the shadows in the room swung to the right with the moving lamp. The blackness in that corner seemed only to swell, refusing entry to the light of the lamp. It grew, like ink poured from a tipped bottle. And yes, a writhing ribbon of deep, unnatural shadow was flowing through the slit window, entering like no mortal assassin could ever hope to.

"Mange of the Old gods," Osment whispered, staring in a mixture of terror and fury. "Jonthrel has found me."

Jonthrel felt his amulet grow heavy against his chest.

"The story, Master Vash. Like one of those formal decrees."

Folotl Vash cleared his throat and began speaking in a rich baritone.

"I gave fifty silver coatls to a whore, sweet Melyne, to slit a liar's throat as he lay with her in a rented bed."

Perfect. These noble types were practically bred for this kind of magic.

"Perfidy drawn by lust falls to treachery. Lo, there is blood" said Jonthrel. The candle's flame flared, and he felt power flowing through Folotl into the circle. He swept his hands above the circle of coins, shaping that power, directing it, and guiding it into the stream of shadow that flowed from the candle.

"I sent a thug to throttle the whore, on the promise that he could keep the fifty coatls I knew she had."

"Greed straddles treachery. Lo, there is blood." Another flare. More essence flowed. More strength to the shade.

"I gave the fifty coatls to the assassin Ilwib Em'eral, and he poisoned the thug with a concoction from the swamp."

"Greed perishes by degrees at the hand of cold apathy. Lo, there is blood." Still, the essences of murder flowed off of Folotl Vash.

Jonthrel puzzled over this for a moment.

"How did you retrieve the bloodcoin from the assassin?"

"I contracted a burglar through the Madame of the Silk Purse to swap the coin for an identical amount. Angering Ilwib Em'eral seemed both unnecessary and unwise."

Jonthrel nodded and gestured again over the circle, clutching his amulet with the other hand. The candle flared again and went out. The tail of that long tendril of essence, imbued with full and final purpose, slipped away under the door.

Osment backed away from the growing shade, which had taken the form of a giant, coiled serpent. He opened his mouth to call for the steward, for the guards, and in that moment the snake struck.

In panic, Osment cast the lantern as he threw his arm up in defense. The lantern passed through the coils, and before it struck the floor the dark serpent's jaws clamped shut on Osment's left arm. The pain of the hundreds of hooked teeth barely registered before the rest of the black beast piled into Osment and knocked him back against his writing table. The massive furnishing shivered from the impact but did not move.

"Help!" Osment cried weakly, gasping in pain. He reached back onto the table and grabbed the small trimming knife with his right hand. In maddened desperation he stabbed at the shade's very snake-like head.

The knife passed through it without slowing, and then stuck meatily in Osment's left forearm.

"With bloodcoin and a proper telling as foci, with a butcher's block as an impetus, and that parchment as a guide, you and I have beckoned, directed, and empowered a shade insubstantial to all but two classes of matter. The first class is the very person of Osment Two-Quills."

"And what's the other?"

"With action comes reaction. Light must cast shadow. Power only comes fraught with weakness. The more singular the power we desire, the more discrete, the more singular the weakness must be. The bloodcoin you've so painstakingly provided renders our shade tangible to any blooded weapon. Just as the promised exchange of those silver coatls ended lives, no weapon that has not taken life can touch the beckoned shade. Asleep in his rooms, Osment Two-Quills will not have a Dharn swordsman at his side. No such weapon will be available."

"This tome magic of yours, these shades," said Folotl. "They wouldn't work too well against a barracks full of soldiers."

Jonthrel considered for just a moment what patronage by the Vash might entail should the current endeavor succeed. A chill ran down his spine.

"If you were paying me to kill a barracks full of soldiers, we would shape the shades differently." He knitted his brows, delighting in the puzzle for a moment. "A shield or sword thrice deserted in battle, perhaps. Or maybe coatls never spent on anything but drink and whoring." He grasped his amulet, and wondered how such items might reveal their natures, their stories. The Afterglow seemed to ripple with the essences trapped here in Taux, so finding focus items shouldn't be—

The Afterglow was rippling. Power still flowed where it shouldn't. Another chill ran down his spine, and Jonthrel felt a sick feeling in his chest that had nothing to do with the amulet he wore.

A sliver of shade, just the tiniest tendril of essence stretched between the circle of bloodcoin and Folotl Vash.

Osment screamed. He released the knife and attempted to pry the serpent's jaws open. His hand found purchase, but he lacked the strength to have any effect at all.

The snake's tail came up and around as the monster sought to coil itself around its prey. It whipped right through the table, the parchments, and the pots without upsetting any of them. It wrapped around Osment once, and then shot cleanly through the table again, further to Osment's left.

It struck his quill, knocking it across the room. The quill-stand remained untouched. The desk, parchments, and inkpots all stood undisturbed.

The quill bounced and skittered, stopping on the floor just a pace away.

Jonthrel clutched his amulet and stared at the second tendril. Their beckoned shade was still somehow connected to Folotl Vash. Faintly, tenuously, to be sure, but any connection could be dangerous.

"Quickly, Master Vash. Did you keep any of the bloodcoin for yourself?"

"Don't be absurd. I have coffers of gold jaguars, and thus no need for a few—"

"Then why..." Jonthrel closed his eyes and concentrated. There had been something missing from the story.

"Why what?"

Jonthrel opened one eye. "Vash, how did you pay Em'eral, the assassin? Did you have him rob his mark, the thug?"

"No. That would have been—"

"But you paid him with the bloodcoin the thug possessed?"

"Yes, is something wrong?"

"I don't know. How did you get the money from the thug?"

"Oh. I slipped that from him myself." Folotl grinned and winked. "I trained as a scout, you know. Have to keep those skills honed should the—"

"Pride robs greed. Lo—" Jonthrel stopped. Lo, there wasn't any blood in that exchange. Not yet.

Osment wondered how something made of shadow could possibly be so heavy.

The weight of the shade began to pull him down as a third coil wrapped itself around his upper body. He staggered forward and toppled within reach of his quill, the only thing in this room besides his person that seemed to be tangible to this beckoned monster.

He had no free hands with which to reach it. His left arm was clamped tight, burning with pain and bloodied from the snake's mouth full of hooked teeth – insult atop the injury he'd done to himself with the knife. His right arm was now pressed tightly to his side by the snake's coils.

Coils which, when Osment lay atop them, passed cleanly through the stone floor.

He struggled and rolled as best he could, his vision blackening as he gasped for breath. With a shove of his tattered left arm, he pushed the beckoned serpent's head onto the quill.

The quill lay flat on the stone floor, but the serpent's head knew no floor. To the beckoned shade, Osment's quill was an immobile object surrounded by empty space, and the quill had a keen brass edge – an edge which had laid ink claiming dozens, perhaps hundreds of lives. An ancient, hereditary assassin's blade could not have had more power of blood behind it than the tip of this scribe's writing instrument.

Jonthrel felt it coming, racing into the Black Gate from the Dharn compound, newly shaped. He leaped away from the young noble and watched as the fat tendril of beckoned essence snapped into the room, whipped once around the circle of coins, shot along the smaller tendril, and then plunged into Folotl's head. For the briefest moment it took on the appearance of a fine quill.

Folotl Vash gasped and stared at Jonthrel. Horror, fury, fear, and betrayal all played across his face.

"You..." he squeaked, his rich baritone gone. He dropped to his knees, and then slumped sideways to the floor. His skin was as grey as if he'd been dead for days instead of seconds.

Jonthrel knew beckoning had risks, but an assymetrical telling shouldn't provide a broad enough channel for the backlash to kill. Unless…unless the writing away of lives, the edicts for which Osment Two-Quills deserved death…if that had all been done with the same writing instrument, then the scribe may have created a powerful focus of his own.

Jonthrel grabbed his cloak and his purse, and then swept the contents of his cupboard into a satchel. He eyed the table with regret. He could ill afford to carry coin brushed by a shade shaped by the quill of his enemy. Wrapping his arm in his cloak, he swept the circle of bloodcoin onto the floor, where they jangled alongside the graying corpse of Folotl Vash. In the fading tolls of each coin, Jonthrel could hear power, anger, fear…and retribution. He now had enemies among both the Dharn and the Vash, and it was probably too much to hope that they'd remain preoccupied with each other forever.

Illustration by Janet Aulisio

THE BEAUTY OF ESSENCE

By Scott Taylor

Sixth Day: Elemental Day

The room, cast in the warm glow of braziers, lined in multi-colored silk curtains, and hung with lewd paintings, was more a prison cell than hall of high priced whores this tepid night. Savino, seated and watched from behind by a few undisclosed men, played a game of falling water as he spun a honey-gold coin down his knuckles and then back up again.

Across from him, his inquisitor stood. She was straight-backed and angular, with the cut of well-used muscles in her arms and shoulders limed in the amber light of the smoldering coals.

Ten minutes—he'd counted every second—had passed as she waited. Finally, still not looking at him, she hissed a sigh before she began.

"Do you believe in love?" Lady Evynhoe asked.

The question was so unexpected that Savino actually paused, something his practiced demeanor almost never did when being interrogated, which occurred far too often.

"Excuse me?" he replied.

Lady Evynhoe turned from where she'd been admiring a watercolor of rapacious debauchery, the ruby-tinted brown of her eyes in heavy contrast to her burnished platinum hair.

"I asked if you believed in love," she repeated.

Savino found his center and smiled, his eyes warming. "You know, I'd have to say I didn't." He paused before providing a wink. "Until very recently."

There was a lengthy pause between them before Evynhoe looked back at the watercolor. "You know what the first lesson my instructors at the abbey taught me?"

He shook his head, the smile fading. "I can't imagine."

"That in every lie, there is surely a seed of truth," she replied.

He shifted in his cushioned seat, his knuckles still flipping the coin as he watched her reach out and run her fingers along a curtain of azure silk that hid leering faces carved into the walls of the luxuriant chamber.

"You play at innuendo and flattery, but beneath the surface love must have indeed found you in the past few days," she continued.

He shrugged, a single chuff of a laugh escaping his lips before asking, "So you've had me summoned to the Silk Purse to ask about issues of the heart, because I assure you more than one man has lost his within these enchanting walls, and I doubt that is a crime."

She nodded, turning again to show him her full form. Without doubt, she could have made a handsome profit among the ladies of the Purse with her body, even if cold and austere. She was tall, slender, and the pale skin of her northern birth was decorated with freckles along her cheeks and across her nose that provided her with a bit of youth some men found irresistible.

Her attire was no less endearing as it was both prudent and revealing. She wore a simple ermine smock of filmy fabric cut low along the neck, and sleeveless because of the city heat, allowing a man's eye to wander to the frosted curves of her small breasts. In contrast, a set of tan breeches could be seen beneath the over-dress, with polished brown boots heavily scuffed along the toes from travel and swordplay. Around her neck a platinum and polished steel necklace of blades lay flush against her skin, a dangerous sign of her devotion to St. Siegfried.

"Actually, I've asked you here because your name has been mentioned by others who have sat in that chair tonight," she said.

"What can I say, I'm a popular fellow."

"And dangerous with a sword, if stories can be believed."

"Well." He smiled. "Even if such tales were lies, there would still be some truth in them, no?"

For the first time since he'd sat down her placid demeanor broke slightly, a hint of a smile turning in the corner of her mouth.

"Indeed…"

"And speaking of blades, I've heard tales that say that necklace you wear cannot hurt you, nor any edged weapon as long as your devotion to your Saint is without reproach," he said.

Nodding, she ran her finger over the razor's edge of one of the upturned blades, the finger coming away without a blemish.

"My calling has its perks," she replied.

"And failings in my minds eye, as the love which you spoke before cannot be had by you without betraying your Saint and thereby losing your invulnerability."

"I suppose, if you consider absolute love and devotion to a Saint a failing."

Smiling, he replied, "That isn't love."

"And you are an expert now? A man who has so recently found love?"

He shrugged and she took a seat, pushed several pieces of yellowed parchment around on a table normally reserved for dancing, and then sighed.

"Whatever the case, I would like to know, if you would avail me, what transpired on the leeward Ullamalitzli court three nights prior?" she asked.

Savino shrugged. "On the Night of Secrets? I can honestly say I have no idea."

Looking up, she nodded before continuing, "I see, and if you weren't at the leeward court that evening, then may I ask your whereabouts, exactly?"

The Emerald Serpent was bursting to the point even the rails of the three terraces were not without a hand, hip, or posterior. Inside, patrons waded through a sea of filled tables, and a dozen barmaids glistened with sweat and dispensed spirits in what appeared to be a never ending mission to drain the bar of all alcohol.

Savino had staked a claim to a wall abutted by a timber support, both his back and right shoulder shielded while his rapier hung free across his left hip. He held no drink and kept his chin lowered and hat drawn down over his forehead as he watched the crowd.

Jarasa, a barmaid so swollen with child she could barely make it through the patrons, smiled on her way past and he gave her a curt nod. He'd been with her months ago, before the child had soured her body, and yet she'd kept smiling at him whenever he was in the bar until he was uncomfortable even seeing her. If she'd just have the overdue baby, perhaps he'd lay with her again to stop her overly obsessive smiles.

After she'd passed from his view, he hissed under his breath, "Where are you, Torrent?"

Below him, a bloom of heat washed over his legs and his already tight lips turned quickly into a frown.

"I don't think she's coming," the distinctly happy voice of Lareo said.

Looking down, Savino laid eyes on the Eldaryn merchant, the little fire-born's copper hair topped with golden wisps and his platinum-rimmed spectacles etched with intricate runes around the edges of their blue lenses. He was paler than usual, however, a tinge of grey set beneath his eyes.

"And how would you know that?" Savino asked.

Lareo smiled, and sweat broke out on Savino's brow from the bloom of heat it caused.

"There is a plot moving in Taux this night, and I think water is stalking her," Lareo replied.

Savino let out a curse before looking back at the crowd. All those who dealt with Lareo understood if he played at riddles it was because he knew something, not because he liked games.

"I'm guessing you needed her for the Vash job," Lareo continued.

Again, a curse came to Savino's lips. "Damn the Saints, Lareo, is there nothing that goes on beyond the Black Gate that you don't have a finger in?"

"Certainly, as water-born Wizards are beyond my reach or wont, but as to the darker side of dealings, I am the foremost expert in most cases. Still, I have to wonder, after what happened on the bridge between you and Yoatl, I'd have thought that the Vash family would have had its fill of you."

Savino shrugged. "I have several outstanding debts, and this job was a brokered deal through Mama Serene, I assume because she'd like to keep Shay out of it."

"And if you took the job, then not only is there profit, but perhaps you wipe some of the tab off the books at the Silk Purse as well," Lareo added.

"You know me too well," Savino replied.

Lareo wrinkled his button nose and adjusted his spectacles. "True, but with a face as fine as yours, I still don't understand why the Purse would be necessary. You can have any woman you wish, and seemingly have."

Savino looked back out at the crowd. "My friend, I don't pay women to sleep with me, I pay them to go away afterwards." Jarasa passed him again and he added, "And to avoid smiles."

Heat bloomed again as Lareo let out the restrained hiss of a laugh and Savino couldn't help but smile.

"You know something, because I like you, I'm going to up the principle on your job," Lareo said.

Savino's eyebrows furrowed. "What does that mean?"

"It means that I know Vash wants a burglary for some illicit coins, but I think there is something else of value that can be had while there," Lareo answered.

Sucking his teeth, Savino looked about the room once more, saw no wandering eyes, and then leaned down until his face trickled with sweat in such close proximity to Lareo's bushy mustache.

"Exchanging money with an assassin is one thing, but outright theft from one is another entirely," he whispered.

"True, but I know you dread pulling off the caper without another set of hands, eyes, magic, or all three, so I can provide those as well as a purse so heavy you can pay off all your debts."

"I'll take debts instead of an assassin's blade, for surely that would be my end once word leaked, and it always does," Savino said.

"So be it, Savino Emantra, but failing to deliver on a contract with Folotl Vash will turn more blades to your back than that of a single assassin, who may or may not ever know who did the deed, because I will be the one to discreetly fence the item in question."

Lareo turned to go, but Savino reached out and caught him, a grimace on his face as he turned the Eldaryn around.

"By St. Erik's thousandth face, Lareo, I see why you are the richest Eldaryn in Taux."

From the tips of his copper mustache to the curls of his upturned eyebrows, Lareo quivered in only half-reserved glee.

"Then you will do it?"

Savino sighed. "Do I really have a choice?"

On the canal, under the light of the Ghost Moon, Savino smelled the earth before he saw the cause. It was oppressive, clinging, and left a layer of paste on his wind-born tongue.

"Lareo, you're going to pay for this…" he whispered.

From the shadows, a figure as tall as he, well-muscled and dark beneath a hooded jerkin, appeared. The set of the hips and the slender hands marked the Jai-Ruk as a female, but it was the thrice-buckled knee-high boots that put a name in his mind.

"Kryranen," he said.

"Savino," a voice a touch deeper than his own but still somehow sanguine, replied.

"Lareo said he'd find someone capable of working as a second story man, but it's well known you only have skills made for the tunnels below the streets," he said.

Beneath the hood, the subtle taper of a chin caught the moonlight as a smile revealed larger than Human canines, something many liked to call tusks, although not to the face of any Ruk.

"I'm capable of work both above and below ground," she replied.

He summoned wind about him, the essence blowing away the stench of her earth in practiced ease. It was a skill he'd learned long ago in his dealing with Dethocrates, and he wondered where the thick-headed rogue was this past week.

"And where is your smaller half?" he asked.

"He had other business, and pot hunting hasn't been good these past months so one must do what is required to keep in coin."

He nodded, looked back up and down the canal, and then pushed off from the wall.

"Well, if I were you, Kry, I'd find him and get a share of whatever mission he's on, because tonight is beyond your scope," he said over his shoulder.

Before he'd taken three steps a hand closed on his arm, fingers strong as iron rods as they turned him around. The earth pervaded the air, but he kept it in check as Kryranen drew close enough that he could see beneath the shadows of her hood to the smooth sandstone-colored skin beneath.

She was no beauty, that word precluded from the souls of her race, but still held well-defined cheekbones, stout jaw, overly full lips, and hair so dark and thick it was like oil dripping from her scalp. Yet her eyes held him, their dark irises like motes of midnight amid the shadows of the hood.

"I need this job," she hissed.

It wasn't a plea; he could hear that in the tone, more simply a devout pragmatism in what was indisputable truth.

"You'll only slow me down, as this is a high acquisition for men beyond your skill," he said.

"Gild the task of thief all you like, Savino, but I need this job," she repeated.

He looked down at his arm, the fingers there acting like a smith's vice, and finally sighed. "We're to make a climb, and for that you'll have to lose those damanable boots."

She didn't smile, but simply released him and nodded. Together, they moved from beneath the towering walls of the northern rim of the Black Gate, whispering voices trailing them from the stone.

The tower was a minaret, stretching seventy feet to the top of its tarnished brass dome that blazed like an open wound in the light of the rising Blood Moon. The structure held a large square base, slightly diminishing for four stories, each set with a single slit window on all sides, before a balcony wrapped it giving access to two more circular levels at the top.

It was the home of Ilwib Em'eral, a trade broker from Zimbolay by day, and if stories at the Emerald Serpent could be believed, a practiced murderer by night. From across the empty street, the tower looked like a Kin obelisk amid the lower structures and walls.

"You have noted that the Tower of Em'eral has no door, yes?" Kryranen asked.

"Which is why I said you wouldn't need boots," Savino replied.

She struck him in the shoulder, the blow making him hiss before he turned to her with eyebrows pinched.

She shook her head, saying, "I'm not a fool, Savino, I understand what climbing means. I'm simply stating that if there is no door, then how does Em'eral enter his own abode?"

Savino rubbed his shoulder. "He is an Aspara, his race blessed with the immorality of being the highest air-born, which also gives power to the rumor of their ability to become both intangible and fly."

Kryranen looked up at the dark balcony as he continued, "Being of the low air myself, I have some understanding of these elemental gifts and find such tales exaggerated, but there are certainly points to be made for how air talents could assist in jobs where victims thought themselves safe and secure behind high walls."

"So you believe the stories that Em'eral has a night job?" she asked.

"I'd not really considered them until this particular task was placed before me, but now I'm starting to be convinced."

She looked at him, saying, "So we climb, but then what happens if we find him home?"

"He won't be. Mama Serene assured me that he'd be entertained at a private party on the third terrace of the Silk Purse tonight in honor of the Night of Secrets."

"Serene?" she scoffed.

"Just because no one wishes to share your bed on the Night of Secrets doesn't mean others should be so unlucky. Besides, I have a high regard for Serene's skill."

"Oh, of that I have no doubt," she replied.

He turned to her and frowned, "Which, I wonder, is more unseemly, spending a night with a fine courtesan or sharing a bed with a rogue Kin-sire?"

Kryranen's blow missed him by a hair's breadth, only his practiced reflexes and a burst of air allowing that. Next came the blade, the thick and short stabbing sword flashing crimson in the moonlight.

"There will be no coin if you kill me!" Savino hissed, the words rising higher in the night than he'd wished.

Somewhere down the street a gang of roving revelers stumbled beneath the light of a burned down lamp, their masks askew and bodies wreathed in golden lilies.

Kryranen hesitated, the blade twitching in her hand before she lowered it, saying, "It seems you are as lucky as they say, Savino, and to be forced to work with you makes me as ill-fated as the rogue Andril the Black Cat."

He smiled, but quickly lost his mirth as the blade came up again and he raised his hands. The procession had begun to move toward them, and both rogues slipped into the deep shadow until they were past. When the last of them drifted out of view, Kryranen turned back toward the tower.

"Let's be done with this so I can find a bath to clean your slithering air and filthy words off me," she said.

"Jai-Ruk's bathe?" he asked.

She eyed him a long moment, a smile playing on the edge of his lips once more, but she shook her head and snapped the blade home in its sheath with a sigh.

"You will die a lonely death," she finished.

He shrugged, edged to a shadowed wall and then slipped across the street. Behind, sounding like a lumbering giant, Kryranen followed. When he reached the base of the minaret he pressed his back against it, whispers slithering into his ears from the stone.

"The tower speaks more than most," Kryranen said when she reached him.

"Take off those damn boots," he replied.

She did so, and he slipped out of his shoes, his night-garb a far cry from his ever-present duelist attire, even his renowned sword replaced by a coal-dusted dirk.

"How well do you climb?" he asked.

"Better than you," she replied.

He laughed, "Is that right?"

Without reply, she jumped two feet in the air and managed to catch a piece of stone that was far too smooth a handhold for even a practiced burglar's hand. Feet splayed, she began climbing, her hands seemingly adhering to the surface.

"Well I'll be..." He shook his head before starting after her.

Each handhold was a precarious maneuver, his air keeping him up on more than one occasion and by the time he'd reached twenty feet Kryranen had disappeared over the lip of the balcony. Moments later, as half a dozen curses slipped his lips, a length of silk rope fell down beside him and he begrudgingly took it.

When he reached the top, Kryranen regarded him placidly, and then waved a hand at the arched opening to the room beyond in a mock invite. Nodding, he moved past her, his hands running up over the sable wood frame before he drew back his hand and pushed air from his palm. The subtle gust pushed back the heavy velvet curtain that served as a door and provided a glimpse of the room beyond.

It was an unassuming chamber, with frescoed walls, a large square rug, and a writing desk set against the curve of a stairwell at the far side of the entry. It was in a perfect position for the person using it to always face the door.

As the curtain fell back into place, Savino turned to Kryranen, asking, "How are you with traps?"

"Not as good as Jelith, but I've been trained."

"If I were an Aspara, I'd trap the floor just inside the entry because I could use my air to glide across it. Can you have a look?" he asked.

She nodded and moved to the curtain, slowly drawing it back so she could get a clear view of the floor in the bloody light of the moon. For a moment she sat there, finally running her hand along the stone as she closed her eyes.

"It is a trap door, ten feet across and five feet wide to either side of the entry," she said.

Savino nodded. "Too far for a stationary leap, and there is not enough running room to the balcony lip for a running start. Well played."

She turned back to him and drew off her hood. Oiled hair spilled down well past her shoulders and she deftly tied it into a knot atop her skull before taking three quick jumps into the air as she stretched.

"Give me your rope," Savino said.

Her eyes narrowed, "Why?"

"Because you can't make that leap, no matter how you try to impress me, and I can. Once inside, I'll go up the stairs to the sleeping chamber above and lower the rope for you to enter there."

He watched as she looked at the polished tile of the round upper levels, no handhold showing at all in the flawlessly placed mortar.

"Fine," she said.

"Good, now draw back the curtain so I have a clear path."

Tossing him the silk rope, she did as she was instructed, and he backed his way against the rail. After three short breaths he ran forward, air coalescing around him and manifesting most heavily on his feet. As he hit the door's threshold he focused his elemental essence downward and slid across the floor like he was skating.

He couldn't maintain the effect long, but it was enough, his feet finally coming to rest on the carpet at the center of the chamber as quiet as a cat's leap. Turning back, he smiled at Kryranen, gave a slight bow, and then bounded quickly up the stair.

The chamber above was smaller, no more than twenty feet across, but more richly decorated. Shelves stacked with scrolls adorned the curving wall behind him, and a large bed hung suspended from four brass chains across from the stair. Beside it was a dark wood rack of cloaks and other clothing, shoes lined perfectly beneath. Rich carpet spread like dark wine across the floor, and the walls were decorated with hangings that covered ceramic mosaics of high mountains and blowing clouds all the way to the vaulted ceiling.

He moved onto the carpet, took one look toward the single window, and then slipped to the far side of the bed where a chest sat with iron fastenings and a saffron-tinged drape of silk lying folded and pristine across the top.

"Savino!" a sheltered call slithered up through the window.

Huffing a sigh, he withdrew around the bed, his gaze drawn to the black velvet cover that lay atop it, a thousand diamond shards twinkling in the endless depths of its inky surface.

"Yes, yes, Lareo, and now I see why you also wanted the assassin's bedclothes," he whispered.

Shaking his gaze away from the twinkling coverlet, he went to the window, leaned out, and saw Kryranen standing below with arms crossed and face dark. He smiled again, waved, but she gave him no reaction until he threw down the rope after securing it beneath his foot and around his right leg.

The slack disappeared, and for a moment he teetered until he adjusted his weight against the pull and leaned back precariously as Kryranen made her way to the lip of the window. When she appeared he loosened his hold and she nearly slipped from the frame before she caught hold and let out several indistinguishable curses.

He suppressed a grin before returning to the chest, a series of fireworks breaking over the night sky from across the canals beyond the ancient stadium.

"That signals the end of the Night of Secrets, and the last call for reverie among the twin houses of the Gate," Kryranen said.

"We'll be done well before Em'eral returns, trust me," he replied.

"Like I did just now with you holding the rope?" she hissed.

He concealed his mirth as he turned to kneel at the chest. He waited there for a full minute, breathing slowly as he repeatedly flexed his fingers.

"Well, do something, as I have other business tonight too!" she said.

"I don't like the silk," he replied.

"Will you move it?"

"Not with my hand."

Tentatively, he put his palm over the silk, the length of his middle finger between the fabric and flesh, and then summoned his air. The silk rose slowly from the surface on invisible fingers, but before it could come completely free, its shape shifted to that of a serpent, crimson fangs reaching out to strike Savino's exposed palm.

Kryranen was faster, her hand shooting out to grab the silk viper so quickly the action tumbled all three of them backward into the chain-suspended bed. Savino hit the gem-studded coverlet first, a thousand needle-like fingers prickling over his shoulders and neck until there was a flash of grey that turned the world to shadow.

He blinked; and then another flash, this one brimming with color, fell from the shadows into him. Managing to push away, his feet drifted over the surface of the shaded floor in a gentle glide.

Kryranen...

He tried to mouth the word but nothing formed in the shadow, although the colorful figure did turn in a shimmering pirouette, licking tendrils of amber, gold, silver, and umber flowing around it.

Savino?

A voice like tinkling crystal filled with hearty wine slithered into his mind. It was somehow familiar, the inflection the same as his ill-gotten companion on this mission.

What happened?

Again, the voice, and this time he was sure it was Kryranen.

Lareo's secret score, that's what happened, he replied.

Then we're...

Inside the blanket, yes, or so it would seem.

The shimmering shape moved forward, the body both lithe and voluptuous, with delicate breasts upturned, angular face and hair spilling down well past its waist. The colors inside it shifted, slithering in patterns like those of the art dealers in the Raised Market who sold sculpture in clear bottles of different colored and layered sands. The effect would have been breathtaking, had he any breath to steal.

She is beautiful…

What?

He blinked, his thoughts betraying him in this new form of fully mental communication.

There is a beauty to this place, he thought.

It just looks drab to me, much like you, Savino, Kryranen's thought touched him coldly.

Looking down he held his hands out before him. They were dull, lifeless things with odd splotches of azure that looked like sickly veins deep beneath the surface. He held no other color, no shine, no tendrils of ether that danced off his skin in playful waves.

Around him, the world was much the same, save for the lurking white forms drifting inside the grey walls of the chamber, their faces sometimes surfacing enough to see a mouth agape in an unheard scream.

This is how he must do it, she thought.

Meaning?

The epically beautiful face turned to him, eyes shining in burnished silver pools with glowing gold irises. *El'emal*, she thought, *it must be how he can find his prey.*

She pointed to the window, and then proceeded to move to it, her wake a shimmering afterglow of cascading energy. He followed her, his range of movement free in any direction with only a thought as though he was flying.

Once to the portal, Kryranen paused only a moment before slipping out into the night. Above, the Blood Moon was hanging low, a wreath of iridescent flame radiating out from it that danced on rooftops in waves that were like the aspect of heat coming off desert sands.

Below, as Kryranen gently descended like a spider down the tower, souls lurked, some bright, some dark, stealing about the streets on night errands or returning home after a long reverie.

Where are you going? He asked.

I have to test this.

Do I dare want to know why?

As I said, I've things to do later.

He followed her until they hit the street and she spoke again.

Do you think they can see us?

Savino landed in front of a large figure marching down the center of the street. It bore a swirling patchwork of skin colored orange, yellow, and violet with licking flame. The burning essence was hot, and the long face held a semblance of beauty, although nothing like that of Kryranen's ethereal self.

There was a moment of pause as the figure stopped, essence blazing once before he, for surely by the set of the shoulders it was male, stepped around the area Savino occupied and then moved on.

He might not have seen me, but I think he sensed something, he thought.

And he moves on toward the Gate with purpose, she added.

Savino turned and raised his gaze beyond the canal. There, over the low tangle of buildings, the white-fire of the failing Blood Moon's radiance played on the shining towers of the Black Gate. Again, his heart pulsed in his chest, but came to a sudden halt when a spine-numbing laugh split the ether.

The chill that went with the laugh leached into his soul, and he slowly looked back to where Kryranen stood glowing in the shadowed street as a thin figure wreathed in violet, so deep it lay against the very foundations of black, moved along the street. An outstretched hand of white digits like exposed sun-bleached bone trailed along the building walls, and wherever it touched the surface, a steaming body of grey-white energy was birthed into the ether.

It's the priestess, Kryranen's mind echoed.

Move back!

Kryranen's tendrils flared a deep ocher as her feet slid toward him, but she stayed close to the ground even as he drifted upward. Around his beautiful companion the newly released spirits gathered, spectral claws dragging against the ebony pavers as the came.

Fly! his mind screamed.

She turned up, looking at him with those golden eyes, and he heard her reply against the growing howls of the dead.

I can't, my essence is tethered to the ground.

A hundred curses swept through his mind, but he flew downward, one of the dead extending a claw as he passed over. Deftly, he landed behind her, his arms outstretched as the circle continued to close.

What are you doing? she formed a mental scream.

Protecting you, what does it look like!

Don't be a fool, we don't have any weapons!

A ghost took a swing at him and he ducked beneath the blow, his left hand going forward to push the enemy back. Instead of making contact with the thing's chest, a flare of blue essence sprang from his palm like a fist and shattered the spirit into a thousand wisps of ethereal white.

Our essence, he thought

What? she asked, taking a step back as two ghosts lunged at her.

Our essence, we can attack with it!

Kryranen's avatar didn't hesitate, her arm creating a wide sweeping arc as a blade of umber energy ripped through the advancing creatures. Screams howled in agony and were cut short, her power turning the area into a cloud of white vapor.

He tried to summon his air again, but this time the essence was lacking both in azure shine and power. A ghost shrugged off his weak blow and came forward with both claws bare. Pushing off the ground, he got four feet high before the ghost lunged, caught his ankle, and pulled him down. Twisting, he let out another blast of essence but a second ghost shook off the blow and ripped a gash three hands wide in his side.

Pain raged through his brain like a lightning storm, and tendrils of inky blue spread from the wound like an ever-growing spider's web.

Savino!

Kryranen was there, her arms blazing with golden light as she turned his attackers to vapor before they could strike again. He fell, the shadow-stone beneath him cool against his back as more essence drained from the wound to create rivers of deep blue and grey in the cracks.

Three more blasts of raw essence and the lonely street was clear, Kryranen kneeling beside him as she reached to lift his head.

The priestess? he asked.

Gone, as she continued down the street on some other errand.

He nodded, the pain in his side slowly fading as the world grew a shade darker.

Savino, why did you come back? she asked.

Her face was now a dusky yellow, eyes polished silver, and hair a flowing sea of dark sienna.

I'm a lot of things, and most of them bad, but I don't abandon a partner.

Without a mouth, she could not smile, but he still somehow sensed it, the swirling patterns in her skin, if that was what it was, turned and looped in a fashion bespeaking mirth.

I guess I shouldn't have listened to Torrent, she thought.

Torrent?

She nodded. *She said you would be the death of me, but now it looks…*

Even as the thought trailed off he finished it, *like I'll be the one dying.*

Reaching out, she placed a honey-hued hand on his wound and he winced. After the initial contact, the pain subsided but he felt a heaviness and corruption in the touch.

Stop, he thought.

She didn't, instead pressing harder until the stone beneath him prickled against his back like needles.

Something is happening, Savino, the wound is closing. Don't move.

He tried to sit up but she put her other hand on him, weighing him down as her silver eyes darkened to steel and burnt umber brows furrowed between them.

But…

His mind was reeling, the corruption like someone pouring sand into his veins, filling his mouth with sawdust, and deadening his ears with mud. If he could have coughed, choked, anything, he would have, but instead he could just lay against the ground as the weight of Kryranen's essence bore him down.

He looked up, watching as the colors in her darkened, the hue seeping down into him, but as it did so he saw traces of azure essence slithering against the stream, somehow making the transfer up her arm until they touched her face, shoulders, and neck with droplets of deep blue.

Finally she withdrew her hands, and he managed to turn his head fully. He could see his own shoulder, now deeply mustard with swirls of violet that bled through it like a painter's brush drawn over old parchment. Pushing up, his hands now yellowed and tipped with blue, reached down to touch the wound, the three scars like a veins of gold glowing there.

She steadied him with a strong hand, and he looked at her. Eyes that were now steely grey were also ringed by a thin veil of blue.

I feel the earth, he thought.

But can you fly? she asked.

With her support, he stood, his arms reaching out from his sides as he felt the conflicting elements inside him clashing. His feet turned deep yellow, and his hands, raised to the crimson sky, became a wash of light blue.

It's working, she thought.

He looked down, and although his feet pulsed as though they needed the earth, his body rose slowly above the pavers. It wasn't an instant thing or easy as before the attack, but it was possible. After a minute of levitation he lowered himself to the ground and held out a hand.

We have to go, he thought.

She looked at the hand, her color slowly returning to the same vibrant levels as it had been when they'd entered the other world.

Take it, he said, waving.

Reluctantly, she did so, and he drew her close, one arm holding her hand and the other wrapping her waist as though they intended to dance. Their eyes were close, and he squinted his as though smiling and she stared at him with a blue-rimmed gold returning to her gaze.

I think we've corrupted each other, he thought.

An answer began to form in his mind from her but he pushed off the ground and the mental thread evaporated as she pulled closer, their course drifting up seventy feet over the shimmering city before he adjusted course and brought them sailing back though the open tower window. Instead of letting her go, he pushed forward to where the bed hung like a wavy field of light.

Savino..., he heard, but the light took them, pushed them out with pins and needles until he blinked away the dark and saw he still held her. Instead of the flawless beauty of her essence, she was Kryranen again, pot hunter, sewer rat, and Jai-Ruk bladeswoman.

Their eyes met for one brief moment, but he released his grip on instinct when he saw her face so close and that was all it took to break the spell. She pushed away, pulling her hood about her angular face as though rain poured down on them both.

"Kryranen..." he whispered.

"Get the chest open, I'll wrap the cursed blanket," she cut him off.

Sighing, he nodded and went to the chest. The silk lay beside it, as mundane as it had been before his air touched it. Stepping fully around the fabric, he knelt beside the chest and pulled forth a small wrap that contained his picks. The lock was stubborn, but he'd been practicing this skill for a century before he came to Taux, and its resistance was defeated before Kryranen had stuffed the blanket fully in her pack.

Inside, a purse lay with a silver tie. He took it, emptied the coins within into a new bag without making contact with them. After that was done he replaced the stolen currency with the ones he'd brought from the Emerald Serpent. Retying the bag, he put it back and almost closed the lid before he saw a piece of paper with a broken seal.

Fingers quick like a viper strike, he unfolded the paper and found a list written in flowing script. *The Vash Ruby, The Crucible of Fire, The Soul of Air, The Seer's Mask.*

He stared at it a moment, whispered each item in turn, and then refolded and tucked the letter away in the chest before closing the lid.

Kryranen waited at the window, face shielded by the cowl.

"You take the rope, once you're down, I'll float," he said.

She didn't argue, and they did the same for the next level as well. When she hit the ground he threw the rope down and then slipped over the edge. His weight was odd, but he was able to adjust his air, keeping himself close to the wall where his fingers could grip it for support as he spider-crawled down to the street below.

When he hit the street he turned, but Kryranen wasn't there, nor was the blanket, and he cursed under his breath, quietly slipping away into the night as the image of her avatar danced behind his eyes.

Mama Serene smiled as she drew Savino into the private parlor after his questioning was complete and the paladin had released him. Smiling, she took a seat on a luxuriant divan.

"What did you tell her?" Serene asked.

He walked to a silvered mirror, the edges cracked in a web of gold, and turned his head one way then another, something about his skin darker than before the festival began. His jaw was also brouder, or so it looked in the mirror's reflection.

"I told her I took a walk among the flowers," he replied.

"Well, you're lucky she didn't know you three days ago," Serene said.

"Meaning?"

"Meaning, you've changed."

He turned, frowning. "I can assure you I haven't."

Serene watched him a moment, a long-nailed finger seductively running down the silken edge of her gown where it cupped her left breast.

"But you have, even if only on the outside. Three days ago, you were a lean rake, handsome to be sure, but always too feminine for my tastes. Yet as you stand there now, I see strength in you, a broader set to your chin, and a weight to your frame that has my jaded heart atwitter."

He shook his head. "Atwitter? I doubt that very much." She laughed, and he joined her in the mirth as the sound of it was infectious. Finally, after the humor had played out, she looked at him long and hard before speaking.

"It would seem your debts are clear, my old friend, so might I interest you in one of my ladies after your long ordeal with the Paladin of St. Siegfried?"

He stared back, something in her eyes pulsing like an ember. At last he signed, saying, "No, not tonight I am afraid."

Her smile returned, and she nodded. "Then perhaps your change runs deeper than I'd thought. Nonetheless, I have a favor to ask of you, if you would hear it."

"Yes?"

"I need you for a private party tomorrow night here in the Purse, and I'll even dress you for it."

"You'll owe me, you know," he said.

She smiled, "Oh yes, but I have a feeling the repaying of this debt will be more fun than I could resist anyway."

"Very well, I shall be here for you as always," he replied.

With a tip of his head, he took his leave and returned to the streets of the Black Gate, a newly formed part of him anchored not only to the earth, but to a soul that had entered his dreams and corrupted his waking thoughts.

Illustration by Jeff Laubenstein

THE FAIREST FLOWER

By Elaine Cunningham

Sixth Day: *Elemental Day*

I am not beautiful, nor have I ever wished to be. Exceptional beauty, in my observation, tends to overshadow any other strength of mind, body, or character a woman might possess. Never have I seen this more clearly illustrated than in Taux's current preoccupation with crowning thier Queen of Flowers. Most people hold strong opinions about the outcome of this contest, and there is much debate about the merits of this or that woman. I disdain such contests and mention this one only to explain why I knew the name Filaria Dharn, thrice-crowned queen of the Black Gate District and reputedly the loveliest woman in Taux, before a murderer's trail led me to her husband's door.

Any investigation is like harvesting wheat—an Inquisitor must pound away until the chaff of rumor and gossip blows away from the grain of truth. It's seldom immediately apparent which is which, so I must work my way through piles of words in search of salient fact.

For good or ill, the gossips of the Black Gate were happy to talk with (and about) "that nice young paladin." ("Lady Evynhoe seems so hard, poor girl. Perhaps if she smiled more....") They especially like to talk about Timar Dharn, a physician of wealthy family, despite their inability to find anything bad to say of him. He met his Filaria at the brothel that employed her, but not in the manner her profession might suggest. Timar was called to tend a dying whore whose many-fathered baby refused to be born. Thanks in no small part to Filaria's assistance, mother and son survived the difficult birth. The devoted physician fell in love with Filaria's compassion and competence before he so much as glanced at her face. To hear it told, her beauty meant little to him, while his family's wealth was nothing to her. They were content in each other. Never was a man more devoted or a wife more constant.

I was curious to meet these paragons, though I fully expected the reality to fall short.

The Hospitalers' clinic is located in a curving alley called the Scorpion's Sting. I pushed my way through the seething festival crowds until I came to a stone building with a narrow front almost entirely filled by a broad door painted in stripes of brown and gold. The painted symbol of St. Shera—the only signage on the clinic—was nearly illegible, thanks to a dozen or so knives and daggers thrust into the cracks between the door's planks. Apparently patients were required to check their weapons before entering. Judging from the rust-colored smears surrounding several of the blades, this seemed a sensible precaution. I, of course, had no intention of relinquishing my sword.

Rows of chairs filled the front room. All were occupied by revelers awaiting treatment. Their ills were about what one might expect: a broken arm, minor knife wounds, the results of various sorts of over indulgence. As I stepped over the drunken youth snoring on the floor, I could not help but wonder what he'd done to merit the insult some scribe of dubious literacy and worse tattooing skills had inked across his forehead.

The Jai-Ruk female seated behind a small table pushed herself to her feet and thrust a battered writing slate toward me. "Put yer name and need at the bottom of the list."

I waved away the registry. "I'm here to see Timar Dharn."

"Are you, now?" sneered a man whose forearm was wrapped in bloodstained bandages. "An' I suppose the rest of us just dropped by to swive the missus?"

An ugly murmur rippled through the room. The Jai-Ruk attendant raised the register high and brought it down on the man's head with force that cracked it—slate, not skull—neatly in two.

"We'll have none o' that," she growled. "You can keep a respectful tongue in yer head or you can find yerself another place to bleed."

The man's muttered apology was lost in a sudden barrage of profanity coming from what I assumed to be a treatment room. The cursing rose into a shriek, which was followed by ominous silence.

My hand went to the hilt of my sword. Before I'd taken a second step forward, the curtain parted and a young woman stepped out. At first glance, I took her for Filaria Dharn. But no—her eyes were merely blue, not the color of a perfect summer twilight or violets in blushing snow or any of the other silly accolades I'd heard, and her blond hair, though longer than mine, did not fall past her waist in waves of shining gold. More to the point, she wore the simple green tunic of the Hospitalers' guild. A physician, then, and not a beauty queen.

The Hospitaler's gaze flicked to my half-drawn sword. One corner of her lips twitched in a fleeting smile.

"Peace, my lady," she said. "You must pardon Hythor. He is prone to colorful speech when his bones are set."

I let my sword fall back into its sheath. "You speak as if this were common occurrence."

"More common than one might think. Hythor is fond of mead, and when he drinks, he walks the roof ridges."

I shook my head in amazement at such foolishness. "And falls, apparently."

"Oh, no. People shoot him down."

My disbelieving stare drew another faint smile from her. She reached back into the treatment room and produced a small crossbow with a short, padded bolt. A spray of blue meadowsweet had been painted on the padded head. Apparently shooting drunken ridge-walkers from rooftops was just another festival game.

She handed the silly weapon to the Jai-Ruk. "Please dispose of this after you've seen to Dinyon. His usual cot is occupied, so a bedroll will have to do. As you can see," she said to me, "we have no shortage of patients today. I am Shayla of St. Amanda. How may I serve you, Lady Evynhoe?"

Given how quickly knowledge of any sort spreads in the Black Gate district, I was not surprised to learn that she knew me. "I need a moment of Timar Dharn's time."

Shayla's gaze flickered, shadowed by some emotion that came and went before I could put a name to it. "He is not on duty today."

"When is he expected?"

"Yesterday," growled the attendant. She stooped and slung the snoring drunkard over one shoulder. "And the day before, and the one before that."

"That will do, Mharra," the physician said, sending the Jai-Ruk a quelling glance. "If you will follow me, my lady?"

She led me into a curtained alcove, unlocked the door on the far side of the room, and beckoned me into the small chamber beyond—a storage room filled with vials and powders and other necessities of the healers' art. She shut the door and put her back to it. Her shoulders squared as she faced me down.

"As a physician, I often ask questions my patients might not understand or consider important. I suspect it is much the same for Inquisitors," she said in a measured tone. "But whatever your purpose might be, I can assure you that Timar's absence from the clinic is not significant. He has many other responsibilities and needed a few days to attend them. That is all."

Her defense of Timar struck me as excessive, but perhaps it was merely her nature to slice bread with a battle-axe. "It seems an inconvenient time," I observed, hoping to draw her out enough to take her measure.

Shayla shrugged. "There is no convenient time to be sick or wounded. Timar hasn't taken an entire day away from the clinic for more than a year. You do know, I suppose, that he holds a council seat among the Red Pillars? That the Dharn family business imports much of the food that feeds Taux's citizens?"

"It's a marvel he finds time to attend the clinic at all."

I put all the admiration I could muster into my tone, but judging from Shayla's sour expression, I fell several feet short of the line that separates praise from sarcasm. I cleared my throat and forged on. "When did he last report?"

Her hesitation was short, but I watched in fascination as several distinct emotions chased one another across her expressive face. She settled, with obvious reluctance, upon simple truth: "The third day of the festival."

While this accorded with the information that had led me here, it did not sing in tune with the tales I'd heard of the devoted physician. Timar was not the focus of my inquiry, but there was something more here than I'd expected to find.

My thoughts must also have found their way onto my face, for Shayla's lips thinned into a grim line. "May I ask what this concerns?"

"I'm seeking information about a patient he saw late that evening—a Lowl named Zhada."

Some of the tension melted from Shayla's stance. "As it turns out, I can help you. I treated Zhada."

I produced a slip of paper I'd appropriated an hour before from a slightly inebriated apothecary. "According to this order for willowbark syrup, Timar was the physician of record. I assume this is his signature?"

Shayla took the slip and gave it a moment's study before handing it back. "It is, but there's a simple explanation. Before the clinic opens, each physician signs ten order slips and gives them to Mharra, our assistant. She fills in the patient's name as needed."

"You must have considerable faith in your assistant."

"She's a good scribe," Shayla said, "but occasionally she uses the wrong physician's slip. There's no harm done, as we only use these slips for willowbark. In this particular case, however, it seems likely that Zhada helped himself to one of the willowbark slips on his way out. I assure you, Timar left the clinic before highsun."

"Did he say why?"

"I didn't ask. Now, what can I tell you about Zhada?"

Since I could find no way to justify further questions about Timar Dharn, I quickly reviewed the facts that had led me here. The physician confirmed what I'd heard and seemed surprised to learn the Lowl was missing. Apparently his injuries were more serious than a script for willowbark suggested, for Shayla stressed that he'd slipped out of the clinic without her knowledge and against her advice.

I thanked the physician for her time and left with nothing to show for mine, other than a profound sense of frustration.

Shayla was no less cooperative than a score of others I'd interviewed, but you can toss only so many small stones into a bucket before the water overflows. Suddenly I'd had my fill of lies and half-truths and "facts" distorted by fixed opinions or self-interest or too much mead. The urge to know the truth of someone—anyone!—burned in me like a three-day thirst.

On the way out, I paused for a quiet word with the Jai-Ruk. "Can you tell me where Timar Dharn lives?"

The brute snorted. "Might be I could. Can't see why I'd want to, though."

I reached for my purse, thinking to offer a few coins for this information, but I recalled the outrage on the Ruk's face when she'd defended Filaria Dharn's honor and decided not to offend her loyalty with a bribe.

"Strange things are happening in this city," I murmured. "Shayla does not say so, but I think she is concerned for Timar's well-being. I suspect you may be, as well."

"I'm getting paid, same as ever."

I adjusted my opinion—and my tactics—a few notches downward. "Just as you were paid for a willowbark script that no physician ordered?"

The scent of fresh-turned soil filled the air as the Ruk's elemental nature emerged in response to the implied threat. She glanced toward the treatment rooms, then gave a curt nod. "Suppose it wouldn't hurt if you was to check on Timar. But before you go, I'll take those coins you decided not to offer."

I left the clinic with a darker mood, a lighter purse, and directions to a nearby shop called The Fairest Flower. Despite the spring festival and the early hour, the shop stood locked and empty. In the narrow walkway between this building and the next, a narrow flight of stairs led to the second floor. I climbed them and pounded on the door until the latch slid back.

Timar Dharn was not, according to gossip, a handsome man, but he was reputedly easy to recognize: hair so red it was almost orange, an overlarge nose, and rather prominent eyes of a peculiar pale green shade. The man at the door fit these particulars, but so haggard was his face and so haunted his eyes that for a moment I could see only the pain and not the person.

His appearance surprised me, which perhaps explains why my first words were as blunt as a cudgel. "I am Inquisitor Evynhoe, and I am looking for a murderer."

He nodded as if he had been expecting this. "I am he."

The paladin on my doorstep seemed younger than most Inquisitors, and I suppose she was as fit and healthy as paladins tend to be. I was too distraught to pay her much heed, though some distant part of my mind took note of her necklace of knives, a dangerous ornament that suggested hubris, or perhaps a limited knowledge of anatomy.

She entered at my invitation and accepted a chair but declined the offer of wine—wisely so, given my confession.

"Before I begin, let us be very clear on one point," I said. "Shayla had no part in this. She merely agreed to take my shift at the clinic so that I could tend a personal matter."

"Did you tell her the nature of your errand?" asked Lady Evynhoe.

I grimaced as the image of Shayla's pity-filled eyes came vividly to mind. "No, but I think she suspected what drove me that day. The truth of the matter, however, was far more complicated than either of us supposed."

"Considering the course this investigation seems to be taking," the paladin said in a tone dryer than dust, "I would be very surprised if it was not."

For the first two years of our marriage, Filaria and I lived a small but rewarding life, I caring for the people of the district, she running the flower shop she'd purchased with money saved during her time in The Silk Purse. Neither of us expected me to inherit the Dharn family fortune, much less the family's council seat, but we had everything we needed or wanted.

When my brothers died in a sailing accident, Filaria offered to see to the sale of Dharn family assets so that we could use the money to further the Hospitalers' work. After a while, it occurred to me that she was spending more time running the business than disposing of its assets, but I didn't mind. Funds were available when I needed them. Filaria was happy and occupied, and she took pride in handling life's practicalities so that I could focus on my work.

For a few months I did my duty with the Red Pillars, but I have no patience for the meetings and the small, petty matters that governance demands. I was pleased and grateful when Filaria offered to attend council and vote in my stead. The council accepted her as my proxy, thanks to the unexpected support of the Vash family. Filaria knew my mind and shared my values, and she enjoyed the complex dance of governance as thoroughly as I loathed it. All in all, ours was an ideal partnership.

Then, four years ago today, she was voted to represent the Black Gate as the Queen of Flowers, and everything changed.

I can't explain why she seemed different after the ceremony, but a change of some sort was profoundly apparent to me. As time passed, this change became more pronounced. She became more distant and distracted as summer faded to winter, almost as if she herself were fading away. Only the coming of the Flower Festival—and her re-election as the Queen of Flowers—revived her.

The more I thought on it, the more I wondered whether perhaps Bram Riviland, the Master of Revels, might have something to do with this. He is renowned for his charm and his merry ways. Filaria spent many hours in his company while discharging her duties as the Black Gate's Queen of Flowers.

Like a worm in my heart, doubt began to gnaw. Perhaps another man had taken first place in her heart. Perhaps the life we shared was not the perfect partnership I fondly believed it to be. Perhaps my wife was not the woman I thought I knew.

Then three days ago, I overheard two patients speaking of Filaria. Both claimed to have been her clients at the Silk Purse. They snickered at their bawdy memories and bemoaned purses too slender to keep pace with her price. Mind you, I have no issue with her past employment, but I could not bear to think that what Filaria and I shared, the life we'd built, might be nothing more than an elaborate business transaction.

Suddenly I could take no more—I felt that I must know the truth or go mad. Leaving Shayla to tend the clinic, I ran to the flower shop and found Filaria's assistant locking up. The shop was completely empty—every blossom had been delivered to a single customer.

I'd come intending to talk with Filaria, not spy upon her, but the image of her meeting a lover in a bower of spring flowers was more than my fevered imagination could withstand. I found the bill of sale and set off for the address written in Filaria's neat, precise runes.

An hour later, I crouched on a balcony outside the window of a discretion-assured rooming house near the Black Gate wall. This particular room was dominated by a large marble bath. To my surprise, Filaria was with not one man, but three. Two of them I knew all too well.

To look at him, you would not know that Tlacolotl Vash was the most powerful member of the Pillar Council. He dressed like a dockworker and his build was so thick and stocky that he resembled a barrel with boots. But his ambitions were boundless, and his views and values were so consistently in opposition to mine that I considered it good policy to vote against anything he proposed.

His son, Folotl, was also familiar to me. Or more to the point, I knew his handiwork, for I've treated many men and more than a few women for injuries they'd received at his hands. I pressed his victims to make official complaint, but so far no one dared.

"Is she pretty, this Yanoan princess?" Folotl's habitual smirk turned ugly. "And more to the point, is she sturdy? Strong enough to take a little damage now and again?"

Tlacoltl regarded his son with open distaste. "The trade agreement with Yanoan is our first consideration. A political marriage is an important goal, but a distant one. When the time for negotiation comes, we will advance the family candidate most likely to close the deal, whoever he may be."

"Whoever he may be." Folotl paused for a derisive sniff. "Might I remind you that all my brothers are wed? Or dead?"

"This is another issue to consider at the proper time."

I would not have thought it possible, but Folotl's smile grew even more unpleasant. "Removing an inconvenient daughter-in-law! Now *there's* a happy thought. I do hope it will be Delitzl's wife—never much liked the wench—but I'm happy to oblige you as needs be."

"Enough of this foolishness. Why are you even here? We agreed you'd take care of Two-Quills."

My breath caught. Osment "Two-Quills" was under my employ. He was a powerful scribe from Zimbolay who worked for all the Dharn business interests, as well as several other merchant houses that opposed a full Vash takeover of the Pillar Council. He was a man of great integrity, a good friend to me and one of Filaria's most chivalrous admirers.

"It will be done, father, I have a pending appointment on the morrow," Folotl replied.

I glanced at Filaria, ready to leap to her defense when she protested this outrage. But she made no comment—indeed, she looked incapable of speech. The change in her horrified me. In a few short moments, her golden hair had gone white as seafoam. Even her eyes seemed devoid of color. She reclined on a chaise of cream-colored velvet, and she was so wan and pale that she almost seemed to fade into the fabric.

The third man, who was cloaked, hunched, and cowled into anonymity, took Filaria's wrist in practiced fashion. "Her pulse is weak and irregular," he said in a dry, sibilent whisper. "The time for renewal is slipping away."

Tlacolotl Vash produced a book from some hidden pocket of his vest—an old book bound in leather the precise shade of dried blood. A gilded sigil on the spine proclaimed it to be the property of Pelantus, the former Vash magus. He offered this treasure to the cloaked man.

"You may use this," he said grandly.

Hissing laughter filled the room. The magus lifted his hands to his cowl and pushed it back, revealing a reptilian face with cold, golden eyes. Only then did I note that his hands, which were narrow and long and of a sun-browned hue, were subtly scaled.

I have little regard for any magus who would align himself with the Vash family, but the water born healing powers of a Candon shaman are formidable. This creature seemed to have Filaria's best interests in mind. As long as he did her good rather than harm, I would not interfere.

The shaman took the book and hurled it into the bath. A splash of water leaped into the air and did not fall, but rather began to swirl and shift to pale azure light.

Folotl chuckled at his father's dumbfounded expression. "He did use the book. If nothing else, the lizard can take instruction."

"Ssssilence!"

The younger Vash lifted both hands in a gesture of mock conciliation.

Turning his back to the men, the shaman reached for the pile of flowers on a large table and selected a handful of yellow jonquils. He touched these to Filaria's hair. To my astonishment, the flowers disappeared with a slight *whoosh!* A faint glow surrounded Filaria, and when it faded her hair had regained a bit of its golden hue.

This went on for some time. Bunches of fragrant pinks restored the color to her lips and cheeks. Blue meadowstars and violets renewed the unique shade of her eyes. Even her garments, which had been the color of watered-down milk, took on spring shades of green and gold and blue.

The truth dawned on me slowly, for the mind is not fashioned to accept any great and terrible loss without a struggle. Mine did not easily accept that focus of the shaman's spell was not Filaria renewed, but a magical construct—a golem of flowers made in the image of my beloved.

I would have left then, but grief held me in a mailed fist. My Filaria was gone, perhaps slain by Folotl Vash in one of his bloody amusements. She had been replaced by this facsimile, this flower woman.

I can't tell you how much time passed, but at some point I realized the shaman had finished his work. The pile of flowers had been reduced to a single spray of bellflowers and the creature in the chair glowed with color and beauty. The Candon took a silver chain and draped it around her neck.

I recognized the amulet that hung from the chain. It was the badge of office that proclaimed the false Filaria to be the Black Gate's Queen of Flowers. She had worn it for three years and would, I was now certain, wear it for another. The Vash clan attempted to control every other aspect of city life, so why not this?

As a Hospitaler I have some small understanding of magic, enough to bind broken bones and torn skin, but I had never considered how powerful the collective energies of the Spring Festival might be, or what use might be made of them. That a woman of flowers might be created to take a place on the Pillar Counsel—and no doubt to pad the Vash fortune from Dharn coffers—would not have occurred to me in my darkest dreams.

"And now to recharge the amulet," the shaman hissed as he took the golem's hand and lifted her from the chair. He glanced at Tlacoltl. "You do realize, I hope, that this is the last time the golem can be renewed?"

Tlacolotl spread both hands in a gesture of careless acceptance. "It will be enough. With the Dharn vote assured, the Yanoan trade agreement will be accomplished before midsummer."

"There should be enough life left in the whore for that. Barely." The Candon nodded.

The older Vash grunted in approval. "Good. It's time we made an end to them both, and once that is done you can begin your hunt for my gem."

"And you will provide the name of the serpent poacher in return," the Candon hissed.

"Indeed," Tlacolotl replied.

"On your way, sweetling." Folotl gave the flower golem's buttocks an ungentle slap.

The creature turned to him with chin lifted high. The steely dignity in those deep blue eyes, so like Filaria's, scattered the pieces of my broken heart. Folotl chuckled and strode for the door.

I kept my perch until the four conspirators left the building, then I scrambled down from the balcony and hurried off after the flower golem, my heart racing with hope and horror.

The whore has that much life in her. Barely.

For once I could feel no outrage over the disrespect shown to Filaria for her youthful profession. If I understood aright, Filaria was alive—barely!—and her memories and intelligence and perhaps even her emotions had given the flower woman this uncanny semblance of life. Vash's final words—*It's time we made an end to them both*—seemed to confirm this conclusion.

The golem slipped into a warehouse near the seawall. It was a Dharn property, one I remembered from childhood visits. Occasionally my father would permit my brothers and me to play in tunnels beneath. The warehouse had been built over a nearly exhausted salt mine, and the tunnels were cool and dry—the perfect place to hang meat for aging, especially in the dampness of Taux. And since many of the old tunnels wandered long-unexplored paths, it would also be the perfect place to hide a captive.

I followed the flower woman through the chill cavern where whole beefs and boors hung skinned and ready for carving, snatching a butcher's knife from one of the cutting tables as I passed. So intent was I on trailing the golem without giving myself away that I paid scant attention to the turns and twists in the tunnel maze. And then I saw my Filaria, and all other thoughts fled.

My flesh-and-blood wife lay on a low, narrow cot, frozen in what appeared to be some sort of magical stasis. The flower golem knelt beside the cot and unclasped the silver chain from her neck. She fastened the chain around Filaria's neck and touched two fingertips to the silver amulet.

A glow surrounded Filaria and the golem. Faint, sweet music drifted from the glowing sphere—the sound of my wife singing softly to herself as she worked among her flowers.

I rushed the flower woman and dragged her away from my wife. She writhed and screamed and punched my thigh with astonishing force. I did not realize I'd been stabbed until she wrenched the knife free.

Searing pain froze me in place for one moment—long enough for the flower woman to roll away and leap to her feet. She faced me in a battle-ready crouch, a knife in each hand.

Again I hesitated, for I couldn't bring myself to kill a creature that wore my wife's face. The flower woman had no such compunctions. She flew at me in a whirlwind of flashing blades. As I held her off with the butcher knife, I blessed my father for insisting upon lessons with Taux's best sword masters. Killing is relatively easy, but it took every bit of skill I possessed to defend myself while inflicting no harm.

Finally the flower golem fell back, her hair disheveled as a madwoman's and her chest heaving with each swift, rasping breath.

"You followed me," she gasped out. "Why?"

Her smirk proclaimed that she understood all too well what drove me. When I did not answer, she said, "You were right, you know. I have been having an affair—or rather, continuing an affair that *she* began." Her gaze slipped swiftly, scathingly, to the place where Filaria lay.

"You lie!"

"Do I?" she taunted. "Or better yet, *can* I? Because if I have her memories, her thoughts, her character, what does that say about her?"

I brushed aside this troubling logic. "Does Filaria still live?"

The golem's hard, mocking smile sat strangely on that beloved face. "There's enough life force left for one of us. And you get to choose."

Before I could respond, the flower woman turned heel and disappeared into one of the tunnels.

I gave chase, but the golem ran like a hare, dodging and twisting through tunnels I vaguely remember from my childhood and tunnels I had never seen. She ran as if all the ghosts of Taux followed in vengeful pursuit, though as for that, one grief-maddened man determined to trade her life for his wife's would be motive enough.

And I *was* determined to kill her. I have never been so intent upon any goal, and if the flower woman knew me as Filaria did, she could not fail to know this.

I have no idea how long the chase went on, or where it led. All that mattered was slaying the imposter so that Filaria might have a chance to live. So when I rounded a corner and saw the flower woman standing with one hand on the rock wall and her head drooping in exhaustion, I did not hesitate.

The butcher knife plunged into flesh that felt solid and real, but I knew to expect this. For nearly four years I had held this creature in my arms, trying in vain to restore the connection we once had shared.

"Timar?"

Her voice was faint and I knew my name would be the last word she spoke. Because I know how to heal, I also know how to kill.

I should have known triumph and relief, but long habits of affection prompted me to catch her in my arms and lower her gently to the tunnel's floor. Despite my rage, I could not help but be affected by the emotions on the dying creature's face: pain, of course, but also deep sorrow. Her fading gaze held mine, and it seemed to me that it held something very like regret.

Slow, measured clapping came from the tunnel behind me. I leaped to my feet and whirled to behold the beautiful, mocking face of the flower woman. And behind her, Filaria's cot—empty.

A terrible cry tore free of my throat. I fell to my knees and wrenched the knife from the true Filaria's heart in the instinctual panic of a child, thinking for a fleeting moment that I could undo what I had done if only I acted swiftly enough.

I threw aside the knife and seized the amulet, praying to every god I knew that the stolen life-force it contained might return to Filaria. As soon as my fingers touched the amulet, I was flooded with memories— Filaria's memories, including the last and worst of them. She had died at the hand of the husband she loved, and she had believed that she deserved his hatred.

"That was too easy," the flower golem said. "Vash was right. You, my love, are an idiot."

I am not a political man and have no mind for the plots and intrigues that characterize life in Taux, but suddenly the design of this thing unfolded in my mind with devastating clarity. This, I realized, was what Tlacolotl Vash had planned, this was his way to "make an end of both of them." Replacing Filaria with a flower woman who would do his bidding gave him a temporary advantage in the Pillar Council, but tricking me into murdering my wife would utterly destroy me.

I think I went a little mad then. The flower golem must have seen this in my face, for again she turned and ran. Again I pursued. She stumbled on the stairs leading up into the warehouse. I grabbed the hem of her gown, but she was up and running before I could gain a more substantial hold. I tossed aside the bit of torn green silk and followed.

We burst into the street just as the sunset colors were fading over the harbor. Just ahead lay a broad plaza where dancers whirled and stomped in time to the music of brass whistles and sitarra. Another few moments and I would lose her in the festival crowd.

A terrible thought occurred to me, something utterly foreign to my nature and training. If a Hospitaler's magic could bind, could it not also unbind?

I gathered all my will, all my grief and rage, and hurled it toward St. Shera in something that was more like a curse than a prayer.

The flower woman stopped short, back arched and arms flung wide. A violent tremor shuddered through her, and she exploded into a thousand flowers.

The music stopped and the dancers paused on a collective *ooh!* of delight at the sudden shower of spring blossoms. Swains left their ladies' sides to scoop up jonquils and violets and pinks, and the musicians struck up the sentimental tune for which Filaria's shop had been named.

A moment passed before I realized the crowd had assumed this to be part of the festivities. Indeed, a passing youth clapped me on the shoulder and remarked on the change from the usual festival fireworks.

I returned to the tunnel to retrieve Filaria's body, but found only the silver amulet, glowing and singing softly in a drifting pile of ash. The light and music faded as I lifted it from the ash. Though I don't claim to understand all that transpired, it seems clear to me that Filaria is truly gone.

I can only hope that she has found peace.

I have heard many strange tales since I became an Inquisitor, few of them entirely true and all of them far more self-serving than Timar Dharn's confession. Oddly enough, it was this utter lack of self-justification that stopped me short of credulity.

"You doubt me," Timar said softly. "I would do the same, in your position."

He pulled a silver pendant from his pocket and handed it to me. "Here is the truth. I assume you will have it from me as I had it from Filaria."

Curious, I took the pendant.

As I child, I once waded too deep into the sea. A large wave engulfed me, lifting me off my feet and dragging me out into the depths. The overwhelming sensations that flooded me when I touched the amulet made this childhood mishap seem a very pale thing.

I saw Timar's story played out, agreeing in every particular with what he had related. I felt his grief and guilt. I *knew* him, as I have never known another living soul. And in this flood of knowledge I received all he had learned of Filaria—including the truths he had learned and could not bear to repeat.

All this, just from touching an amulet.

What a blessing such a thing might be! In the right hands, this amulet could free the falsely accused and bring the guilty to justice. My mind whirled with thoughts of what I might accomplish.

"Do not hold it for long," Timar said. "It was fashioned to drink the life from one soul and feed it to another."

I set the amulet down, for I did not doubt him. In the short time since I had entered his home, Timar's bright hair had dulled to the color of dust and new lines had carved deep paths on his grief-ravaged face. Clearly he had been diminished by the amulet's power. Most likely his fate would be shared by everyone who held it. But I did not fear for myself. I was young and strong, and in all candor, no paladin expects to live to old age.

So I reached for the amulet again, curious to see if Timar's memories could be shared a second time.

A very different mind overwhelmed me—a mind that, it pains me to admit, was far less noble than Timar's.

The cynicism was not unexpected, nor the devotion to duty and a determination to prove worthy. But since all was open to me, I saw with new eyes my humiliation at being assigned to the "murder" of a woman long dead, my deep resentment of the people who insulted my intelligence by spinning lies no half-wit would believe. I saw behind my fascination with Filaria's amulet a willingness to harm people, guilty and innocent alike, to gain useful information. And to my shame, what bothered me the most was knowing that the next person to touch the amulet would see me in the harsh light of truth.

The amulet clattered to the table. Timar looked up. His gaze sharpened in understanding.

"The memories will dissipate soon enough," he said. "No one need know what you saw just then."

Before I could respond, Timar's expression changed; the sympathetic physician disappeared, replaced by the doomed man. His shoulders rose and fell in a sigh of resignation. "Will you report me to the constable or take me in yourself?"

I gathered my wits and rose to my feet. "Many people saw the flower golem explode; some will recognize her face. I will report Filaria's death as the result of an unexpected confluence of festival magic—a tragic but accidental occurrence. There is truth in that. You are no murderer. No one could know that better than I."

Timar nodded, but I doubt he heard one word in ten. I have never seen a man who cared less what became of him.

"Take the amulet," he said. "It will be safe in your keeping."

Saints forgive me, but I was tempted.

I picked up the amulet and gripped it in my fist for a long moment—long enough, I hoped, for him to know the truth of me—and through me, his own true measure. When I reached for his hand, he pulled away.

"Keep it," he repeated. "Never again will I be tempted to know another person's truth."

I dropped the amulet on the table. "And that, good sir, is precisely why it must stay in your keeping."

Illustration by Jeff Laubenstein

A VIEW FROM HIGH GROUND

By Mike Tousignant

Seventh Day: The Eight Queens

The woman was frozen in a single moment, hips and arms mid-motion, her face brimming with laughter. She promised the viewer excitement that would never be forgotten, and her audience was rapt with fascination, likewise frozen upon the canvas.

The paladin cleared her throat. "Are you ready to answer my questions?"

Dethocrates turned away from the painting, moving stiffly. His head was bandaged, and his right arm was in a sling, but he smiled as he answered. "On the Night of Secrets, I spent my time watching the fireworks, then drinking at the Emerald Serpent. Others will remember it; I believe I was leading the house in a chorus of cat-strangling, and Quilan was gracious enough to let me run up a prodigious tab."

"I wasn't going to ask you about the Night of Secrets," she said.

"Lady Evynhoe," Dethocrates said, sitting upright, "I am well aware of exactly what murder you are trying to solve. My location at the time is well established; there is little I can say that will help you find who killed that poor, innocent, eater of souls."

"From what I understand," she said, "you crossed paths this week with another remnant of the old city."

Dethocrates nodded. "You speak of the cult."

"I speak of the bracelet."

The Jai-Ruk raised an eyebrow. "Do I seem knowledgeable in the arcane arts?"

The paladin smiled. "I have heard that you and an accomplice intruded on a Vash social event on the same night that something very precious, and reputably magical, vanished, not too long ago."

"That night also saw a hideous abomination menace the party and then fly away after stealing Vash's dollie. Obviously, that's your prime suspect." Dethocrates stood up. "May I leave now?"

"Tohil told me."

There was a pause.

"Arcxas's eyes," Dethocrates cursed, and then coughed. "Apologies, my lady."

She nodded forgiveness as Dethocrates sat back down. "He told me the basics of the situation," she said, "but there is much he didn't see. He says that you saw everything."

Dethocrates chuckled at that. "I wish I had. I saw *more*, perhaps, but not everything."

Evynhoe leaned against the wall. "Then simply tell me *more*."

Dethocrates nodded. "To tell the truth, I had been hoping to relax this festival season. I had a surplus of money, which is rare for me, and wanted to spend the nights drinking and feasting. When all of this started, I was enjoying a simple, easy, job of street performing."

"That's what you and Fynn were doing on the morning before the Serpent Dance?"

"What else would you call it? I was paid to play the dumb thug; if there was trouble in the audience during the performance, it's hardly my fault, and the assailants were masked, to boot; I would be unable to identify them."

"If street theater pays so well," Lady Evynhoe asked, "why the need to run up a tab only a few days later?"

"Repaying an old kindness," Dethocrates replied, "is rarely cheap."

Lover's Day had been everything a romantic could desire; clear, warm, and filled with the sight and smell of flowers of all types. By midmorning of the next day, however, gray clouds stretched across the sky, threatening to dampen the Serpent Dance later that evening. The people of Taux paid it little heed, tidying up their homes and shops, decorating them with the finest blossoms they could find. Later in the afternoon, the serpent dancers would award a feather to those with the finest flowers, and there was fierce competition in some neighborhoods to snare the honor.

On one busy street in the Turquoise Tortoise District, a handcart overladen with expensive Tungese Lotus blossoms carefully rolled along, flanked by two guards. On the corner ahead, an Eldaryn street performer and his pet monkey had attracted a small crowd of onlookers, many of them wearing elaborate festival masks. As the cart approached the crossroads, the monkey suddenly dashed away and assaulted a Jai-Ruk crossing the street, causing him to drop the crates he was carrying. The cart's driver stopped short, narrowly avoiding colliding with the large earth-born porter.

The Jai-Ruk roared with anger, kicking one of the crates and attempting to grab the capering monkey. Its owner ran over, hat in hand, muttering apologies and trailed by a bloom of heat.

"Oh, I'm so sorry, sir!" he said, words coming out in flickers and sputters. "He's never like this—it's a big day, after all—and with the crowd-"

"So dat's yer monkey?" The Jai-Ruk asked, smelling of tilled earth. "Good. Sell 'em to me - I'm gonna fry 'em up and eat 'em!"

The monkey howled, and its owner found courage, the air becoming further charged with heat. "Now, see here, you big bully! There's no reason to talk to anyone like that! I'll have you know—"

At this point, both of the guards interceded, trying to get the argument to move aside. As they did so, two masked figures silently stepped out of the shadows; a slim woman on one side, a young teen on the other. While the driver was distracted, they grabbed up several bundles of lotus blossoms and disappeared down opposite alleyways. When the driver turned at the shadows leaving his cart, the Jai-Ruk, Eldaryn, and monkey also disappeared into the gathering crowd, the driver shouting after them, the onlookers uncertain how much was performance and how much was crime as the guards accused each other of failed duty.

Several minutes later, beneath a secluded arch of leering faces near the Black Gate, the flowers were given to a new owner, herself masked, and Dethocrates was dividing up the fee among his compatriots.

"A fourth for Fynn, a fourth for Analyse, a fourth for Ixti, a fourth for myself, and a treat for the mastermind." The monkey, perched on

Fynn's shoulder, screeched and caught the tossed fruit, peeling it as Fynn and Analyse strolled away.

The boy, Ixti, marveled at the coins he'd just received. "I can't believe stealing flowers pays so well!"

Dethocrates patted the boy on the back. "Just promise me that this was the most dangerous thing you'll do all week."

The boy shook his head. "It's too late for that, Dethoc," he said. "The dare's already been made. Me and six others are going into the Haunted Temple District tonight."

Dethocrates sighed. Every year, on the night of the Serpent Dance, street urchins of the Black Gate who had reached thirteen years would dare each other to trek across the city to the haunted streets of the Ghost Towers. The few who lived there were more desperate and more dangerous even than those who lived within the Black Gate, to say nothing of the things that did not *live* in the temples.

"It's dangerous enough in the Black Gate," Dethocrates said, "between the monster stalking the streets and the kidnappers everyone keeps talking about. Do you really need to go hunting across the city for more trouble?"

"It's not that dangerous," the youth said. "The Bloody Lady is just a story people made up, and the same's probably true of the kidnappers. As for the temples, people need to know I'm brave! How else am I going to be a famous swordsman someday, like Xavier Crane, or maybe Savino Emantra?"

Dethocrates stifled a scoff at the mention of Savino. "The nature of your expectations," Dethocrates began, "is a subject for another time. For today, understand that I will literally give you all the money I just made if you return to the Gate right now and don't leave again for the rest of the festival."

Before Ixti could respond, a figure stepped out of the shadows. The man was tall, dark, and beautiful, with an unmasked face as cold as the death-filled stones of the city. A sword hung from his belt, hilt untied. "Dethocrates," the man said, "we need to talk."

Ixti gasped before taking off at a run in the opposite direction; Dethocrates stayed where he was, making no sudden movements. "It's not every day," he said, "that I find myself in the presence of an Angel. I hope you're not here on a commission?"

Shay Gatewell, the Angel of Death, shook his head. "This isn't paying business, but family. The Madame of the Silk Purse has requested your presence at a chocolate house nearby. I was told to mention certain…obligations."

Dethocrates nodded. "At the very least, I owe her a conversation. Lead on, Cold Shay."

The two walked through quiet side streets for several minutes, until Dethoc posed a question. "Shay, when you were a stripling, were you ever dared to visit the Ghost Towers?"

Shay nodded. "Yes."

Dethocrates waited then pressed, "Did you go?"

"No."

Dethocrates laughed. "I suppose your mother would have sent Xavier Crane after you to drag you home by the heels."

Shay's teeth set, and Dethocrates kept his eyes on the street.

"It's been a while since I've spoken to him," Dethocrates tried to change the subject. "By the Saints, he's a good man. Is he still a favorite of you mother?"

"He was until a few days ago, when a necromancer sucked him into the walls of the brothel," Shay gritted out.

Dethocrates cursed under his breath as Shay's hand glanced against the hilt of his rapier and he thought a quick prayer to Saint Erik to let the ill spoken words pass. "I'm sorry to hear that…I—"

"Forget it."

The rest of the walk was in silence.

A few minutes later, Dethocrates and Shay walked through a doorway into a room crowded with chocolate drinkers. The air was filled with the scent of champurrado mixed with the blossoms in the windowsills and on counters, and with a dozen pleasant conversations. A masked woman in the corner waved to the two as they walked in. Shay simply nodded and departed; Dethocrates walked over and took a seat across from the woman.

"Dethocrates!" the woman said, smiling beneath the mask. "You're looking well." She gestured, and two steaming cups were brought to the table.

"As are you, Lady Gatewell," Dethocrates replied, blowing on the drink to cool it.

"Always so formal," Mama Serene said, sipping her drink slowly. "I hope this discussion hasn't inconvenienced you."

"Not at all," Dethocrates replied. "My afternoon is open, and it has been some time since we talked. Of course, I'm sure the inconvenience is going to come later."

The Madame of the Silk Purse nodded at this, but was silent. She stared into her drink for several minutes before speaking.

"This has been a rough summer," Serene said, "for the Silk Purse, and for the whole Black Gate. Monsters and worse have been haunting us, but the rest of the city doesn't care." She gestured around to the room's other patrons, mainly merchants. "Do you think anyone here has found a loved one reduced to bones? Or had a child vanish into the night? No, the other Red Pillars don't care, as long as the trouble is contained to the Black Gate."

"And so, as always, we must take care of our own," Dethocrates said. "I assume that's why I'm here? I'm not some steel-hearted slayer of monsters, to avenge the dead; I'm simply a skilled liar, and a few worse things besides. Hopefully, that's all you'll need."

Mama Serene smirked at hearing this. "I believe that is the most humble I've ever heard you. I simply need some help getting through this festival in one piece, and hoped you could look into a problem for me. Do you remember one of my girls, named Melyne?"

Dethocrates nodded. "If I've heard right, she's one of those who left your service after…after that night."

"That is true," Mama Serene said. "She was scared of the building, and I can hardly blame her. I asked Tohil to keep an ear out for her, in case she found herself in trouble, and that's what happened. She rents a regular room at the Broken Eye for her business; this morning, they say Emmanuel Burgunzi was found with a slashed throat in a room that she rented."

"The fat man's layabout son?" Dethocrates whistled. "This could be bad for her. I assume you wish me to bring the lost lamb back to the fold?"

The lady nodded. "She has a daughter, as well. I can make sure they're somewhere safe, until the matter settles."

"Arcxas's eyes, children complicate things," Dethocrates said casting his gaze around the crowded building, down at his cup, and finally drained it in silence. Then, he looked across at the lady who had helped him once, when nobody else would.

"I have a few people I can talk to," he said. "I make no promises that I can find her before anyone else, but I'll find her nonetheless."

"Good," Mama Serene said. "If you need an extra sword, I'm sure Tohil would be willing to help."

Dethocrates stood, making a slight, formal bow. "Hopefully, that won't be necessary."

Dethocrates stared into the alleyway and cursed.

The woman had been lovely, he could tell. Not one of the great beauties of the age, but still lovelier than the Black Gate deserved. This beauty was marred now, by blue lips, bruised throat, and bulging eyes.

Kneeling, Dethocrates slowly closed the sightless eyes. He'd spent hours combing the Black Gate, asking around, calling in favors, paying for drinks, using up money meant for his own debauchery. He'd walked paths to and from places she'd been spotted a half-dozen times, looking for new routes as the rain started and stopped. Finally, three blocks from the hovel she lived in, he'd found her. He looked around the alleyway, noting where piles of refuse had been knocked over. He could see that there had been a struggle, and that the woman's pockets had been emptied. The stones around him whispered of her death, but he did his best to put that out of his mind; as on the rare occasions that he heard the city's stones clearly, they always lied.

"Is she gone?" a voice asked.

Dethocrates whirled around and saw Ixti standing two feet behind him. "How long have you been following me?" he asked.

"Since the Raised Market. I don't have anything better to do until tonight. Who was she?"

"Her name was Melyne," Dethocrates said, standing. "She found herself mixed up in a murder. It seems she was taking alleys, to avoid being seen, and someone throttled her for her coins; the only question remaining is—"

Dethocrates was cut off as one of the piles of trash moved. There was a groan, and the pile rolled over, revealing a man who'd been obscured by garbage.

Dethocrates stepped closer, pulling refuse off of the derelict. Dirt caked him from head to foot, obscuring how old he was, or what his country of origin might be. Still, when Dethocrates looked into his face, the man looked back, his eyes clearly seeing what was around him. Dethocrates hoped he was dealing with a beggar, not a madman.

"Did you see anything, stranger?"

The man slowly sat up, clutching his throat. "Saw the girl die," he said, his voice raspy and dry, "and what came after."

Dethocrates reached for the skin of walking-wine on his belt, as the city had few clean sources of water, and put it to the man's lips. It was coarse stuff, but the man drank it eagerly. "What do you mean, came after?" Dethoc asked.

The man looked around; the grime on his face made it hard to tell if he showed fear. "Woman cut through here with a girl. Man came in after her, a big man. He grabbed her, no talkin or nothin, just grabbed her, and choked the life out of her. The girl kicked him a few times, but he just pushed her into the wall, knocked her off her feet. The woman died, and he went through her pockets, found more coins than a woman like that should have been carrying and then left, like it was nothing."

Ixti looked around the alley as the man talked, face somber.

"Do you remember what the man looked like?" Dethocrates asked.

The beggar nodded. "Aye. Ruffian in one of the local gangs. I remember him well. But that's not the end of the story."

The man looked at the alley's mouth. "The girl stayed behind, weeping. That's when they showed up. Four of 'em. Didn't say much. Two had knives, one had a club, and the other had a sack. Just saw the girl by herself, knocked her out, tossed her into a sack, and were gone."

"Kidnappers," Dethocrates muttered. "Were any of them wearing medallions? Designs of any sort? Specifically, a jaguar?"

"Yeah, one had a tattoo, like a cat. Coulda been a jaguar."

"Arcxas's eyes," Dethocrates cursed. "They're cultists."

Ixti leaned over. "Cultists? To the old gods?"

Dethocrates nodded. "All the trouble in the Black Gate started with a man who claimed to serve a jaguar god. He started pulling people out of the city stones with a magic bracelet, including the Bloody Lady. He may have died at the hands of Tohil, but those he freed are still out there with the bracelet."

"So, they're the people who originally owned the city?"

"And if they're the kidnappers, I'm guessing they're none too pleased at the way the newcomers treat it." Dethocrates helped the beggar to his feet, then reached into his pouch, pulled out ten coatls, and handed them to the man. "Thank you for your troubles, stranger. I would be grateful if you could do one more favor for me—go to the Silk Purse, and let them know that Deth needs Tohil. You may then use this money as you wish. I suggest starting with a bath; there are several experts on such matters on the premises."

The man looked at the silver coins, his eyebrows lifting as he first mumbled the words 'Silk Purse' and 'experts' then fully forming, "Deth needs Tohil," before finishing with, "Understood."

Ixti looked up at Dethocrates as the man left. "You trust him to deliver the message?"

Dethocrates nodded. "He may look like he slept in the swamp, but he was smart enough to stay alive when five killers came through the alley, and smart enough to tell me what happened. That means he knows me as folk of the Gate. My message will get to Tohil. Now, I just need to find another sword-arm somewhere."

"You need Tohil for what?"

"Since the Silk Purse is involved, I know I can trust him in this, and I'm going to need a Sturgeon. If it's the cultists, they're probably hiding in the Ghost Towers, and he might know where. I've got just enough money left over to hire a third man to come with us."

Ixti looked excited. "We're going to the Ghost Towers? That's great!"

Dethocrates put his hand on Ixti's shoulder. "No. Three men are going to the Ghost Towers. *You* are not. You are going to find the other six who made the dare and keep them in the Black Gate for the rest of the festival. I'll even pay you to stay out, if that's what it takes."

Ixti shot Dethoc a nasty look. "You better pay me a lot."

The floodgates had opened, and the rain was pouring now. In other districts, the Serpent Dances were bravely carrying on in spite of the weather, refusing to behave as if all wasn't well. No such dances went on among the Ghost Towers, though. The occasional wilted flower or stolen bouquet was on display in some parts of the district, but where the three armed men walked there was little sign of life. Rain spattered against the cold and empty stone, and handfuls of desperate vagabonds crouched inside the abandoned buildings, sheltered against the weather but hounded by restless spirits.

Tohil led them through the gloom. He'd explained that the Sturgeons knew where the cultists gathered, but that removing them wasn't a priority. Increase Coin walked just behind him, hand never leaving his sword hilt. In the rear walked Dethocrates, leather satchel strapped to his back, looking behind every few seconds, eyes adjusting to the increasing dark.

"I hate this part of town," Increase Coin muttered.

"From what I recall," Dethocrates said, "you hate this whole city. That's what you say, every time you make port. Yet you keep coming back, and you'll take money to walk through this district nonetheless."

"The money's good in Taux," Increase Coin said. "Good enough so that I'll put up with the ghosts, but never good enough that I won't complain about it. That goes double for the Rollin Shear job you've proposed for the end of the festival, Tohil."

Tohil harrumphed.

"We're not here for ghosts tonight," Dethocrates said. "We're here for former ghosts, made flesh again. The people who used to live in this city return."

Tohil stopped short and turned around. "I don't know what the people we're after were like in the old days, but I know what they're like now. They're not here to resume their lives; they're here to hurt the city. My city. I've got no qualms putting this group down. By the way, we're here – it's the temple at the end of the block."

Dethocrates studied the outside of the structure, as well as the buildings nearby. "Any idea how many we might be dealing with?"

Tohil shrugged. "My guess would be about a dozen, but there could be a lot more. Four to one odds are our best bet; I'm not sure how I feel about just walking through the front door."

"We're not here to slaughter them all," Dethocrates said, "just to rescue any kidnapped victims, and maybe grab the bracelet if we're lucky. My hope is, if we come at them from all sides, and put up enough of a show of force, they'll break and run."

Increase Coin crossed his arms. "So, we're not just storming through the front door?"

"One of us will have to," Dethocrates admitted. "However, another of us, a daring Jai-Ruk skilled in archery, is going to get to the temple's second floor from a nearby building, and provide cover. Meanwhile, a cunning mercenary from Zimbolay will sneak ahead, take out any sentries, and find a less obvious entrance. Once these two are in position, they'll wait for the third man."

Tohil interrupted. "Would this third man be a thick-skulled guardsman who was duped into walking through the front door alone?"

"I was thinking that he was a stalwart defender of the people, fully confident that his allies would be ready to help him achieve a quick victory," Dethocrates said.

"My 'allies' are a paranoid sailor and a swindling burglar," Tohil said, unenthusiastically.

"Good company for a brothel's champion," Increase Coin added.

Dethocrates spoke before the Sturgeon could reply. "I know that you have little reason to trust me, other than Mama Serene, but I will have your back. I can get up to a higher floor, and cover you from there. Find a dry spot to try and get warm – I know you fire-touched folk aren't at your best in the rain – then give the two of us ten minutes to get in position. Once the time has passed, draw your blade and walk right through that door. I promise, the first to come after you will die by my hand; that should buy you a moment or two, and Increase will come at them from another angle. They've just got their lives back; I don't think they'll be too willing to give them up."

"Or," Tohil said, "several decades spent screaming inside stone has driven them so insane that they don't care." Despite the reluctant words, he nodded. "You have ten minutes. Don't make me regret this."

Increase Coin nodded and then vanished into the dark of a side street. Dethocrates quickly found loose stones that let him climb up onto the roof of a nearby shack. Moving carefully in the rain, he crossed the roofs of the street, crouching low when he thought he might be in view. Soon, he found himself separated from one of the temple's windows by a few feet of open air and pouring rain. Taking deep breaths, Dethocrates tried not to think about the air, or the water; he thought about the stone under his feet, and the stone of the temple. He made the distance seem as small as possible in his head, and then, he jumped.

Rather than easily clearing the distance, Dethocrates's hands barely latched onto the window. The air in his lungs wheezed out as he slammed against the side, afraid for a moment that the slickness would make him slip off, but he held firm against the stone as his element connected to it and adhered. After waiting several breaths, he slowly pulled himself up, first only to eye level, to see if he'd been noticed.

He had a clear view into the main room of the temple. The room had been cleaned, and furnishings salvaged to make it livable. Torches burned in sconces along the walls, casting long shadows on the ceiling. He saw a score of people, men and women, conducting a prayer ritual. Almost directly below him, four children were tied up, guarded by three of the cultists. One man, wicked knife raised in his hand, led a prayer from the temple's altar; behind him loomed an obsidian jaguar statue. On his wrist, he wore a golden bracelet.

Once he was certain that his arrival was unnoticed, Dethocrates raised himself up onto the window ledge. He pulled the leather satchel from his back, and slowly withdrew his bow and string, leaving the arrows inside for now. As he strung his bow, he watched the ritual; the people of Old Taux chanted in a language he couldn't understand. He could also hear a reverberation to the chant; at first, he thought this was just an echo, but his blood went cold when he realized that he could hear the stones of the temple echoing in perfect rhythm.

As he watched the ritual, thoughts raced through his head; thoughts about the people of the old city, and the ordeals they had been through; worries of all the factors that could cause the plan to fail; and the lies of the whispering stone beneath him. Then, the man leading the ritual gestured to the prisoners. One of the cultists grabbed a girl, and even in the dim light, he saw the resemblance between the girl and the dead Melyne. The view of her released his introspection until all that remained was the plan; he fit an arrow to his bow, and waited.

Thunder rumbled in the distance, and the temple's main door slammed open, Tohil appearing in the doorway. The man leading the ritual saw him first, and pointed, shouting in rage. Tohil drew his sword, and shouted, "Sturgeon! Let the prisoners go!"

At the same moment, on the other side of the temple, one of the cultists cried out and fell over. Increase Coin stood behind him, blade drawn. The cultists grabbed weapons and approached the invaders.

One of the cultists closer to the entrance had been armed, ready for trouble. He raised his club and shouted, charging at Tohil. Dethocrates whispered a prayer to Saint Erik, and let his arrow fly. The charging man cried out as the dart struck him in the back; he stumbled, fell, and stayed down. As several others approached Tohil, the Sturgeon kicked a nearby chair at them; most stepped back, but one tripped and fell over, and Tohil stabbed him as he fell. Two cultists moved to either side of the chair; another arrow took out one of them, while Tohil lunged at the second.

Dethocrates then turned his attention across the temple, where Increase Coin was pressed by four of the cultists. Backed up to the wall, he grabbed a torch out of a sconce; surrounded by angered Humans, the torch's light flared brighter, and Increase swung it in front of him, leaving brief circles of light behind it. An arrow took down one of the cultists; the one next to him turned to look at his fallen comrade and Increase shoved the torch into his face. He screamed as he fell, and the remaining two cultists quickly stepped back. Increase Coin grinned and advanced.

The leader of the cultists began shouting over the din. He pointed at Tohil, and Dethocrates could hear the stones begin to murmur. He took aim at the leader, but ducked when he heard the rushing air of an arrow from below. The missile grazed his forehead, and as he ducked back he saw a cultist with a bow crouched behind furniture.

Dethocrates drew back another arrow when a dark figure caught his eye among the chaos. A curse slipped his lips as Ixti, dressed for night work, dashed through the shadows toward the now-neglected prisoners. The boy produced a knife and started cutting through the bindings when the cultist leader's eyes fell on him; he abandoned his chanting with a punctuating roar.

"Ixti! Look out!" Dethocrates shouted. The archer fired on him again. He rolled, stumbling out of the window. He caught onto the ledge with one hand, only his elemental connection to the stone keeping him there, but the satchel of arrows fell. He gasped, clenched his teeth and heaved as his muscles strained. His off hand, still holding the bow, caught in the angle of the window and he used the crux to pull himself back into the frame. There, amid the splattering rain, he saw the leader slash Ixti across the chest with a curved dagger.

Dethocrates's roar shook the temple. In a moment, he was in motion, bow in hand, leaping into the room below. He fell close to the archer, and in one arcing swing brought his full weight into a strike with his bow. The man's skull gave way and he tumbled to the stone floor with a thud. Rising, Dethocrates gripped the bow like a club, advancing on the leader and Ixti's fallen form.

Two more cultists charged and the earth stank of the depths as he beat them down, bones shattering and screams cut short with crushing finality, but the leader stood his ground. He turned his blade backward against his naked arm and whispered prayers as Dethocrates approached. He grinned confidently as he chanted, but the stones beneath Dethocrates didn't move, or so much as whisper. The man's eyes grew wide as his prayers went unanswered; he looked down in horror at his now empty right wrist, the bracelet gone.

Dethocrates bore down on the man with a great leap, the bow singing in the air before it struck. Blade met wood, but the earth was overwhelming and the blade fell away, even as the bow snapped in half. Dethocrates cast aside the remnants of his improvised weapon and grappled the man, twisting his knife-arm until it snapped. The knife fell, but the man howled a defiant curse through the pain and bit Dethocrates on the shoulder. Dethocrates roared again, raised the man over his head, and pitched him back against the altar. The impact crumpled the body as it tumbled head-first onto the flags with a sickening thud.

Cultists shouted and screamed, some clawing at their faces to be ended by Tohil or Coin while others fled through unseen holes to the streets beyond.

Dethocrates shook violently, his breath coming in great gasps before he shook the darkness of the deep earth away and stumbled over to the prisoners. Ixti, blood trailing from him, lay with the children, his hands clutching the leader's bracelet in his hands.

"I got their magic," Ixti wheezed, "I stopped them."

Dethocrates carefully picked Ixti up in his arms. "You did," he said. "Nobody can say you're not brave, Ixti, or a man of the Black Gate. Now, try to keep quiet; I'm getting you to a healer."

Tohil finished untying the children who looked fearfully up at the man but more so at Dethocrates. Coin walked over to them, knelt down, and extended his hand to Melyne's daughter.

"You are safe," he said. "I knew your mother, and I promise, you'll be safe with me. Take my hand."

Dethocrates watched the kindness with a furrowed brow, but in Taux there were more relations and secrets than anyone could ever know. He made no comment as the remainder of the party moved to the door, Ixti's ragged breathing hissing softly in his ears.

Dethocrates coughed, clearing a rapidly-tightening throat, then continued. "Tohil and Coin brought the children to the Silk Purse and I got Ixti to the Hospitaler's Guild; the last of my money going for the boy's treatment."

The paladin had been quiet through most of the Jai-Ruk's story, only occasionally asking for more information. "What about Melyne's killer? You said the beggar had an idea what he looked like; have you found him?"

"As it turned out," Dethocrates said, "I just missed him. On the Night of Secrets, before the celebration, I went to settle my accounts. There, I learned that Master Dharn, the man who treated Ixti, had also treated a man matching the killer's description. He had come in earlier that day, suffering from poison; his life could not be saved."

"Any idea who killed him?"

Dethocrates shook his head. "Probably another in his gang, jealous of his success. Does it matter? A rich man's son dies in a rented room; the next day, the woman he was with tries to hide from the scandal, gets mugged, and dies in an alleyway; the next day, her mugger dies under care in a healer's bed. Death, you may have noticed, whispers to all of us in the Black Gate."

"Actually," Lady Evynhoe replied, "the dead man in the room wasn't the real Emmanuel Burgunzi; just a charlatan putting on airs."

Dethocrates nodded. "Of course," he said. "A little deception was all our fable was missing."

"This leaves me with one last question," Lady Evynhoe forced a smile. "The question you've known I was going to ask since you started telling your story. What happened to the bracelet?"

Dethocrates kept himself very, very calm. He thought of the stones beneath him, which were thankfully quiet, and tried to emulate their silence and coolness. "I took it from Ixti; after the Dharn released me, I walked with it for most of the night. Then, I tossed it."

Evynhoe was silent for a moment. "You tossed it?"

"Yes. I stood on the Wayside Bridge and threw it." This was true. He simply did not mention that he threw it to Shay Gatewell, and that Shay caught it.

Evynhoe leaned against the wall. "Very recently you were involved in an incident where a magical gem disappeared. Within two days of that event, ships in the harbor were shattered by a flash freeze in the night."

"So I have heard," Dethocrates said.

"This very week, you were involved in an incident where a magical bracelet disappeared. Within two days, a monster summoned by that bracelet was slain."

Dethocrates shrugged with his good arm. "As much as you want there to be a connection," he said, "there isn't, no more than there's a connection between the monster and Melyne. I'm sure you're aware that sometimes, puzzles and mysteries have extra pieces. As I said before, I didn't see everything; I'm sorry that I can't be more help to you, but that's all I saw. Do I remain a suspect despite this?"

Lady Evynhoe shook her head, thoughtfully, and then moved to open the door. As Dethocrates walked through, she added, "Just so you know, while you're innocent of the crime I'm investigating, you'll likely have to pay a fine."

Dethocrates turned, puzzled. "What are you talking about?"

"It is my understanding that street performances require permits, and as far as I can tell, you have none." Her expression blank, she closed the door.

Illustration by Jeff Laubenstein

ANOTHER WORD FOR RAIN

By Dave Gross

Fifth Day: Saint's Day

Atzi awoke in darkness, sweating from the drink and trembling from the nightmares. She'd dreamt her former neighbors stood over her, shaking their heads. Some spoke in strange accents. Others had familiar voices. She couldn't understand most of the words, only a few phrases.

"No use to us."

"No good to anyone like this."

"No use at all."

They wet their fingers on their tongues and bent down to wipe their spittle on her body.

Atzi shuddered at the wet trails on her skin until an insistent pain distracted her. Something hard pressed into her ribs. She rolled away from the source of the irritation and heard the clink of a clay bottle rolling out from beneath her. She smelled the sour, yeasty pulque. The cactus liquor left her mouth feel like mold. She reached after the sound of the bottle, yearning for the last remaining drops. Her fingers barely touched the side before it slipped away.

She struggled to rise but failed. Instead she lay back on the cool stone floor. Reaching across her thin chest, she felt the tender spot where she'd slept on the bottle. She rubbed it, wincing. As the unfamiliar pain ebbed, the familiar ones rose: the aches in her wrists and elbows, her shoulders and hips. The hollow in her belly. The hollow in her heart.

For a while she only breathed. The odor of pulque was heavy in the air, but soon she smelled stone and earth. She tried to remember where she had gone. She recalled wandering the raised market, standing aside to watch as flower dancers passed, mute while others cheered, alone while others embraced. She remembered the celebrations at Emerald Serpent, where she was unwelcome, and the Silk Purse, where she never dared to go.

She rubbed the rheum from her eyes and saw strange patterns crossing her hands and arms. Looking side to side, she saw no light. Everywhere else was utter darkness. She looked back at her hands. The gray shapes moved as she turned her wrists.

She wiped her arms, but the patterns remained. They shed no light, but she saw them as clearly as dawn seeping through the cracks of a hovel. She thought of her dream and of her neighbors' wet fingers. She thought of ghosts.

Atzi scrambled to her feet. She slipped barefoot in a cool puddle. She fell to the stone floor, protecting her head with one arm. Her elbow slapped into the viscous mess on the floor. She smelled the stench of vomit. Even in her panic, she hoped the mess was not her own. The thought of a stranger sleeping near her in the dark changed her mind. She hoped it was her own.

Disgust and the thought of cracking her head on a stone corner slowed her panic. She wiped her elbow across the stone floor and stood again, arms outstretched. She felt her way through empty air. Her breath came quick and shallow. She yelped when her hands touched a carved stone wall.

Her fingers navigated the shapes: waves and serpents, sheaves and bushels, human figures and naked skulls. They found a rectangular cavity, and within it a stiff, beaded sheet of fabric. She pressed her palms against the brittle garment until she felt what lay beneath it. Bones.

She was in the catacombs.

When Chicahua first announced they would move to the city, Atzi had been frightened by the tales she had heard of Taux. It was known even in their distant village that the place was accursed because of the catacombs.

In the days of Atzi's great-grandmother's grandmother, the Moon Priests and Tome-Mages of Taux commanded the tunnels built beneath their city. They desired to perform a great ritual. For what purpose, Atzi could not say. Yet it was known that this ritual caused

the death of every living soul within a hundred miles of the city.
Ghost villages surrounded the empty city, the blackened ashes of their
previous inhabitants blasted to the walls of their hovels, the boles of
the swamp trees.

For years none dared approach the city of Taux. Then scouts
returned with tales that the city was not destroyed. It stood empty but
for the Lowl who scavenged the abandoned houses.

Before what was left of the Tolimic people could reclaim their city,
invaders from the New Kingdoms claimed it as a free city for trade
among their foreign lands: Thalonia, Gariny, Dravaria, Zimbolay,
Findalynn, Arcania, and some place called the Opal Gates. Those
names frightened Atzi almost as much as the tale of Taux.

By the time Atzi and Chicahua carried their meager belongings
to the city, foreigners had claimed all the richest houses. They staked
out entire neighborhoods for themselves, leaving the haunted streets
of the Temple District for the Lowl and Tolimic refugees. Those who
prospered might hope to move their families to the Harbor district.
Those who proved most ingenious or useful to the foreigners might find
a place of service in the Turquoise Tortoise or Gold Jaguar districts.

Chicahua was neither ingenious nor especially useful to the
foreigners, but he was strong and hard-working, so he found work
in the Harbor district. The pay was only enough to rent a modest
home in the Haunted Temple District. At night they heard the
whispers from the carvings on the streets. Atzi wept and pleaded
with Chicahua to return to their village. He pleaded with her to
be brave and promised that, in time, they would grow used to the
strange sounds as all their neighbors had.

And, in time, he had been right. After the birth of their daughter,
Teyacapan, Atzi came to hear the mutterings of the city's dead with
little more fear than at the cry of a distant jaguar or the rumble of an
approaching storm. But that had been when she lay beside Chicahua at
night, Teya cradled between them, neighbors with their own children
lying in houses to either side of them.

Ten years later, Atzi enjoyed no such comforts. Teya was gone.
Chicahua was gone. Atzi was alone in the dark subterranean passages
of a haunted city.

The pulque that had soothed her mind during the festival now
punished her body. Her head throbbed. Her back ached. Blind and

lost, she searched the unseen passages for any sign of light, for anything she could see except the dull gray marks upon her arms.

She searched for hours, turning back when she came to a dead end. A few times she screamed as she trod upon a brittle mess on the floor or walked herself into a sudden cul-de-sac.

Sometimes she fell to her knees and wept until she felt invisible eyes boring into her neck, judging her. She wiped her tears, licked the moisture from her hands, and stood again.

Her tongue grew thick. Her parched throat narrowed. She began to think she would die there in the dark. She began to think that was just as well.

She screamed again as she felt hard claws and a warm belly scuttle over her naked foot. A dozen more tiny creatures followed, a few climbing her garments, scratching and biting at her legs until she slapped them off. One clung to her hand. She tried to fling it away, but it locked its teeth into the thick of her thumb and held fast. She smashed it twice against the wall. It fell away, its squeal dwindling to a whimper.

Still screaming, Atzi ran through the rats' nest, one arm raised high, the other straight forward, until her foot struck stone and she fell onto a stairway. She heard distant singing and saw a blue-green wall tickled by light.

On hands and knees, she climbed. Halfway up the stairs, she paused to dispel an unbidden memory of Teya's first awkward climb up the four steps to their shack beside the Harvest Temple. A convulsion wracked her body. She swallowed the memory with the bile of her empty stomach and resumed her climb.

Atzi emerged in one of the city's aqueducts, crouching beneath the low curving ceiling. The wall she had glimpsed was furry with mold above a runoff grate through which she smelled the rich ordure of the city sewers. She followed the damp channel toward the daylight.

Sprawled in the tunnel entrance lay a fat-bellied Findalynn man. In one arm he cradled a green wine bottle, the cheap kind wound inside a jacket of reeds. He spied Atzi emerging from the shadows. His song dribbled away.

He pinched his oily mustache as she approached, his lips smiling for a moment before forming a plump little moue. He blinked, shook his head, and smiled again.

"What is this?" he said. "A flower spirit emerging from the pure springs of Taux to soothe my weary—?"

"Give me a drink." Atzi reached for the wine bottle.

He moved the bottle away. "Give me a reason."

"I'm thirsty."

"So am I." He snaked a hand around her calf.

Atzi grabbed the wine bottle in both hands and drank. The wine was sourer than pulque, dry and tannic. It was gone in two swallows.

The man's hand moved higher. He pulled it back when he touched the wounds the rats had left. He looked surprised at the blood on his fingers. "You're bleeding."

Atzi swung the bottle down on his head. A brawler's confidence swelled in her chest. "So are you."

The glass didn't break, but a trickle of blood ran down the man's brow and into one eye. He wobbled, belched, and looked up at her with a confused expression. She hit him again. He slumped.

Atzi tipped the bottle to eke out its last few drops. She dropped it into the man's lap and walked out into the light.

The sun hung directly above the city, throwing narrow frames of shadow around the stone buildings and the gray wooden shacks at their feet. From every direction came the sounds of people talking, children playing, cart wheels rolling across the streets. A crier shouted something about a murder in the Black Gate District. Behind it all, Atzi heard a faint susurrus of whispers from the carved walls.

She was back in the Haunted Temple District, where she had once lived. Yet the last she remembered of the night before, she had passed beyond the Black Gate into the raised market, watched the flower dancers in the Ullamalitzi stadium, drew away from the celebrants at the tavern and the brothel and then…

The rest she didn't remember, except for the nightmare of disappointed neighbors murmuring over her.

Atzi knew she couldn't have stumbled all the way across the city before succumbing to sleep or pulque—she hardly knew the difference anymore. Somehow she had crossed the entire city wandering blind through the catacombs.

A boy ran into Atzi. Menial labor had hardened her body, so the impact startled rather than hurt her. The boy shook his head as though he'd banged into a wall. He looked nine or ten years old. Atzi knew that probably meant he was seven or eight. Children of the Haunted Temple always looked older.

The boy pushed off of Atzi's hip and ran away clutching a feathered doll, the sort given to those with the finest blossoms at the Dance of Serpents.

"No, bring it back!" A girl appearing about eight pursued the thief. She'd scraped both knees black and red. A bright trickle of blood ran down her shin. She stopped before Atzi and looked up, eyes shimmering with tears. "He took it."

The sight of the girl made Atzi's stomach tighten. She swallowed to keep herself from vomiting. Atzi tried to walk around the girl, but she stepped in front of her. The girl raised her arms as if to be lifted and comforted.

"I fell," said the girl. The tears began to streak down her dirty face.

Atzi swallowed to keep from vomiting. "Nobody cares."

She pushed past the girl, moving fast. She had to get away before the crying. If she heard the crying, it would be too much.

A pulque vendor led his donkey through the crowd, heading north toward the bridge to the Harbor District.

"Wait," Atzi called out to him. "I want a drink."

The vendor turned. Atzi recognized him at the same moment he recognized her. He shook his head. "I ought to call the Sturgeons." He pointed at her and shouted to all nearby. "This woman steals! She owes me for two gourds of pulque!"

Atzi gave him the fig and walked away. No one stopped her, but everyone stared. She felt their disapproving stares like wet fingers on the back of her neck.

"Here," called a man from a painted shop under a yellow-and-white awning. A few customers sat outside, drinking chocolate and nibbling on snacks from the little dishes they used to protect their drinks from flies. The proprietor was a stout man of blended Tolimic and Zimbolay features, a touch of frost on either side of his curls. He held up a clay cup, its surface beaded with moisture. So cold. "Have a drink."

In six swift steps, Atzi moved beside him and took the cup in both hands. She drank with a thirst so deep that she drained the cup before she realized it wasn't pulque.

"Water!" She raised the cup, half intending to throw it in his face.

"Not so fast," he said, catching her wrist. He took the cup from her hand. "You need more water and some food. Come inside."

Atzi was ready to walk away when a passing woman cupped a hand to her mouth and said, "Don't waste your time, Khamisi. She has no money. She's a thief."

Atzi spun around to glare at her accuser. She didn't know the woman. She was only repeating what she'd heard the pulque vendor say. She raised her chin and sniffed at Atzi.

Atzi took a step toward her. The woman hurried off, pushing through the crowd. A warm hand encircled Atzi's upper arm, holding her back.

"Is this true?" said the man who had given her water. The woman had called him Khamisi.

Atzi whirled to face him. She pulled her arm away. "Are you asking whether I'm a thief?"

"I'm asking whether you have no money."

"What if I don't?"

"If you don't, then you are not a customer."

"I don't have any money."

"Then you are not a customer." He shrugged, and his frown became a smile. "Today you are my guest and must share my supper. It is only soup, but it is good."

"I don't want—"

Before Atzi could finish, the girl with the scraped knees pushed past her and raised her arms to Khamisi. He lifted her up and gave her a squeeze before holding her at arm's length and tsking at her scraped knees. She sucked her lip and made her eyes big for him.

"But before that, we must clean these dirty knees. What do you say—?"

"There! There she is!"

Atzi turned once more toward the street. There standing beside a pair of Sturgeons was the Findalynn she had struck. Blood streaked across his forehead and cheek. He cradled his empty wine bottle in one arm, pointing at her with the other. "There is the ghost woman!"

One of the Sturgeons crooked his finger at her.

Atzi took a deep breath. Her body tensed, ready to run. She felt as hollow as an empty gourd.

The Sturgeons put their hands on their weapons. The older one said, "Don't make us run."

The younger one added, "It's too hot. We'll be angry."

Atzi released her breath. She felt as heavy as an empty wine bottle.

The Sturgeons had rounded up dozens of others from the district, mostly Tolimic but also a few half-breeds and Lowls. Their clerks wrote down their names and the locations of their homes or—as often as not, "no home." Atzi was placed in the latter group and left to wait in a pen outside the watch post while the Sturgeons interrogated the others. They waited for hours, while the heat of the sun settled like a blanket over the city. Atzi began to wish she had drunk a second cup of water before the Sturgeons arrested her.

The other homeless were drunks, brawlers, and thieves. One was a broad-shouldered bully who squatted beside the water pail, demanding a fee for each drink. The poor paid him. The destitute wheedled and pled. From them he extracted favors for tiny sips.

Atzi's tongue swelled. Her head grew dizzy.

As the sun melted into the western sea, the bully eyed Atzi and waved a ladle of water at her. She glowered at him until he drank it himself and turned away.

Atzi wondered whether the others would help overthrow him if she started by kicking him in the neck. They wouldn't, she decided. They would watch him beat her until the Sturgeons broke up the fight. They would steal a drink while she fought.

Maybe she could steal a drink as well.

Atzi moved, ready to rush in and kick the bully. Another prisoner started at her approach, alerting him. He turned, crouched low to guard his pail. His arms were thick and muscled. He sneered, his face like one of the masks carved into the temple walls. When his gaze locked on Atzi, his fearsome expression faltered. He choked and backpedaled, almost spilling the water pail as he tripped over it.

Atzi ran to the pail and scooped water into her mouth with both hands.

Instead of driving her off, the bully scuttled along the margin of the pen, moving as far away from her as he could manage. The others did the same, everyone competing to get the farthest away.

Atzi lifted the pail in both hands and drank. In the rippling surface of the water she saw her face. It looked thinner than she'd ever seen it before. Her skin was covered in gray lines like the glistening track of a snail. The writing did not glow, not like the crescent of the Ghost moon floating above her shoulder. It looked as though someone had wiped a finger across a dusty mirror. The lines looked less like stains on her skin and more like windows revealing something beneath it.

A sudden rapping on the bars of the pen broke her reverie.

"That one," said a Sturgeon, pointing at Atzi. "Bring her inside now."

The Sturgeons questioned her in a lighted room before moving her to a dark cell. They looked at her and whispered among themselves. She couldn't see the Sturgeons well, but standing beside one of them she saw two pale gray figures. One was a Thalonian man, his hair and clothes damp. The other was a Tolimic boy of perhaps fifteen. Perhaps thirteen.

Atzi didn't know how she knew, but she knew they were ghosts. She didn't know how she knew, but she knew the Sturgeon with the raspy voice had killed them.

The Sturgeons left her alone in the dark for hours before taking her back to the lighted room. They sent for a Tome-Mage. While they waited for him to arrive, they took turns asking her the same questions.

"Where were you on the Night of Secrets?"

"Tonight is the Night of Secrets," said Atzi. "Isn't it?"

"Where were you during the Dance of Serpents?"

"The Black Gate District."

"Did you go to the Emerald Serpent? Were you inside the Silk Purse?'"

"No. I watched the Serpent Dance. I think I saw the fireworks."

"Were you there to pick pockets? To steal?"

She shook her head.

"Answer the question."

"No," she lied.

"Where did you wake up?"

"Somewhere beneath the city. It was dark."

"How did you get there?"

"I don't remember."

"You were drunk."

She shrugged.

"Answer the question."

"I was drunk."

"Who was with you?"

"Nobody. I told you that already."

"What were you doing in the Black Gate District on the Night of Secrets?"

"I wasn't there on the—What day is this?"

"Answer the question."

"I thought tonight was the Night of Secrets."

"Where did you get those marks on your body?"

"I don't know."

"How long have you had them?"

"Since I woke up," she said.

Was that true? She wondered. How long had she had them? She remembered the dream, the whispers, the feeling of wet fingers—or were they tongues?—upon her skin. Had the ghosts marked her? Or had they wiped away the dust to reveal a mirror underneath?

"I don't know."

They took her back in the dark cell. Someone had left a pair of maize cakes on the straw pallet. There was a pail of fresh water. There was an empty pail that stank.

Atzi ate the cakes, drank some water, and lay down to sleep. She woke, or thought she woke, to the sound of whispers. Three ghosts stood by her bed: a sick woman, a young man, and an old man.

"They left me here," said the ghost of the sick woman. "They knew I needed medicine, but they didn't care."

"Nobody cares," said Atzi.

"I spat on the fat guard with the monkey on his shoulder," said the ghost of the young man. "He beat me to death in this cell. Nobody stopped him."

"Nobody cares."

"You don't care either," said the ghost of the old man.

"No," Atzi agreed. "I don't."

Another ghost walked through the wall. "I hanged myself in the next cell."

"Nobody cares," said the ghost of the sick woman. "She doesn't care."

"She's no use to us," said the ghost of the old man.

The ghost of the young man began to weep. The ghost of the sick woman shook her head. They faded away.

Atzi lay on the pallet and tried to sleep. She couldn't sleep. She lay there for hours, maybe more than a day.

A jailer came by, leaving the outer door open. Morning light spilled through the bars of the cell. He passed Atzi two more maize cakes. He poured fresh water through the bars into her pail. She asked him what day it was.

"Saints Day," he said before catching himself. "I'm not supposed to talk to you."

"Is a Tome-Mage coming?"

"I'm not supposed—" He shut his mouth and left her alone.

Throughout the day, Atzi heard doors open and close. She heard many voices, some meek, others angry, as those who had been rounded up were released one by one. She ate half of one of her cakes and saved the rest for later. She drank a little water. She traced the path of the gray characters on her arm. She tried to read the messages on her legs and belly, but she could make out only incomplete phrases: "…angry when I burned our supper and took…" "…always hated me, so when I met her…" "…lost, he said he would take me home but…"

After reading the last phrase, Atzi tugged down her clothes to cover as much of her skin as she could. She didn't want to know any more about what had happened to the ghosts.

She heard the Sturgeons arguing even before they opened the door. "I know this woman," said a voice she thought she should recognize. "If none of the mages wants to see her, I say let her go."

Keys jangled in the lock. "She still can't account for the night of the murder, or the one afterward. She's been in fights."

"Do you seriously think she could kill someone like *her?*"

The outer door opened, and Atzi closed her eyes against the light. It was a strange light, not the yellow rays of midday nor the red glow of dusk. There was blue and green in that light, and a kind of grayness. A storm was coming.

When Atzi opened her eyes, a Sturgeon and a jailer were opening her cell door. Instead of letting her out, the Sturgeon stepped inside.

"Do you remember me?" said the Sturgeon. His eyes looked tired, and more than a day's growth of beard covered his dark scarred cheeks.

With reluctance, Atzi nodded.

"It's been a while, so I wasn't sure you'd remember. I'm Tohil, I searched for your girl," he said. "Teya."

Surprised to hear him say her daughter's name, Atzi felt her lips tremble. She clenched her teeth to stop it.

"I looked for your husband, too."

"I remember," she said, hoping saying it would make him stop talking about it. There was nothing he could tell her that she didn't already know.

No one knew where Teya had gone. She had been playing in the street before Atzi called her in for supper. She asked the neighbors where she had gone. No one had seen her going off with anyone. When Chicahua came home, they went together, asking all the neighbors. After a few frantic hours, they went to the Sturgeons.

The Sturgeons didn't care about one Tolimic girl, no matter what this man before her said. They said they would search, but Atzi knew they never had. If they had searched, they would have found her. They would have found something.

Atzi and Chicahua had searched every night, together at first. They had asked all their neighbors for help. A few searched with them, at first. But one by one they gave up. Then Atzi and Chicahua searched separately to cover more streets, to ask more people whether they had seen the girl alone or with someone who led her away. No one had seen anything.

One night Atzi came home to collapse on the floor of their little shack. When she woke up, Chicahua was gone. She went out again, day and night, asking neighbors and strangers the same questions over and over. Have you seen a little girl? Have you seen a man? Nobody had, they said. They grew impatient. In time, even before Atzi asked, they said, "I don't know anything."

And so Atzi stopped looking. She took menial jobs in the Harbor District, nothing that paid well. She spent her earnings on food and pulque. At first, she drank only enough to help her sleep. Each week it seemed to take more and more. Soon she needed a drink to start the day, and then she needed a drink with lunch. After that, she had a drink instead of lunch, and when she returned the foreman sent her away from the docks.

The Sturgeon, Tohil, stood a while, looking down at her from across the cell. She looked down at the straw.

"Is there anything you can think of about the last few nights that you didn't tell the others?"

Atzi shook her head.

"Do you have someplace to stay?"

Atzi started to shake her head, but then she realized they might not let her go if she had nowhere to stay. "Yes."

"Where?"

He had caught her lie, but then she remembered the vendor who had given her water. "A man named Khamisi. He invited me to be his guest."

Tohil narrowed his eyes and drew in a long breath between his teeth. "I know the place. I'm going to look for you there," he said. "When I do, I want to find you."

Atzi nodded. She stood up, and Tohil led her out of the jail.

To the east, dark clouds crawled toward the city. Behind them, to the west, the molten sun sank into the ocean. The long crooked finger of the Star Tower pointed to the sky. Atzi saw no omens there, only the pitiless stars.

"One more thing," Tohil said. "Lay off the pulque."

Atzi scoffed, amazed at his condescension.

"Seriously," he said. "You're no use to anyone drunk."

Atzi shuddered to hear him speak the ghosts' words. Despite the warm air, she hugged her arms as she walked away.

After the first street, she realized she was heading toward her old home. She turned around to see the Sturgeon had followed her, watching to see where she would go. Avoiding his gaze, she turned back and walked toward Khamisi's.

Thunder crackled to the east. Storm clouds crossed the eastern wall to loom above the Haunted Temple District.

The first cold raindrops shocked Atzi. She hurried on, eyes searching for the yellow-and-white awning she had seen earlier. If she could get inside, even for a few moments, she hoped she could persuade Khamisi to let her stay long enough for the Sturgeon to leave her alone.

Another rumble of thunder trembled through the streets. The drops became a drizzle, and the last rays of sunset drowned in the shadows. People cried out, covered their heads with anything close at hand, and ran for shelter.

A woman screamed. Atzi turned to see her pointing back at her. She looked down to see the ghost marks on her arms had become visible in the gloom.

People fled from her. The heavier the rain fell, the more her ghost marks seemed to shine. Soon the street was empty except for Atzi and one other. The girl who had skinned her knees a few days earlier stood staring at her.

From beneath the awning, Khamisi called out, "Tepin! Come in out of the rain."

Tepin looked up at Atzi. The rain trailed like tears down her face, but she wasn't crying. She raised her arms up to Atzi.

Atzi didn't move. For a moment she couldn't remember whether she had heard the man call "Teya" or "Tepin." Atzi wasn't drunk. She knew Tepin wasn't her daughter.

The girl didn't look anything like Teya. She was the wrong age. Besides, Teya had never been so quick to cry, nor so slow to obey when called out of the rain. Yet she had not come in when Atzi called her in for supper on that first day of her absence. She was never coming home.

"Can't you hear him calling?" Atzi said. "Go inside."

"I can't," said Tepin. She moved closer, raising her arms higher.

"Get inside," said Atzi. She no longer wanted to go inside Khamisi's shop, not even to elude the Sturgeon. She just wanted to get away from this little girl, this phantom of her loss. "There's nothing wrong with you. You don't need to be held."

"I know," said Tepin. "You're the one who's hurt."

Atzi had a mad thought. Maybe she could wave away the ghost like wood smoke. She could dispel her with her hands. She reached out.

Before she knew it, she had the girl—the warm, living girl—in her arms, hugging her tight, both of their bodies heaving with sobs.

Khamisi took a step out of his shop. He stood there watching, his clothes growing heavy with rain as his mouth opened in a perfect O. His gaze drifted left and right of Atzi and Tepin, to a gathering crowd surrounding them.

Atzi turned to see ghosts oozing out of the alleys and windows, the sewer channels and storm drains. She heard their whispers. She felt their cool hands upon her shoulders. She listened to their complaints, nodding as she realized how she could once more be of use.

Atzi carried Tepin to the shop and set her down just beneath the awning. Atzi remained outside with the ghosts and the rain.

Khamisi said, "Come in and dry yourself. I still have some of my wife's clothes."

"I can't stay," said Atzi. She turned back to the ghosts. "I have to look for something."

"What?"

"I don't know." Atzi looked down at the ghost characters on her palms. "They will tell me."

Tepin tugged on Atzi's hem. "But first, soup."

Atzi tried to smile, but it fell to pieces in the rain. Laughing or crying, she let Tepin pull her into Khamsin's shop. She dried herself and put on another woman's clothes. She ate soup with another woman's husband and another woman's daughter.

The ghosts waited.

Illustration by Todd Lockwood

SOUL OF FIRE

By Martha Wells

Sixth Day: *Elemental Day*

Jelith asked, "Why are we in a brothel?"

Lady Evynhoe eyed him. "I will ask the questions."

"Are the questions to do with brothels?"

A small collection of men stood by the door, and one turned an amused snort into a cough.

They were in the Silk Purse, in a room lined with lustrous drapes and rich brocades and overstuffed cushions, salacious paintings on the walls. Jelith was not a frequenter of brothels, but also not as puzzled as he pretended. It was still an odd place to be questioned by a Paladin. "If you were in my position, you would ask the same," Jelith leaned his elbows on the table, as if he and the Inquisitor were about to have a scholarly discussion. "You would think it odd. You would ask yourself—"

Lady Evynhoe advanced on him. "You are a treasure hunter."

"No." Jelith tried to be helpful. "Perhaps you have the wrong person?"

She took a seat opposite him at the table, her expression clearly indicating that she thought he was a very clumsy liar. "You are Jelith the Kin, who hunts treasure with one Kryranen, a Jai-Ruk."

"We do not hunt treasure, we hunt the past," Jelith explained, unperturbed. "We are scholars."

Lady Evynhoe lifted a skeptical brow. "Scholars who find treasure."

"It turns up occasionally, and it would be strange to ignore it." Jelith spread his hands. "I can show you our writings, they are extensive." He dug into the pouch on the table and pulled out their latest notes and conclusions from their explorations into Taux' catacombs. It was a sizable sheaf.

Lady Evynhoe lifted the first page, her eyes narrowing, a faint line of consternation between her brows. Jelith kept his expression mild and helpful. Yes, it would be a bit much to claim he had whipped it all up just to fool her. "That won't be necessary." She pushed the papers back. "Were you and your associate Kryranen on the leeward Ullamalitzli court three nights ago, during the Night of Secrets?"

"Ah, no." That one he could answer with truthful confidence.

"Then where were you?"

"At work." Jelith shrugged. "Where we always are."

The story that Jelith had no intention of telling started when he and Kryranen were accosted twice.

It was on the second day of the Festival of a Thousand Blooms, the day of the Dance of Serpents, when each district would have its public dances and the carefully constructed feathered serpents would wind through the enthusiastic crowds. Of course the day had dawned with rain, which would make everything unpleasant for the celebrants.

Jelith and Kryranen were not much for dances so they were working in the catacombs as usual. They had spent much of the morning in unproductive delving, and were preparing to move to another section. Jelith had found a passage beneath a wall with incomprehensible, but strangely alluring, symbols and writing on it. While he had searched beneath the stone, Kryranen had spent her time reading through their notes and books, trying to match these symbols to others in the catacombs and looking for patterns. Jelith had discovered the passage held nothing and led nowhere, and his dark skin was covered with rock dust mixed with sweat. Kryranen had found no patterns or meaning and her brown skin and the dark fall of hair was also covered with rock dust and sweat. They both had pounding headaches and were ready to leave this section and perhaps never visit it again.

"We're so close," Kryranen said, frustrated, as they trudged up the ramp toward the corridor that would take them to the next probably equally disappointing section. "I feel it."

Jelith felt it too. Every time he probed the rock, he heard the voices, tasted the old blood, and sensed…something, just out of reach. He nodded wearily. "Perhaps when we can try that chamber down—"

The figure stepped out of the shadows into the light of their lamp. It had been concealed near the left hand column wall. Jelith flinched back. Kryranen half-drew her sword.

The problem with the catacombs was that they were generally known to be empty and haunted, so they tended to be occupied only by mad people drawn to emptiness and ghosts, or actual ghosts, or those who enjoyed preying on mad people. Jelith and Kryranen were the only ones down here who fell into none of those categories. So coming upon another living person suddenly was often not a pleasant experience.

It was a Human woman, dressed in stained and worn clothing, her face haggard with premature age. None of this was unusual in Taux. But what made Jelith stare were the patterns that crawled across the bare flesh of her face and arms like fading gray snakes. He thought they were actually real serpents at first, that she had been attacked or enspelled by some horrible Haunted Temple District curse. But there was something familiar about the writhing images. It was like the visual representation of what he felt and saw in his mind when he pushed his awareness into the stones of the catacombs. He said, "I think the lady is ghost-ridden."

Kryranen peered at the person more closely. "So she is." She sheathed her sword. "You're lucky it's us," she told the woman.

The woman swayed. Her eyes were vague and wary, but Jelith thought that she was looking past them, not at them. Her voice rough and harsh, she said, "I've been told to give you a message."

"Told by who?" Kryranen asked.

The woman stepped closer. She smelled strongly of pulque but if Jelith was this ghost-ridden he would drink too. She said, "Someone who no longer lives. She no longer has her name."

"Oh." Jelith was not a great believer in listening to ghosts, feeling their motives were not to be trusted. Most of them seemed to be mainly interested in making more ghosts. But turning the woman away felt as though it might be a bad decision. On impulse, he said, "We will hear the message."

Kryranen muttered, "We are not going to want to hear this message."

Jelith muttered back, "I know that, but the message is here, and so are we. There must be a reason."

Kryranen eyed him with derision.

As if they had not spoken, the woman said, "She says that he will force you to bring him the object, but if you carry it through earth it will destroy you."

Kryranen had been right, Jelith hadn't wanted to hear this. "Who will force me to bring what?"

The woman took a step backward, shaking her head in confusion. "I only know what I'm told."

Jelith scratched his chin. "Ah." That seemed unsurprising, ghosts being what they were. "Well, at least we are warned."

Kryranen sighed. "It could be worse, I suppose. 'You're going to die, no matter what you do.' That would certainly be worse."

"True," he agreed. "Your command of the obvious—"

"Is often better than yours, yes, sadly," Kryranen retorted. She asked the woman, "Where were you when you were given this message? Here?"

Some of their words must have penetrated the woman's ghost-and-pulque haze, because she was staring at them as if she had never seen the like before. It was probably a new achievement, to be thought odd even by the ghost-ridden woman. They were an odd pair anyway, a short Kin and a tall Jai-Ruk, but their shared interest in the past and its scholarship made the denizens of the Black Gate consider them even more strange. She shook her head, as if hearing a voice inaudible to normal ears, and said, "I was in the Gold Jaguar District. The fourth house on the curve of the Street of Bitter Stars. In the courtyard with the acacia tree."

"We don't know anyone in the Gold Jaguar District," Kryranen said. The woman was backing away. Kryranen took a step forward. "Why would one of their ghosts—"

The woman bolted into darkness. Jelith swore and Kryranen rolled her eyes in annoyance. They followed the woman, fearing she would run into a wall and kill herself in her unsteady condition. But the slap of her bare feet against the stone stopped and they couldn't find her, no matter how hard they searched.

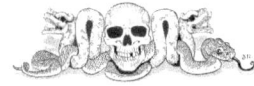

The second accosting was not so amicable.

After they had searched for some time and found no sign of the woman, Kryranen said, "She's gone to deliver her next message. I don't suppose we'll find her unless she wants us to."

Jelith agreed. They knew these catacombs as well as anyone living could, and if they couldn't find her, she was truly lost, or avoiding them deliberately. He shrugged and they went back to work.

They were in a junction room that had a passage leading off it at each of three cardinal points and one wall that was an intriguing slab of solid stone. Kryranen had marked it as worth investigation by close examination of the maps they had made. Some exploration in the passages and rooms around it had led her to suppose there might be a cavity or passage behind the slab. Or there might just be solid rock, of course, but it was worth a look.

Jelith stood in front of it, hands flat against the rock, carefully extending his senses into it. Kryranen sat on the paving stones behind him, her maps spread out around her, checking over their notes from previous explorations in this area. She said, "There has to be something here."

Jelith countered, "We both know there does not have to be—"

Their lamp flickered. The air was dead and still and Jelith turned just as Kryranen looked up.

It was not the return of their ghost-ridden friend. A man stood in the room, though Jelith had not been aware of even hearing a step on the stone. He looked Human, and nondescript for Taux, with dark hair, dark eyes, and light brown skin, though there was a cast to it that seemed unhealthy, as if the blood did not flow as vigorously beneath it as it should. He was dressed very richly, in loose pants and a long jacket of silken materials, with heavy metal bracelets and rings and other jewelry, but his clothes were disheveled as if he did not take much care for his appearance.

It was only after this inspection that he sensed the man was High Earth.

Humans, if that was what he truly was, were not meant to be High Earth and it was extremely rare to encounter one, if ever. Jelith was so distracted by the strange essence that it almost obscured the whole fact of the man's sudden appearance.

Kryranen was not so distracted. She was on her feet in an instant, one hand on her sword. "Well, this is a day for surprises. Who are you?"

The man said, "I wish to hire you."

Kryranen frowned, still uneasy. "For what purpose?"

Instead of answering the question, the man looked at Jelith. "You are High Earth, and can move your body through stone."

"Not as such." Jelith was taken aback. "You are High Earth yourself, though you appear Human. You must know that it is not so easy."

The man tilted his head, his opaque gaze fixed on Jelith. "You have done it before."

Jelith waved a hand in dismissal. "Not voluntarily. Perhaps in a life or death situation—"

"This will be a life or death situation."

Jelith went still for a moment, then glanced at Kryranen. Her expression said she shared his view of their erstwhile employer. She asked the man, "What do you mean?"

Emotionless, as if he spoke of something of no particular import, he said, "If you don't accept my commission, I'll kill you."

They both just stared at him. Nonplused, Jelith said, "You escalated that quickly. You haven't even told us—"

A crack sounded as shards of rock peeled off the far wall. Jelith shouted, "Run!" almost before his mind understood what was happening. Fortunately Kryranen moved and thought even faster.

She ducked as the shards shot toward her head, drew her sword and knocked the lamp over. Jelith turned for the nearest passage and bolted down it into the dark. Kryranen had picked another passage but they both knew where they were going. Their plan if attacked was always to split up and head for their meeting point.

Jelith darted around a corner, through a chamber and into another passage. The dark was complete but he clicked his tongue, using the echo to judge his distance from the walls with his bat-like ears. It was something their pursuer, no matter how High his Earth, couldn't emulate unless he was hiding a pair of Kin ears in his clothes.

Jelith went down a ramp, around, and up again. He ran his hand along a wall, feeling the marks he and Kryranen had left here over the years, something else the stranger wouldn't know about. Kryranen, though she had only Middling Earth affinity, could do the same with ease, and had a much better sense of direction than he did underground.

He came up into the level not far below the surface where tiny shafts riven through the rock above provided pinpricks of daylight. Pausing to listen, he heard no sound of pursuit.

Kryranen waited at the next junction of passages. Not breathing hard though in a shaft of light, he could see sweat beading on the brown skin of her arms. She lifted her brows, asking silently if anyone had followed, and he shook his head. They took a dark passage down to what appeared to be a dead end, and Jelith felt for the hidden catch they had found beneath one of the facing stones. He pushed it until it clunked and the stone slab moved, pivoting out with only a faint whisper of sound.

Jelith pushed it back into place until he felt the old locking bolts slide home. He pulled on his eye protectors as they hurried up the ramp toward the failing evening daylight at the top. They burst out into a bare open court that formed one of the many hidden entrances to the catacombs—and the earth-born man stood in the only opening.

Jelith stumbled to a halt, Kryranen beside him. They were several hundred paces from where they had started, and on the far edge of this part of the catacomb courts. There was no way the— Jelith elected to call him a 'terramancer'—could have followed them, no way that he could have known where they would go without magical aid. And even getting here so fast without knowledge of the secret way was impossible. "This is not good," Jelith muttered.

"You think?" Kryranen said.

Then the wall behind them exploded.

Jelith felt the shift travel through the stone and had an instant's warning, just enough to harden the skin of his back and to fling himself on top of Kryranen. She trusted him so well she folded as soon as she felt his weight, letting them both drop down to the pavement. She tucked her head down and he huddled over her as razor-sharp shards sliced through his shirt.

As if continuing their earlier conversation, the terramancer said, "Perhaps it would be more accurate to say, 'I want you to do a favor for me.'"

The cuts stung all down Jelith's back and his head pounded. Kryranen looked up at him, watching his face for a cue, as if she actually believed he had some sort of plan. Her faith in his intelligence was gratifying but worrisome, as he had been hoping to buy time for her to form a plan. He said, "We often hire our services to those wishing to find lost objects. There was no need for violence."

The terramancer said, "I have no intention of paying you, except with your lives."

"No, really?" Kryranen muttered under her breath.

Ignoring her, the terramancer continued, "I want you to enter the sealed chamber in the grand hall of Kree-tath House and bring out the object inside."

Kryranen said, "There's a sealed chamber in the grand hall of Kree-tath House?"

The wall behind them rumbled and more shards rained down. Jelith hunched his shoulders and winced. Kryranen murmured, "Apparently so."

Still speaking to Jelith, the terramancer continued, "I will meet you there tomorrow, on the third night of the festival, after midnight. You will enter the chamber while your companion waits with me. When you bring out the object, I will let you both leave." He stepped forward. "If you refuse, and try to flee, I'll hunt you down. Do you understand?"

Jelith said, "Perfectly." He waited a moment but when he lifted his head, the man was gone.

Jelith sat up awkwardly, and Kryranen pushed to her feet, looking around. She said, "Did that just happen?"

"Evidently." He gestured to the debris of rock surrounding them. "It did happen fast, didn't it?"

She shook her head, and reached down to haul him to his feet. "Let's get your back fixed."

Jelith was tended to by Timar Dharn at the Black Gate Hospitaler's Guildhouse at the edge of the Raised Market, and washed the dust and blood away in the fountain in the courtyard behind the building. Timar's work was clean and quick, as usual, but the man seemed distracted although he provided no reason and Jelith didn't press the issue.

By the time they were done, the evening was shading into night and all the lamps were lit, flickering reflections in the water. The stones were damp with rainwater and they could hear the music and loud talk from the nearest public dance. As Kryranen put salve on Jelith's many cuts, she said, "What are we going to do?"

Jelith had been asking himself just that question. The answers were all unsatisfactory. Very unsatisfactory. "I'm going to bring him the object."

Kryranen made a noise of impatience and frustration. "We can't. This is what the ghost-ridden woman came to warn us of. 'If you carry it through the earth it will kill you.' The ghost who spoke it to her knew this would happen."

Jelith hesitated. Kryranen had not understood him, and perhaps that was for the best. "Perhaps she meant something else."

"Perhaps you were hit on the head and your wits were knocked out through your ear," she snapped. She finished with the salve and set the jar aside, wiping her hands on a cloth Timar had provided. "He is High Earth himself, and he must have been able to enter the chamber or he wouldn't know this object is really there. There must be some trap or danger he fears."

That was all sadly obvious. Jelith pulled his shirt back into place and shifted around on the bench to face her. "It has to be an object of power or value." Neither of which truly interested Jelith, but it might also be something that would provide clues to Taux's past. Perhaps he would be able to at least get a good look at the thing, to pass on whatever information it gave him to Kryranen, before it killed him.

Kryranen grimaced in frustration. "There is a reason he approached us."

Jelith let out his breath, and made himself participate in the logical discussion she wanted to have. "He needs someone of High Earth to enter this place, and in the trade of art and artifacts, my skills are well known."

Kryranen nodded. "He does not wish to go to anyone from a prominent Kin family with relatives in the city."

Jelith feared this was the key. "We are no one of importance. We have no powerful friends to go to for help."

"If he kills us, no one will miss us."

Jelith stared at her in dismay. Kryranen shrugged philosophically. She was right, he just hadn't liked to hear it stated in such bald terms. He said, "We are known to be strongly attached to one another, so it is possible to control one of us by threatening the other."

Kryranen's mouth twisted. Jelith wanted to take her hand, or another such sentimental gesture, but while their friendship ran deep and strong, they had never made such overtures to each other. He saw no way out of this and he feared she was not willing to accept that. So what he said was, "We won't do it. We'll think of a way to appease him."

The silence stretched. He looked away, fixed his eyes on the damp weeds growing at the base of the courtyard wall. The fountain water trickled in the quiet. She was staring at the side of his head and he feared what it was telling her; if she could see his whole face, there was no hope of concealment. He never lied to her and he was terrible at it anyway.

She said, softly, "You think I'm a fool?"

"I don't." He still couldn't look at her. In a last effort, he tried, "I know appeasing a man such as that will be difficult, but perhaps we can—"

"You mean to bring him the damn object."

"I don't wish to die. But I don't wish you to die."

"I won't let you do it. And you know I can stop you."

"You could kill me," he said. As a joke, it was not a very good attempt.

It was her turn to stare at the cracked pavement. She said, "We're letting him intimidate us. We can't give up so easily."

That…might very well be true. Jelith let his breath out and tried to be optimistic. "We'll go to this place now, and look at the situation. Perhaps the spirit who spoke to the ghost-ridden woman meant that there is a trap that may be sprung if the object is moved or touched. We can look for a way to disarm the trap."

Kryranen's tense posture relaxed a little. "Perhaps you're right, we'll do that."

They would do that. But he thought if a spirit had gone to such trouble to ask a ghost-ridden woman to warn them, then the spirit would have told them to look for a trap.

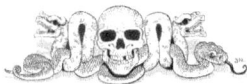

They made their way into the Haunted Temple District, the dark silent walls of stone looming over them. There were no celebratory dances or blossoms and feathers here. They stuck closely to the shadows, wary of ghosts but more wary of being caught by the Sons of the Moon. For Jelith, the myriad scents of Taux' stone faded to be replaced by the blood and hot iron that seemed to cling to every wall in this quarter.

The House of Kree-tath was actually a temple, named for a powerful ship captain, one of the first of the interlopers to enter Taux after its population vanished. Kree-tath had tried to take this temple for his palace, but it had rejected him. Violently, so the story went.

Kryranen went first, slipping through the gate in the thick wall to an outer courtyard which held nothing but the long empty square of a reflecting pool. The walls of the temple itself were a very dark stone, and it was hard to make out any detail in the light of the approaching Ghost Moon. Jelith could tell the great dark mass had rounded walls, but that was all.

Kryranen groped for the doors covered with slabs of verdigrised copper and finally found a handle. As she pulled it, she whispered, "It's just occurred to me this chamber may be hard to find. He said it was in the entry hall, but is it below the floor, or in a wall?"

They slipped inside, the interior strongly smelling of dust but no urine or food rot or any other sign that someone had come to try to emulate Kree-tath's attempt at ownership. Jelith answered, "Perhaps our 'employer' expects us to search the entire place first."

Kryranen fumbled open the slide on the dark lantern. "Or perhaps..." As the candlelight illuminated the chamber before them, she added, "Or perhaps it's very obvious."

They were in a large round hall, stretching up what would be three stories in a normal structure, with several arched doorways leading off it. In the center sat a huge stone object the size of a well-appointed hut, and round as a melon. Jelith circled it with sinking heart. It was made entirely of black stone shot through with silver and gray metallics, and it was obviously a container for something extremely deadly.

"How do you think Kree-tath decorated around it?" Kryranen asked, seeming uncomfortable with his silence.

"Very carefully," Jelith said. He laid a cautious hand on it. The stone was cool and dry. Maybe too dry, considering Taux' damp heat and the recent rain. He extended his awareness into it, but its scent was oddly neutral. There was none of the terror or rage or decay that clung to every wall of the ghost towers that he had touched before. He pushed deeper into it and sensed that the wall was not thick, that there was a chamber beyond. It was not that different than probing the wall of an ordinary house and feeling the room just past. It meant that forcing himself through the stone would not be nearly as dangerous, but it also meant...He said, "Either our employer is wrong and this is just a decorative object, or there is some powerful magic concealing the powerful magic."

Kryranen frowned. "Hmm. Maybe this isn't it. Let's search the rest of the place and look for another likely chamber."

They made a dispirited search, walking through the rooms on this level and the two above. There were many large rooms, though no outside windows, only openings into the central well to provide limited ventilation. The place was the size of a small palace, but Jelith could not see it ever becoming a comfortable home, with or without angry ghosts.

They came back to the giant ball in the central hall, and stared at it glumly. The light of their lamp caught along the silver veins and sent glints chasing up the dark walls. If there was a trap, it was not apparent. Such a container needed no guards or traps, except to protect it from those with High Earth.

"Why did he want us to wait?" Kryranen wondered. "Why tomorrow, why not today?"

Jelith shook his head. "I'm going to step in and have a look. Perhaps it will become apparent." As he had told the terramancer, he did not make it a habit to move his entire body through masses of rock, and it was not an easy thing to do.

Kryranen frowned at him. "You want to die a day early?"

"The warning was to refuse to bring the object out," he retorted. "Not to refrain from looking at it."

"Yes, well." They both stared at the sphere.

Reluctantly, Jelith said, "So, here I go."

He extended his hands and walked into the curved wall. The taste of blood burned like hot iron in his mouth and his head filled with the screams of the dying. He came out the other side and staggered, sick with it.

The space should have been dark, but it was softly lit by a blue glow. The light emanated from an object set on a short pillar in the center of the room. Jelith stepped forward cautiously. It was no more than a bowl, as big as his cupped hands, of the kind of rough pottery he and Kryranen had found heaped in broken pieces in many of the rooms they excavated. They thought it must be the pottery used by the poor of Old Taux, as it was not that much different from that used by the poor now. It was ordinary, except that it glowed. He lifted a hand toward it and heat scorched his palm.

Jelith stepped back, swallowing hard. It was like fire itself was imprisoned in the bowl. The blue glow was not some soft light, it was the essence of intense heat.

He looked around the room, squinting to see the faded paintings. And his heart sank.

They were of burning cities. Towers, walls, fleeing people, all consumed in towering waves of fire, as a man-figure lifted the bowl and aimed it at the ranks of his enemies. The mural was painted in slapdash fashion, the colors garish, with none of the artistry normally seen in Taux decorative painting. It was a hastily painted warning, like someone flinging a board down over a hole in a floor to give some caution to the next passerby. One image caught his eye, a depiction of the Blood Moon with the bowl below, fire raining up from it like a fountain.

The chamber must have been constructed by some mage-priests of Old Taux to conceal this object. Perhaps they had meant to retrieve it at some point and use it for war…Or perhaps they had simply been unable to destroy it and wished no one else to use it against them. The Blood Moon seemed to mark some indication that its power would be especially deadly on that night. That had to be why the terramancer wished to wait until then; any earlier, and the object would not be at its height of power. And how did he mean to control the thing? Did the man know? Or was he simply mad for the destructive power it would wield?

Jelith tried to approach the bowl again, but he could come no closer than a few paces without prickles of pain in the skin of his hand. In fact, the prickles were starting to grow all over his body. The breath in his lungs grew warm, and his head swam. He turned for the wall and half-fell, half-lunged into it.

It resisted him for a moment with the terrifying sensation of hands dragging at him. Then he tumbled through.

He stumbled out, gasping a breath of the warm, damp, yet sweet air of the outside world. Kryranen caught his shoulders to steady him and swore. "You're hot! Are you burned?"

"It was a near thing," he admitted, bracing himself against her. He had no desire to touch any of these walls again. "The object inside is magical, some sort of repository for fire."

As he described the room and what he had found, Kryranen's expression became even graver. She cursed vehemently. "How does he think he can control this thing?"

"Does he seem to you a person of rational thought and reasoned consideration of his own limitations?" Jelith shook his head. "Perhaps he has no need to control it. Perhaps freeing it from the chamber during the correct time of the Blood Moon is enough to set it off and destroy the city. That may be his goal."

Kryranen sighed agreement. "Jelith…"

"I know," he told her. They did not think of themselves as heroes, only scholars. But this was not something he could contemplate releasing on Taux, or on any part of the world. If the terramancer did not kill them immediately—which they had no reason to suppose he wouldn't, even if they did as he wished—he would surely kill them when he did whatever it was he meant to do with this object. Jelith straightened up, feeling his skin tight and dry even from short exposure to that magical heat. "We need to find out where this man lives."

Kryranen said, "Perhaps the ghost who wished to warn us knows."

Jelith had thought it would be difficult to find the house, but once they reached the Gold Jaguar District, the fourth house on the curve of the Street of Bitter Stars proved to be the only one with empty dark windows and an air of disuse and past disaster. "This is probably it," he said to Kryranen.

"Probably," she agreed.

They slipped through the unlocked gate and found the courtyard with the acacia tree. It was empty of everything but a stone bench, and littered only with wet leaves. It didn't look as if anyone had been sleeping here. Jelith put his hand against the stone of the wall, cautiously at first, then with more decision as no spirits immediately shrieked in rage at him.

"Can you tell anything about it?" Kryranen asked. "Was it a spirit of old Taux, or someone more recent?"

"I think it must be recent." Jelith frowned. "The stone is oddly quiet."

"As if something banished the old ghosts?" Kryranen said thoughtfully.

He turned to look at her, as best he could in the flicker of lamplight. "What makes you say that?"

She lifted her brows. "I don't know."

There were still people out, determined to enjoy the dancing no matter how wet, and as they went a short way down the Street of Flowers they found a vendor selling sugar candies and sweetened waters out of a handcart. They stopped to question her, but also to buy candy, because they had had no dinner and Jelith was ready to drop.

"It was a tome-mage's house," the woman told them when Kryranen asked. "He lived there with a wife, and children and servants, up until last year."

"And what happened then?" Jelith asked.

"No one knows," she said, "One day they just weren't there." She filled a cup for another patron and dropped the coin into the pouch at her waist. "A few months later, I heard tell they found bodies in the house's well, so it was a terrible thing, whatever it was."

They walked away down the street, no better off than they had been before. It was late at night, they had walked all over Taux, and a madman wanted to kill them. Jelith was too weary by this point to continue. "Let us go to work as usual tomorrow, and perhaps we will think of something."

Kryranen hesitated, her face drawn.

He hoped she would agree. It was mostly that if tomorrow was to be his last day alive, he wanted to spend it doing what he loved best.

"Very well," Kryranen said, "But I may be late. I want to speak to some people in the Raised Market. Perhaps..."

"Perhaps..." Jelith agreed, though he thought there would be no hope.

By late afternoon, Kryranen hadn't come to the catacombs.

Jelith didn't fear that she had abandoned him. He did fear that she had conceived some plan she felt too dangerous and ill-advised to share, lest he object and find a way to stop her. He gave up on work and went to search.

When he went to the Emerald Serpent to see if anyone had news of her, he found Quilan the tavernkeeper had a note that said only that Kryranen had heard rumor of something that might assist them in their work and had gone to try to find it, that she would meet him at the place they had been told to go at the High Point of the Blood Moon, nearly three hours after midnight.

Jelith was at the ill-fated house of Kree-tath at the appointed time, but Kryranen did not appear. He paced around the stone chamber, torn by intermittent bouts of hope but mostly fear. Fear that whatever she had attempted had killed her, fear that the terramancer had somehow encountered her and killed her. The distant sound of fireworks over the river told him he didn't have much longer to wait for the terramancer's appearance. He tried to form alternate plans, and finally decided the first one he had conceived was the best: he would conceal himself in the temple foyer and attempt to kill the terramancer when the man arrived.

He was trying to make some sort of arrangement where he could de-stabilize the blocks above the entranceway as a trap, but it was difficult to do so without antagonizing any of the violent ghosts that lurked just below the surface of the stone. Then he sensed stealthy movement in the court outside the doors.

He braced himself, then Kryranen's voice whispered, "It's me."

Jelith opened the door all the way and let her in, swinging it shut behind her. "Where—What—" he demanded, not sure what he wanted to ask first.

Breathing hard, Kryranen held out something to him. It was a blanket, of night-black velvet, sewn with hundreds of tiny diamond shards. "Very pretty," he said, baffled.

"It's magic," she said hurriedly. "It takes you into another plain of existence, where everything is insubstantial. I think you can use it to bring the fire object out without being hurt."

This did not do much to assuage Jelith's bafflement. "Not to sound ungrateful, but that only solves half the problem," he said. "Our employer will have it then, and will kill us, which at least means we will not be around to see what he intends to do with the fire object, but—"

She clarified, "While you are in that plain, no one here can see you. Well, hopefully the terramancer can't see you, but perhaps you can kill him."

It was a better plan than Jelith had come up with. He said, "But where did you get it?"

"I'll tell you later." She pressed the bundle into his arms. It didn't feel magic; it felt soft and heavy, like very expensive velvet. "Careful, if you hold the fire object too long while in the other plain, a bit of its essence may come into you."

He stared at her in horror.

"I know," she snapped. "I would go get the fabled magic blanket that doesn't do that, but—"

A faint crack from the walkway alerted them. Jelith said, "Tell him I am already in the chamber," and threw the blanket over himself.

For a moment he felt like a fool. He believed Kryranen, but still, he felt like a child pretending to be a ghost. Then the world faded to gray, the light of his single lamp became a glittering yellow gem, and the temple walls rose up forever, onyx streaked with silver. Figures writhed across them, shapes and patterns like runes he couldn't read, but he knew they were revenants of the passion and anger and fear of the people who had worshipped in this place.

He turned his gaze on Kryranen, who...looked like Kryranen, though she blazed with a gold and ocher light, mingled with wisps of purest azure. She glittered as though she were made of insubstantial glass. He had always known her to be beautiful; this view of her simply seemed to show the beauty from all angles at once. Marveling, he looked down at himself. He was shot through with red and gold lights, the colors of the earth's deeps, shifting and changing. The blanket still clung to him, a weightless drape like gossamer.

Then the temple doors opened. For an instant Jelith thought that the being that stood there must be one of the temple ghosts. It was man-shaped but dark, inert, like a body composed of clay. Or a dead body. But as it moved forward he saw there was a spark of light inside it.

It said, "Where is Jelith?" The words floated in the air, so Jelith saw them as well as heard them.

Kryranen said, "He's inside the chamber. He will bring you the object, as you asked."

The "man" moved closer to her, advancing as she backed away. Jelith tried to step forward, realizing only then that his feet were stuck to the floor. He dragged one leg forward and it was like his body was made of lead. Struggling, he dragged himself awkwardly toward Kryranen. As the terramancer drew closer, he saw the light within its dull body was shaped like a knife. And from the position and angle, the knife must be driven hilt-deep into its chest.

The man's body looked like inert clay because it was; the man was dead, killed by the dagger driven into his heart and animated by whatever dark force controlled him though it. There, like a wisp of black smoke, a tendril of shadow slithered away from the man like a tether in the direction of the bay.

It explained how the revenant had expected to handle the fire object. He was already dead, so presumably would be unconcerned by being burned by it. And perhaps a dead body could no longer be forced through the solid rock of the chamber, no matter how high the Earth of its former owner had been. That was why he had needed Jelith.

As Jelith forced himself closer, he saw another shape clung to the revenant's back. It was as insubstantial as his own form, but he could tell it was a woman, dressed in a light loose garment for sleeping, stained dark with her own blood. He said, "You sent the warning." He looked toward the revenant and Kryranen, but neither had reacted. His voice must be as insubstantial as his body.

She whispered, "My husband was given an artifact, a stone knife, said to be from the house of a powerful priest or mage in the Ghost Towers."

Jelith said, "I think I see it." If it wasn't the knife buried in the body's chest, then that was a very strange coincidence.

The woman drifted closer. "He used the power of his High Earth to delve into it, and it took possession of him and made him stab himself. Then it entered his body."

"It killed all of you." Jelith could see it, faded figures fleeing through a house, stalked mercilessly by the body of the man who should have been their protector. He could see the spirit of the mage-priest, too, a roiling cloud driven mad by whatever force had killed it.

"Yes. And now it will destroy everyone in the city," she said, and as if the effort had proven too much, she grimaced in pain and faded away. "Free him," a voice said in Jelith's ear.

As if their conversation had taken only a heartbeat, the revenant was saying to Kryranen, "Then there is no need for you." He lifted a hand to reach for her throat.

Jelith acted by instinct, stretched out his insubstantial hand as if to grip the dagger. To his surprise, his fingers curled around the cold stone hilt.

The revenant clawed at his hand but his fingers passed through Jelith's flesh without purchase. Jelith pulled the dagger free and the body collapsed in a dark heap. He remembered what Kryranen said about the transfer of essence while inside the blanket's plain, and knew he had to rid himself of this dagger immediately.

Jelith lurched forward, letting his leaden body topple. He drove his hand as far into the stone floor as his arm would reach, then released the dagger and withdrew. He righted himself and swept the blanket off his body.

As soon as he did, it was only an armful of velvet, though cool where it rested against his skin. He was standing back where he had started, as if he hadn't moved at all. Kryranen looked down at the dead terramancer, then turned to stare at him. "Did you do that?"

"Yes." Jelith moved forward, picked up the lamp and held it so he could see the dead man's face. It was younger than it had appeared before, slack with death. "He was an animated corpse. There was a dagger in his chest, imbued with some magic."

Kryranen's brow furrowed. "What did you do with the dagger?"

"I put it into the floor. I only hope the ghosts are not antagonized further by—"

Behind them, something heavy slid across the stone. They turned to look, and nothing was there.

Kryranen took the lamp. "I think we've overstayed our welcome."

They hastened to leave the temple to its ghosts, and while Jelith told Kryranen what the spirit had said, they did not slow their steps until they were on the outer edge of the district. Even this late, after the turning of the Night of Secrets, there was still a small after party in the Black Gate's Raised Market, and he thought they perhaps deserved a break.

He said as much to Kryranen, who nodded and added, "We need to take the blanket to Lareo first. I only borrowed it."

She didn't look at Jelith as she said it, though her face was hard to read in the dark. He thought the borrowing was more complicated than that. "This sounds like a good story."

Her voice dry, she said, "When we can sit down and have a drink I'll tell you of it."

Illustration by Todd Lockwood

FOUR FACES

By Todd Lockwood

Second Day: Dance of the Serpents

The city of Taux carried forward with its celebration, despite the fact that two ships lay broken at the bottom of the bay, crushed by the sudden freezing of the harbor three nights ago, their cargo of wine and food spoiled or inaccessible. Several of the quays were damaged as well, which slowed down the delivery of party goods. A downpour ruined the flowers of the previous day's celebration, and dampened the mood of the throngs who gathered to watch the Dance of Serpents this evening. Their dogged insistence on *cheer* didn't strike Torrent as noble so much as fatalistic self-delusion.

These people are crazy, she thought. But then, what else could they do? If nothing more, the heightened level of activity made it easier to lay low, blend in.

That's what she'd been doing for days, and it wore on her. Vash patrols pursued her relentlessly, seeking the gem she carried. Last night she attempted to recover some goods and clothing she'd left behind in a hostel and discovered magical traps woven into her clothing—spells inked with water, or she'd never have sensed them.

It could only mean one of two things: that a Candon Shaman had entered the city. Or worse, that a Wizard stalked her.

She couldn't defend herself from a Wizard even if her gem was completely charged—which it wasn't. High Water didn't normally involve itself in Human doings, though. It was beneath them.

A Candon made more sense, but a Candon was bad enough. The lizard people didn't venture out of their fetid swamps without reason.

If the Vash had enjoined a Candon *Shaman* to find her, she was in deep trouble. His affinity to water would exceed her own.

She abandoned her things a second time.

Then there were the dreams.

At first she thought them to be echoes of her experience with the gem, the fight with the Vash tome-mage and his golems, but the dreams weren't populated with any of those characters. Instead, bloody footprints, ghosts screaming out of the stone, and a ragged figure with rotting limbs who followed, followed. Then she heard rumors connecting similar dreams to a dark priestess, "Yaretzi," come from beyond death to steal souls, and dreamers who went missing, their personal effects found in piles of ash and dust. She'd wake in whatever bridge span or hollow that served as her bed, shaken to her core. Then she'd move to a new bed until daylight dispelled the apparitions.

With the last of her coin, Torrent hired a leathersmith in a shop outside the Black Gate to repair her vest. She didn't have enough for a new shirt. The proprietors allowed her to wash up in a back room as she tried it on in front of a shop mirror. The work was good, but when she stepped closer to tease some of the tangles out of her hair, she gasped in alarm.

That wasn't her face—not the face she expected to see. A faint web of lines surrounded her darkly circled eyes, and her black mane was salted with white hairs. The change was not so great that most people who knew her would even notice, but Torrent saw it, and she guessed the cause. Using the magical gem had wracked her with pain and left her unconscious for hours when the deed was done. She'd asked herself at the time what price the conduit pays for channeling such power. Now she knew.

She'd never thought of herself as vain, but this was alarming. Before she hit the street again she pulled her bandana down a little lower on her head.

Torrent looked around at the city, bustling with preparations.

"I hate you, Taux."

She chose a shadow across the street from the Emerald Serpent, and waited for a Candon to appear. She figured he'd show up sooner or later. Anyone seeking information in Taux knew that the Eldaryn merchant, Lareo, operated from a table in the back of the tavern. She would love to speak to Lareo herself, to learn what she could about the situation—even though such a conversation would come with a price. Probably a very high price.

It was too risky, and you never knew when that conniving little pimple might sell you out for a greater prize.

Just before sundown, she sensed water. Alerted, she studied every passer by. One figure didn't fit the panoply of summer garb and festival attire. Swathed in great volumes of cloth, face hidden by wrappings across chin and mouth and a hood lowered well below the eyes, he might have passed for a beggar, bent and broken. But no beggar would wear so much in the summer heat. The voluminous hood and robes that dragged on the cobbles might disguise the shape of a Candon. This creature moved with the shambling gait of the swamp-dwellers, a deceptive rocking slowness that she knew could turn to fury at the pulling of a blade. She reached out with her sense of water to see if he had a signature she might remember and keep watch for.

He stopped and turned to the street, scanning left and right as if someone had called his name. She put a post between them and stood still. When next she peeked out, his back vanished through the tavern doors.

The explosion of a rocket and an eruption of cheers startled her. Then drums sounded from down the street, around the corner of the square. Bass drums throbbed in low notes as steel drums rang like the musical offspring of hammer and anvil. Zimbolayan djembe beat in round staccato notes that popped like maize in a hot skillet. Dancers appeared, arms feathered to appear as wings, stepping high, bowing low. Children skipped and danced along the perimeter. The rain that had fallen all day in mists and drizzles parted for a minute or two, and then the Serpent appeared.

Raised up on poles by the performers beneath, it undulated up the street, head now dipping, now moving side to side. Multicolored, festooned with the feathers of parrots and touc-bills—red, green, black and purple and fiery blue. Lanterns inside the paper maché head lit the eyes, giving it a demonic aspect. A noise-maker growled with menace from within. The performers had cleverly arranged for gouts of oil from the mouth to burst into flame, too. But for the misty damp air, Torrent might have wondered how they kept from immolating themselves in their paper Coatl. It was grand spectacle, to be sure.

As it twisted up the square, Torrent felt a sting at the periphery of her heightened awareness, and she looked back to the Emerald Serpent. The Candon stood in the doorway, amber eyes glinting out of the shadow of his hood. Surrounded by women in scanty festival attire and Lowl in loin-cloths alone, Kin in masks decorated with feathers and flowers, Ruk and Humans in absurd masks depicting horn-bill and monkey and jaguar, the Candon only looked slowly around the square. Once again, she sensed something unright in the air, a menace she couldn't define, much like the spell secreted in her abandoned clothing. As his gaze turned toward her it only grew in power. He'd created some sort of summoning spell, some means of finding her out, but with what magic?

Water. It was water. The air was filled with it; everything in Taux was coated in it. He used it like a spider uses her web, feeling everything that touched it, a mist of rain turned into a net cast wide.

Torrent reached for the pouch in her shirt, but hesitated to stick her hand inside and touch the gem. Would he sense that too? Would that be like striking one of the bass drums that even now came alongside her position, obscuring him from view? She concentrated on her low-water affinity, seeking a shape or idea or strategy she might use to dispel his magical web, but to no avail. He had formula and structure in his magic. Torrent had only instinct and wiles. She pulled her hand out of her shirt.

His head snapped in her direction, if only for an instant before the dancing Coatl came between and blocked his view. Had he seen her? A gout of flame surged from the Coatl's mouth again, effectively negating his questing magic, and Torrent seized the moment. She sprang from her post and joined the throng next to the serpent's head, wishing she had a mask to blend in with the other celebrants. She could see the Candon's feet beyond the Serpent's body, moving with her, following the snaking paper-and-feather Coatl as it danced through the square. She felt him feel her. He knew she was here and who she was. She loosened the ties on her sword, but knew instinctively that his magics would negate her mundane blade if she raised it against him.

Only the press of the crowd kept him from closing on her. A group of Aspara dressed as parrots floated through his web, blocking his path, obstructing his magic. He drove through them in pursuit, eliciting curses. Had he seen her? Or only sensed her presence? Torrent felt that it was the latter, and worked to keep the serpent's head between them, but through the dancers surrounding her she spied his feet and the hint of a tail lashing beneath his robes. Fire blocked his supernatural sight, but only momentarily.

A palanquin bourn by four Ruk crossed the path of the dancers then, one of the rides-for-hire that allowed a person to cross the city with anonymity. Water flooded Torrent's wits. She knew that current well: Cenoté of the Grim Mask, out on some errand even on this night. Her presence drowned out all else. A great flood—a Wizard's aura—battered the Candon's magic with an overabundance of the very thing it sought: currents of elemental water. Torrent caught a glimpse of him bent in pain with his hands over his head as she ducked under Cenoté's palanquin and followed it out of sight.

The litter stopped at a maskmaker's shop on the outskirts of the Black Gate district, and Cenoté passed inside after a quick exchange of coin. The windows of the maskmaker's shop were open, so once the street became quiet Torrent availed herself of them, taking care not to disturb any of the vessels arranged on the sill.

This was Cenoté's home. The home of a Wizard. Torrent was certain of it. A shudder swept her from head to toe. She sensed her power in the moisture of the air. Overwhelming but sublime, like a tide that quietly raises all boats regardless of their weight, a current that moves and dislodges with gentle force. Not a tidal wave, but an eon of wet embrace or churning presence.

A lantern burned in the entry, so Torrent pulled furniture into the obvious walking paths and then extinguished it. Before she could make sure the door was barred, voices sounded from the other side. She ducked into a shadow.

"I've more ale. Spend the night," said a voice small and wavery as a key rattled in the lock, and then the door pushed open.

St. Erik's balls! She'd hoped to speak to the Wizard alone, but two silhouettes filled the doorframe, one small and thin and incongruously supporting the other much larger shape. Muttering voices. A sniff. Then they passed beyond light into the black of the chamber. More muttering, and then a crash of broken glass before the little shape shouted, "Oaf!"

"Whawassat?" asked the big shape.

"The lantern! Curses!" The light of the Ghost Moon beamed through the windows and illuminated the little man where he lay entangled on the floor beneath the much larger form of a drunken sturgeon. The little man wore a mask of elaborate design, perhaps accommodating a large nose. Torrent pressed the tip of her sword to his chin as a warning.

"I need a mask," she said.

The sturgeon growled, but the little man quavered, "S'all right, A c-customer."

"Exactly," said Torrent, pulling her sword aside and hefting the little man to his feet with her free hand. She didn't want conflict. "We're all friends here."

"Are we?" said another voice from the stairwell, smooth and languid as a wave upon the beach. A figure came down the stairs bearing a lantern. Torrent retreated into shadow again, fearful of the power she sensed. She stared at Cenoté in wonder. The Wizard was tall and slender, moving like seaweed in gentle surf, her skin pale as northern ice, hair like blue algae that flowed about her shoulders as if on an ocean current. She took a robe from the little man, still in his mask, as he warned her of the broken glass. Only as the Wizard poured into her robe and the small man led her around the table did Torrent realize that she'd previously been nude but for a loin clout and her plain driftwood mask.

Several times she'd crossed paths with Cenoté in the streets and felt her aura, like a current deep and strong. She questioned her own presence here, though she knew not what else she might have done. Cenoté's arrival in the square probably saved her life.

The big man stumbled to his feet, mumbling, "Mistress. Sorry to disturb your rest." Torrent recognized him: Tohil. One of the city Sturgeons. How odd to see him so inebriated.

"You weren't the first," said Cenoté, turning toward Torrent and extending a hand.

"Come, child," she said.

"This *child* could have killed you in your sleep," said Torrent with reflexive bravado, but immediately regretted the words. She was out of her element, even so close in proximity to one who embodied her element perfectly.

Cenoté sat on a stool at the table and said, "Could you?"

Torrent deferred to the question with silence, and sheathed her slender blade at last. The Wizard nodded gently and said, "Come, Hunhau. Ale for our guests, please."

The little man made a huffing noise and removed his mask, his dark brows pinched in anger or fear. Or both. The nose revealed was exceptional. Torrent wondered if "Hunhau" might be Tolimic for "giant nostrils," but she held her tongue, turning to Cenoté. "I need your help."

"There's daylight," said the nostrils. "And knocking."

Torrent ignored him.

Cenoté laid her fingers on the table. "Hunhau?" When the nostrils seemed confused, she added, "The ale?"

He glanced at Cenoté sheepishly but then glared at Torrent with all the force his dark eyebrows could muster before scurrying up the stairs.

Cenoté watched until he disappeared, then she turned to Torrent. The grim mask tilted slightly.

"Water stalks you," said the Wizard.

Torrent felt the blood rush from her face. "How do you know that?"

"In the square—a web of rain knew you well enough to seek you out."

Tohil stared at Torrent with changed appraisal, even though one eye seemed drunker than the other. This one could be trouble yet.

The small man—Hunhau—returned, his arms full of cups and a pitcher. Shortly he had poured a drink for Tohil, Torrent, and himself, but not for Cenoté.

"Won't you drink with us?" Torrent asked.

"I will. Hunhau, my cup."

The little man set a cup in front of Cenoté, but did not offer to fill it with ale. Instead, Cenoté crooked a finger toward the windowsill. From each cup and bowl there rose a thread of sparkling water that twined through the air with movement worthy of the Night of Serpents, coiled above her cup, and rained gently into it.

Torrent nodded. "So it's true. You are a Wizard."

"That is why you've come." Cenoté lowered the mask from her face and laid it on the table. "To see for yourself."

The lines of her neck and face were long and elegant, her cheeks high and angled, the curve of jaw and chin and nose smooth, elongated. Where her eyes should have been were only angry red holes, two cauterized wounds that tugged at Torrent's heart. There was no expression on that face that she could read...unless it was sadness contained in glacial ice.

Silence dragged out until Torrent felt that she must fill it somehow. "I came for—" she began, but then her words seemed inadequate, neglectful of this beauty and sorrow. She took a draught from her cup to fill the gap in her words. The ale was good. Very good. She hadn't eaten since yesterday, but she set the cup down and took a deep breath. "It's true I need a mask. I must be on the streets tomorrow night. I was told yours are the best."

The little man dismissed her with a wave of his hand. "We've none left, nor materials to make more. We are enjoying the festival."

"I've coin," she lied.

Tohil made a strangled noise and Torrent cast another glance at him. He *was* going to be trouble. Every instinct told her so.

Cenoté lifted her cup, not to her lips but to her ear, as if it spoke to her in a soft elemental voice. Only after long seconds of concentration did she take a sip. Emotion writhed across her face. She set the cup down awkwardly and took several moments to compose herself.

"The name you use is Torrent," she said. "What you have is cursed."

Torrent leapt to her feet with a cry of surprise. Tohil lunged, reaching for his sword, but Torrent grabbed the big man's sweaty wrist, instantly connecting with the water in his body and depriving his brain of blood. Drunks were so much easier to handle. He toppled the pitcher of ale before collapsing unconscious on the floor.

Hunhau looked angrily at the spill, but moved to put himself between Torrent and Cenoté. "How did you do that?"

"What do you know of what I have?" Torrent demanded. "Tell me!"

The Wizard only gestured to the table and waited, her face unreadable.

"St. Erik's pustulent cock…" Torrent muttered. Could she trust this Wizard? Had she made a mistake coming here? She reached out with her water-sense, but she felt no malice. Only great power. She reached into her shirt to pull out the canvas bag. Untied it. Let the gem slide out into her hand.

"I can't give it to you," she said.

"I would not touch this thing you carry for all the lives in Taux, for that would be its cost." Cenoté tapped the tabletop. "Put it down. If you still can."

Torrent let the ruby roll out of her hand and onto the table, the simple gold casing glinting in the lantern light, the salamander within pulsing with its strange light.

"It has awakened," Torrent said. "But I don't know if that's a blessing or a curse."

"You have used it." Cenoté's voice a mixture of concern and rebuke.

"It was that or die." Torrent looked down at the thing, recalling the power she had wielded when it was fully charged—power like unto a Wizard! She'd frozen the entire harbor in service to a scheme of the rogue Savino. But afterwards she was hunted, displaced, homeless and hungry. If it had remained dead she might well be quit of it. But it recharged slowly, revealing its true potential, and the Vash family who still wanted it back would never stop pursuing her.

"Have you not felt its toll?" said the Wizard, with arctic cold in her tone. "This is Cizin, the Life Thief. One of the four vile objects created by tome-mages to rape the Afterglow of magic. They opened the door to darkness and brought destruction to this city. Another has awakened. More—" Cenoté paused to shake her head. "More will be found if evil has its way. This must be destroyed."

"Oh, I agree." Torrent sat down. "But not before I've done what I must, Wizard. Cizin, as you call it, belonged to Tlacolotl Vash and he wants it back. Preferably with my corpse. I'd rather not let that happen."

"A Vash? And you came here?!" Hunhau squeaked. "What if they've followed you? You've put Cenoté in danger!"

You know nothing about danger, Torrent thought.

"Peace, Hunhau. She had no choice," the Wizard said gently. "Cizin grants power, but at a price. It feeds on the water of life. It has begun to steal yours, Torrent. But you already know that, don't you?"

She'd felt the damage the first time she used it. The effects she'd seen in a mirror this morning only proved the truth of it. "Vash will have my life first, unless I can shake him off my trail for good. I'm out of choices, Wizard. Cursed or not, the stone evens the playing field. With it, I can defeat him."

"Then you mean to kill him, don't you," said Hunhau. "That's a terrible plan. Killing a Vash will only bring the rest down on you."

Tell me something I don't know, Torrent thought. How she wanted to drop this disagreeable little man with the giant nostrils down beside his sturgeon friend.

"Men are the least of what hunt the Cizin," said Cenoté. "Should Yaretzi reclaim it—"

"You mean the dead priestess? She's after me too?" Fear and anger and desperation squirmed inside her weariness like snakes in a bag, and she could only laugh long and loud. "Oh, this just keeps getting better. Savino, I'm going to rip your ears off."

"You have to leave," said the little man, his eyes wide.

"How? Trade in and out of this stinking city has all but stopped, and the Vash family watches every quay. I'm trapped here." She turned back to Cenoté. "I need your help." She pointed at the gem. "Unless you want this in worse hands than mine."

The blind Wizard remained silent for several long moments, and seemed to stare at Torrent even without eyes. Then she reached for her mask, and the little man placed it in her hands. "A filled basin, please Hunhau," said the Wizard.

"I have no wood. I'll have to run out—"

"Stay, Hunhau. Just the basin, please."

The maskmaker's eyes darted between the two women before he scurried out of the room, leaving a silence that Torrent once again felt obligated to fill. She collected the spilled cups and pitcher and set them upright again. The maskmaker returned just then and saw what she did. "I don't have more," he said with a note of scorn.

"This will do," Torrent said, touching the spilled ale. It gathered toward her fingertips into a ball that floated in the air as she raised her hand, then poured into her cup.

The little man's expression softened and he glanced at Cenoté. "A Corsair!" The Wizard nodded. Torrent smiled at his changed demeanour and quaffed the ale at last. Gods, but she was hungry, and it *was* good ale.

Hunhau filled the basin with water, stealing glances at Torrent and the Wizard. Cenoté pointed to a stone vase in the shadows, filled with clustered pink flowers on long red stems. Torrent had failed to notice it before. It was unnatural, the blooms waving gently in the air like sea anemones wafting in a current. "Bring that closer, if you please."

The blossoms snapped shut at Hunhau's approach, and he turned to Cenoté. "But…these were a gift from—from your—"

"Their intention," said the Wizard, and Torrent's brow puzzled into a frown. But Hunhau seemed satisfied, and he moved the vase closer. Then with a gesture Cenoté caused the flower stalks to lift from the vase and lay themselves across her outstretched hands. The blooms came alive, opening and closing as if in time with her pulse.

"Not flowers, then," said Hunhau, voicing Torrent's thoughts. Cenoté clapped her hands, and the stalks and flowers crumbled into particles like sand that fell to the table. Torrent reached out to touch them. They *were* sand—or that which remained when life and water were stripped from something living. She felt a wave of resolve move through the chamber, a tide of power that put pressure in her ears. She shivered despite the humid summer night air.

Cenoté lifted the stone vase, and now Torrent saw that it was covered with runes and carvings of bones and skulls. It wasn't pretty, but perhaps that was not its "intention." The Wizard lowered it into the basin of water, where it dissolved instantly into a black skin on the surface of the water.

The feeling of power surged through the room, like a tidal wave that stirred only her arcane senses. It swallowed sound and blurred sight. Hunhau seemed oblivious to it, but Torrent gripped the table edge to brace herself.

A face appeared in the water—a man's face, solid and stern. Eyes snapped open, the deep turquoise of moonlight shining through a wave, and fixed on the Wizard.

"Who's that?" Torrent said, but could barely hear her own voice. Hunhau said something, but she couldn't make it out. She looked to Cenoté in fear.

"Water remembers," said the Wizard, to Torrent, her voice rising clearly above the non-sound that obscured all other sound. Then she blew on the face and it wisped away. "This brings a gift to aid you now, Torrent, should you use it wisely. Behold!"

Torrent stood frozen in wonder as Cenoté's fingers danced above the basin. The black skin on the water swirled and roiled, gathering into a convex oval the size of a face. It lifted above the basin without so much as a drip, and hovered there beneath Cenoté's outstretched hand. "Hunhau. One of the best wrappings, please."

The little man presented a large square of silk to Torrent, and she released the table to take it even though the tide still dizzied her. She approached the basin and extended the silk beneath the mask on her two hands.

"Only you may touch it," said Cenoté. "Keep it covered until you wish to be masked."

Once it was hidden in the folds of fabric, the tide of magic in the room dissipated all at once. Torrent gasped for a breath as equilibrium returned.

"It's warm," she said at last. "I feel—life."

"It's a copy of life." The Wizard touched the water in the basin, without causing so much as a ripple. "The spell lasts from sunset to sunrise, once put to a face. Three times, the mask will give you the appearance of whomever you last touched, and the final face will be yours until sunrise."

"I owe you—"

"Destroy Cizin."

Torrent swallowed. "I can't—Not yet." The ruby pulsed, casting fractured red light on the table. Mocking. She looked up at the Wizard. "But I swear that I will."

Cenoté nodded once. "Try not to use it."

"It barely has any charge at all. Not enough to do anything—" She paused as Cenoté removed her finger from the basin, reaching out over the gem with a single drop of water clinging to her fingertip. She gasped in unison with Hunhau as the drop fell and landed on the stone.

Blue light surged through the gem and dispersed the faint ruddy light the way blue sky chases away a crimson dawn. Torrent felt the surge of an invisible, but troubled, elemental tide, Cenoté's chords of power connected to it. Taut. Strained. She felt the gem almost as if she were touching it; Cenote battled with its very essence. It pulsed a beautiful sapphire blue for a beat, two, but then red swirled through it like blood in water. The blue vanished, and the Wizard swooned. Torrent leaped to catch her.

The ruby pulsed anew with blood-red intensity. Not fully charged ,but power to tempt her. Tears brimmed unexpectedly in Torrent's eyes and she fought them back. Not gratitude, not fear or anger, not…anything. Overwhelmed. "You didn't need to do that. I'd have managed without."

Cenoté seemed frail, almost insubstantial in her arms.

"I wanted you to see its nature. Cizin seeks evil, as evil will seek it. It will turn good into darkness. Do not use it unless you must."

Then Cenoté laid her hand along Torrent's cheek and said, so quietly it might have been a murmur of rain. "Sister."

Torrent slipped back into the dark streets, her two magic treasures hidden in her shirt, and Cenoté's last word echoing in her head. The rain broke, though the sky still hung low enough to be visible in the light of the city. If the Candon was anywhere near, she didn't sense his subtle web. Perhaps he needed wetter conditions. Or perhaps he prepared another, more devious attack.

The revelries were far from over. Laughter sounded from the direction of the Black Gate. She passed a group of staggering drunks singing a dockworker's chantey. She found revelers passed out in a doorway and tried to rouse them, urging them to find a berth indoors somewhere. Anywhere. They wouldn't budge; one of them might have been dead already. She considered searching them for coins, but that seemed like low behavior when her first thought had been for their safety.

She did it anyway, and found no coin at all.

At last she climbed a trellis to the third-floor balcony of a tenement house in the lower quarters, thinking to break in and spend the balance of the night indoors. No light showed under the door, so she tested the doorlatch. Locked, and probably also barred.

Exhausted beyond words, she huddled into a corner to think, stomach growling. A mist began to fall.

She didn't mean to fall asleep.

The dream sky drizzled down rain. A voice barren as a dry riverbed whispered out of darkness. "Cizin," it said. "I smell you, Cizin." Bloody footprints. Ghosts swarming out of the stone to follow.

"Someone holds you, Cizin," said the voice, the sibilance of gravel sliding over sand. "Hold her for me."

"I can't give it to you." Torrent clutched the canvas bag, the ruby within pulsing red light through the fabric, between the gaps in her fingers.

A silhouette appeared over the balcony's rail. Matted hair straggled from beneath a sodden hood to crawl over pointed shoulders. Green rags dripped from bone, arms and legs that were mere remnants of rat-chewed flesh. Spectral figures clambered after. The apparition reached up and pulled back the cowl that covered its face.

Torrent bolted awake and realized two things immediately; the gem was not in the bag, but in her hand. And the creature from her dream stood on the balcony in front of her, not eight feet away.

With a cry she sprang to her feet, sword drawn, staggering back to crash into the wall.

The monster had no face at all. Dried flesh held what was left of the lower jaw in place below a black hole where forehead, eyes, nose, and cheeks should have been, the brainpan an empty hollow. Only the lower teeth and the mummified skin of her lips remained. A voice came out of the void nonetheless.

"I am Yaretzi. Cizin is mine. Give it to me."

Torrent froze in confusion, sleep fogging her mind. Not sleep; something else.

Another spell.

The Candon? She didn't have time to consider it. The dead priestess lurched toward her, one arm raised, fingers questing like mummified worms. Torrent stabbed the thing in its non-face and felt the point of her sword pierce the skull in back. She yanked it out again, but the creature took another step, laughter rasping out of the hole. "I am death," she said. "*You cannot kill me.*" Torrent dodged past the monster, swatting the outstretched arm aside with her sword tip, but the creature stepped across her escape route before she could make the next move.

Yaretzi reached out with her other hand and nearly brushed Torrent's left shoulder. Burning cold braised her even so, and with the gem in her hand Torrent sensed the destruction of water, a sudden desiccation that she only countered by directing water from her body and from the air to replenish the wound.

The priestess paused, the ruined head cocked to one side. "*Interesting,*" she said, the whisper of leaves in a dry gutter.

Then she advanced again. Torrent stabbed her in the chest, but the sword encountered little more than fabric and dust. She pulled the sword loose and stepped back before a knobby hand could make contact.

"*Cizin is mine,*" the Priestess said again, the sound of coarse sand in an hourglass. "*I will have it.*"

Torrent feinted to the right, then dashed past the Priestess on the left, making for the railing, but held up at the sight of Yaretzi's Ghosts, wispy tattered creatures with hollow eyes and gaping mouths, all lamenting as they clambered over the rail. *Could I leap through them?* she thought, but three stories separated her from the street; if she broke a leg she'd be helpless. She turned to face Yaretzi, sword held forward. The ghosts swarmed around her, clouding her vision, but the gem gave her no power to dispel them. She slashed desperately at the Priestess, and fabric like cobwebs fell away, chips of dried flesh chattered to the stone. She heard screams and knew they were her own.

"*Give it to me!*" the monster demanded with the rage of a desert windstorm scouring a dry oasis. The priestess caught hold of her sleeve and before thought could intervene Torrent pressed the gem into the void of the thing's hollow face. Boil! Freeze! Do something!

In that instant Torrent knew that Yaretzi had once been a creature of water like herself or Cenoté, but the curse had stripped her very essence away. The blood that puddled at her feet was a mockery. The dead Priestess contained no water to manipulate, only a tar-like sludge in the deepest recesses of dust and stringy sinew. Yet a perversion of her power remained. Whatever the opposite of water might be, the opposite of life—that was her weapon now.

Only the charge Cenoté put into the gem saved Torrent's hand from the burning cold. She tore water out of the air, directed it through her hand like a fountain into the void in Yaretzi's head, causing the horror to reel backward for half an instant. The water spilled back out of the cavity, turning Yaretzi's laugh into a bubbling hiss.

Torrent spun, jumped up on the railing, coiled her legs to leap as far as she could. Yaretzi's Ghosts grabbed at her like spider threads, but the dead Priestess brushed her leg with one hand briefly before she pushed off with a cry of pain.

She hit a balcony one floor down on the building across the narrow way. The railing cracked her across the ribs and drove the breath from her body. The bannister failed and she tumbled to the street below in a shower of wood and splinters.

Her leg screamed. She directed her senses to the spot and knew that flesh crumbled. With a shout she drew every ounce of the energy Cenoté had put into the gem and directed it toward the wound. All of it and a little more. She pulled clean water out of the sky and through the wound at such a volume that it ripped her boot open. Desiccated flesh tore away, leaving a gaping hole in her calf.

The crumbling stopped, but the pain continued. She barely summoned the strength to rise to her feet.

The gem was all but dead again. Torrent put it away and stood in agony, limping toward the sunrise as Yaretzi's angry cry rattled from the balcony behind her like stones falling into a deep, dry well.

The sun touched the western horizon, and the Ghost Moon rose in the east. The last of the sun vanished, and the Night of Secrets began. Then the Blood Moon rose.

Blood would follow the Ghost tonight.

The spell lasts from sunset to sunrise, once put to a face, Cenoté had told her. *Three times, the mask will give you the appearance of whomever you last touched.*

The last person Torrent touched was Yaretzi.

She'd felt the Candon as well, through his magic at work in the falling mist. It lulled her to sleep and then quested through her dreams until it found the gem, and caused her to grip it so he might follow it like a beacon. She was certain of that. Yaretzi's appearance disrupted his attack. Only blind luck saved her.

If nothing else, it was elegant proof that they weren't in league with each other.

Her leg throbbed. She'd fashioned a bandage from her sleeves, but blood oozed out and filled her boot. She could only use her water affinity to staunch the flow if she concentrated on it, but she'd spent the day on the move. The wound weakened her.

At the sun's failing light Torrent decided to find the Candon first. Or to let him find her. She couldn't run forever. Twice now he'd demonstrated his ability to locate her with spells hidden in rain. He knew who she was. The air had dried out, though. Perhaps this night wouldn't serve his magic as well.

She stayed on the dry rooftops and out of the damp streets, moving away from the sounds of revelry at the Emerald Serpent and the Silk Purse. She listened to her water affinity carefully.

And found him.

He shambled toward her in an empty street below, his hood turning from side to side. Then he stopped, and his head tilted upward. Torrent withdrew from the roof precipice. She dared one more glimpse, and saw him weaving his arms about inside their giant sleeves in fluid patterns. Ripples of subtle power washed past her and she ran to the far end of the roof to escape them. He knew she was here.

As she swung her game leg over the parapet of the roof to start climbing down, she heard a familiar, sibilant demand.

"*You cannot avoid me forever, Corsair.*" Yaretzi was at the far end of a side street, at the head of a string of bloody footprints reflecting the lights of the city beyond. "*I will have my gem back, along with your soul.*" Her ghosts raised their spectral arms, pointing, repeating her words in whispers.

Torrent withdrew again and started across the roof to another side, away from Yaretzi or the Shaman—but stopped herself.

She saw a chance.

The last person Torrent had touched was Yaretzi.

She pulled the silk bundle from her shirt and unwrapped Cenoté's mask. Cool and soothing to the touch, black as a deep pool, it tickled her water affinity so perfectly that she gasped in astonishment. Would this thing she contemplated even work? She had no time for debate before the Candon turned the next corner. She put the mask to her face.

It fused with her, covering her eyes and nose and mouth, and she panicked at first the way a child does when thrown into deep water for the first time. Then water moved over her, and she inhaled deeply. It was entirely different from the power she felt in the gem. Cizin was nothing like unto a Wizard. Where Cenoté's mask soothed and cooled, the gem violated. Torrent understood that now with clarity.

Her vision cleared. She felt a transformation and, looking down at herself, saw the dead Priestess' withered limbs and tattered clothes. She half expected to feel pain, but the mask was imbued with Cenoté's calming presence.

Dear conniving St. Erik, she muttered, *give me the wits to pull this off.*

She ran as fast as her wound allowed to an alley between two buildings, and made careful descent to the ground by way of downspouts, vines, and windowsills. Then she went forward to meet the Candon. When she stepped out of the shadow of the alley he was but two doors away.

"*Candon,*" she said, attempting to mimic the dry hiss of the dead Priestess. The voice she heard *was* Yaretzi. The mask provided even that.

The lizard Shaman pulled up when he saw her, and amber eyes flashed deep in the hooded cowl.

"*You and I seek the same thing,*" she said to him.

The Candon studied her silently for several long moments, and Torrent wondered if he'd seen through her disguise already. He shuffled backward a step, giving her hope that her appearance provided exactly the shock she wanted. She took a step toward him, and he took another step back.

"You are Yaretzi," he said, his voice like the bubble and splash of a pond skinned with algae.

"*In life I was Yaretzi,*" she said. "*But now...You and I, we both seek the same thing.*"

"And that is?" Caution in his tone, he took half a shambling step forward.

"*You know of what I speak, Candon. That which your web of spells sought these last few nights.*"

Again he stood silent, seemingly at debate with himself. "You don't know what I seek," he said warily.

"*Perhaps I don't. But I know what your spells seek. One of them interrupted me last night, and allowed my quarry to waken and escape.*" A touch of truth to prick his interest.

He stood a little taller, allowing more of his crocodilian physique to inform his thick robes. "It was you who interrupted *me*, hag."

Torrent paused, not sure what to say next, worried that she would overplay this delicate hand. She swallowed. "*I don't want another conflict. I will give you the gem if you will allow me the girl's soul.*"

"The gem!" hissed the Candon.

"*Yesss, Shaman,*" Torrent whispered, as if hunger guided her words. "*I but need you to hold her with your magic so I may have her flesh. In exchange, I will allow you the gem you seek.*"

"How do you know about that?"

"*In life I was water-born, Shaman. Your spells give your secrets away to one who knows how to read them.*"

The Shaman stood straight, increasing his height by a foot, and pulled the wrappings off his nose and mouth. Gray-green scales winked in the dim light, the amber eyes in the shadows behind grown wide. The teeth he revealed were sharp as needles. "So long as I get the gem."

"*Why does it matter to you so?*"

He hesitated a moment, then answered. "It will buy me information. Leave it at that."

Torrent laughed, but the sound coming from her throat was the scuff of paper on paper. "*I will lead you to her. Simply immobilize her so that I may have what I seek.*"

The Candon nodded slowly. Torrent turned and imitated the dead priestess' lurching pace as she moved down the street. Tendrils of the Shaman's magic reached out to her. She sensed them, but Cenoté's mask overflowed with water energy. Would it be enough? She needed her lies to keep him off balance a little longer.

Looking back, she saw bloody footprints in the cobbles behind her. Did the mask provide those too? Or was it her own blood, oozing from her throbbing wound? As if to consider the same question, the Candon kneeled down and touched a footprint.

His head snapped up. "YOU!" he said, and charged.

Fear numbed the pain in Torrent's wounded leg as she bolted for the corner. The Candon threw a manipulation at her, cramping her legs. Torrent stumbled and barely managed to stay upright. She opened her water affinity to dispel his attack, but he was strong where she was weak, prepared where she was merely responsive, and the gem that might have helped her was spent. She drew her slender curved sword but he twisted the muscles in her arm and she dropped her weapon to the cobbles. He nodded his scaly head and her abdomen clenched, doubling her over in pain. She fell to the paving and crawled backward as he advanced, horrible talons emerging from his sleeves. Fought her way upright again. Cancelled an assault on her brain that might have given her a blinding migraine. He was powerful. She couldn't take much more of this. She stumbled backward to the intersection of the two streets.

Where a fog of ghostly forms appeared.

Torrent turned the corner. On the other side, the dead face of Yaretzi stared back at her.

She recoiled, even as Yaretzi withdrew from a vision of herself in horrendous ruin. The dead Priestess stood transfixed long enough for Torrent to dive into a shadow. The Candon turned the corner behind her, and barrelled full on into the Priestess with intent to rend her limb from limb.

He knew his mistake only when Yaretzi grappled with him, trying to win through his thick clothing to touch flesh. He howled in surprise and fear.

Torrent stepped behind him and pulled his hood back, revealing the long back-swept reptilian head and knobby hide. She retraced her steps, found her sword, and for good measure stabbed him in the back of each leg to disable him. Then she pushed him hard, as hard as strength would allow, so that he stumbled into the dead Priestess.

Water swarmed to the Candon from every direction, as if his instinctive response to Yaretzi's attack was the same as Torrent's had been. Cleansing water, to battle the un-water that was her death magic. It tore at Yaretzi, scouring chunks of shrivelled flesh off her boney arms, ripping the skin from her lower jaw. She reeled back a step, but grabbed hold of the Shaman's wrist. He shouted fear and anger, and more water poured from the crumbling wound.

Yaretzi's howl of surprise became a dry wind of anger and fury. She slipped inside the Candon's defense and gripped his face, and with an unworldly scream his flesh blew off of bone as dust and ash, and then his skull dissolved, falling into his robes.

Torrent assumed the Candon's appearance as she ran, Yaretzi's angry screech shivering in her shoulder, in her leg, and in her soul. She ran until she encountered a mob of revelers.

"Candon!" screamed one of them, and the throng parted in fear, but Torrent careened into them, first striking a small boy. In the confusion of tumbling bodies, she took on the boy's appearance. Shouts of surprise followed. Where did the Candon go? Was that an illusion? Several even cheered drunkenly as if it was all part of the Night of Secrets, a show for their entertainment. The shriek of Yaretzi changed the tone again.

Torrent limped into the broader road and down a crowded street, Yaretzi's anger fading behind her.

She had spent Cenoté's magic. The Candon was dead, the gem was dead, but the Priestess still followed. And she could not be killed.

Torrent climbed once more to the rooftops, scarcely strong enough to pull her own weight over the last low wall. Exhaustion wracked her. The gaping hole in her leg throbbed, her shoulder burned.

No sleep. No sleep until dawn. She needed healing, but knew not who to trust. Cenoté perhaps. She rubbed dust out of her eyes. Closed them for just a moment. A moment too long.

"Foul wretch," said Yaretzi in her dream, plodding through the dank streets. *"Go ahead and sleep. Dream my dreams. I have nothing but time. I will have my gem, but I will make you suffer a long, long time for what you have done to me."* Her ghosts swarmed around her, peering into windows, touching the stones of the city with wails of despair, repeating Yaretzi's words in hushed echoes.

Torrent awoke to the sound of rockets exploding, and scrambled to a sitting position. Sword still unsheathed and in her hand, she scanned the rooftop frantically for Yaretzi in the dwindling, crackling light.

She was alone.

With a grimace, she levered herself against the parapet and upright, then set out once again. She mustn't sleep. Not tonight. She caught her reflection once in a rain gutter as she dipped water to slake her thirst. A small boy, perhaps ten years in age, carrying what for him was an overlarge sword. She would wear that face for the rest of the night. Two days ago, the face she wore was not her own. With dawn's light, Cenoté's magic would end. What face would she see then?

She must survive the night to find out. For now, she had one imperative.

Keep moving.

Illustration by Jeff Laubenstein

PROMISES

By Juliet McKenna

First Day: Lover's Day

Out in the camp, Zhada would have been awake at first light. Back in Taux he could sleep late by Lowl standards. He could also sleep secure in the knowledge that every room in this tenement housed allies; fellow Lowl, a handful of Jai-Ruk and the couple of Humans bold enough to join their venture hunting vicious winged serpents in the Ebon Swamp through this past half-year.

But now the serpents were mating and breeding. More dangerous than ever, the males fought off rivals while their mates guarded the eggs which would hatch the next crop of fledglings. When Zhada and his hunters returned in the autumn they'd find more than enough young serpents to replace those they had taken. Though that wouldn't make them greedy. Cull too many and the current high prices for dazzling scaled leather and iridescent feathers would fall.

He tossed the thin sheet aside, washed, and dressed in the fine new clothes which he had sent the Human lad Papan back to the city to order on his behalf, in time for the Festival of a Thousand Blossoms.

A crisp white shirt with maroon-enamelled tags for its laces. A cream waistcoat embroidered with black vines and crimson flowers. Scarlet breeches and a high-collared coat with no need for padding to suggest muscular shoulders. Years of swordplay had honed his impressive build.

Studying himself in the mirror, Zhada smoothed down the persistent tuft of black fur between his pointed ears. He wondered idly if the tailor had realized he was sewing these fine fabrics for a Lowl. There was no particular reason why the man should have guessed that from the measurements he'd been sent. Below the neck both races shared the same physique, though a Lowl generally topped a Human man by at least half a head. A dog-like head, thanks to Vitcoska, demon queen of the distant fire mountains, who'd had the insight long ages ago, to blend the best qualities of man and canine.

Now Zhada had proved to any ignorant Human who assumed his kind had no more wits than a dog, that a Lowl could equal any trader in this city of merchants and adventurers drawn from every nation and race dwelling on either side of the great ocean.

He smiled in his kindred's lolling-jaw fashion as he left the bedchamber and padded in stocking feet down to the boarding house's kitchen. Mistress Talleran was busy preparing breakfast for her many guests.

'Good morning and fair festival.' She looked up from stirring a pot of spiced beans and shredded meat. Flatbreads were already stacked high on the scrubbed table.

'I polished your boots.' She gestured with her wooden spoon. His footwear stood behind the door.

'Thank you,' Zhada said, surprised. 'You didn't need—'

'It was my pleasure,' Talleran assured him. 'Now, eat, and you can go courting.' She set a full bowl on the table.

'Thank you.' As Zhada scooped up the piquant pottage with a piece of flatbread, leaning over the bowl to be sure not to stain his shirt, he eyed his boots.

The scuffed and stretched leather was gleaming. Mistress Talleran must have risen before dawn to polish them since she'd already been in her nightgown when Zhada and his associates had arrived the night before.

He finished his breakfast and reached for his footwear. 'I appreciate this, truly,' he said as he pulled the boots on. He had resigned himself to their shabbiness in contrast to his new clothes. Sending his measurements to a tailor was one thing but Zhada wasn't prepared to risk blisters from a shoemaker trying to fit a foot outlined in charcoal on the back of a letter.

Talleran took his empty bowl away. 'It was little enough to do. Now go and get your flowers.'

'I will, and thanks again.' Zhada ducked his head as he would to a Lowl elder before heading out through the hall and down the old house's broad steps.

Humans and Lowl weren't so different, he reflected. They all understood the offering and repayment of favors – at least, the honorable ones did. Like Mistress Talleran cleaning his boots to show she appreciated his loyalty as he brought his people and their newfound coin back to her boarding house. And Zhada did that because he'd been made so welcome when he had been living hand-to-mouth as a hired sword.

At least, Humans like Mistress Talleran understood such things on this side of the Black Gate, where they rubbed shoulders with Lowl, Jai Ruk, Kin and Eldaryn not to mention Humans with skins as varied in colour as the fur on a Lowl's head, from palest gold to glossy black.

Zhada strode through the erstwhile Ullamalitzli Stadium. The hucksters and peddlers who thronged the terraces rising formidably high on either side were busy preparing for the festival. Over the next seven days the raised market's men and women would take more coin than they could expect to see between the celebration's end and midwinter. As long as Taux's six saints blessed them. Passing by the Silk Purse, he noted the fragrant queyaia garland around the statue of Saint Shera's neck, beseeching her favor.

He soon reached the flower seller close by the Black Gate where Papan had brought his second letter. 'Filaria Dharn, Queen of the Black Gate!'

'One moment.' The lovely and pale woman said as she settled a sheaf of speckled nufi flowers in a heavily pregnant woman's arms, enough to decorate a whole room with the symbol of wedded bliss.

'Fair festival.' Filaria sent her on her way with a smile and turned to Zhada. 'Step this way.'

Zhada sniffed at her hard tone, but perhaps the stress of the festival was more than most flower venders could take. He followed her into the small shop erected in the angle of two walls carved with contorted limbs and grimacing faces. The Lowl had never understood why the first, long-lost, inhabitants of Taux had favored such decoration, but he'd grown used to it in time.

The beautiful flower seller hesitated as she picked up an elegant bouquet of pink shirrima and creamy ixcamai, their stems bound together with mimazul vine's feathery green fronds. 'Are you sure you want to carry that through the streets out there?' Filaria motioned towards the city beyond the Black Gate's grinning maw. Her face was wan, and her eyes less vibrant than he'd remembered when last he'd seen her.

Zhada nodded as he counted silver coatls. 'Why wouldn't I?'

'There's some—' Filaria broke off and shook her head. 'Never mind.'

'Thanks and fair festival to you, as well as luck in this year's pageant.' Zhada paid her and took the flowers. She gave him a smile, but it felt cold, and outside the rumble of thunder rolled in the distance.

Sighing, he put the dire mood she'd given him out of his mind and went out through the gate, glancing thoughtfully at the Humans he passed on his way to the Turquoise Turtle District. Were they looking askance at a Lowl carrying the flowers traditionally given to a beloved betrothed? Was arriving on Master Mesare's doorstep with this particular bouquet too presumptuous?

Zhada had no doubt that the marriage he was intent on would be the talk of Taux for a year. Those who considered Lowl no better than dogs would be scandalised. Obscene jokes would swirl around the taverns.

But Asalyan's family had never shown him such disdain. Zhada had been welcomed warmly each time he returned from the Ebon Swamp. Surely not just because they all profited as the merchant's son, Icael, sold winged serpents' hides on the far side of the ocean for a king's ransom.

Zhada squared his shoulders as he approached the house. He tugged on the bell-pull.

'Master Zhada. Fair festival.' The lackey greeted him with a broad smile. 'You're here to see Asalyan?' If anything the grey-haired Human's smile broadened as he looked at Zhada's flowers. 'Shall I find a vase of water for those?'

'If you please.' Zhada surrendered the bouquet.

The lackey beckoned the Lowl inside. 'She's in the conservatory. You know the way.'

Zhada nodded. 'Thank you.'

The glass-walled room overlooking the garden was filled with flowers and not just the blooming vines and shrubs in bright-glazed ceramic pots. A dozen or more hopeful youths had already brought bouquets to show their respectful adoration of Master Mesare's beautiful, golden-haired daughter. Zhada wondered which particular blossom conveyed their equal desire for her father's well-filled strongboxes.

Well, any man of any race would be drawn to Asalyan, as quick-witted and sweet-natured as she was beautiful. But she had been his friend since childhood when his family had lived in the house behind this one. She had become so much more than his friend since his business dealings with her father had enriched them all.

Asalyan looked up from the book she was reading. Zhada was startled to see she had visibly lost weight since he had last been here. Dark shadows of weariness stained her eyes, all the more noticeable given her unhealthy pallor and he was reminded of the look of the flower seller. Two years ago, she had been the Turquoise Turtle's Queen of Flowers, riding the blossom-filled barge down the canal to the harbor, carrying all the district's wishes for the year to come. Now she looked as if she'd be lucky to see the year out.

'My love? Are you ill?' He hurried to sit on the bench beside her, reaching for her hands.

She returned his clasp with reassuring firmness. 'No, I'm just tired.'

'Why?' The hackles on the back of Zhada's neck were rising. To a Human nose, Asalyan would be her usual fragrant, powdered self. With a Lowl's far superior senses, he could smell something very wrong. Not an illness. She wasn't sick, which prompted a sigh of relief, but an eerie scent of death hung around her nevertheless.

Asalyan bit her lip. 'I've been having such bad dreams. But it's just silly.'

'What are you dreaming of?' Zhada stroked her hand.

'Death.' She pressed her lips tight together to stifle tears. 'I see such dreadful things. People screaming in terror as the very life is sucked out of them. Men and women collapsing into heaps of dusty bones. Bloody footprints cutting across the dust.'

She shook her head and straightened her back. 'Dreams cannot hurt me. This will pass.'

'We can hope so.' Zhada felt uneasy all the same. He recalled stories of households plagued by dreams in the Haunted Temple District. Such nightmare visions were supposedly sent by Taux's first denizens. Their souls had been trapped in the buildings' very stones by whatever magical catastrophe had killed everyone overnight, leaving the city deserted until explorers had discovered its ruins, Zhada's own grandfather among them.

'Excuse me.' The lackey returned with the vase of flowers and coughed discreetly at the door. 'The master would appreciate a few moments of your time.'

Asalyan cupped a hand around Zhada's neck, her fingers caressing his fur. She drew his head down to plant a soft kiss on the top of his muzzle. 'Go and see what Papa wants. I'll find a nice place for those gorgeous flowers.' Weary as she was, her eyes shone as she recognized the particular blooms he had brought.

'I won't be long,' he promised.

'The master's in his study.' The lackey led the way.

'Ah, Zhada.' Mesare stood rather than sat behind his desk. He barely glanced up from the sheaves of paper scattered across a handful of open ledgers. 'I won't keep you long. I'm sure you want to go and enjoy the festival—'

'I was hoping to spend the day with Asalyan.' Zhada spoke more sharply than he'd intended but those rival flowers in the conservatory made him uneasy. 'Am I not welcome?'

'What?' Mesare stood up straight, looking puzzled. 'Of course you're welcome. You're my trusted business partner and my daughter's favoured friend.' He gestured in the direction of the conservatory. 'I was hoping you'd take her out into the city to raise her spirits with some festival fun.'

'I misunderstood.' Zhada ducked his muzzle, abashed, before he cocked his head, ears pricked. 'What can you tell me about these dreams tormenting her? Are all your household suffering?'

There was no scent of death hanging around the lackey or in this room. The Lowl wanted to know why.

Mesare ran a hand over his bald head. 'I take it you haven't heard of the undead priestess loose in the city?'

'What?' Zhada barked.

Mesare waved to an empty chair. 'Sit down, please.' He slumped into his own seat. 'They say her name is Yaretzi and she's the horror Asalyan is dreaming of, and no, none of the rest of us are plagued with such ghastly visions.'

Zhada sat and listened, appalled, as the Human merchant told a scarcely believable tale of treachery, evil magic and murder.

'This revenant is sucking the essence of life from those it slaughters? It's still wandering the city? What are the Red Pillars doing to hunt it down? The Sturgeons? Vitcoska's teeth, can't the Wizards kill it?'

The Lowl couldn't help a shudder. Natural magic, like the spark of fire all Lowl carried within them was one thing. The arcane sorcery of the Star Tower's Wizards was something else entirely, to be held at arm's length if not shunned outright. Until the need for such power outweighed the risks of unleashing it.

The merchant sighed, exasperated. 'The city's high and mighty are bickering and dithering. Of course they want rid of the monster. The festival's distracting the populace but it won't take many more deaths for panic to sweep through the streets. But every power in Taux wants to be sure that they'll get the credit for destroying Yaretzi. So they don't dare act before they can be certain of success. No one's willing to risk the blame of a failed attempt provoking her to mass-murder, and to make matters worse the Order has brought in a Paladin to subdue the creature, or so it is said.'

Zhada's lips curled back from his fangs in a humourless parody of a Human smile. Lowl didn't play such games. If a sabre-toothed lion skulked near their nomadic settlements, ready to pounce on the unwary, then all able-bodied adults formed a hunting party. Kill the beast and the menace was gone.

Well, indecision among Taux's rulers wasn't his principle concern. Asalyan's suffering was.

'Is there some way to ward off these dreams, so she may sleep untroubled?'

'Apparently not, though the priests assure me that as soon as Yaretzi is destroyed, Asalyan's torment will end. Meantime, I hope to see her strength restored by other means. There's been discreet talk among the wealthy of a new healer in the city.' Mesare shuffled his records of coin on hand and debts owed. 'His services are costly, granted, his cures for all manner of ailments verge on the miraculous—'

'Tome-mage fakery,' Zhada snarled. While true Wizardry was the blessed gift of a birth to High Water, the deceits of lesser mages were as contemptible as their spells were ineffective.

'Do you think me such a fool?' Mesare was more surprised than annoyed. 'Trust me, I've tested these claims as thoroughly as Zimbolay gold. I wouldn't trust my daughter to him otherwise.'

Zhada ducked his head a second time. 'Forgive me.'

Mesare grunted. 'I have secured her an appointment with this new healer for tomorrow morning. You can call tomorrow noon and see the results for yourself. Meantime, you entertain her while I muster the price. Make no mention of that, my lad,' the merchant added. 'I don't want her fretting. We can always earn more money. She is an irreplaceable treasure.'

'Indeed.' Zhada rose, privately vowing to discover how much this so-called healer was charging. If the man helped Asalyan, Zhada would insist on bearing the cost alongside Master Mesare. If on the other hand, he was some conniving tome-mage, Zhada would recover the merchant's money, with hefty interest paid in blood or coin as the confidence-trickster preferred.

The Lowl returned to the conservatory to find Mistress Mesare with a gossamer shawl and a parasol for her daughter, to protect her complexion from the strong sun.

'Go out and have some fun. Perhaps the exercise will help you sleep,' she urged Asalyan.

'Please?' Zhada held out his hand.

'Oh, very well.' Asalyan rose and entwined her fingers with his.

They spent the day wandering the city and admiring the festival flowers. Zhada chose a route leading through the Turquoise Turtle's prosperous streets into the wealthy enclaves of the Golden Jaguar District and then wandering the more modest byways of the Serpent Wall neighbourhoods. All this to lead Asalyan as far from the Haunted Temple as he could.

Did that offer her some respite? He couldn't tell. Returning her home though, as the sun sank towards the sea, Zhada saw apprehension overshadow her. He noted her shifting uneasily in her seat as they passed an otherwise pleasurable evening, dining with her parents and enjoying festival visits from Master Mesare's closest business acquaintances. Those gentlemen and their wives mostly managed to conceal their surprise at finding a Lowl treated as one of the family, keeping their feelings hidden from Human eyes if not from Zhada's nose.

He could smell something else as well. As the dusk darkened to night, that intangible scent of death strengthened around Asalyan. By the time that decorum demanded he return to his lodging, Zhada had silently promised himself he would act. Some healer restoring Asalyan's strength could be no more than a temporary measure. He must put an end to these dreams, which meant putting an end to this undead priestess.

On the second morning of the festival, The Dance of the Serpents, Zhada woke as early as he would have in the Ebon Swamp. He dressed quickly in plain leathers and went out into the Black Gate without waiting for breakfast. Even so, he realised with a sinking feeling, he hadn't risen early enough. Serpent Chieftains must have risen before dawn, assuming they'd been to bed at all. The men and women who would carry the fantastically adorned heads of the gigantic feathered serpents were already chivvying their neighbours to work. Once they had put the final touches to the great coils, the festival snake would be raised high on poles and carried, swaying and dancing through the city streets.

Zhada glanced up at the sky as he dodged between people hurrying to and fro with baskets of ribbons and gaudily-dyed chicken feathers. It would be such a shame if their hard work ended up sad and bedraggled but he'd wager those first wisps of dark cloud heralded rain.

'Watch your step!' came a voice with a thick Tolimic accent, far older than most newcomers to Taux.

Zhada was taken aback as much by the speaker's tone as his words. His hand went instinctively to his hip even though his sword hilt was securely knotted to its scabbard as the law required.

The Human sneered. 'That's better, dog.'

Before Zhada could find an answer, another voice challenged the Human.

'Get back to your slums, black rat!'

Varrach. If Zhada were to make a list of the Lowl he never wanted help from, Varrach would be at the top.

'I've no quarrel with you.' Zhada told the Human. He raised both hands, partly to show he wasn't holding a dagger and mostly to be ready to disarm this inexplicably aggressive man if he produced a blade.

But the Human had already turned his attention to Varrach. Worse, a dozen men in the same shabby, baggy black garb were emerging from the crowd. They all wore belted black surcoats adorned with a pale circle.

The contrast with Varrach and his swiftly gathering supporters couldn't be more marked. Shoeless and bare-chested, with tattoos to feign a pelt covering their torsos and only a loincloth to cover their manhood in the summer heat, these Lowl scorned their humanity in favor of what they asserted was their true wolfish nature. Zhada found their attitude as wilfully stupid as it was insulting to Vitcoska.

The tan-furred Lowl taunted the black-clad man.

'Running scared, are you? Looking for somewhere to hide hereabouts? Too many bloody footprints circling your usual midden?' Varrach took a swift step forward, fist clenched and muscles bulging. 'Or are you the ones who led her here? Who's paying you to make sure she slaughters Lowl and Kin and Jai-Ruk instead of Humans?'

The black-clad man squared up to the tattooed Lowl. 'Holy Yaretzi only kills those who deserve to die. If she's hunting you dogs down, that proves you're guilty of something.'

'It's Humans who deserve to die!' Varrach snarled at the man, before raising his voice to be heard more widely. 'They brought this disaster down on our city. They roused the Dread Priestess's wrath! Why haven't they put an end to her yet?'

The Lowl answered his own question, bitingly cold. 'Because they're happy to see us culled. All the races stronger than weakling Humans—'

Turning his head to assess his audience's reaction was a mistake. The black-clad leader punched Varrach hard in the side of his jaw, a golden bracelet catching the daylight beneath his dark sleave. Inside half a breath, his gang attacked the other Lowl who proved only too willing to answer such violence with equal savagery.

Innocent bystanders with laden baskets shouted as they were jostled. Serpent dancers hurrying past yelled protests as they were swept into the mêlée. Screams and fury spread as festival food or serpent plumage spilled on the ground, trampled underfoot.

Zhada skirted the spreading brawl, heading for the Emerald Serpent as quickly as he could. He didn't want to be rounded up with Varrach and his troublemakers when the Sturgeons arrived. He wanted answers and hopefully he'd find them in Taux's oldest inn.

The tavern was preparing for the long day and night ahead. Spectators and participants alike worked up a mighty thirst on this day. Maids and potboys mopped the floor, wiped the tables and straightened the chairs, working around a few early drinkers already propping up the bar.

Seeing Lareo sitting in a corner, Zhada raised a hand. The Eldaryn beckoned him over with a smile. Zhada took a seat and gestured at the table, empty but for a cup and a flagon of fruit cordial.

'You're not trading today?'

Lareo wasn't an Emerald Serpent soak. He was one of the regulars trusted to run his business from the bar; buying and selling all manner of curious and valuable things which he kept in cunningly crafted boxes of little drawers and cantilevered shelves.

From time to time, some would-be thief would assume the Eldaryn was an easy target; barely chest-high to a Human and so old that his once-fiery blue hair had faded to palest gold. Such bandits learned their mistake the hardest possible way. There were always people in the Emerald Serpent who owed Lareo debts of coin and honor which guaranteed him their immediate, unquestioning help.

'I honor the saints by sitting idle through the festival,' he said comfortably. 'So the youngsters can try to satisfy my customer's more obvious requirements, and my customers can reflect how invaluable I am when they need something more unusual.'

The Eldaryn took his tortoiseshell-rimmed eyeglasses out of his blue silk shirt's breast pocket and perched them on his prominent nose. 'You look gloomy for a pup let off his leash.'

Few people dared speak to a Lowl like that but Lareo had known Zhada's father since before his mother had whelped him.

'Tell me about this priestess.' Zhada leaned forward, elbows on the table. 'Who are these fools in black saying she's preying on the guilty? What do they know?'

'The Sons of the Moon are back?' Lareo groaned before waving Zhada's explanation of the fracas away. 'They're a Temple District gang with a new leader with a talent for lies. As for Yaretzi, they know nothing more than anyone else.'

'Varrach says—'

'A dry skull has more brains than Varrach.' Faint sparks crackled amid Lareo's shock of hair; a sure sign of Eldaryn anger. 'If Yaretzi truly was hunting down sinners, everyone's life would be easier. The Red Pillars could bait a trap with juicy criminals. But there's no link that anyone can see between the unfortunates who have died. Not beyond the dreams of dusty death and bloody footprints that plagued them before Yaretzi struck.'

'What?' Zhada yelped.

'What?' Lareo looked at him, startled.

As Zhada explained Asalyan's suffering, Lareo's expression grew solemn.

'I must put an end to this horror.' Zhada saw Lareo chewing on a tuft of his still copper-bright moustache. 'Do you know how to do that, old imp?'

'No more than anyone else.' But the Eldaryn wouldn't meet his gaze and Zhada could smell his evasion. Not a lie but not the whole truth.

'Please, I beg you.' The Lowl extended his hand across the table. 'She's the love of my life.'

Lareo's ruby eyes misted behind his spectacles. 'You remind me so much of your father, pup.'

He sighed heavily. 'I don't know how Yaretzi can be destroyed. Believe me, if I did, I'd sell that knowledge to the Red Pillars for a pile of gold jaguars as tall as you.'

He leaned forward and lowered his voice. 'I have heard tell of someone vastly learned in death magic, however, who might be able to hazard a guess.'

'Who?' It took all Zhada's self-control to whisper.

'There's a Wizard who trades in souls,' Lareo said reluctantly. 'He lives in caves beneath the Star Tower—'

'Under the seabed of the bay?' Zhada shivered. To be below such a vast expanse of water? The elemental spark within him flickered queasily.

'I did think of going to ask, but there was no one I could trust to guard my back.' Lareo looked steadily at Zhada, 'but I'd trust you.'

Zhada nodded. 'Very well. Let's go.'

Lareo raised a long-nailed forefinger. 'Not so fast. I have to send the Wizard a message and get an answer. I must know we'll be welcomed, and not going to our own deaths.'

'How long will that take?' Zhada clenched frustrated fists.

The Eldaryn shrugged. 'Go and take Asalyan to watch the serpents dancing and come back around noon? With luck, I'll have heard something.'

Zhada shook his head. 'She's going to see a healer.' He related what Master Mesare had told him of the newcomer to Taux.

Lareo's eyes gleamed with interest. 'That could be worth knowing.'

'I thought you weren't trading through the festival,' Zhada retorted.

'I'm not trading trinkets. There's always a market for information.' Lareo clapped his hands briskly. 'Go and enjoy the festival. I have letters to write and messengers to pay.'

'Add a few coppers from me,' Zhada said quickly, 'for the latest news of Yaretzi. I want to know everywhere she's been seen, everyone she has killed.'

'Yes, yes.' Lareo waved him away.

Reluctant, Zhada left the tavern. Outside, there was no sign of the Sons of the Moon or Varrach's gang of Lowls. Not beyond a few smears of blood, a black sleeve torn off a tunic and the breeze making playthings of tufts of tan and gold fur, so he guessed the Sturgeons had broken up the brawl.

Flanked by good-humoured crowds, the first of the Black Gate's dancing serpents was being raised high on its poles. Zhada was in no mood to laugh and clap. He made his way moodily out through the Black Gate and into the Turquoise Turtle District.

He briefly considered calling on his family's man of business, to ask the current value of the properties his father still owned in the city. Zhada would sell them all, if that was the price of Asalyan's health. But of course, the man would be celebrating the festival with his family.

So Zhada would just have to be patient. He could do that. Lying in wait for prey, he could spend hours at a time motionless and silent. Though that was different. That was his choice. As he walked aimlessly through the city streets, barely noticing the festival all around him, Zhada chafed at this inaction forced on him by other people.

Master Mesare had told him to call after noon. The last bell's chime was barely fading when Zhada arrived at the door. To his astonishment, the merchant answered it himself.

'Ah, lad, now, you're not to worry. Asalyan's much improved—'

'Can I see her?' Zhada's foot was already on the step.

'No, she's not here,' Mesare said hastily. 'She must stay in the healer's house until her cure is complete. He has a magic garden—'

'How long?' At least Zhada could smell the truth on the merchant, as well as the Human's relief.

Mesare hesitated. 'A few days. Till the end of the festival at most.'

Zhada nodded. 'Can I go and see her?'

Mesare shrugged. 'I don't see why not.' He gave Zhada the address.

Swift and single-minded, the Lowl headed to a high-walled house on the street which divided the Golden Jaguar District from the Serpent Wall neighbourhood.

Well-dressed men and women were making their way to the same door, attended by servants and bodyguards. Sturdy Jai Ruk carried curtained litters bringing more prospective patients.

Waiting his turn was another exercise in patience, though he did see several patients come and go. Zhada caught the robust scent of good health replacing the ominous reek of illness which had hung around them on arrival. Whoever this mysterious healer might be, he wasn't a fraud.

Finally the Lowl reached the head of the line, knocked on the gate and was invited into an anteroom.

'I'm here to see Asalyan Mesare.'

'No, I'm sorry, that's not possible.' The handsome Human shook his head emphatically. 'You're not a patient and we don't allow visitors.'

Zhada took a closer look at the Human. Though he couldn't put a name to him, he was sure he recognised him from the Black Gate's less than respectable corners. He reached for his purse. 'How much?'

To the Lowl's surprise, the lad shook his head again. 'No exceptions.'

'No exceptions,' a heavy-set Jai-Ruk echoed. Zhada hadn't even noticed him enter the anteroom through a curtained door.

Someone hammered on the outer gate.

'You have to go,' the Human told Zhada. 'You're preventing the sick being healed.'

'You have to go,' the Jai-Ruk agreed.

Zhada nodded curtly, barely managing not to snarl. But that was merely one of the differences between Lowl and the dogs they resembled. Vitcoska gave Lowl the wits to assess a situation. He could leave this Human groaning on the floor and give the Jai-Ruk a bloody nose, but brutalizing this mysterious healer's servants in order to see his beloved would surely anger the man. Could he withdraw his healing magic as easily as he bestowed it? Zhada couldn't do anything to put Asalyan in danger.

'I'll be back,' he growled as he left.

Even though rain was now falling, the city streets were full of dancing serpents. Zhada barely spared them a glance as he forced a path though the crowds, taking the most direct route back to the Black Gate.

But Lareo wasn't in the Emerald Serpent. The bartender handed Zhada a triple-sealed note from the old Eldaryn.

'Meet me at the city end of the Baymourn Bridge at sunset. Come prepared.'

Prepared for what? Zhada asked himself that question for the hundredth, no, the thousandth time, while he waited by the bridge, watching the sun sinking amid the dark rags of cloud left by the afternoon's downpour.

Well, Wizards were still mortal, for all their fearsome magic. Hopefully they were as vulnerable to an unexpected blade as anyone else. As well as his sword and daggers, Zhada had concealed several throwing stars in purpose-sewn pockets in the sleeves of his thick leather coat.

'Fair festival!'

He turned to see Lareo hurrying along the road, wearing hobnailed boots and an oiled leather jerkin. The old Eldaryn was silhouetted against the uncounted lanterns in the city proclaiming Taux's refusal to let bad weather spoil the celebrations.

Zhada hurried to meet him. 'Where are we going?'

'This way.' Lareo glanced around. Satisfied that the bridge was deserted, he led Zhada into the closest mighty pillar's shadow. 'Can you lift this slab, pup?' He rapped a flagstone with his metal-shod walking cane.

Squatting down, Zhada studied the unremarkable paving around the pillar. It took him a moment to realize that one edge of the slab Lareo had indicated was bevelled to offer a handhold. He braced himself and heaved, nearly falling over as the stone rose as easily as a wooden trapdoor. Stone steps spiralled down into the darkness.

'Come on.' A flame kindled at the top of Lareo's cane, striking gold shimmers from the brass eagle's head handle.

'I'll go first.' Zhada led the way.

As they descended through the first full twist of the stair, they left the last fading daylight behind. Another turn and Zhada halted as a grating noise filtered down from above. The slam of the slab closing itself sent a cold shock down his spine.

Lareo managed a hollow laugh. 'I don't suppose a Wizard wants any passing drunk wandering in.'

'Probably not.' Zhada forced himself to continue down the dank stone steps.

By the time they reached the bottom, he had counted eight hundred and forty seven of them.

'I don't fancy the climb back up.' Lareo tried to make a joke of it.

Zhada had more immediate concerns. The Eldaryn's flame had dimmed markedly. 'Are you all right?'

'I will be,' Lareo assured him.

Zhada could only hope so. 'Which way now?'

He gestured at the cavern ahead, black openings offering routes into unknown caves. His ears twitched at the plinking of water dripping into unseen lakes. Had the day's rain already filtered down through these rocks? If not, could rising water cut off their retreat? The sooner they got in and out, the better.

Before Lareo could answer, eerie laughter echoed through the caves. A cold glow, pale as bone, lit one passage and left all the others in even deeper darkness. Zhada's nostrils flared at a charnel reek blended from death and magic. But it wasn't the same death magic which had besieged Asalyan.

He had vowed to fight that threat, he reminded himself, even if he must fight fire with fire. The Lowl of the plains knew all about deliberately burning a broad swathe of good pasture to drifting grey ash to save their encampments from some furious blaze racing across the grasslands faster than a spiral-horned elk.

'Stay close.' Lareo headed for the luminous tunnel.

As they went onwards, Zhada tried to count his strides, just as he'd counted the steps of the stair. The further they went, the harder it was to keep track. He was chilled to the bone and short of breath even though the level rock underfoot made for easy walking.

How long had they been in these caves? Panting with exertion, he saw his exhalations hanging mistily in the air, as though this were a winter's morning. He tried to call on the spark of fire within himself to counter the deadening dampness. To no avail.

He heard a clack of metal on stone behind him as the old Eldaryn stumbled. The flame Lareo was carrying died.

'What's amiss?' Zhada rasped.

'A– a moment.' Lareo leaned heavily on his walking cane, almost doubled over.

Zhada stooped to put a supportive arm around the Eldaryn's shoulders. He caught a whiff of sodden embers and realised with horror that the elemental fire within his friend was nigh on quenched.

'You can't go on. It'll be the death of you.'

Before Lareo could respond, that eerie laugh echoed through the caves, following by a mocking voice.

'*Oh dear, this will never do.*'

A faint hint of gold warmed the pallid light clinging like moisture to the tunnel walls. Zhada realised his own breathing was coming a little easier. 'What's happening?'

Lareo forced himself upright. 'I believe the Wizard realizes he cannot profit by seeing us die.'

Zhada didn't find that particularly reassuring. Whatever a Wizard gave, a Wizard could easily take away. 'How much further?'

'*Not far.*' The eerie voice assured him.

'Come on.' Gritting his teeth, Lareo pressed on, leaning heavily on his cane.

Zhada had no choice but to follow.

At least the voice hadn't lied. The tunnel turned a final corner to reveal a large chamber with a pool of glowing water at its centre. The glow was the same dead bone-color and the stagnant water reeked.

The Wizard sat beside the pool with a loom to his other side – or her side. Zhada couldn't tell. Between the oppressive weight of water smothering Vitcoska's legacy of fire, and the death-stench blunting his nose, his keen Lowl senses were failing him.

The Wizard's face gave no clues, completely concealed within the voluminous hood of a black robe trimmed with gold. Zhada wondered how long the sorcerer had been hiding down here. That robe was old and tattered around the hem, and spotted with pale mildew.

By contrast, the tapestry on the broad loom was pristine, though he couldn't make much sense of the incomplete picture, with barely a handspan of multi-coloured weft visible between the lower roller and the empty warp threads above.

Zhada tried to make out the detail of the other tapestries hung on the cavern walls behind the Wizard. He could see costly silver thread reflecting the cave's cold radiance to highlight countless shades of blue and grey. The weaver's skill depicted a man with skates for shoes descending a stair with torch in hand.

The rest were lost in shadow. Zhada took a step forward, trying to see more clearly. He wondered who wanted such striking furnishings for a room. What deal had they struck to have such a tapestry made, and why?

The folds of the hood turned towards them. 'Your message said you had questions.'

'We want—' Lareo had to pause to catch his breath.

The robed figure raised a pale, withered hand. 'Before you ask anything, we must agree on terms.'

Zhada could only tell that the hand belonged to a living person older than any he'd ever met. He was relieved. He'd half-expected a skeletal limb.

'Go on,' Lareo invited, wheezing alarmingly.

'I will answer three questions,' the deathly voice said calmly. 'In payment, you may choose either to surrender your soul to me when you die, or to swear a binding vow to bring me certain things which I require. The choice is yours but in either case, the oath will keep you honest. If you promise to meet my needs but fail to deliver, your soul will be forfeit regardless.'

'What—?'

Zhada fell silent as the cold white hand pointed a long finger at him. 'First and foremost I require Death's Kiss seeds from the Ebon Swamp.' Then the Wizard pointed at Lareo. 'I also have need of Eldaryn White Fire. If you cannot deliver these, our conversation is at an end. You may discuss this if you wish.'

The pale hand's fluttering gesture dismissed them to the far side of the cave. Lareo stumbled and Zhada barely caught his arm to save the

Eldaryn from a nasty fall. The Lowl winced as he realised how dulled his reflexes were, trapped under the bay's water.

'I can get Death's Kiss seeds, provided this Wizard is prepared to wait,' he assured Lareo in an undertone. 'When winter's chill sets in, the vines fall dormant.'

They had learned that much on a hunting trip when the Human lad Papan had stumbled into an unsuspected thicket of the deadly crimson flowers. Everyone had been amazed to see him not drop dead within the next breath. Alas, Suntar the Jai-Ruk had lost his life proving that, as the days warmed, the vile plant's deadly reputation was well-earned. Judging by the dead birds which they had learned to look for, the hotter the weather, the further its evil influence reached. That was another reason for leaving the Ebon Swamp to the feathered serpents and its other denizens at the height of summer.

Zhada realized his wits were wandering and concentrated on the matter in hand. 'But what is White Fire?'

Lareo's drawn face was ghastly with shock. 'He must know that we never share it.'

'What is it?' Zhada persisted.

'It is—' Lareo struggled with his conscience '—an Eldaryn secret. A powder that burns with no need for a match once it's touched by air. It will even continue to burn under water.' He shuddered. 'Every Eldaryn in Taux would turn against me.' Lareo grasped his hand and Zhada felt the old Eldaryn tremble with emotion and exhaustion.

'But only if they know. We can surely swear this Wizard to secrecy. Remember why we're here,' the Lowl pleaded. 'To learn how to kill Yaretzi. Sell that secret to the Red Pillars and you'll secure enough in their favor to buy off any amount of anger elsewhere.'

His voice shook with desperation. 'Or you can tell me where to find this White Fire. I'll risk Eldaryn wrath to steal some and save Asalyan.'

Lareo looked at him for a long moment. 'I can get some, though it won't be easy,' he finally said. 'To save an innocent.'

As they turned to face the Wizard, the robed figure shook with unkind laughter. 'Very well. Now, the third thing—'

'A moment.' Zhada raised a commanding hand even though he felt as if lead manacles weighed him down. 'You've already asked us to undertake two perilous quests but we have no guarantees that your answers will be worth more than a wilted blossom.'

Zhada had no hope of sniffing out whatever truth or falsehood lay beneath that black hood.

'We will ask our two questions,' Lareo rasped. 'If your answers meet our needs, we can come to terms over a third trade.'

The black robed figure shook with an emotion Zhada couldn't fathom. The only sound to break the silence was the steady drip of water into the pool. They waited so long; the Lowl was convinced the Wizard was going to send them away empty–handed—

The eerie figure laughed. 'Very well. But first you must swear. Vow to deliver what you have promised in return for my answers, on forfeit of your soul should you fail.'

'I vow to bring you Death's Kiss seeds—'

Zhada swore the oath and Lareo stumbled through the words after him. As they spoke, the radiance in the stagnant pool grew stronger and stronger. The aura of death in the cave grew so oppressive that Zhada reeled. Lareo collapsed onto his hands and knees.

'Very well.' As the Wizard spoke, the eldritch light faded and the intangible menace receded.

Zhada helped Lareo back to his feet.

'Who's going first?' the Wizard inquired amiably.

Zhada found this good-humor the most worrying thing they'd encountered.

Lareo coughed like a man in the throes of consumption. As he drew himself up to his full height to address the Wizard, Zhada could see what the effort cost him.

'How can the Princess Yaretzi be killed, or destroyed, whatever the word might be for sending an undead creature to oblivion?'

'A good question,' the Wizard approved. 'Yaretzi is a creature sustained by suffering and pain. To kill her requires a weapon consecrated to life and light which can nevertheless cut her down, because you may be assured she will fight back.'

The hooded figure cackled. 'A pretty puzzle since the whole purpose of a weapon is to slay the living, so any such blade is inevitably imbued with death.'

Zhada swallowed a growl. It's an answer, and puzzles can be solved, he reminded himself. Meantime, he needed to know how to protect Asalyan.

'Why does Yaretzi torment her victims before she kills them, with dreams and visions of death?' the Lowl demanded. 'Assuming that is how she marks her prey?'

'You think you can ask two questions for the price of one?' The Wizard chuckled again. 'No, you're on the wrong scent entirely. Yaretzi's black sorcery stirs the ancient souls trapped within Taux's stones. Those who dream of their torment are merely more sensitive to such arcane voices. But Yaretzi is drawn to kill those who have such dreams because she finds the anguish of the living far richer and more satisfying for her undead appetites.'

The hooded figure leaned forward, continuing to explain with relish. 'That's why she is killing so many within the Black Gate. The stones of the old Ullamalitzli courts are soaked in the abject terror of those who lost the sacred game in Taux's days of yore. Amid the anguish of defeat, they knew their fate was execution. That's why those courts were called the garden of death.

'Yaretzi drinks that torment in like fine wine, compared to the stale dregs of the Haunted Temple District where victims dragged to the sacrificial altars were either drugged or resigned to their doom. Still sweating from the game though, the losers would desperately hope for some escape—'

The Wizard broke off, leaning back. 'That's enough of an answer to prove my knowledge's worth. Now, let us agree to terms for a third question.'

What could they ask which might lead them to this weapon? Or should they ask how to lure Yaretzi, once it was found?

Before Zhada could decide what they needed to know most urgently, Lareo spoke up.

'No, thank you. Our business is concluded.'

'What?' The Wizard's wrath echoed around the cavern.

'We have sworn to deliver two things in return for two answers,' the Eldaryn said doggedly. 'We will fulfil our end of that bargain. You cannot compel us to ask more questions.'

Zhada longed to ask Lareo what in the names of all the saints and demons he was playing at. Angering a Wizard could be lethal.

'We will take our leave—' As Lareo tried to bow, he slumped to the floor.

The aura of death in the cavern strengthened. The Wizard's white hands gripped the arms of the chair, as though the sorcerer was about to stand. Bone-white wisps of mist rose from the seething pool. Globes of malevolent darkness surged up from the depths and swirled around in maddened circles. Zhada glimpsed eerie outlines of contorted faces in the waters and vapours alike.

The Lowl scooped Lareo up into his arms and staggered back down the tunnel. The Wizard's outrage pursued them.

'*You asked me three questions. You owe me three things. I want one of Yaretzi's bones. Bring that to me or face my vengeance!*'

Zhada kept running. The light oozing from the walls was fading fast. Was that the Wizard's doing? Incoherently begging Vitcoska for guidance out of this hellish labyrinth, he stumbled onwards, clutching Lareo's limp body.

Whether or not his prayers were answered, the further he got from the cavern's deathly pool, Zhada felt the fire within him strengthen. Better yet, he felt Lareo's breathing deepen.

Finding a dry patch, he lowered the old Eldaryn to the floor. 'Are you alright?' There was barely enough light to see his face. 'I hope I'm following the right passages.'

Lareo gestured with his walking cane. 'Look for my marks.'

Zhada saw a pale scrape on the stone, where Lareo had drawn a line through the mold with his iron-shod cane.

'I brought a candle and matches as well.' Lareo laughed feebly as he reached inside his jerkin. 'It doesn't do to rely on magic for everything.'

'I'll remember that.' Zhada took them from the Eldaryn's shaking hands.

It took four attempts to light the candle. By then, Lareo had succumbed to exhaustion again. Zhada picked him up, cradling the senseless Eldaryn with one arm and holding the candle in his other hand. It gave just enough light to show the trail Lareo had marked back to the spiral stair.

By then the candle was a guttering stub. By the time Zhada reached the top step, he was crawling on his hands and knees with Lareo slumped across his back. The heavy stone blocked their exit.

Zhada laid Lareo down and tried to lift the slab but he didn't have the strength after the sapping effects of being so far underground and so deep below water. He sat in the darkness, desolate. How could he save Asalyan if he starved to death under this rock?

'*Remember what you owe me. All that you owe me.*'

Magical radiance outlined the stone. It rose and sunlight flooded the stairwell as the slab fell back.

Sunlight? Zhada picked up Lareo and stumbled into the open air, incredulous. The sky was bright with dawn. They had been underground all night and now another day was in full bloom, one that would culminate in the Night of Secrets.

As Zhada headed for the heart of the city with Lareo in his arms, he vowed to find some way to use the secrets they had learned. As soon as he'd gotten some sleep.

He woke to find Lareo looking down at him. For a moment, Zhada couldn't remember where he was or what he had done. Then he dredged up a vague recollection of laying the unconscious Eldaryn down on the bed in his tenement room. Zhada had stretched out on the floor, so exhausted he could have slept on a mattress of razor thorns.

Zhada ran his long tongue around his teeth and grimaced. 'I haven't felt this bad since I was last fool enough to drink myself senseless.'

'I've had worse, though at my age, that's to be expected.' Lareo grinned, though he was still wearily pale with bloodshot eyes.

Zhada struggled to his feet and went to the washstand to lap cold water from the ewer. As he gazed out of the window, he saw the sun at its zenith. They had slept until just before noon. He could only hope that Asalyan was still safe.

'Why didn't you let me ask where we could find that accursed weapon?'

'That blessed weapon,' Lareo corrected him. 'Because we already know, between us.'

'How so?' Zhada asked with rising hope.

Lareo sat on the side of the bed, feet swinging. 'I made some enquiries about this healer you mentioned yesterday. I've heard from several reliable sources that the man's power stems from an ancient

Tolimic wood and obsidian sword. It's a marvel, apparently. A weapon which cures instead of wounding.'

'A weapon imbued with life,' Zhada said slowly.

'And you know where to find it.' Lareo jumped down to the floor. 'So we must establish the price for borrowing it. However high that might be, it's better than owing that Wizard a third favor.' He shuddered.

'I'll pay whatever the Healer asks,' Zhada promised. 'Come on.'

Outside, the Black Gate was largely empty of yesterday's crowds. Most folk were sleeping off yesterday's excesses or preparing themselves for the Night of Secrets. Festival tradition allowed men and women alike to slip away from burdensome obligations under the cover of masks and darkness.

That wasn't all that happened under cover of this particular night. Zhada glanced warily to either side as they walked past the Silk Purse. Old grudges often saw unsanctioned duels fought in the moonlight. Any swordsman worth his blade spent this particular day alert for veiled hostility which might hint at challenges to come.

They reached the Black Gate itsef without incident. Once they were in the city beyond, Lareo waved down a carriage for hire with his eagle-headed cane. Zhada gave the driver the healer's address.

The line of wealthy folk willing to empty their purses for a cure was four times as long as it had been the day before. Zhada ignored them all, pushing forward to hammer on the door while Lareo was paying off the carriage driver.

The handsome young Human opened the door a crack. 'You? I told you, she cannot leave. Her cure isn't complete—'

Zhada shoved the door open, easily overcoming the Human's belated resistance. He looked around for that Jai-Ruk, ready to knock him to the floor as well.

When the curtained inner door opened however, a man entered the antechamber, extravagant robes swishing around him. He was tall, lean and dark-skinned, seemingly akin to men and women Zhada had met from Zimbolay. But those folk had dark eyes while this man's heavy-lidded gaze was as brilliantly blue as the summer sky over the grasslands.

He looked down his long nose at Zhada. 'You're the lover, I take it?'

'You're the healer.' The Lowl had no doubt of that. The room was suffused with the fresh, green scent of life, as magical and as vibrant as the peak of springtime.

The tall man was also holding an ancient Tolimic weapon, though Zhada wouldn't have called it a sword. The long blade was made from polished wood with razor-shards of obsidian embedded along both sides. The hilt was long enough for a solid two-handed grip and bound with what looked like snakeskin, though not from any serpent he'd ever encountered.

Zhada eyed the weapon warily, even though the healer wasn't holding it ready for use. It might not be steel but the Lowl had no doubt it could inflict lethal wounds. Good, because that was exactly why he needed it. But would this man surrender the shard-edged blade, even for a little while?

'Forgive my intrusion,' he began stiffly. 'I need a Tolimic blade such as you have there. I will pay whatever price you ask, to use it for a night and a day.' That would surely give him time to track down Yaretzi.

'No,' the man said bluntly.

Zhada coughed. A deadly scent rolled off the healer, momentarily penetrating the all-pervasive breath of life. Zhada tasted powerful death-magic though this was very different to the malevolent vapours surrounding the Wizard under the sea. This evil was as ancient and dry as a long-sealed desert tomb opened by robbers.

Quicker than conscious thought, Zhada sprang, He pressed the man hard against the wall, one forearm under the man's chin ready to choke the breath from him and his other hand forcing the Tolimic sword away.

'Who are you?' he snarled. 'What are you? Where is Asalyan? If you've harmed a hair on her head—'

'You'll do what?' the healer sneered. 'Kill me? Try it and see how far you get. Have you never heard of Kalomir Bouchtat, seven-deathed Lich Lord of the Nightmare Army?'

Before Zhada could say that this boast meant nothing to him, another voice spoke. It wasn't the man who'd been guarding the door. He couldn't have said if it was male or female, young or old.

'Honest Lowl, you have my word. Your beloved Asalyan is perfectly safe and well. She is resting in our garden.'

'Provided you do as we say, she will remain safe and well.' The tall man smirked at Zhada, clearly unconcerned at being menaced.

That much was true, Zhada could tell, although the stink of deceit hung around the Zimbolayan like stale sweat.

'Can't we just be friends?' the new voice pleaded.

Zhada looked down as the vivid scent of life overwhelmed Kalomir's ominous magical scents. Was he going mad, or was the Tolimic weapon somehow speaking to him?

'It's the old sword talking,' the man who'd been watching the door confirmed. 'Curious, ain't it?'

Zhada looked around to see the gatekeeper standing with upraised hands, making no move to challenge Lareo for a firestick which the old Eldaryn had drawn as he stood guarding the closed door.

'You, fire-born.' Kalomir nodded at Lareo. 'You've heard of me, I can see it in your eyes. Call off your dog and explain to him precisely what 'undead ruler enduring for millennia' means.'

'I have heard of Kalomir Bouchtat,' the old Eldaryn said cautiously. 'As to believing that you are him—'

'Let me tell you why you are here, by way of a trifling display of my powers.'

The healer shoved Zhada away with a contemptuous flick of his wrist. Though Kalomir took him unawares, that shouldn't have been enough. His strength was far beyond what the Lowl would have expected for a man of his stature.

Zhada retreated cautiously to stand beside Lareo. The Eldaryn lowered his weapon as the gatekeeper crossed the anteroom to stand beside the Lich Lord.

'That's better,' the disembodied voice said cheerily. 'Now we can all be friends.'

Kalomir laughed, mocking. 'Allies perhaps, as long as that suits us all. So you want to kill Priestess Yaretzi?'

'Why do you say that?' Zhada demanded.

'Two millennia of experience with Human – and other – natures.' The Zimbolay Lich angled his head, sardonic. 'Your beloved is tormented by dreams of Yaretzi. Her anguish will soon lure the monster to kill her. To save Asalyan, you must destroy the priestess. You need my sword to do that. Tell me I'm wrong,' he taunted.

'You're not,' Zhada replied through gritted teeth.

'I never am,' Kalomir said smugly.

'Oh, now that's not quite true,' the sword began. 'Remember when—'

'Enough.' Kalomir smacked the blade against the wall. 'Though I am curious to know how you learned that I have the very weapon you need?'

He looked from Zhada to Lareo and back again, fine black brows arched, questioning.

Zhada and Lareo shared a glance and both stayed silent. Zhada knew precisely what Lareo would say. Caught at a disadvantage, only a fool gave up any information without extracting the best possible price.

Kalomir shrugged. 'All in good time. Now, you may thank your lucky stars that I also want Yaretzi destroyed. So I need some brave warrior to do the deed.' He smirked at Zhada again.

'Why?' the Lowl demanded. 'If you're all-powerful.'

'That's for me to know and you to wonder.' Kalomir dismissed the question with a wave of his hand.

The sword piped up. 'He's a mage not a warrior. You should have seen—'

The Lich Lord quickly spoke over it. 'One doesn't become an undead lord enduring for aeons by taking any unnecessary risks. Now, can we come to terms?'

Zhada's hackles rose at this echo of the Wizard's words under the bay. 'Perhaps,' he growled.

'Very well.' Kalomir smiled complacently, as though he had already got his own way. 'Since you know this city, I'm sure you can discover the place Yaretzi calls her Garden of Death. We will all go there together and when Asalyan's distress draws the priestess—'

'No.' Zhada shook his head in absolute refusal. 'Asalyan goes nowhere near her.'

'Foolish hound.' Kalomir's face hardened, cruel. 'You seem to think—'

'Oh, we don't need to take Asalyan,' the sword chirped helpfully. 'Any one of the nightmare-afflicted will do to lure Yaretzi. We have any number here to choose from.'

'How fortunate,' Lareo said drily.

Zhada caught the sour whiff of Kalomir's irritation.

'Quite so.' The Lich Lord continued as though there had been no interruption. 'I must speak with Yaretzi for reasons which do not concern you. Once my business with her is concluded, you can use Tezcatlecuhtli here to destroy her once and for all.'

He waved the sword which promptly spoke up. 'I can do it, have no fear of that. Meantime, your beloved will be quite safe. The Garden of Life I have made for her here will ward off Yaretzi—'

Kalomir shook the sword to silence it, fixing his icy blue gaze on Zhada. 'Do we have a deal?'

Zhada longed to say no. He had already sworn to risk his life for one Wizard today. But he had promised to save Asalyan too.

'As long as no harm comes to her,' he said slowly. 'Otherwise I will hunt you down and tear you limb from limb, eternal undead lord or not.'

'I would expect nothing else.' Kalomir smiled with cold satisfaction. 'To keep you honest, Andril here will stay with Asalyan. If for some reason I fail to return, with Tezcatlecuhtli in my possession, he will cut your beloved's throat. No Garden of Life will keep him out.'

'Then I'll send a man to watch over the bargain,' Lareo said quickly. 'And to escort Asalyan home, as soon as you return.'

Kalomir shook his head. 'I don't think—'

'If you want to know where Yaretzi's Garden of Death is, that's my price,' the old Eldaryn said, unblinking.

'That's fine with us,' the sword said happily. 'I'm sure she'll be glad of the company.'

And Zhada knew that Lareo would call on all the power the Eldaryn had to save Asalyan from any treachery while he was away.

'Then we have a deal.' Zhada said, though his mouth was so dry he could barely speak.

Waiting in the darkness of the deserted ball court, Zhada wondered how Kalomir had put up with two thousand years of Tezcatlecuhtli's company. The Lowl had endured barely an hour of the sword's irrepressibly cheery prattle and he was ready to bury the blade in the Ebon Swamp. The wretched thing didn't even need to pause for breath.

Asking the artifact to stay silent, to avoid alerting Yaretzi hadn't helped either. Now Tezcatlecuhtli was somehow speaking directly into Zhada's mind, relating yet another tale of an evil the Lich had slain in order to prolong his own accursed existence.

Which was the answer, of course. As they had agreed on their tactics for this encounter, Kalomir had been forced to explain his tie to the blade, and that explained in turn why he was holding Asalyan hostage, to ensure Zhada wouldn't put a quick end to the Lich's unholy undeath.

He had to admit Kalomir was indeed an astute judge of character. If he hadn't made that promise, after hearing the Lich boast of his malevolent plans for Taux, Zhada wouldn't hesitate to take Tezcatlecuhtli as far away as needs be to see Kalomir crumble to dust. Before handing the blade over to some priest or other, who could put up with its endless burbling as a toll to balance the healing it could do.

But he had promised. So all he could do was hope that the enchanted blade's influence would continue to frustrate the Lich's lust for wielding death and destruction. At least he had learned that much from Tezcatlecuhtli's incessant stories.

'I didn't tell you how we saved the people of Oxachtli from the Devouring Slime, did I?' the voice exclaimed happily inside Zhada's head. 'As it turned out, the abomination was an emanation from the para-elemental plane of—'

Zhada did his best to ignore the sword's latest tale of ancient death and sorcery. Crouched in the shadows, he fixed his gaze on Kalomir and the ghastly apparition that was Yaretzi, her skeletal form draped in a robe of venomous green scales, blood puddling around her fleshless feet. Zhada was fervently grateful that a hood concealed whatever horror her face had become.

She was gesturing with bony white hands, animated as she talked to Kalomir. Zhada didn't speak Old Tolimic and besides, the moaning from the stones drowned out their words, so he had no idea what they were saying. That didn't matter. What mattered was being ready when the moment came for him to strike the monster down.

He watched the cowering shadow that was the Human named Demorn. Zhada didn't know who the man was, and didn't much care, beyond pitying his abject terror when with characteristic malicious glee, Kalomir had explained his role as bait to draw Yaretzi to the old ball court. The Lowl's nostrils twitched. The wretched man's bladder had just yielded to his fear. But Kalomir had promised them all, Tezcatlecuhtli included, that Demorn wouldn't be killed. That was the sword's price for playing its part in this plot.

'Now!' Tezcatlecuhtli's yell made Zhada's head ring.

Kalomir was surging backwards, carried on a blast of air toward the shadows where Zhada lurked. He was dragging Demorn with him. Yaretzi was following, impossibly fast. Her clawed hands reached out to seize Demorn's flailing feet. The stench of rotting blood made Zhada retch.

He ran straight for her regardless. His snarls echoed back from the carved walls, even louder than the wailing souls. Yaretzi's hooded head shifted from Demorn to Zhada. No, he realized an instant later, all her attention was fixed on Tezcatlecuhtli. The monster was recoiling. The Tolimic blade's exuberant vitality must be anathema to such a loathsome creature of death and decay.

Summoning all his strength and will, he ran faster. So fast he felt his heart hammering within his chest. As Yaretzi turned to flee, he gripped Tezcatlecuhtli's hilt tight in both hands. Before the undead priestess could escape, he sprang, raising the blade high above his head. He smashed the weapon down into the angle of her hooded head and the bony shoulder beneath her scaled robe.

The obsidian shards sliced through the leathery garment like a razor through silk. Collarbone, ribs and breastbone shattered like white ceramic, shards flying in all directions. Yaretzi screamed as the weapon's murderous arc ended, the blade biting deep into the bones of her spine and pelvis.

The hood dipped as the creature looked down and then spoke to Kalomir. Zhada looked down and to one side, not wishing to catch even a glimpse of whatever lay under that hood. He tugged but realized the weapon was stuck fast amid Yaretzi's ghastly bones.

Kalomir answered her, and whatever his actual words, Zhada could hear the smug satisfaction in his tone. The Lich put his hand on Tezcatlecuhtli's hilt. 'Time for us to go.'

'You're not going anywhere without me,' growled Zhada.

'Hold me here and Asalyan dies,' said Kalomir coldly. 'I told you how this magic works. As soon as I take Tezcatlecuhtli away, the priestess will die. But I suggest you stay here to make sure of that.'

The Lich raised his voice over Yaretzi's shrieks. 'You want to be quite certain that your beloved is safe, don't you? I mean,' he mocked Zhada, 'you don't trust me, not really. Let's be honest.'

Zhada tightened his grip on Tezcatlecuhtli. Why was the infuriating blade silent, precisely when he could have done with its inconvenient candour betraying Kalomir's true intentions?

The Lich tugged harder on the weapon's handle. 'Let me go and Yaretzi dies.'

'We will go together.' Zhada released his hold.

Kalomir swept the weapon upwards, his unnatural strength freeing the wedged blade.

As soon as Tezcatlecuhtli was clear, Yaretzi sprang. Zhada was taken wholly by surprise. The monster knocked him backwards, clean off his feet. As he landed flat on his back, her clawed fingers dug deep into his shoulders. Her bony feet scrabbled at his legs.

Why wasn't she dead? He'd all but cut her in half. Then he heard an ominous clicking. It was a moment before Zhada realised that was the sound of bone striking bone. Tezcatlecuhtli's indiscriminate magic was already mending the damage he'd done to the ghastly priestess.

A stink of rancid death choked him as she murmured threats of unknown horrors. Blood spattered across his face, stinging his eyes, blinding him. Zhada thrashed desperately trying to free himself. To no avail. Yaretzi's undead strength was as formidable as the Lich Lord's. Somewhere in the shadows of the ball court, he heard Kalomir laughing. 'Of course, I didn't say how soon Yaretzi would die, did I? Threaten me, dog, and see where it gets you, fool!'

Kalomir's taunting chuckles faded as he departed. Zhada spared half a breath to promise himself a reckoning with the Lich. To secure that, he must survive. He had to keep fighting to destroy the priestess until Kalomir took the Tolimic blade too far away to heal her. At least the magic was healing him just as fast. But could he kill her before he took a fatal wound without even realising it?

Zhada brought his fists up between Yaretzi's bony arms and thrust his hands forward. Broken bone lacerated his fingers. He ignored the pain, taking firm hold of the undead priestess's exposed spine on the one hand, and of her shoulder blade on the other. Turning all his rage, and his fear, for himself and Asalyan, into the endeavour, he tore open the gash Tezcatlecuhtli had cut through the monster.

Dry cartilage snapped and cracked bone shattered. He felt her arm come away from her ravaged rib cage completely. Still blinded by tears, he hurled the bones into the darkness. At least that got rid of the fingers digging deep into his sword arm. Zhada flung out his hand and braced himself against the blood-soaked sand. With a mighty effort, he shoved, digging his booted heel into the ground as well, and twisting his hips. If he could throw the creature off with a wrestling move—

Yaretzi collapsed like a stack of firewood knocked by a careless passer-by. Zhada scrambled out from underneath the lifeless bones. Was it finally dead? Had Kalomir carried Tezcatlecuhtli far enough away to draw the weapon's life-essence out of the monster?

He looked at the hooded skull, motionless on the ground. Drawing back his foot, he kicked it as hard as he could. The hood flew off as it smashed into the Ullamalitzli court wall with a sickly crunch.

Zhada fell to his knees, still struggling for breath. The death reek was slow to fade.

'Are you alright, Master Lowl?' a voice quavered in the darkness.

'Demorn?' Zhada was astonished. Why hadn't the Human fled as soon as he'd had the chance? Then again, why should he want to have anything more to do with Kalomir, who'd used him to lure the monster here?

'Can you sense anything of Yaretzi?' Zhada demanded. 'Any hint of the nightmares that have tormented you?'

'No, not in the least. I feel better than I have for days.' Demorn's wonder echoed around the empty ball court.

'Then it's done.' Zhada breathed with fervent relief.

Now he had to catch up with Kalomir. He used the last of his strength to struggle to his feet. As he turned to head for the exit, bone crunched beneath his boot. He looked down and remembered the bargains he and Lareo had made to get him here. Stooping, he picked up a small bone, from a finger or a foot, he guessed. It would be as well to have that in reserve, when it came to settling accounts with the Wizard under the bay.

He growled deep in his throat as reaching down sent daggers of pain lancing through his shoulder. Blood slid down his arm. His own fresh blood, not Yaretzi's clotted sorcery.

'That looks bad, Master Lowl,' Demorn said nervously. 'Shall I take you to a healer? One who won't ask questions,' he added meaningfully. 'Unlike the Sturgeons.'

It took a moment before Zhada grasped the little man's meaning. Night of Secrets or not, the city's peace-keepers couldn't turn a blind eye to potential evidence of an illegal duel. And it wasn't as if he had another believable explanation to offer.

'Quickly then,' he said to Demorn. Meantime, he could only hope that Tezcatlecuhtli would be true to its word, and keep her safe from Kalomir's malice.

Though as he followed the scurrying Human out of the Ullamalitzli court, satisfaction warmed away his pain. He had fulfilled his promise to Asalyan. First and last that's what mattered most.

Illustration by Jeff Laubenstein

THE DRINKER OF DEATH

By Dan Wells

The Distant Past

Kalomir Bouchtat, seven-deathed lich lord of the Nightmare Army, looked down at the sword in his chest. He blinked in surprise—a quirk of muscle memory, since his dead eyes had no need for moisture. It was an old sword, a Tolimic sword, a wide wooden blade set with glittering shards of razor-sharp obsidian, and it sliced through his shoulder and ribs so cleanly he barely even felt it. Even now he couldn't see the line of its passage, despite the weapon's width. It protruded from his long-dead chest like the branch of a tree, the wood somehow—impossibly—still alive, green shoots and tendrils twisting out like the new growth of a spring sapling. He watched a pale green vine wind up from the handle and wrap around the wrist of the man who wielded it: Ordoun, one of Kalomir's lieutenants, who had drawn the sword from hiding only moments ago, and betrayed him with this vicious attack.

Except Kalomir wasn't dead. He actually felt pretty good.

"Let me get this straight," said Kalomir. He could destroy this man with a snap of his bony fingers, but his curiosity got the better of him. "You're betraying me, right?"

"I am destroying you, foul creature," said Ordoun boldly. "Your war of vile conquest is over, and the world is safe from the grip of your necromancy."

"That's what I thought," said Kalomir, studying the sword. Ordoun held it firmly in place, right through the lich's sternum. Kalomir frowned. "I guess I'm just....I mean it's not a very effective weapon, is it? It doesn't even hurt."

"Delicious," said the sword.

Kalomir's eyes widened. "It talks?"

"It is Tezcatlecuhtli!" shouted Ordoun. "The most powerful artifact of the Tolimic Empire, the slayer of death, and you will fall before its power, villain!"

"Absolutely delicious," said the sword. Its voice was cheery and amiable, bizarrely out of place in the war tent of an undead overlord. "I haven't eaten this well in centuries."

"I think I'm still confused," said Kalomir. "You're trying to kill me, right?"

"That...." Ordoun's bravado faltered. "That was the plan, yes. I...." He wiggled the sword a bit in Kalomir's chest. "Tezcatlecuhtli? You okay?"

"This lich," said Tezcatlecuhtli, "is fantastic. It's like a...what do you humans eat, grain? It's like the grainiest grain you've ever tasted. It's like the essence of grain itself, condensed into an elixir of pure grain-ness."

Kalomir smirked. "Seriously, where did you get this thing?"

"In the deepest catacombs of the God-King Barrows," said Ordoun, "beyond the mountains of Skywrath in the Motionless Plains. Standard stuff. The witch-woman told me this would work."

"How did you have time to go that far?" asked Kalomir. "You've been sending battle reports from the western flank every week for months."

"I pre-wrote them all," said Ordoun. "Had a friendly messenger bring them in for me."

"Clever."

"Thanks." Ordoun frowned nervously. "Aren't you mad? I mean, I kind of figured you'd be dead by now, or I would be. Thought I had just one blow, had to make it count, but you're...."

"Believe me," said Kalomir, "I am going to *literally* eat your soul, but first this is pretty surreal. You've got to give me a minute to let it sink in."

"Nope," said Tezcatlecuhtli, "sorry, no soul-eating for you anymore. You're cut off from the plane of shadow, or what you call negative energy and death."

Kalomir's eyes widened—another old habit—as the full import of the sword's statement struck him. "Cut off? You mean, completely cut off?" He tried to reach out with his mind to the vast skeletal hordes that filled the fields outside the tent, waiting on his command to launch another wave against the failing defenses of his latest target kingdom. He couldn't even tell if the skeletons were there anymore. "No," he said, feeling the power slip away from him as the sword drank ever more greedily. "No! My army!"

"The witch-woman was right!" cried Ordoun. "The Nightmare Army falls!"

Kalomir roared in fury, drawing his own sword and plunging it into Ordoun's heart. The traitorous lieutenant staggered back, losing his grip on Tezcatlecuhtli, and stared down at the blade in his chest. He didn't die either.

"This is getting weird," said Ordoun.

"I don't think either of you are grasping the full ramifications of our situation," said Tezcatlecuhtli. "I'm an incredibly ancient, incredibly powerful artifact that feeds on death magic and turns it into life magic. It's like how you feed on grain and turn it into running and fighting and…human-ing."

"Your knowledge of human beings is severely lacking," said Kalomir.

"You're the most powerful lich I've ever encountered," said Tezcatlecuhtli, "and consuming your connection to the plane of shadow is causing me to produce more life magic than I can reasonably contain."

Kalomir looked down, seeing new young plants growing up between the rugs laid out on the floor. Even his chair and table were growing, sprouting leaves and tendrils as if they were new green wood.

"That's why I'm not dead," said Kalomir. "You're producing so much life magic, you're keeping me alive even without the necromancy that *used to be* keeping me alive."

"Exactly," said the sword. "And the same effect is keeping him alive even with a sword in his chest."

"Huh," said Kalomir. "Well, that's easy to fix." Even without his necromancy he was still a potent Aspara air born, intimately connected to the plane of air; he summoned a ball of wind, and Ordoun shouted as he realized what was happening, but it was too late: Kalomir released the air in a massive burst, blowing Ordoun backwards into the wall of the tent, the force of the gale tearing the tent up from its stakes and carrying both man and fabric away in a flapping, screaming arc. The heavy body fell to the ground as the tent blew away, and

Kalomir watched in satisfaction as the traitor flew beyond the reach of Tezcatlecuhtli's life-giving aura, dying instantly as he did.

"That wasn't very nice," said Tezcatlecuhtli.

"Shut up," said Kalomir. He turned slowly, observing the destruction around the now-wall-less war tent. His army, the greatest necromantic war-host ever assembled, was crumbling to dust, wights and wraiths and skeletons and more all sinking to the ground or disappearing into the air as the sword hungrily, relentlessly, devoured the magic spells Kalomir had used to bind them. Armor fell empty to the ground; weapons clattered to the stones amid the debris of ribs and skulls and femurs. "I gave up everything for this," Kalomir whispered. "I was going to rule the world."

"I'm sorry," said Tezcatlecuhtli. "I mean, I'm not sorry about what you've lost, because destroying dark magic is my entire purpose in existing. But I am sorry that you're sad; I don't like people to be sad. Even evil liches."

The circle of destruction spread out from the central war tent like ripples in a pond, undead creatures and constructs tumbling like discarded toys, and in their wake the life magic churned and bubbled, raising up trees and grass and bushes so quickly that Kalomir had to step aside to keep from being caught in their swift-sprouting branches and carried up into the sky. Soon his entire army was gone, and in its place a forest stood, tall and green and vibrant.

"I am going to break you," said Kalomir to the sword. "I'm going to snap you in half, and wear your shards as trophies on my crown."

"I don't think you could," said Tezcatlecuhtli. "And even if you could I don't think you'd really want to. I'm the only thing keeping you alive."

"I can use my powers—"

"You're cut off from your powers," said the sword. "As soon as you get far enough away from me to access them again, you'll be too far for me to keep you alive. You'll die instantly, just like your friend."

"He wasn't my friend."

"He should have been, he was a nice guy."

Kalomir scowled, staring up at the towering trees around him. "Can I at least take you out of my chest?"

"Yep. You could even set me down if you wanted, just don't get too far."

Kalomir grasped the sword's wooden hilt, feeling the power flow through it like music through an instrument. He braced himself for the pain and pulled it free, but it didn't hurt at all, and left no hole or scar to mark its passing. He ran his finger over his chest, feeling the long-dead skin grow soft and pliant as living flesh. He didn't even look like a lich anymore. "You didn't even cut my clothes."

"I'm not a weapon," said Tezcatlecuhtli.

"So what now, I just…carry you around? I keep you with me and I'm fine?"

"For most people, yes," said Tezcatlecuhtli. "You're different, because you're technically dead. If you want me to keep you alive—and I assume you do—you need to keep me topped off with death magic."

"You're running out?"

"I can hold a little, but the excess just flows out whether I want it to or not. As this sudden forest can attest."

"And the only way to get more death magic is to…." Kalomir sighed, and if he'd had a heart it would have sunk. "You need me to find more undead and slay them."

"That's what I was made for."

"But the undead are my allies," said Kalomir. "I like the undead—I don't want them slain, I want them to take over the world."

The sword sounded hopeful. "Enough to let yourself die?"

Kalomir stared at the ground, dark and black between the roots of the trees. "No," he said at last. "If they're going to take over the world, they're going to do it with me as their ruler."

"I don't really condone that," said Tezcatlecuhtli.

"And I don't condone you," said Kalomir. "But it looks like we're stuck with each other."

"So where does that leave us?"

"As heroes," said Kalomir, though the word itself sickened him. He shook his head in resignation, and trudged off through the thick foliage. "Come on, I know a zombie cult in the Nublar Highlands that ought to keep us going for a few weeks."

"Hooray!" said Tezcatlecuhtli. "Time to smite some evil!"

"Only until I can figure out how to survive without you," said Kalomir. "Then I break you and go right back to being evil again. I just hope it's soon…."

*T*wo *Thousand Years Later*

*F*irst *Day: Lover's Day*

"**A**nother day, another adventure!" Tezcatlecuhtli was practically beaming, and Kalomir rolled his eyes.

"Another day with your relentlessly cheerful nattering," said the former lich. He stepped out onto the deck of the ship, watching the distant line of land grow larger in the morning light. "Is there some way, after two thousand years, that you could maybe just be quiet for a day? Or even an hour? I'd take an hour."

"I've given you an hour before."

"Never," said Kalomir. "I've been keeping track. At this point I'd voluntarily help an orphanage for a single hour of silence."

"I like orphans," said Tezcatlecuhtli. Kalomir groaned inwardly, knowing all too well the statement that would follow. He said it along with the sword in almost perfect unison: "I mean, I don't like the fact that they're orphans, but I like being able to help them." The sword's perpetually peppy mood somehow managed to brighten even further. "Hey! You agreed with me!"

"I was mocking you," said Kalomir. "There's a difference."

"Someday," said the sword knowingly, "you'll come around. No one can slay monsters and save innocent lives for two thousand years without a little bit of friendliness and good intentions rubbing off."

Kalomir didn't respond out loud, but simply shook his head as he watched their destination grow closer and closer. Coming around to Tezcatlecuhtli's way of thinking was more of a concern than he dared to admit. Two thousand years of slaying the undead, of seeking out monsters and necromancers and creatures of the night, and destroying them. He'd become a folk hero, the legend of the Ghost Who Walks spreading far and wide across the world, until he could arrive in a new city, in a country he'd never visited, and be regaled by the local barkeep about the mysterious stranger who wanders the shadows making the world a safer place. It made him sick. He'd started reminding himself, through actions as well as words, of his real nature and goals: fostering death before he was finally forced to attack it; hurting an innocent for every monster he slew. More importantly, he'd been gaining knowledge from every mage and witch and necromantic coven he destroyed, slowly building not his power, for the sword still cut him off from it, but his notes and knowledge about the nature of that power. Always working toward the single goal of escaping the sword and his cursed dependence on it. Only when he could sustain himself through necromancy, again a proper lich, would he ever be free to conquer the world again.

And that was what had brought him here: the city of Taux, the Living Crypt, the place of the Wailing Stones. It was here that the ancient priests had constructed Tezcatlecuhtli, as a weapon against the forces of darkness, and it was here that those dark forces had eventually won, long ago casting out the sword, before more recently destroying their own city in a mystic apocalypse so terrible that the souls of its denizens were still trapped in the streets and buildings. Many times he'd thought of coming here, hoping to find the lost secrets of the old Tolimic necromancers, but he could not choose where he went—his path across the world was dictated by the rumors he followed, always moving from one undead creature to the next. Tezcatlecuhtli couldn't feed without their energy, and Kalomir couldn't live without Tezcatlecuhtli, so around and around he went, chasing one nightmare after another. Only now, when the word reached him of a dark priestess stalking Taux's alleys, could he risk the trip. He hoped he could find what he needed, and kill the priestess for sustenance, before his endless need pulled him away again.

"That city looks terrible," said Tezcatlecuhtli. "We can do so much good here! I want to hug somebody. Go hug somebody and tell me what it's like."

"I'm not going to hug anybody," said Kalomir.

"Hug that sailor," said Tezcatlecuhtli. "Hey, sailor! Can we give you a hug? We love hugs!"

"We don't love hugs," said Kalomir. The sailor looked at him suspiciously, then crossed to the other side of the ship. "When will you realize," asked Kalomir, "that they don't know you're a sword? No one can tell where your voice is coming from—they think I'm a crazy person with two voices."

"I'm sorry I embarrassed you."

"I don't get embarrassed."

"Then why does it bother you?"

Kalomir ground his teeth together. "Just…stop talking. We're almost there."

The city of Taux grew larger as the ship drew near, and as they passed through the wide, moon-shaped bay the buildings began to rise up before them like ancient monoliths—first the wizards' spire, on its isolated island, and then the great towers and pyramids of Taux itself, the stones dark in the dawn, their carvings intricate and beautiful and indefinably unsettling. It was a city of death, and Kalomir couldn't help but feel at home as the gloom settled over him. He felt a flash of malicious glee: Tezcatlecuhtli would hate it here.

"Oh my," said the sword. Its voice was surprised, and Kalomir knew its mood well enough to identify its pleasure at sensing food. Death magic was nearby.

"The priestess?" asked Kalomir.

"I don't think so," said Tezcatlecuhtli. "Only if she's way, way more powerful than we thought she was."

Kalomir grinned wolfishly. "An entire cult, perhaps?" That would be a boon in two ways—a dark priestess that powerful would make a more satisfying meal for the sword *and* a greater source of knowledge for Kalomir.

"I think…." Tezcatlecuhtli paused. "I think it's the city."

"What do you mean?"

"I mean the city itself," said the sword. "It's infused with death magic—it's drenched in it. I can feed on it from here, and we're still a boat length from the dock. I can—oh, that's good stuff."

Kalomir looked at the sword's wooden hilt, and saw new shoots of green growing out of it.

"I haven't eaten this well since…well, since the day I met you," said Tezcatlecuhtli. "I wish you could taste this, because it is seriously wonderful. I mean, death magic is evil and terrible, not wonderful, but it *tastes* wonderful."

"The grainiest grain," said Kalomir.

"You told me that was a bad analogy," said the sword.

"It is," said Kalomir. The sailors heaved their anchor overboard, and the ship drifted to a stop. Already he could feel himself invigorated by Tezcatlecuhtli's feasting—his senses sharper, his muscles stronger, his reactions quicker. In every way he felt more alive, and he loved it and hated it at the same time. "Your bad analogies are one of the only things I like about you."

"You like me? I like you too."

"I don't like you at all," said Kalomir, "I just like the reminder that you're fallible. I'm going to beat you someday."

"I disagree with your dreams," said the sword, "but following your dreams is awesome, so you should get some better ones and follow those instead. Holy mother of heaven and earth, this city is delicious."

Kalomir walked down the gangplank and onto the wharf, and from there into Taux itself. Every step seemed to fill him with vigor and light, and he clenched his teeth into a scowl. Filthy children, half-naked and scrawny, called out for alms as the wharf bustled around them, sailors and merchants and longshoremen and more all pushing and shoving in a hundred different directions. Men and women of every nationality carried boxes of spice from far continents, crates of fruit, bolts of silk, cages full of wild birds and screeching, hairy beasts. Crippled beggars reached out with pleading hands, cruelly ignored; Kalomir thought about how easy it would be to make one or a dozen or a hundred of them disappear, stolen in the night for unspeakable necromantic experiments, but it was still an unreachable dream and he pushed it from his mind. Some day he would return and destroy this city, but for now....

"Please," groaned a man, reaching out with gnarled fingers. "Have a pity on a blind man. I lost my sight in battle, and my legs as well. I can't work, and I—wait."

The quaver in the man's voice changed so abruptly Kalomir couldn't help but slow his walk and glance back, wondering what had happened.

"You should help him," said Tezcatlecuhtli. "Helping makes me happy."

"I think someone already is," said Kalomir.

The man was blinking his white, useless eyes, and Kalomir watched in wonder as pupils began to form in the center of the milky surface—black at first like deepening pools of ink, then slowly rippling, expanding out into a dull green iris. The man blinked again in shock, squeezing his eyes shut, and when he opened them again the irises were a brilliant viridian green.

"The—" The man stuttered in surprise, shielding his face with his hands. "The sun!" he cried. "I can see!"

A crowd had gathered now, stopped around the man, and Kalomir slunk to the shadow of a nearby wall. "I've seen you heal injuries like that before," he muttered softly. "Why him, out of all the hundreds of cripples and beggars?"

"I didn't heal him," said the sword. "At least, I didn't heal him *on purpose.* But I do admit that it looked like my work."

"Is there another of you?"

"Not that I know of," said Tezcatlecuhtli. "If there were, the odds of it being in the possession of someone as secretive as you are incredibly small. Surely we would have heard about it."

"And yet none of the stories of Taux tell of its random, mysterious healing powers," said Kalomir. The rags by his feet stirred, and he looked down to see another beggar stirring from the bottom of the pile, boils fading on his skin with miraculous, almost comical speed. "Blast it, Tez, it *is* you. Stop healing everyone, you'll get us noticed."

"I'm not doing it on purpose," said Tezcatlecuhtli. "It's just happening. There's so much dark magic in this city I can't help myself. You have to understand—even the cobbles in the road are haunted. But maybe...."

The sword drifted away into thought, and Kalomir shook his head angrily, walking quickly away from the healed beggar now struggling to his feet. "Don't you even think about it," said Kalomir gruffly. "I know that tone of voice, and I know what it means, and whatever plan you're concocting I order you to stop it immediately. We can't afford the notoriety—"

"I *wasn't* doing it on purpose," said Tezcatlecuhtli, "but I totally should be. Watch this." Kalomir stumbled a step as an invisible wave of magic burst out from the sword in an expanding sphere, a wall of living magic so powerful plants sprouted up in the gaps of the stones as it passed. Kalomir couldn't see the effect, but he could track its movement as it passed each new person: their backs straightened, their eyes brightened, their pace quickened as the very stuff of life itself burned through them like a healing breeze. Flowers too, probably for some huge festival rose up on sagging stalks with blooms vibrant alive. "Oh, I *like* this city!" said the sword. "Let's do another one!"

"No," hissed Kalomir, clamping down on the sword's hilt as if it could stifle the voice. People were watching him now, though he hoped it was merely for his odd behavior, and not because they'd identified the source of the healing. "Our entire way of life revolves around staying hidden—no one can know who we are or what we do!"

"But what we do is awesome," said Tezcatlecuhtli, "and who we are is hardly a concern anymore—do you honestly think anyone would recognize you at this point? Two thousand years ago you were the world's most infamous villain; today you're a bedtime story. You don't even look like a corpse anymore."

"Yes, but I am," said Kalomir. "And that means we have to keep moving to stay alive, always running to the next source of death magic. Do you really think they'll let us leave once they get a taste of free magic healing?"

"We won't have to leave," said Tezcatlecuhtli, "this city's practically gushing with death magic. It's like we've found a spring of pure water in the desert, except that the pure water is evil." It let out another healing wave, and Kalomir quickened his step running deeper into the city. "Delicious, delicious evil."

"That's great for you," said Kalomir, "but what if someone takes you away from me?"

"Will you miss me?"

"I'll die, you idiot. They take one step out of range and I'll crumble to dust."

"You know I would be sad if *anyone* died," said the sword, its voice somber, "but you have to admit, I could probably get a lot more good done in the world if I wasn't being wielded by an evil lich."

"Oh, so that's where we're going now, is it? Two thousand years of killing monsters and suddenly I'm not righteous enough for you. We get all kinds of good done in the world."

"You just specifically told me to stop doing something good."

"That's one incident," said Kalomir. "And I think it's justified considering that you just told me you wanted me dead. I thought we were friends."

"No you didn't," said Tezcatlecuhtli.

"I thought we were allies then."

"We should be," said Tezcatlecuhtli. "Look at me: I'm healing people just by walking past them. You're practically running through a slum, and I'm making the people we pass so healthy—without even trying—that I'm even saving them from starvation. Think about that: we could solve this city's disease problem *and* hunger problem. Just by walking around!"

Kalomir stopped.

"That's only going to intensify the effect," said Tezcatlecuhtli. "I'm an artifact of goodness and purity, Kal, you know that. It's time to stop running from it. We could really make a difference here."

Kalomir's mind raced, struggling to adapt to this new situation. The sword was right: it would keep healing people, passively or actively, as long and as diligently as it could. Goodness was its nature. But power was Kalomir's, and even if healing power wasn't exactly the kind he'd been looking for, it was all he had, and he would be foolish not to use it.

And Kalomir was no fool.

"You're right," said Kalomir. "We're going to stay, and we're going to heal people."

"Hooray!" cried Tezcatlicuhtli. "Wait. Why does you being good make me so scared?"

"Because you're smarter than you look," said Kalomir. He turned at the next street, made sure his coin pouch was still safe around his neck, and walked purposefully toward the center of the city. "We're going to start a hospital."

The sun dawned bright on The Dance Of Serpents even as clouds threatened to soak the city by late afternoon.

Kalomir heard a knock on the door, and looked up cheerfully. "Come in!"

"I hate you," said Tezcatlecuhtli.

"I know."

The door opened, and the local man Kalomir had hired—a shady trickster named Andril—peeked his head in. "The next patient is ready, Doctor." Kalomir knew little about the man, but he'd seen from their first meeting that Andril was no stranger to confidence games, and Kalomir needed someone willing to go along with his 'hospital' without asking questions. Kalomir nodded sagely.

"And the complaint?"

"Certainly not nightmares."

"I see," said Kalomir, disappointed. "Well then. Did he pay?"

"Well enough," said Andril. "Not as much as the asking price—"

"Send him away," said Kalomir. "The spirits require more of your precious—how do you say? Jewels."

"No!" shouted Tezcatlecuhtli, "bring him in, bring him in we'll heal him for free bringhimin—" Andril left and closed the door, and the sword sneered with all the vitriol an inanimate artifact of righteousness can possibly summon. "I hate you."

"You said you wanted to help people," said Kalomir. "That's exactly what we're doing."

"Rich people," said Tezcatlecuhtli.

"Rich people get sick, too."

"That defense only works if you're also healing poor people."

"I am healing poor people," said Kalomir. "Just…very specific ones."

"Your hospital is a sham," said Tezcatlecuhtli, "and your shriveled veneer of kindness is an abomination. I can't even sense anyone in the center of this wretched courtyard, let alone help them."

"That is entirely the point," said Kalomir. "Do you know how hard it was to find a courtyard this big?" It had taken almost the entirety of the previous day, in fact, and cost him the sum total of his money, but now he had a walled cottage in the center of a courtyard so wide Tezcatlecuhtli couldn't reach out and heal anyone unless they came inside—and no one came inside unless they paid. Well, almost no one.

"Yes!" cried Tezcatlecuhtli suddenly, and Kalomir could sense a wave of life magic rippling out from him. "Be healed, my friend! Rise up and walk, or whatever your problem is. Consumption, maybe?"

"Another of Andril's 'friends?'" asked Kalomir.

"If he sneaks them through the gate I'll heal them," said Tezcatlecuhtli, "and if you don't get paid a cent for it I'll be that much happier."

"You realize Andril's probably making just as much money as we are," said Kalomir. "I'll bet you a sick orphan that the man you just healed is the man I told him to send away—Andril took whatever money he had and kept it for himself."

"At least he's helping them," said Tezcatlecuhtli. "You're just sitting here, hoarding an endless resource like some kind of…I don't know. A very bad word."

"Do you know any bad words?"

"None that I'll say."

"I'll have you know that I'm not hoarding you," said Kalomir. "I'm aiming you. This way we can be sure that you're healing the right people." He couldn't help but smile as he said it, and was rewarded with another furious outburst from Tezcatlecuhtli.

"I don't need to be aimed, I'm like…air. I'm literally like air in this city: there is enough of me for everyone, I don't cost anything, and *everyone needs me*. You're hoarding air. You're telling people they're not allowed to breathe."

"They breathed just fine before you showed up."

"You're a monster."

They heard another knock on the door, and Kalomir dared to hope. "Come in!"

Andril peeked his head through the door, looking completely innocent. "Another patient." He grinned. "Nightmares."

"Perfect," said Kalomir, a wide grin spreading across his face. This was exactly what he'd been waiting for. "Send him in."

"It's a her," said Andril, and disappeared back out the door. Kalomir arranged the desk and chairs again, though they were already perfect, and glanced out the window. Tezcatlecuhtli's influence couldn't reach beyond the far walls of the courtyard, but everything within the walls was teeming with life energy; what had been a wide lawn only hours before was now practically a jungle, and Kalomir could hear Andril speaking softly as he led the new patient through it.

"…so don't be alarmed if you hear two voices," Andril was saying. "The spirits are very active here, operating in a system we can't fully understand." He arrived at the door and led the woman through. "Doctor Kalomir, this is Asalyan."

The woman who stepped through the door was pretty, and well-dressed, but her hazel eyes were bloodshot, and her face was gaunt from lack of sleep. "Hello, Doctor."

"Thank you for coming," said Kalomir, gesturing to a chair. And then, though he already knew the answer, he asked: "What seems to be the trouble?"

"Don't tell him anything!" shouted Tezcatlicuhtli. "I've already healed you! Run, and tell the others not to pay him. Tell them we'll heal everyone for free!"

"Are those the spirits?" she asked, shooting a glance over her shoulder at Andril, but the con man had already left the room—no doubt to fleece a few more patients and short Kalomir on the money. Kalomir didn't mind; as much as he loved tormenting Tezcatlicuhtli, the real prize was here. The nightmares.

"Ignore them," said Kalomir.

"I can make myself impossible to ignore," said Tezcatlicuhtli.

"Pay closer attention," said Kalomir. "Have your healing powers done anything to cure her?"

Tezcatlicuhtli paused, and when he spoke again his voice was dark. "What's wrong with you, child?"

"It's...." Asalyan hesitated, sitting lightly, and raising a hand to her forehead. She was exhausted—not physically, for Tezcatlicuhtli had already healed her physical fatigue, but mentally. Emotionally. She was haunted, just like the rumors had said. "I'm not getting any sleep," she said softly. "I have nightmares—horrible nightmares, of screaming and wailing and suffering. It's the voices in the city stones, I think; they're calling to me. Sometimes I think...I don't know. Sometimes I think they want me to join them. To pull me right in to the walls." She lifted her feet slightly, resting all of her weight on the chair, as if trying to avoid any direct contact with the dark stones of the floor.

"We heard about this," said the sword, and Kalomir hastened to talk over it.

"We have heard many things about these nightmares," said Kalomir. "It seems that they plague many people in this city, and that they arose only recently. Can you tell me anything more specific?"

Asalyan nodded, visibly bracing herself to discuss a topic she was obviously uncomfortable with. "It's almost like...they're hungry. Sometimes when they get to be too much, and I wake up in a sweat, sometimes I feel hungry, too. Not for food, not for anything, just... empty. Like a deep, black pit that wants to be full, to fill itself up with everything it can find—people and colors and sounds and everything—but it will never be full. The people in the stones, the souls we hear crying in the night, they want...I don't know what they want. They want that hunger to go away. They want existence to stop tormenting them." Her eyes looked up, dark and ghostly. "They want nothing and everything, all at once."

Tezcatlecuhtli piped up, slowly putting the pieces together. "Isn't this what we heard about the—"

"Excuse me," said Kalomir, "I need to consult with the spirits for a moment."

"Of course," said Asalyan.

"You mean me?" asked Tezcatlecuhtli. "Are we going to talk somewhere in private?"

"Please shut up," hissed Kalomir, walking to the far side of the cottage. There was a folding screen in the corner, providing a modicum of privacy, and Kalomir disappeared behind it with measured patience. "Could you possibly be any more oblivious?" he whispered angrily. "I realize you hate my methods, but do you have to act like such an idiot around the patients?"

"This is one of the longest conversations we've had with another human in almost six hundred years," said the sword. "It's not like you've given me a lot of time to practice my conversational skills."

"Then shut up and let me do the talking," said Kalomir. "Yes, to answer your blunt question, this is almost exactly what we heard about the dark priestess. The Jaguar cult we killed in Mahe, the ones who gave us this lead, said that the people in the stones wanted to come back to the real world and devour it, and then last night in the temple the old apothecary told us that the priestess was targeting people who had been afflicted with nightmares—nightmares he had been completely unable to cure. Now a woman comes to us with nightmares about the people in the stones trying to devour the world, and yes, congratulations on your deductive reasoning, I think they're related."

"So you think the pretty lady with the nightmares can lead us to the priestess."

"I think the pretty lady with the nightmares can lead the priestess to us," said Kalomir.

"She's bait," said the sword. "You know I don't like it when you use people as bait."

"And you know that it's historically one of our most successful methods," said Kalomir. "With all the death magic in this city clogging up your senses, we have no way of tracking her on our own. This hospital gives us the chance to gather as many of the nightmare victims as possible, and then when she comes for them—

"Wham."

"Wham?"

"Wham is a great plan," said Tezcatlecuhtli.

"Wham is fine," said Kalomir, "but first we have to talk to her."

The sword sighed. "Just kill the priestess and be done with it. Your obsession with interrogating all of these monsters before we kill them is going to get you killed yourself."

"You know that I need to know what they know."

"No you don't."

"They might be able to save me," said Kalomir.

"I've already saved you," said Tezcatlecuhtli. "I've kept you safe and alive for two thousand years. Just give it up and be a good guy."

"This priestess is different," said Kalomir. "The jaguar cult said she might be one of the ancient Tolimics reborn—one of the people who created this haunted city in the first place. She could be more valuable than anyone else we've talked to."

"For certain very evil definitions of valuable," said the sword.

"Just work with me, okay?" said Kalomir. "Help me collect as many of these nightmare victims as we can, and while we wait for the priestess I'll let you heal as many people as you like, absolutely free of charge."

"I do like healing people," said Tezcatlicuhtli.

"You do."

"But you have to promise to protect the bait. No harm can come to anyone involved in this."

"I promise," said Kalomir.

"Are you crossing your fingers?"

"How do you know about crossing fingers?" asked Kalomir. "You don't even have fingers."

"Just promise me."

"I promise," said Kalomir. He composed himself and stepped out past the screen to the main room. "Thank you for your patience," he told Asalyan. "It seems that the spirits have a special request for you."

By dusk they'd collected two dozen nightmare victims. Kalomir had dropped his exorbitant fees in exchange for Tezcatlecuhtli's cooperation, though he assumed that Andril was still charging them on the sly. When the sun went down Kalomir sealed the gates, and gathered his new guests in the central cottage to wait.

They did not have to wait long.

"She's here," said Tezcatlecuhtli. "On the southern wall."

Kalomir went to the window, but the courtyard had grown so full of plants that it was impossible to see what lay beyond them.

"Who's here?" asked Asalyan.

"Nobody you need to worry about," said Kalomir.

"An evil Tolimic priestess brought back from death to consume your souls," said Tezcatlecuhtli.

Kalomir grimaced. "That's…hardly worth their…concern."

Asalyan raised her eyebrow.

"As long as you stay in this cottage you're safe," said Tezcatlecuhtli. "I—" He stopped and corrected himself. "The spirits will protect you."

Kalomir moved to another window, craning his neck to see through the ferns and foliage, but they were completely hemmed in.

"Eastern wall," said Tezcatlecuhtli. "She's just circling us, looking for weak spots."

"She knows they're here," Kalomir whispered. "Why doesn't she come for them?"

"I think she can sense me," the sword whispered back. "Or at least my area of effect. If she comes within the circle of life magic she'll be drained of power, and she doesn't dare."

"Then stop it," said Kalomir. "We need her to get close."

"I can't," said Tezcatlecuhtli. "There's too much power in this city. I can't stop absorbing the death magic—I'm practically drowning in it—and that's creating more life magic than I can hold in."

"We need to get close," said Kalomir.

"Just chase her down," said the sword. "Move toward her and the circle moves toward her; if you go fast enough you'll catch her and weaken her too much to get away."

"I don't want to kill her until I talk to her," said Kalomir. "Can't we sneak up on her? We used to be able to sneak up on people."

"Not in Taux," said Tezcatlecuhtli, and his voice sounded so much like a shrug Kalomir wanted to punch him. "I'm sorry."

"Then what good is it to have everyone—never mind. Come with me." He stepped outside, gathered a ball of elemental power into his palm, and launched himself up into the air. He could see the priestess on a far wall, framed in the moonlight, bent and misshapen and vile. Kalomir's heart softened, and he felt the old, familiar longing for necromantic energy. He landed lightly on the roof of the cottage and called out to her. "Excuse me!"

The crooked form of the priestess looked up, stretching out a bony finger. "Who dares address the Princess Yaretzi?"

"My name is Kalomir Bouchtat, seven-deathed lich lord of the Nightmare Army. I seek your counsel."

"A lich in the heart of a garden of life?" Yaretzi hissed. "You insult me with your lies."

"That's kind of the problem," said Kalomir. "I need to know how I can—"

"Silence!" Yaretzi shouted. "Give me the souls in your garden, if you be so dark, and then we can discuss your needs and my counsel."

"You promised," Tezcatlecuhtli whispered.

"Just bait," Kalomir whispered back.

"Just what?" asked the distant priestess.

"'Just wait,' I said," Kalomir called out, "'Just wait.' I'm considering your offer."

"Don't do it," said the sword.

"I'll give you one," Kalomir shouted. "The one with the most nightmares. Do we have a bargain?"

The priestess stared at him for a moment, then hissed again. "Not in a garden of life. Come beyond the Black Gate, to my garden of death. Come where the very stones cry out in terror." She cackled. "A seven-deathed lich should have no fear of that."

"One hour," said Kalomir. "Don't be late, or I'll consume the soul myself."

"One hour," said Yaretzi, and leaped down from the wall to the darkness beyond. The moonlight gleamed slickly off the dark, wet footprints she left behind.

"You said we weren't going to hurt anyone," said Tezcatlecuhtli.

"We're not, we're just going to…endanger them slightly."

"You promised."

"They're already bait, it's just that now one of them will be…more bait. More…bait-y."

"The Black Gate is on the other side of Taux," said Tezcatlecuhtli. If we go there with one of our nightmare patients, we'll be leaving 20-something more nightmare patients behind. The one we take as bait will be the safest one."

"Yaretzi thinks the magic is in the garden," said Kalomir. "Just like Asalyan did, and all the others. Andril doesn't even know the truth, and he works for us. We'll leave them here, protected by fear and rumor, and by the time Yaretzi figures it out she'll be dead."

"She's already dead."

"You know what I mean."

"She wouldn't enter the garden because she could sense my aura of magic," said Tezcatlecuhtli. "When we meet up with her again she'll just sense it again, and she still won't trust you, and your plan will fail, and she'll come right back here and kill everyone."

"But I have to talk to her to figure out how to get away from you."

"But you can't get away from me until you talk to her."

"I feel like we've been wrestling this same stupid problem for two thousand years." Kalomir scowled. "We need a solution."

"What if you set me down?" asked Tezcatlecuhtli.

"Are you kidding?"

"You don't have to be holding me for the magic to work," said the sword, "you know that. You could leave me here on the roof of the cottage and go anywhere in this garden without dying—as long as you stay within my aura you're fine."

"What if someone steals you?"

"Who's going to steal me in the middle of the night on the roof of an enchanted garden?"

"We're not having this meeting in an enchanted garden," said Kalomir, "we're having it in the poorest, scariest, most dangerous-part of what is already the most dangerous city in the world. I'm not going to just leave the most powerful magical artifact in recorded history discarded on the ground."

"Then find somebody you trust to hold it for you."

"The only person I even know is Andril," said Kalomir, "and I wouldn't trust him for half a heartbeat—I'd die before the second half."

"How about Asalyan?" asked Tezcatlecuhtli. "She thinks her life depends on you, she wouldn't betray you."

"Her life for mine," mused Kalomir. "It's no good—my life is worth more, it's a terrible trade." He stopped suddenly, his mind racing. "But if I found someone who valued her life even more than I value my own…."

"Oh no you don't," said Tezcatlecuhtli. "I know that look, and it is invariably followed by evil, evil things."

"She had a lover," said Kalomir, "the Lowl who came by earlier today—gruff, humorless, inordinately dedicated to her. What was his name?"

"I think it was 'Shut up you evil bastard, I'm not going to let you hold a woman hostage.'"

"No, that doesn't sound like a Lowl name at all."

"His name is Zhada, and he's far too righteous to work with you."

"More righteous than you?" asked Kalomir. "Listen, it's perfect. He's even looking for the priestess—he already wants to kill her, and we're giving him the opportunity to help. I'll even let him do it himself if he wants; you get the good stuff either way."

"So you're going to track him down, threaten to kill the love of his life, and then trust him to keep you alive."

"I told you," said Kalomir, "I'm going to trade her life for mine. Which means I'm going to pay Andril to kill her if I die."

"Here," said Zhada, pointing angrily at the ancient ball court. It was a recessed pit set into the stone, accessible only by ladder, and they had all climbed down together: Kalomir, Zhada, and the bait. "The spirits are strongest here—in the days of the old Tolimic Empire the losing ball players were sacrificed, and their terror runs deep in the stones. This is where she'll come."

"Her garden of death," said Kalomir. "Perfect."

The Lowl glared at him, anger boiling so close to the surface he seemed more wolf than man and the heat from him was palpable. "You made a promise," he said, more calmly than Kalomir would have expected. "Asalyan will be unharmed."

"As long as I'm equally unharmed," said Kalomir. He stalked to the end of the court and found a small alcove, buried in shadow and hidden from view. "You can hide here with the sword, and I'll stand out there, on the edge of its range."

"If you don't keep your promise," said Zhada, "I want to be clear that nothing will stop me from killing you."

"Get in line," said Kalomir. He unbuckled the sword belt from his waist and held it out, but kept his grip tight on it when the Lowl tried to take it. "Since we're being clear: this sword is my life, and Asalyan is yours. Take it from me and she dies. The man I have guarding her has the morals of a sea monster."

"You will live," said Zhada, "and I will slay Yaretzi. And then when Asalyan is safe our agreement ends."

And then you won't be bound to protect or help me, thought Kalomir, reading the unspoken subtext from the Lowl's intense stare. *He'll never forgive me for threatening his love.*

Fine. As long as he helps me now.

"You're very focused," said Kalomir, slapping him on the shoulder with his free hand. "Very single-minded. That's good. Now stay here in the shadows, keep me alive, and don't move until I give you the signal." He hesitated another moment, his hand still clenched tightly around Tezcatlecuhtli's hilt, the time dragging out uncomfortably long. "Promise me."

"I promise," said Zhada.

"Are your fingers crossed?" asked Tezcatlecuhtli.

"I promise," said Zhada again, more harshly this time.

Kalomir stared at him, gritting his teeth, and finally let go of the sword. "Hide," he said simply. He turned around, grabbed his bait by the arm, and walked several paces into the center of the ball court.

"Stop there," Tezcatlecuhtli called out. "You've got maybe two more steps forward before you die."

Kalomir looked down, and marked a line in the grime with his foot.

"Are you going to kill me?" asked the bait.

"Demorn, isn't it?" asked Kalomir.

"Yes," said the nervous man.

"Demorn, no, I'm not going to kill you. For a few years at least."

"What happens in a few years?"

"I'm going to raise up an army of darkness and lay waste to your entire civilization, burning everything in my path and reanimating your ash and bones to serve me eternally."

"That's...." Demorn swallowed, obviously struggling to keep from collapsing in fear. "When did you say that was coming, exactly?"

"At the current rate, another two thousand years."

"Aha." He was trembling, and Kalomir relished the feeling of power. "And, um, what are you doing now?"

"Now I'm…keeping a promise to a friend."

"You have friends?"

Kalomir grimaced. "Don't rub it in, Demorn, nobody's perfect."

He heard wet footsteps, limping and dragging across the court, and a ghostly chorus rose up from the stones at the dark priestess's coming.

"Lord of the Nightmare Army," said Yaretzi. She lurched out of the shadows, somehow both shriveled and larger than life all at once. "I've been asking about you."

"Hear anything good?"

"You're a children's story," said Yaretzi. "Nursemaid tales to frighten children."

"It's not easy becoming a myth," said Kalomir. "At least give me some credit for that."

"You've been gone a long time."

Kalomir nodded. "Not quite as long as you. It looks like we're both making a comeback."

"You want to raise an army," said Yaretzi dismissively. "I want to raise a civilization."

"The greatest civilization in history," said Kalomir. "But, to be fair, I had the greatest army, so…we're more or less on equal footing."

The priestess took a step forward, leaving a dark bloody print, and Kalomir had to struggle not to point out the juxtaposition of word and image.

"Is this my victim?"

"Yaretzi, meet Demorn; Demorn, this is the evil monster princess Yaretzi."

Demorn peed himself.

"That's how they say hello in his culture," said Kalomir. "Now: before you get him, you owe me some answers. Tell me how to escape from life."

"Join my brothers in the stones," she hissed, taking another eager step forward. She was now only four paces away from him—just two paces from the edge of Tezcatlecuhtli's bubble of magic. If she got too close she'd sense it and flee. Kalomir stepped over his safety line in the grime, hoping to stop her. He held his breath, but didn't die.

He only had one more step.

"I have my own preferred method of undeath," he said calmly. "What I need is a method of death that doesn't involve death magic—

no necromancy, no skeletons, none of that. Nothing that your—" He hesitated, wondering how much to reveal, and decided he had nothing to lose at this point. "Nothing that your ancient Tolimic life magic could devour."

Yaretzi leaned forward, her hideous interest piqued. "You know of the death drinkers? You are more knowledgeable than I thought."

"I know many things," said Kalomir. "I know that the 'death drinkers' were a powerful tool against darkness, and I am playing a very dangerous game with darkness. I am not a man to make a move with so simple a counter."

"Every move has a counter."

"Then tell me the counter for life," said Kalomir. "Tell me how to find a dark power that the death drinkers cannot steal."

"We thought we found a way, once," said Yaretzi. "It didn't end well."

"What happened?"

She leered at him wickedly. "You're standing in it."

"The apocalypse of Taux," whispered Kalomir. "What went wrong with it? You were there, you have to know. Tell me how to do it again—how to do it right!"

"We tried and we died," said Yaretzi. "I can no more tell you how to survive it than a dead man can tell you how to survive the blade that took his head."

"You must know something."

"I know that I am hungry," said the priestess, stepping forward once more. She was barely a single pace from him, a hair's breadth from Tezcatlecuhtli's aura. Her voice drifted through the air like poison, so close that Kalomir could feel the wind of it like dust from an ancient tomb.

He savored it.

"P—please don't kill me," whimpered Demorn.

Kalomir closed his eyes, sighing, wishing he'd been able to learn more, but he was out of space and out of time. He threw himself backward with a burst of air, dragging Demorn with him, and as the priestess lunged forward in chase Zhada barreled in from the opposite direction, a howl of battle on his fangs. The priestess felt Tezcatlecuhtli coming and shrieked in rage, turning to flee, but the Lowl was already upon her, his speed and reflexes almost impossible to follow. Zhada brought the sword down in a terrifying slash, burying the obsidian shards deep in the monster's chest, and she screamed in fear.

And then looked at the sword in confusion.

"Why didn't that hurt?"

"It hurt like hell," said Kalomir calmly, walking back toward the fallen priestess. "You just won't actually feel it until I leave." He put his hands on Tezcatlecuhtli's hilt, shocked at the sense of comfort it gave him to touch it again. He switched back to a more modern language for Zhada's benefit. "It's time to go."

"You're not going anywhere without me," growled Zhada.

"Hold me here and Asalyan dies," said Kalomir. "I told you how this magic works. As soon as I take Tezcatlecuhtli away, the priestess will die, but—I suggest you stay here to make sure of that."

"Vile, wretched man!" cried Yaretzi.

"Flattery will get you nowhere," said Kalomir, and turned back to Zhada. "You want to be quiet certain that your beloved is safe, don't you?" He looked at the Lowl and felt a pang of regret, mixed with a moment of terror. "I mean, you don't trust me, not really. Let's be honest." And Kalomir wondered, again, if he could trust Zhada. Did he really value Asalyan's life that much? Enough to protect a lich he hated?

Zhada tightened his grip on the sword's hilt, staring at Kalomir with a look of unfiltered hate. Kalomir gave him one last promise, desperately hoping that their agreement would hold. "Let me go, and Yaretzi dies."

Zhada paused, staring. "We will go together." He released his hold on the sword.

That's what you think, thought Kalomir, and swept Tezcatlecuhtli up and out of the dark priestess's body. In that same instant Yaretzi sprang, not at Kalomir but at Zhada—she needed blood, desperate to heal herself, and Kalomir had none. The leap took Zhada by surprise, nearly ending his life right there, but he recovered quickly and fought to defend himself, growling just as viciously as the snarling priestess. Kalomir turned and walked away, whistling idly as he swung Tezcatlecuhtli in his hands. "Of course," he called over his shoulder, "I didn't say how *soon* Yaretzi would die, did I? Threaten me, dog, and see where it gets you." He shook his head, and couldn't help but laugh. "Fool."

"You should help him," said Tezcatlecuhtli. "He helped you, and now she's going to kill him, and you promised me no one would get hurt."

"I am helping him," said Kalomir, climbing the ladder to the edge of the ball court. "I'm taking you out of range, thus killing the priestess while leaving the Lowl who wants to kill me alive but injured, thus allowing us to escape before he has a chance to take revenge. It's all going perfectly to plan."

"You're evil," said Tezcatlecuhtli. "You're evil and you're horrible and I hate you."

"You don't hate anyone," said Kalomir, pausing at the edge of the court to look at the two fighters rolling desperately in the filth. Demorn was cowering in the corner behind them. "You just hate my methods."

"I hate them intensely," said the sword.

"You're going to hate it even more when I tell you we're leaving Taux," said Kalomir.

"No!"

"Yes. The death you've devoured here should keep us going for a month at least, and we have work to do."

"So you learned something from the priestess."

Kalomir nodded, and started walking away. "Nothing you'll like."

"You never learn anything I like," said the sword, but then paused. "I take that back. You learned a valuable lesson here today."

"Bite your tongue."

"You kept your promise, even though you didn't have to. You kept everyone alive, Asalyan and the bait and everyone. Even Zhada."

"I didn't learn a lesson."

"Of course you learned a lesson."

"Don't cheapen this with a moral," said Kalomir. "We helped some people and killed a monster. That's it."

"You learned the true meaning of friendship," said Tezcatlecuhtli. "Or at least most of the meaning. Certain shades, of some aspects, of most of the meaning of friendship."

Kalomir paused, looking back. Yaretzi and Zhada were both weakened, but alive. Zhada was losing. Kalomir took a single step backward, moving Tezcatlecuhtli out of range, and the undead priestess collapsed like a lifeless doll.

"That's going to be a mess to clean up," said Tezcatlecuhtli.

"Leaving messes is what we're best at," said Kalomir. He turned toward the Black Gate and started walking. "Time to leave another one, but first...." He sighed. "First let's go back to Andril and free that girl."

"That's another thing you don't have to do," said Tezcatlecuhtli. "You're nothing but a big old softy."

"Shut up." They were slowly moving back toward the crowded regions of the city, the erotic sounds of the Night of Secrets moaning around them, and Kalomir tried to look as inconspicuous as possible as he walked without a lover. High above, light bloomed amid the crimson stain of the Blood Moon, fireworks turning the night to the next day of the Festival.

"Come on, Kal," said Tezcatlecuhtli loudly, "it's hug time. Find someone and give him a hug for me, come on. That seemingly lonely guy right there. Ooh, or her! She'll give you a hug."

Kalomir looked at the homely prostitute they were passing. "Yeah, she probably would."

"So do it! It's a celebration."

Kalomir shook his head. "How about I just let you heal the living daylights out of everyone we pass."

"I'm doing that already."

"But how about I approve of it?"

"You'd do that for me?"

"Just this once," said Kalomir, and shook his head. "Just...don't tell any necromancers about it or anything, okay? I've got a certain reputation to uphold."

"Your secret's safe with me."

Illustration by Todd Lockwood

WATER LISTENS

By Julie Czerneda

Second Day: Dance of the Serpents

Rain is a gossip.

It travels over Taux, missing no crack or crevice, gathering stories. On a balcony, it collects perfume from a warm, bared neck. It tumbles across a patio to find spilled drinks. In a temple doorway, it tastes tears.

Being Taux, in every alley, rain washes away vomit and piss, sweeping them to the gutters with perfume, drink, and tears.

And, in Taux, the rain always finds blood.

On the second night of the Festival of a Thousand Blooms, rain chattered and muttered, a din where it struck tile or empty table, a quiet murmur where it slid through leaves and abandoned flowers. It ran from Taux down twisted streets, puddles and runnels catching fire from torchlight while hiding potholes, so late-night revellers both laughed and cursed it as they danced around their wet and bedraggled serpents.

Here and there, unnoticed, unremarked, the rain washed footprints of blood from the cobbles. It lifted and nudged dried bone, this pile once a child of golden curls, that one an old woman with bracelets of onyx and gold, another from a man who'd been, earlier that night, lover and dancer and thief.

Replete, the rain coursed away through pipes to flood catchments, or sank under streets into lost catacombs, carrying Taux's secrets into the dark.

Rain streamed into an open window as well. The window was lined with wooden cups and ewers and vases, no two the same, and not a drop escaped or overflowed to dampen the masks lining shelves below the windowsill or reach the floor. In no other way strange, the window overlooked a small courtyard, tidily kept. The courtyard and its building were too near the Black Gate to house anyone of wealth or nobility or consequence. Hunhau the maskmaker lived and worked here, an honest man and a simple one.

Except that the vessels in his window had been made by the blind Wizard he'd found at tide's edge and now loved with all his heart.

Her name was Cenoté.

And she listened to rain.

"Lis-shen to that!" Tohil threw his massive right arm around his companion's shoulders as they staggered by another group of dancers. "The lot of them. Drunker than a Korys sniffing bankilal! Haven't they not-notished the rain? Issh raining, you know." This with profound gravity.

It was assuredly raining, which intensified each and every stench in Taux—and they were legion—and the Sturgeon's arm must weigh more than he did, but Hunhau nodded agreeably. The mask he wore was Cenoté's gift and cleansed the air before it could assail his too-sensitive nostrils. As for the arm, well, better the mighty Tohil lean on him than fall flat in one of the greasy puddles underfoot. There'd be no picking him up again without help.

Hunhau craned his head to watch the dancers, who moved to flute and drum with admirable grace, all things considered. The Turquoise Turtle District's serpent had been larger, as befitted the home of last year's Festival Queen, with coils held high above spectators and bedecked with feathers sturdy enough to survive the day's frequent downpours, but this one, the Black Gate's, had a certain disreputable charm despite the conditions. Perhaps it was the Jai-Ruks scrapping to see who'd take over the tail section.

Tomorrow was the Night of Secrets, when almost everyone in Taux would don a mask and dare, oh so many things. For most of Hunhau's life he, like every other maskmaker in the city, had slaved till the last possible moment before that night to fill orders, then collapsed in a heap.

Until Cenoté. Having watched him sleep through the rest of the Festival their first year together, she'd pointed out, her voice the calmest of seas, that if he made extra masks throughout the year, wouldn't the sale of those be sufficient? He could enjoy himself instead.

And he did, thoroughly. Even now, the dancing, the revels, the crowds of the festival remained a novelty. He'd pulled Tohil from beer stalls and wine shops to see as much as he could. Best of all, Hunhau thought, wincing as he found himself bearing more of his friend's weight, tomorrow he could go out and see the masks he'd made in use, knowing all were his best work, not his sloppy worst. Not that he was a prideful man, but there was satisfaction—

Tohil's foot found a puddle, and his lurch sent both men staggering towards the dark shadows along the wall. Before they could reach them, the Sturgeon pulled up short. "'Ware, friend," he warned, all trace of the affable drunk gone. "Can't rissshk the dark. Summing hunts the streets. Summing evil."

Anything Tohil, with his long experience with Taux's darker side, named as evil must be vile indeed. Hunhau had had his own brush with foulness and shuddered, thinking of the creature Cenoté had found and fought below the Ullamalitzli Tournament Field. It had appeared a child…

A child who feasted on the souls of the dead.

"What hunts?" he whispered urgently, wishing for larger eyeholes in his mask as he peered around.

"Saintsssss high and low, Hunhau, I'll not name her." Lower. "I dare not."

Her? Realizing who—or what—Tohil meant, Hunhau was beyond grateful to see his courtyard gate ahead. The tale of Yaretzi the Blood Priestess, who'd stepped from the walls of the Silk Purse, had seemed just a story over the day's first cups until he'd looked into his friend's haunted eyes. If that's what walked the streets?

No one was safe, especially an off-duty, drunk, and, mostly, weaponless Sturgeon. Not that the streets of Taux ever were safe, but in Hunhau's firm opinion, the danger posed by a cutpurse or assassin paled in comparison to the murdering undead.

"Come," the maskmaker urged, forcing cheer into his voice. "I've more ale. Spend the night."

Whatever his friend grunted, Hunhau took for agreement, taking hold of Tohil's arm with both hands and tugging to hurry the man along with about as much effect as a kitten swinging on a bull's tail. Once they made their way through the small courtyard, he propped Tohil to lean comfortably against the wall. With a heartfelt sigh of relief, he went to open the door.

Only the door was already ajar; the shop inside dark.

Which wasn't right at all. Cenoté might need no light, but she never forgot he did. She kept the lantern by their worktable filled with oil and lit, during the day as well because the shop was on the first floor and shadowed except for an hour in the morning.

Hunhau stopped babbling to himself and reached blindly to shake Tohil. "Something's wrong," he whispered, fear flushing the remaining drink from his blood. "Maybe it's the priestess—" A loud snore made him jump.

When his friend didn't budge to a stronger effort, the maskmaker shook his head, then removed his mask to sniff.

Flowers! His eyes watered and he slapped the mask back on as quickly as he could. Of course the air stank of flowers. Taux was awash in every sort of odorous floral arrangement, as overwhelming as they faded and died as when fresh and loved. How could a useful scent make it through that reek?

There was nothing else left. Hunhau gathered his courage and slipped through the open door.

Saints, it was black as a Corsair's heart inside. He steadied himself. He knew this room, every wood scrap he'd not yet swept, every basket leaning in corners. Stools, though? Unsure where he'd left those in his eagerness to meet his friend, the maskmaker slid a sandaled foot forward with care as he reached for the lantern.

Instead of glass, his fingers found the cool softness of flower petals. Hardly had Hunhau gathered himself from that surprise when Tohil burst through the door and crashed right into him. They fell with paired shouts amid the clatter of wooden bowls and, yes, that was definitely the lantern smashing.

"Oaf!"

As the maskmaker struggled to free himself, a thin, very sharp blade settled lightly under his chin and a woman's voice, not Cenoté's, not in any way hers or warm, found his ear.

"I need a mask."

Dreadful dreams stole into her sleep, poisoning every night. She'd battled to stay awake. How long since she'd slept? Zhada had noticed—nothing escaped his keen senses or knowing heart—but hadn't asked what she couldn't answer. He'd done what he could. Taken her into the sunshine, offered his warmth, and for a few blissful moments, she'd felt safe.

Not now. As the sun had set, nightmares rose before her waking eyes until Asalyan Mesare could barely discern what was real. Flowers became bone. Food became rot. The faces of those she loved lost their skin and hair, eyes dropping from their sockets, flesh shrivelling into corpses before her. Too exhausted to weep, she curled into a ball in the shadows of her own bedroom, knowing there was nothing she could do—nothing her dear father or any healer could do—but wait for the end.

For there was a purpose to her torment. She felt it, hated it, fought with all her might against it. But there was nothing she could do, nothing *it* would let her say.

As she suffered, *something* fed.

When she could suffer no more, it would come to consume her.

Leaving footprints of blood.

He'd left her alone, going out to celebrate like some oaf of a youth. He'd thought of no one but himself, was the truth of it, and this—THIS—happened!

Torrent and her cursed stone. At least she'd left.

Leaving a mess, Hunhau muttered to himself, someone had to clean. Doubtless she was famous for it. He finished sweeping broken glass and sand into the flat pan, tipping it into the bin of shavings and other refuse to be dealt with in the morning. When he straightened, broom in one hand, pan in the other, he stole a look at Cenoté.

She sat, as she had for the past hour, still as a becalmed sea. To be fair, Cizin had done this, not Torrent. Taken her strength.

Or was it something more? Pale lips, skin like mother-of-pearl, a strong, elegant sweep to neck and jaw and cheek, a graceful nose. Above, still-red scars surrounded and lined the gaping holes where eyes had been, as if a burning hand had reached in and dug them out.

He could read her lips, the way a sailor learned to read the sea. Discover her mood in curve or line. Know if she were tired or focused. Feel the joy in the small, rare dimple. What Hunhau saw now? Sadness.

"I'm sorry I left you," he ventured.

She'd set aside her mask, as had he, this being their private space. Now her head turned, blue-green hair slipping like silk over a shoulder. "This was your day, Hunhau. You work very hard. You deserve to have fun."

Fun? Tohil lay comatose—not from drink, though entirely likely given the big man's consumption these past hours, but from magic. Magic dealt by the stranger who'd entered their home while Cenoté slept. Not that the Wizard had been in any danger, as it turned out, but it was, also in Hunhau's firm opinion, the principle of it all. Torrent had no right…

Even if she'd every right, he was having the locks changed after the Festival.

For what good that would do. "You work harder," Hunhau said, for that was true. "Next year, Cenoté, you should come with us." Though they both knew she hadn't for good reason and wouldn't, ever. The blind Wizard wasn't comfortable in crowds, nor was it safe for her, Taux's only Wizard outside the Tower, to expose herself. Determined to cheer her up, the little maskmaker struggled valiantly on, "There's so much—" to see, he almost said, and finished "—so much going on."

"I've watched the Festival from the Star Tower, Hunhau." Cenoté sounded amused. "Though until today, I hadn't appreciated how difficult it is to dodge giant serpents in the streets."

Broom and pan clattered to the floor. Hunhau barely noticed dropping them, so bone-deep was his shock. "You went—out? Today? Alone?!" But he'd locked the door.

"Hardly alone. I hired a pannequin."

The door unlocked from inside; Cenoté wasn't a prisoner, she was—what? His thoughts seemed stuck in glue. A murderous dead priestess roamed the streets; Cenoté had hired strangers to do the same.

Which might be fine, were she anyone else, save Cenoté hadn't taken a single step outside without him since washing ashore on the tide.

Or had she?

How could he know? Hunhau sat heavily on a stool, flattening his hands on the tabletop as if he could capture its strength. Why should he? He lived with a Wizard, he reminded himself, not a child. Had fooled himself, thinking he mattered. Misjudged his importance, in the scheme of things. Good thing he had his own friends, he thought.

Tohil, that great lump, snorted and twitched as though chasing a felon. Hunhau held back a sigh.

Cenoté's fingertip found the back of his right hand, traced the knuckle gnarled from a break in his youth, leaving a cool that soothed behind. Hunhau looked up, surprising the saddest of smiles. "Truest of friends. Do you doubt me?"

Something dark left his spirit, then, something that hadn't belonged there, and the little maskmaker dared touch her hand in return. "Never," he vowed with all his heart. "Come. To bed with you. It's been a long night." Longer for her, and more taxing, so he added, "We'll talk in the morning. You need to rest."

"I cannot. You will not," she guessed.

Well enough. He braced himself, expecting the worst. She'd gone to chase the priestess, he just knew it. Risked herself without him. "Then tell me."

Cenoté nodded, aiming empty eyes at what he couldn't see. "After you left, I heard a voice in the rain. A voice I'd lost long ago. His name is Mulac."

Hunhau shot a disturbed glance at the little cups on the window sill. "A threat?"

Soft and low. "A lover."

Oh. He blushed so violently his nose felt swollen. Worse, he was certain she could tell. "What—what did the—ah—Mulac—ah—" The maskmaker stammered to a halt. He'd not expected anything so—ordinary—as a lost love. Or rather, a found one.

Hunhau coughed and recovered his voice. "Well. It is the festival. An excellent time for such, ah, encounters." As if she was anything so ordinary as a woman.

But what did anyone truly know of Wizards?

Cenoté sighed, and he heard in that small breath the ebbing tide as it slipped away from land, dragging flotsam back to sea. "I went where he bid me. He wasn't there." She crooked a finger and the last of the pink "flowers" popped free of its stalk, somersaulting along the tabletop until it found her hand, nestling in her palm like a bird in its nest. "Only this, left for me to find."

The face in the basin, revealed when Cenoté had used her magic to create Torrent's mask. A man's face, older. Fierce, but Hunhau remembered somehow hearing a laugh, full and rich. "But—" His was a romantic heart and kind, and all he could think was that flowers—of any sort—were in no sense sufficient after Cenoté had dared go out alone to meet this Mulac. "Why?"

"Perhaps, seeing I am not what I was, he chose not to reveal himself."

Hunhau bristled. "Then he's a fool!"

Not quite a dimple. "Never that. Circumspect, yes. Aware, always." Now the dimple. "Annoying. I choose to believe Mulac saw I am less, and refused to put me in danger."

Putting a slightly better light on the matter, Hunhau supposed. "So he gave you flowers." Or, as she'd put it, their intention. "I'm sorry."

"Don't be." The dimple deepened and the curve of her lips held satisfaction. "After all this time, I've proof Mulac lives. That he's here, in Taux. A powerful Wizard, Hunhau, able to demand answers from the dead? It means we are far from alone, you and I, in our fight against what would destroy this city again."

Hearing that "we," Hunhau straightened his shoulders and nodded briskly as if the notion of a mysterious Wizard ally in the city—where Wizards didn't come—and a necromancer on top of it all—was actually a comfort and not simply terrifying. "I imagine the two of you—when this is over—" he stopped.

For Cenoté had closed her fingers over the flower. She opened her hand, tilting it to let what was now sand slip down to the table. "I am not what I was. When this is over, so will I be," said with such calm acceptance, tears sprang to Hunhau's eyes and he couldn't have said another word.

Understanding what he hadn't before.

Cenoté had washed ashore, into his life, not to survive.

But to end with her enemy.

The Garden of Life had been a courtyard, once. Despite flower and green leaf, despite frilled canopy and silk-cushioned lounge, and oh, the small but elegant fountain—which was a nice touch—Asalyan guessed the space had been used, and recently, to house livestock waiting for slaughter. Strangely suitable, given the healer, Kalomir, seemed to her a similar layering of too-obvious compassion and hidden—what? Cruelty, she thought, well-practiced and preferred. Yet, like the courtyard's new garden and the care she'd received, cruelty left behind.

Was that what it took, to understand an affliction like hers? There were others here. She'd bumped into one, a man named Demorn, and seen her own horrors in his eyes.

The dreams were gone, at least here, at least for now. Asalyan knelt by the fountain, watching birds sip and bathe without other visions to torment her. She'd passed exhaustion so long ago. This moment's peace was a gift.

It wouldn't last, or couldn't, away from this place. Kalomir knew that as well as she did, or he'd let her go home. She leaned forward to gaze at her reflection. Tidy. Tired.

Terrified. She brought the ixcamai flower from her pocket and put it to her nose, breathing deeply of its rich perfume, doing her best to fill her thoughts with its promise instead of fear. To cherish forever.

If only Zhada were here.

Asalyan's lips twitched. Then again, he'd be able to scent exactly what the courtyard had been, flower or no flower, and not let her stay another minute. His heightened senses connected him to the world in a way she'd always envied. She learned, every moment they were together, to better use her own, to reach for that connection herself. When they were together and alone, she felt transcendent, as if their love bonded them not only to one another, but to nature itself.

"Milady?"

Asalyan looked up, surprised to see a small, bespectacled Eldaryn approaching. He had the bright red hair of his race and clearly the affinity to fire. Plants shrivelled and scorched as he brushed by them, for he came in a hurry.

"Are you Asalyan Mesare? Of course you are," he answered himself, coming to an abrupt stop with a short bow. "Fair Festival, Asalyan. My name is Lareo. I've come on behalf of a mutual friend, to be sure—to see that you're all right."

"Fair Festival." She got to her feet, hugging the cushion in sudden hope. "You mean Zhada, don't you?" She looked over his head at the now-closed door. "Is he here?"

"He was."

Something wasn't right. Asalyan stooped to look the smaller being in the eyes. She wasn't only a merchant's daughter, but his heir and right hand. Truth be told, her ability to read faces far surpassed her father's and was already a major asset to the family business. What she read now had her nod graciously and move to the lounge to sit, offering a place to her visitor, even as her heart pounded. "He's in danger," she said, outwardly calm.

"You both are. The city is." His eyes were keen and kind. "You know of what I speak. The Blood Priestess."

"She's real, then." Asalyan clasped her hands together and controlled her voice. "I'd hoped I was going mad." Oh Saints. "Zhada—he's on the hunt."

"Yes. Not alone." Lareo hesitated. "Kalomir, your healer, went with him. They've come to an arrangement."

Hunt alone, Zhada had told her. Then it's your decisions that matter. When she'd challenged him, worried at the thought of him returning to the swamp, he'd admitted a partner could be of use, but such a person would have to be utterly trustworthy or expendable. There were too few of the former and he was, he'd admitted, grinning that Lowl grin she so loved, too soft-hearted.

He wouldn't have taken Kalomir willingly on this hunt. Unless... "Tell me everything, from the beginning."

Lareo wanted to refuse. Asalyan could see it and went on, "Zhada is my life, as I am his. He is remarkable in every way and I'd back him against any living foe without hesitation. But this? I've fought this priestess in my dreams and failed every time," she assured him, letting her despair show. "I know what he faces. Tell me, please, why I should hope."

But as the Eldaryn nodded and began the tale—of bargains and weavers and magical swords—Asalyan's heart sank further and further.

Oh, Zhada, my dearest friend and light of my life, she thought. What have you done?

The next day, Hunhau didn't leave the shop. He didn't open it either. He saw Tohil off to work, for though the Night of Secrets was ostensibly lawless, there were those who'd prefer not to have mobs break into their homes and had the means to hire. The Sturgeon had slept on the table till dawn, Hunhau having managed to get a pillow under his big head and a blanket over his shoulders, then had awakened with an oath, looking wildly around the shop as if Torrent would still be there. Breakfast had restored his good humour, along with there being no apparent damage.

Having locked the door behind his friend, Hunhau put his back to it, gathering his courage. Tonight, Torrent would seek her escape. He wished her luck. An abundance of luck and a very great distance between them, so long as she carried Cizin the Cursed. The other side of the ocean would do nicely.

He'd clean, that's what he'd do. There were cobwebs in the rafters older than he was, and the floor hadn't been sanded since—well, it could use a going over. He'd dust and sand and clean and keep himself and Cenoté safely inside.

Until someone—anyone—took the Blood Priestess off Taux's streets.

Deep beneath the city, the Weaver ran his fingers along a particular thread, so, and waited.

Watchers in the Star Tower stared from on high, messengers dozing at their sides. This was the night named by portents and they would be ready.

While Cenoté sat by her window, waiting for rain, expecting tears.

Night of Secrets?

Night of Salvation! Asalyan stood, holding her shaking hands in front of her, staring at them as if they weren't hers at all. They didn't feel like hers, being light and free. Nothing did, and everything was. "He's done it!" she cried as Lareo stirred from his pile of cushions to stare up at her.

"You're sure?"

She closed her eyes and waited, then opened them with a laugh. "Nothing haunts me. Nothing hunts me. She's dead!" Or whatever happened to evil undead beings. "Zhada did it!"

"He was of some use," said a deep, dry voice. Kalomir stepped from the dark shadows into the lamplight of the walkway, his strange sword hanging loose in one hand.

Asalyan's eyes narrowed. "Why are you here and he is not?"

Lareo moved to stand in front of her, valiant if small, and spat a ball of flame. "There was a bargain, Lich Lord!"

"When I left our doggy friend he was alive." Kalomir examined the nails of one hand. "I've no idea what happened after that. My part in things was over. I don't linger."

"Where?" As if she asked about a new tea house, not her beloved. Never reveal the strength of your desire, her father had taught her. Now, she thought, more than ever.

Kalomir smiled. "No place for a fine and gentle lady such as yourself."

"I know where to start looking," Lareo said, reaching back to take her hand. "Come!" He pulled her with him and she didn't resist or spare the so-called healer another glance.

As they left the Garden of Life, Asalyan's shoulders stiffened at the sound of laughter behind them.

"It's morning, my friend."

Hunhau startled awake, his mask falling to the floor. As he struggled to make sense of why he was sitting on a stool in front of the door, he realized two things, his behind was numb and Cenoté was smiling.

More than smiling. He squinted at the dimple in her cheek and asked stupidly, "Why are you happy?"

"We all should be, Hunhau. Taux is threatened by one less evil." She bent to put a small bowl of foam-topped cocoa, seasoned no doubt with his favourite hot chillies, in his hands then straightened, arms out swept. "Yaretzi was slain last night."

Careful of the bowl, Hunhau scrambled awkwardly to his feet. "How—who? Do you know? Was it Mulac or..." He found he couldn't say her name.

Cenoté's arms fell to her sides. Her smile faded. "There was a price. I know not who paid it." Empty eyes turned to the window. "The Sea be gentle."

Hunhau sighed, and then brightened a little as he considered the sea or, more precisely, the beaches east of the harbor. This was the Day of Reflection, when the streets would be almost empty as Taux's inhabitants rested after the debauchery of the Night of Secrets. Families would take a midday meal together before visiting their Saints to make their offerings. It was hardly chance that those offerings were more generous because of the night before, Festival planners having strong ties to the clergy. What mattered to him, however?

Ttoday every other maskmaker in Taux would be closed.

"I think I'll see if there's wood to be had on the beach."

The dimple returned. "What of the Festival?"

"I've had my share." He drained his cup, licked foam from his lips, and headed for the stairs.

It wasn't until Hunhau heaved his basket over his shoulders and stepped out into the courtyard that he remembered the other part of the Day of Reflection.

This was the morning the Sturgeons patrolled not for the living, but to find and, more or less discreetly, remove the dead.

He would look for good pieces, fine pieces, the little maskmaker decided. He'd save the very best to carve in honor of the one who'd saved Taux from the Blood Priestess.

Assuming there was a face left to mask.

He hadn't been there. But he'd fought there. Asalyan stood in the bath and waved away her servants, unable to bear their kindly ministrations.

She and Lareo had searched the ball court, clotted with filth and dying flowers. He'd discovered the pile of dust no rain would touch and set it ablaze.

She'd found the blood—so much blood—and Zhada's knife.

No body, Asalyan reminded herself as she dried her skin, and then dressed slowly. He'd fought there—and won, she added with a hot flash of pride. The Eldaryn had studied the blood, the dreadful dried pool, the smeared length and drips, and claimed Zhada had been dragged away. He couldn't say if the Lowl had been alive. Neither of them believed Zhada would leave his knife behind if conscious.

Sorely wounded, she decided, and taken. But where? Asalyan slipped the knife within the wide band around her waist. She had nothing to wear suited to hunting a wounded Lowl through the back streets, but today her family would make its offering to Saint Shera of the Happy Hall, patron of hearth and home, travelers and lovers. Her father, overjoyed at her recovery, had understood when she'd asked to remain by herself.

Not a lie, though hardly the full truth.

On the Day of Reflection everyone dressed in a subdued manner. How better to blend into the crowds than to appear as a dutiful celebrant should? She topped the dark blue silk of her belted robe with a light, sleeveless brown tunic and pushed her hair within a cap subtly embroidered with flowers. Pinning the last of the creamy ixcamai flowers to the cloak, she bent to weave the rich gold laces of her sandals from ankle to knee, then stood to be sure the robe split to reveal her shapely legs. An old merchant's trick: dazzle to distract.

She mustn't be recognized. Her father, dear as he was, nor any of his clients, would not approve of the heir to the business wandering unescorted through the Black Gate but that's where she had to go. The clothes—and legs—might spare her from a casual glimpse, but anyone taking a second look at her face? Being crowned last year as Queen of the Festival might have been good business, but it wasn't good now.

Asalyan tucked Zhada's knife into her wide belt. She had an idea about that too.

The pickings on the beach had been, well, picked. Oh, he'd found five pieces of driftwood that might reasonably do, but from the smouldering piles and scattered broken bottles, more than a few of the night's revellers had gathered around bonfires. Such waste! Hunhau tsked to himself.

Not that he regretted coming. The air over the sea was kind to his too-sensitive nose, except by the fire pits, and being here reminded him of finding Cenoté. Of the day his life had changed forever.

And for the better, he told himself, despite the occasional terrifying magical encounters. What else did one expect with a Wizard under the same roof? Though he hoped, sincerely, they were done with such matters for now. As for her view of the future, well, that wasn't now, and mightn't be ever. He'd have his say, that was for sure.

Hunhau put on his mask and climbed the rocks back up to the bridge, whistling cheerfully under his breath as he made his way home. It would be a hot day, and a sticky one. After putting away his finds he'd invite Cenoté out for a flavoured ice. No child could enjoy the simple treat with more pure delight than—

"Maskmaker?"

Even in broad daylight, a whisper from a strange doorway was enough to make Hunhau duck his head and walk faster, wood clacking in his mostly empty basket.

His steps developed an echo, lighter and close. He lengthened his stride, which wasn't easy on a cobbled street fraught with potholes. The basket began to bounce on his shoulders.

"Master Hunhau. Please wait! I know of your work."

Meaning a complaint or praise? Still, Hunhau stopped in his tracks and turned. Oh, he knew that face! "Why—you're Asalyan Mesare!" Last Festival, he'd waited in a corner an interminable time while the dressmaker attended to the merchant's daughter and her peers; though he'd come for Cenoté's new robes, she could hardly serve him first. "What are you doing here?" Here being out of her district and well into a part of the city where lovely young women—especially those alone and without weapons—tended to disappear. Forever. Worse, Asalyan wasn't merely one of the most beautiful women in Taux, her merchant father was wealthy enough to attract kidnappers. After a frantic look around for either her guards, none, or anyone of the other sort, thankfully none—yet—he took her arm and pulled her with him just as quickly as before. "We have to get you home!"

She pulled back. "I'm coming with you. I need a mask." Her face was pale and set, not with fear, but determination.

A second desperate request in less than a day? Hunhau didn't believe in coincidence. Or he believed much less in it, having lived with Cenoté. He gave in. "To my shop then," he said heavily. "But please don't be kidnapped along the way. Your father will have my head."

"Give me your basket."

He blinked.

"Trust me." She began to pull at the shoulder strap, so he shrugged the other free. "Watch." The merchant's daughter put the tall basket on her back, leaning forward to balance its weight. "What do you think?"

She was clever, he gave her that. From a distance, she might pass for a servant. A far better one than he could ever hope to hire, such being his usual clientele, or that would be on this street with him. "I think we should hurry," he suggested, already breaking into a sweat.

He had wood to make a mask, he consoled himself. Provided they survived the four streets and three turns left to get home. Oh, and made it through the Black Gate without being noticed.

Much to Hunhau's surprise, they did make it through the Black Gate.

Then were noticed.

A lanky Lowl, one of the kind who tried to burn, cut, and scrape all vestige of humanity from his body—failing miserably but that never stopped them—stepped in their way.

"Fair Festival," Hunhau ventured, looking up and up. Saints, the thing was huge. "If you'll excuse us?" He went to move around the creature.

It growled, a low, wet growl that did, indeed, have nothing Human about it.

Asalyan growled back, a shrill singsong that went up a scale, then down. Hunhau wasn't sure if he was more shocked or the Lowl. As the creature straightened with a confused frown, the merchant's daughter, basket and all, took a step forward, pushing into his space. "Out of my way, cur," she said, cold and hard as ice.

The Lowl opened his mouth to answer. She stepped again, this time close enough to reach out and push, which she did, hard, with both hands. "Begone!"

The push, despite her effort, did nothing to move the much bulkier Lowl. Astonished, Hunhau watched as the creature closed his lips over what were very nasty fangs, then bent at the waist and sulked away. If he'd had a tail, it would have been tucked between his legs as he disappeared into an alley.

"Blessed Saint Shera." Asalyan took a deep, shaking breath and touched the flower on her cloak as if it were a talisman. "Zhada told me what to do if Varrach ever accosted me. I never thought I'd have the courage to try it."

"I wouldn't," Hunhau admitted and she almost smiled. Almost. He gave her troubled face a deeper look and sighed to himself. Desperate indeed. "You're in luck," he said as they started walking again. "I'm the only maskmaker in Taux open for business today."

"I hadn't thought of that," she replied shakily. "I just remembered the amazing masks you made for my dressmaker's children. Seahorses? Each a different colour?"

"Ah, yes. Those." Hunhau blushed, grateful for his own mask. Cenoté's work, not his. She made masks for children all year long, taking nothing in return; masks better than any other maskmaker's, intended for no other purpose than play. "Come. You can have something to eat while I work on your mask."

"I'm not hungry."

"And I'm not quick." When they entered his courtyard, Hunhau took back his basket.

Before they reached the door, it opened in welcome. Cenoté stepped aside to let them through. "Fair Festival," she said pleasantly.

"And to you—" Asalyan looked to Hunhau uncertainly.

He understood. Cenoté's mask was a hideous thing, a hunk of raw grey driftwood tied to her head with leather straps. Deep gashes implied eyes and mouth, yet hid both in ominous darkness. Her robe and sandals, on the other hand, were both fashionable and the finest Hunhau could afford, and her hair poured over one shoulder like a blue waterfall. Confounding first impressions, though tall and graceful, she looked shorter, her shoulders and back stooped.

A scholar, dressed like royalty, in a beggar's mask.

"Cenoté, this is Asalyan Mesare. She's come to us—" he paused to let her answer.

"Forgive my intrusion, Cenoté," the merchant's daughter said graciously. "I've come for a mask, most urgently. I care not what it looks like, so long as it—so long no one can recognize me. I'll pay anything."

Before Cenoté could be gracious in return, Hunhau put down his basket with a thud. "We don't do enchantments." Which wasn't strictly true, after last night, but that had been Wizard's work, not his. He knew better than claim a mask was magic, no matter how many other maskmakers would, if the price was right. That was the short path to a knife in the gut, once the "magic" failed.

Asalyan looked ready to flee. "'Enchantments?!'" The revulsion in her voice was more convincing than any argument.

"My mistake." The maskmaker removed his mask, wrinkling his nose at the smell from the flower pinned to the young woman's cloak but risking it so she could see someone's face. "We get asked. It's not—" he coughed "—something we do."

He was pleasantly surprised when she didn't appear to notice his oversized nose. Then again, a merchant's daughter would have excellent manners.

"And my mistake as well. Your pardon." Asalyan sighed. "I'm not saying this well. I need to go to the Silk Purse, without anyone telling my family." When his eyes widened, she blushed prettily. "Not for—not that there mightn't be—I've a friend I'm told went there, last night and I—" The blush extended down her neck. "Not that I—oh, bollocks," she swore suddenly, her color fading to normal. "My friend Zhada was injured last night. He was taken to the 'Purse—they have a healer!" As though Hunhau would argue what he and everyone else in the Black Gate knew. "The man who helped him—Demorn—sent me a message this morning. Where Zhada was. To come as quickly as I could." Her lower lip began to tremble and huge tears filled her eyes. "He said…Zhada's not doing well."

"He fought Yaretzi," Cenoté said abruptly. "For you."

"How—?" Asalyan stared at the Wizard, and then shuddered. "Yes, for me. I'd had the dreams for days. The healer said the priestess was coming for me next. I don't know how Zhada found her or how he defeated her, but he saved me. He saved Taux."

"And paid the price. We will help you."

He'd been right to think her coming no coincidence; the how of it was, thankfully, beyond his ken, being the purview of Wizards. Hunhau went to the basket and picked out the worst piece of wood. "Only one kind of folk aren't marked going into the 'Purse," he informed Asalyan. "But it's risky."

The merchant's daughter nodded, lips firm. "A courtesan?"

Hunhau couldn't help his chuckle. "Dear lady, those are marked most of all."

Cenoté offered her hand to bring Asalyan to sit by the worktable. "Hunhau is right. The only people unnoticed come to the kitchen for scraps. Madame Serene is a kindly woman."

Not a description he'd have applied to the formidable owner of the city's most famous bordello, but Hunhau wisely didn't argue. Asalyan looked anxious as it was. She had a right to be. "So," he said, making it cheerful. "Leper or madwoman?"

"There is only one choice." Cenoté touched the centre of Asalyan's forehead. "If you are sure?"

Determination burned in the younger woman's eyes. She laid her hand over the flower on her cloak. "I must get to him. I'll do whatever it takes."

"Then prepare," the Wizard told her, "to go back."

To remember madness, all one need do was walk too close to Taux's haunted stone. Asalyan sought it, ran her hands along it, drew it into herself like a lover and made it real, again. The blood priestess had put nightmares into her sleeping mind. The voices of the dead called them forth until the real world, streets and flesh and flower, faded behind dusty bone.

What kept them back, what controlled them so she still knew who and what she was, and why, oh why, this?

Even as she sobbed and cried out and struck at the air, another, newer memory battled the old and kept her from falling past the edge. Cenoté's voice. It ebbed and flowed through Asalyan's thoughts, cleansing and sure. *Yaretzi cannot harm you. She cannot touch you. Let your scars become your armour. Love shall be your shield.*

Hearing that voice, the words repeated over and over, she steadied inside, though outwardly she staggered from the main street, past a statue hung with flowers, into a cramped alley. She wasn't alone. Three lepers, one pulling himself—herself—along in a cart, were already at the back door of the Silk Purse. A man, well-dressed and groomed, sat on the ground, booted feet spread wide, slowly drawing a knife across the bared skin of his arm. All wore masks that matched hers, crude in design, inscribed in red with the sigil of Saint Amanda of the Virgins, patron of Healers.

Contagion, that meant. Pity.

Most of all, a final warning. Harm those protected by the Saint and never again be healed.

The mask was a key to get by the watchers outside. Who weren't, Hunhau had warned her, fools. A mask and an act would fail. Any who passed those cynical eyes met Madame Serene's healer and daughter, Shayla Gatewell, waiting to inspect any who came to her so masked, ready to condemn any who blasphemed her gracious Saint.

A young boy slipped out the door, moving in and out of shadows, favoring one leg. He passed by her and their eyes met.

His weren't young at all. She'd been mistaken.

Asalyan waited her turn, flinching at visions. The blood priestess had given her so very many; now, unleashed, they cried out for mercy, for death, for anything but what Yaretzi gave them. How close she'd come to being such, sent to torment an innocent, to pull suffering from a soul until it could—

"Peace. You're safe here. Peace. Saint Amanda, aid me! Will! Benbe!"

The voice was higher than Cenoté's, younger, filled with compassion and urgency. Closing her eyes, Asalyan stumbled towards it. She tripped over a step or body, and found herself caught and held tight. "I have you," the voice said as a second set of hands took hold, lifting her. "Easy. What's your name?"

"She's taken it," she heard herself whisper, then whimper, "Make her stop. Please!"

"I'll do my best." Louder, to someone else, "Another victim. Take her upstairs. Gently."

By instinct, Asalyan kept her eyes closed, but she hardly needed to see. It was a game she'd play with Zhada, to learn her surroundings through scent alone. Now spices and roasting meats painted a kitchen; a brief rush of perfume and rich smoke meant passing a door to a common room as it opened and closed; incense and candle wax—coupled with climbing—painted floors and corridors with openings into more private spaces. Finally, sickness, almost masking the scent she knew best of all.

"Zhada!" Asalyan squirmed free, surprising whomever carried her. She pushed through a beaded curtain, and there he was, lying on a frankly magnificent bed.

Like a corpse prepared for a funeral.

She was at his side in a heartbeat, hands trembling as she tore aside the sheet to feel for a pulse at his neck. Nothing! She flung off her mask to lean her cheek over his half-open mouth to feel for a breath, waiting, hoping. Was that? There! Asalyan sank down on the side of the bed, overcome by relief, her hand on Zhada's broad chest. "He lives."

"Barely. You must be Asalyan."

The merchant's daughter looked up.

A tall woman, dressed in the garb of a healer, stood in the doorway. She waved away the men who'd accompanied her and let the beads close behind her. "He called your name, during the fever. I'm Shayla Gatewell."

Asalyan bowed her head. "Please forgive—"

A smile dismissed her apology. "There's nothing to forgive. Trust me, I've more than I can handle left by that foul creature. I can tell you've been touched and take hope, truly, seeing you've recovered." The smile vanished as she stepped to the bedside. "I wish I could say the same about your friend."

Asalyan turned to look more closely at Zhada. Neat bandages covered his shoulder and upper chest, but what soaked through them was yellow and stank of rot. His skin was covered with a fine sheen of sweat and his eyelids moved constantly, as though he tracked something unseen. She went to take his hand, only to find the right one clenched into a fist, tendons and bone standing out in relief. His wrist was—it was shot through with black! Her eyes shot up to the healer's.

"His wounds were deep, but nothing to such a strong and healthy Lowl." Shayla pointed to the fist. "I believe there's the answer. The man who brought him couldn't be sure, but thought Zhada took something from the dead priestess. Saint Amanda save me from idiots. Short of cutting off his hand," she went on bluntly, "which would kill him in this state, we can't take it away."

"We must!" Asalyan tried to pry his fingers apart, but they were like stone. With a cry of despair, she leaned forward to press her lips to his cheeks, his wide nose, his slack lips. He was always so warm. Now he was as cold as something dead.

Shayla put her hand on Asalyan's shoulder. "I haven't given up—"

"Wait." Barely discernible, but yes! Nostrils flared, seeking a scent. The merchant's daughter tore the flower that meant cherished from her tunic and brought it close. Exquisite, the senses of a Lowl.

And scent was everything.

A breath, deep enough to move his chest. There! The flicker of an eyelid, the slow movement of a tongue. "Zhada," Asalyan whispered, her tears raining on his dry, cracked lips. "You've won, my beloved. Don't let her steal you from me now." His tongue, thick and stained, moved to touch the drops.

"Blessed Amanda the Merciful." The healer came close, checking pulse and still-dazed eyes with trained surety, muttering a prayer under her breath that seemed more demand than gratitude as she squeezed drops from a sponge into his open mouth. After what seemed an eternity, Zhada's mouth closed and he swallowed. "Well done," she told him. "Well done."

Shayla stood and beckoned Asalyan to the far side of the room. "We've a chance, if he'll drink. Take this."

Asalyan accepted the bowl and sponge. The golden liquid in the bowl gave off a faint, heady aroma. As she sniffed, the room seemed brighter, freed of its sickness if only for a moment.

"What ails your love isn't a sickness my skill can cure," Shayla warned her. "What saps his strength is magic. Only magic can save him."

Asalyan nodded, unsurprised. "He will be saved," she vowed, calm and sure. "Where do I find it? This magic."

The healer's eyes warmed. "I can see why a Lowl might choose you. The magic we need will come to us. A gem that can be imbued with great power—and it will be, three days hence. Zhada must last till then," almost stern.

The Eight Queens. The final day of the Festival. It seemed an eternity.

Whatever it took. Asalyan brought the bowl close to her breast. "He will," she said, knowing it was true. "For me."

Rain skirted the city, dancing to thunder and tossed by wind. Droplets carried grim tales of swamp snake and black mire, and giggled mightily over a ship caught by the gale. Sailors sank to the depths. Snakes slithered. All the while, Taux partied, for weren't the streets now safe?

Safer, at least.

In a quiet room, on a magnificent bed, life flickered, almost spent.

The Weaver chuckled and plucked playfully at a thread.

And on the seventh day, as on every seventh day since coming to Taux, the blind Wizard Cenoté went to pay her debt.

He didn't go in, he'd never gone in—except the once at the beginning and all those times in his youth didn't count now at all—and Hunhau the maskmaker felt almost queasy as he stepped through the side door of the Silk Purse at Cenoté's side. Why she'd asked him to join her this time he didn't know, couldn't say, and refused to guess.

Other than it had nothing to do with pleasure.

She'd been quiet, since they'd sent the merchant's daughter on her quest. Intent. She'd taken nothing but water, nor slept as far as he could tell.

Cried. She'd done that. He'd heard the dry, racking sobs and laid there in helpless pity. Was it dread for those they'd masked and sent into peril?

Or regret, for the man who'd sent her flowers' intention.

Regardless, she'd risen, as always on the seventh day, ready to visit the physician of the Silk Purse. He'd summoned the litter, their bearers cheerful as only the young could be after six days of Festival.

Then she'd asked him to come with her, instead of waiting outside.

Hunhau headed for the private rooms, realizing all at once he did so alone. He turned to see Cenoté sweep aside the white linen curtain that led into the public portion of the 'Purse and step through.

Making no sense, or too much. He hurried after her.

The room was dimly lit and would reek of incense, should he remove his mask. Low tables ringed a circle where a dancer stood as still as her audience, eyes fixed on Cenoté. The ancient stone walls of the room curtain were draped with hangings of emerald, saffron, and azure silk, tumbling to stacks and piles of cushions, most of those occupied.

Except for one wall, left bare and stark but for a small table laid with flowers and flanked by tall candles. Hunhau dodged pillows and legs to catch up, for despite being blind and in an unfamiliar room, Cenoté moved with long sure strides.

While the room's inhabitants stared in disbelief.

She reached the wall and he dared run. Did she mean to do magic, for surely this was the dreadful wall within which Yaretzil had immured her victims? Only in Taux—and the Silk Purse— would business as usual continue near such a site.

Hunhau came close, then waited. Cenoté, having stopped before a section of bare stone, raised her hands, silk falling away from bare too-thin arms. She touched here, then there, her head cocked as though listening.

"Can you help them?" he whispered in an agony of hope. And wasn't alone. Others approached, some frowning, some with hands clasped almost in prayer. He lowered his voice to barely audible. "Or are they—gone?"

Cenoté lowered her arms and turned from the wall. When she spoke, it was in a clear ringing tone. "Those within sleep. Do not listen to the liar," and Hunhau heard the warning crash of surf. "Do not succumb to fear. Your friends are at peace and safe, for now."

Then she took his arm. "Let us tend to ours."

Madame Serene herself, buxom and olive-skinned, with curves that made Hunhau regret his long absence, met them at the curtain. "Fair Festival," she said, her smile as false as a mask's. "Everything is ready." To Cenoté. She didn't—quite—frown at Hunhau.

Something was wrong. Something more. The laughter and music, the voices raised and murmuring were as false as the Madame's welcome. Hunhau touched Cenoté's hand in mute warning.

Her mask tilted towards him, but she spoke to Madame Serene. "Do not doubt Hunhau. I may need his help, this time."

The Madame's turquoise-lidded eyes slid to the closed door to the blue room, then back. "You know who's put herself here." Without doubt. "She's a right nuisance, but—" louder "—we're always pleased to serve justice and the will of the city."

Hunhau felt his heart start to race. What was going on? Who was here?

"I must not be disturbed." The Sea was in Cenoté's reply, rising in a dangerous swell.

For some reason, Madame Serene's smile grew wider, and real. "I've made sure of that." She snapped her fingers and a tall shape detached from the group watching a listless dancer. A tall shape dressed in the scant silk and fine chain of a very expensive courtesan, muscles gleaming with oil.

Hunhau blinked. "Savino?"

Putting a long finger over lips red with carmine as he swaggered close, the duelist flexed an arm bare but for tattoos and three silver bangles. "Triumphant-Joy's the name. What do you think?"

"You look very—ah—unrestricted," the maskmaker said cautiously, grateful for his mask.

"Please escort your guests upstairs, 'Joy," Madame Serene ordered. "No need to linger here. Do enjoy," to Cenoté, with a graceful nod. To Hunhau, "Don't wear him out, now. He's booked for the rest of the Festival."

Offering his arm, Savino smiled with astonishing charm. A charm not to be trusted, Hunhau thought nervously. Nonetheless, he copied Cenoté and laid a hand on what felt like braided steel, managing a chuckle. "Dear Madame, surely we can't promise that."

Madame Serene laughed. "Give it your best, little man!"

"Triumphant-Joy" led them upstairs to the private space of the Silk Purse, dimly lit and, Hunhau feared, redolent of incense as well as other aromas. At the first landing, a pair of gorgeous twins waited to let them pass, their eyes wide. Savino cheerfully planted a kiss on the top of Hunhau's head and they giggled.

He was never, the maskmaker knew, going to hear the end of this. Especially if Tohil found out.

The room they sought was at the far end of the second corridor, the portion of the 'Purse reserved for those who expected and paid for privacy. Some brought their own guards, who stirred at their posts until Triumphant-Joy blew them a kiss.

Never, ever, hearing the end of it.

The door they sought was covered in a beaded curtain and would appear unguarded to those unaware of how many peepholes the Purse contained, or the number of blowguns waiting at the ready. Some darts were tipped with laxatives or other sure-to-embarrass deterrents. Others, poisons guaranteed to drop a maddened Jai-Ruk. Without alarming the authorities. After all, love's ardent exertions caused many a heart to fail.

Cenoté took her hand from Savino's arm and stepped through first. The men followed.

"You!" said Asalyan, rising from her seat on the large bed in the centre of the room.

A bed, Hunhau saw, that already had an occupant. A good-sized Lowl, young and, once, well-featured. For if not dead, he was within a final breath of that end, his body wasted to bone. Most of what showed of his skin was black with rot.

"I told you help was coming," another woman said with relief. "Hunhau, welcome."

He bowed his head in respect. "Healer." Memory trapped whatever else he might have said. For the last time he'd been in the same room with Shayla Gatewell, the then-apprentice had been helping Physician Itzamna treat Cenoté's dreadful wounds.

"Just forget I'm here. Truly. I've promised the Madame not to be involved." Savino, having produced a sword from somewhere in his adornment, took a post facing the bead curtain, his back to whatever might happen inside the room.

Shayla came to Cenoté and offered her elbow, then guided the blind Wizard to the dying Lowl. They conferred in low voices. Asalyan stayed nearby, listening intently. He must be her friend, Zhada. Her love, Hunhau corrected to himself, recognizing the desperate hope in her face.

He looked away, diligently studying the wine-red woodwork. He'd started to count the coupling positions along the upper fresco when Cenoté called his name.

Hunhau went to her side. He couldn't help but stare at Zhada's face. Black clawed its way up the Lowl's throat and down his broad forehead. Only the wide nose and muzzle remained still free of it.

"He can hear you." Asalyan laid her hand against Zhada's jowl and his eyelids struggled to open, but failed. Her eyes lifted. "If Zhada could speak, he would apologize for his condition." The words were even and steady. "If he could move, he wouldn't be here. He is a hunter and a warrior, like the man at the door. He has stayed alive this long—like this—for me." She took a deep breath, then finished. "If you can't cure him, I ask, as he would, that you help him die."

The healer closed her mouth over whatever she'd have said when Cenoté nodded. "Let us begin. Shayla?"

The woman reached to her neck and pulled a chain. At the end was a too-familiar gem, blood red and set in gold. The maskmaker gasped. "How did you—? That belongs to—"

"Peace, Hunhau. This isn't Cizin. This is its opponent, K'in the Light Bringer."

He couldn't have told the difference. The gem was as dull as Cizin had been. "I used it to make the last of the elixir yesterday," Shayla explained as she unfastened the stone and held it out in both hands. "Saint Amanda blessing on you," she added huskily. "Nothing else worked."

"Saints do not care for me," Cenoté replied absently, cupping her own hand briefly over the stone, but not, Hunhau noticed, touching it. "I pay my debt." She removed her mask, passing it to his keeping, then, raising her hand, brought one finger to her mouth.

Biting down, hard enough to draw blood.

But blood wasn't what welled up. Asalyan's eyes grew round as a drop of clear water appeared on Cenoté's skin. The blind Wizard held her finger over the stone, letting that drop, then the next and the next, splash onto the red facets.

Each sank within.

With each, the red faded. By the third, it was gone, replaced by vivid blue. Cenoté bent forward and touched the gem with the tip of her tongue.

The blue began to pulse with light, soft and mesmerizing.

As Cenoté straightened, the line of her mouth one of exhaustion, in Hunhau's worried opinion, Shayla breathed a sigh of wonder. "Then accept my thanks, as always, Cenoté. I've prepared more elixir. It only needs the gem."

The Wizard shook her head. "The drink cannot help him now. Hunhau?"

He swallowed. The reason she'd wanted him here was at hand. "What do you need me to do?"

Her smile warmed his heart, even as it warned he was right to be anxious. "Be, as always, my strength. I must remove the poison Zhada holds in his hand."

"That hand?" He looked down at the Lowl. Fist was more like it, and a tightly clenched one. As he looked, the flesh seemed to melt away, leaving only a cage of bone fingers. "Oh my."

"Shayla, give K'in to Hunhau to hold."

He put Cenoté's mask on a nearby table, and then stepped up to take the stone. It was—it was warm, in his hands, like spring sunshine given form, and for an instant he wanted nothing more than to stand and hold it, like this, forever.

"Asalyan, stay with Zhada." Cenoté leaned over the Lowl, her ruined face close to his, and spoke. "Brave hunter, the time has come to finish this chase. Trust us at your side." She straightened and reached out. Hunhau put his free hand in hers.

"Now, Hunhau! Press K'in to Zhada's hand!"

He obeyed. His fingertips brushed cold bone and it was like being dropped into a nightmare. His mask—surely it was alive and trying to eat his face! His face, wasn't it falling off, leaving the white of bone behind? Bone like the shards he'd seen in Cenoté's poor face—

Even as he drowned, Cenoté's hand in his became a rope, pulling him towards safety. Towards what was real, for the dire visions were, he took a breath, lies. The poor Lowl, to suffer through this? Hunhau pressed the stone against the fist, blinking away sweat, determined not to fail.

K'in's glow brightened, as if responding to his courage. There was a flash! Hunhau was thrown back, but held onto the stone. He watched with regret as all light within it vanished. The blue faded to dull red once more.

And Zhada's hand opened.

On his palm rested a small fragment of bone, weathered and grey. Black rot grew from it into his skin, into all of him, for what this bone had been—what it was—was anathema to life itself.

Before anyone else could move, Cenoté sent her fingers racing along the Lowl's arm, to his wrist, finding his hand. She snatched up the bone and took two quick steps away. Then brought the foul thing to her mouth.

"Cenoté, no!"

Even as Hunhau protested, he saw her swallow. "Come for Yaretzi if you dare, Weaver," she said then, and he heard the triumphant cries of gulls.

Did the ground beneath them tremble?

"Look! You've saved him!" Asalyan exclaimed. They all turned to the bed. It was true. Health flooded through the Lowl's body, restoring flesh, driving out the rot.

His eyes shot open and there was rage in their depths. With a hideous growl, Zhada lunged off the bed. At Cenoté!

Hunhau threw himself towards the two, shouting, "Savino!"

But the Lowl wasn't mad. He stopped short and dropped to one knee before the Wizard, head bent in a supplication rare in his kind.

Cenoté reached out, found his face, then slipped her hand beneath his chin. He rose as if lifted. They were the same in height, the Wizard pale as a statue, the Lowl flushed with vibrant life, and stood as if learning each other.

Then Cenoté smiled and tapped the Lowl lightly on his broad nose. "It's the last day of the Festival, Brave Hunter. Shouldn't you be taking your beloved to see the sights?"

Zhada blinked as though startled, then spun around. Asalyan stood by the bed, tears streaming down her face even as she smiled at him too. She opened her arms and he stepped into them like a man entering paradise.

Which was all very well and good and lovely, but Hunhau was far from happy. She'd eaten a bone. An undead bone. To keep it from something called "Weaver" and he didn't, not in any way, like the sound of that. There was noble and there was risky and this, he just knew, was risky.

Oh, and there was the dimple in her cheek, meaning Cenoté was well aware of his opinion and amused. Which could mean she'd taken no risk she couldn't manage, but he still planned to be wary—

"This is a private party," Savino said in that cheerful happy-to-send-you-to-hell tone of his, one arm out to block the door.

The would-be intruder stared at him in disbelief. "There's nothing private from me! You know who I am, fool. Step aside!"

A rasp as Savino produced a second blade from his scanty silks. "The name's Triumphant-Joy and you aren't welcome here, Lady Evynhoe."

Few clients were aware of the peepholes in the Silk Purse. Fewer still knew of its other useful attribute. Before Hunhau realized what was happening, Shayla smoothly recovered the spent gem and steered her charges out of the room through an exit that hadn't, to his eye, been there before.

Almost at once, it wasn't.

He retrieved Cenoté's mask as Savino continued to block the view of the room, helping her with the straps. "Shouldn't we be escaping?" he whispered in her ear. "I've heard this name. She's a paladin."

"Why? We rented the room," she replied. "'Joy, please allow this person to enter. We've nothing to hide." A note of something grimmer. "And it's time I met this Lady Evynhoe."

Savino stepped aside with a mocking bow. The paladin burst through the bead curtain, gave the well-used bed a dismissive glance, then focused on Hunhau. "Show your faces."

He held his breath as he began to remove the mask; it was that, or pass out from the scents in the 'Purse, let alone this room.

"We will not," Cenoté declared calmly. "Leave be, Hunhau."

Relieved, he dropped his hands.

The paladin looked more puzzled than concerned. "Do you not respect my office?"

Savino snorted.

"Why should we …" Cenoté tilted her head "…when you do not?"

Offense warred with curiosity. "Before I have you taken downstairs for questioning, tell me why you'd say that? I've devoted my life to the search for justice. Tonight, I'm here to find the one who killed Yaretzi. My purpose is worthy."

Hunhau very carefully did not look at the section of paneling through which that "one" had just slipped away.

"Yaretzi was already dead. Her slaying was as much a mercy to her as to the citizens of this city."

"We can't have killers running loose!?"

"It's Taux," the maskmaker heard himself say.

"The place doesn't matter. Justice is what matters."

The grotesque mask moved from side to side. "That is what you believe. But you were sent not to bring justice, but to find that which could be used to again destroy this city, by those who lust after the magic of the Afterglow Sea!"

"What are you saying—"

Cenoté was as relentless as the incoming tide. "Did they not ask you to find her remains, once you had her killer?"

The paladin's face might have been of stone. "Those instructions were secret. Given to me by—" She put hand to sword hilt and Savino came to alert. "How could you—Saint Siegfried the Just, how did you—"

"That is the only reason you were sent," Cenoté told her. "Any part of Yaretzi, in the hands of a necromancer, would grant a power neither you nor any of your kind could stop. That power would be used to find and rekindle the remaining cursed objects within Taux. Once done?" Cenoté swept her arm to encompass the room. "What happened here before will be but a shadow to the destruction to come. I ask you, Lady Evynhoe. Is this your justice?"

"No." The paladin's eyes fixed on Cenoté and her hand left the hilt of her sword. "No, it isn't. This—something wasn't right. There were so many cases, why this one? Why me?"

"I can tell you." Madame Serene stepped into the room. "Triumphant-Joy, your next clients are downstairs." Savino smiled and blew Hunhau a kiss before leaving. "Lady Evynhoe, they picked you because you are the best. You've been used. Do you see that now?"

The paladin nodded slowly, her eyes taking fire. "They picked the wrong knight," she said grimly. "I will have answers. There will be justice!"

"When the time's right. Which it isn't," Madame Serene said sternly. "Trust me on this. Stick your head in that jaguar's mouth and you'll be supper, nothing more."

The paladin stiffened. "Thank you for your opinion, but the sooner I take my questions to my Order, the better!" She dipped her head to Cenoté. "We will speak again." Turning, back stiff as a board, she marched from the room.

"I wouldn't hold your breath waiting for that conversation," Madame Serene said oddly, then cast her eye around. "I trust you enjoyed yourselves?"

Hunhau heard the dimple in Cenoté's voice. "Give me some moments to rest here, and I will be back in seven days."

"And we will, as always, be grateful." Madame Serene bowed her head. "Take care, my friends. This isn't over."

"No, it isn't." Cenoté put her hand on Hunhau's shoulder, a weight and responsibility he gladly bore. "I may not keep watch any longer," she said gently.

"But I will listen."

Rain is the gossip that never lies.

It finds the truths others hide in shadows, flushes out secrets, and makes no judgement. Good washes away as easily as evil, both tumbled through gutters and down empty streets, their stories, ultimately, flowing into the sea.

And into a window, lined with little cups.

Illustration by Jeff Laubenstein

A CONFLICT OF AIR

By Rob Mancebo

Seventh Day: The Eight Queens

A huge crowd was packed into the wide common room of the Emerald Serpent. The final evening of the festival of flowers had brought out the city's exuberant population *en masse*. Tohil pushed his way through the crowd purposefully. With no tables open, he navigated toward the packed bar. Any patrons who didn't spread before him, he simply brushed aside. In a city rife with daring duelists, Tohil was seldom challenged. Those who had dared to assay the metal of the guardsman over the years had been killed or terribly crippled.

As he bumped a shoulder in passing a group packed in at a table, Tohil heard an indignant curse in a strange accent. A hand caught his arm with considerable power. The big guardsman almost smiled as he wheeled.

The person who had arrested his progress stood up, ice blue eyes coming level with his own. All of Tohil's seething anger puffed out like a candle in a summer breeze. The tall, inhumanly slim girl who faced him with her white cloak tossed back to clear her sword for a draw was a Farian.

Tohil stood locked in quandry. Even if he could bring himself to draw his blade on a woman-child, to kill a Farian would doubtless bring the ancient people's wrath down upon Taux like a plague sent from the heavens.

Tohil nodded a grudging bow while grumbling, "Your pardon, I didn't see you."

The girl defiantly pulled her sword out of its pearl mounted sheath to display a hand's breadth of blade that shimmered in the lamplight of the tavern.

"That would be unwise," he warned.

"You do not insult a ship's captain and live!" she snapped.

"There was no insult," the guardsman told her in a calm tone he had used to quell a thousand and one fights. "The room is crowded, that's all. I didn't see you."

"Draw your blade!" she insisted.

"No."

"Then by the seven islands of hell—" she flashed out her sword, but Tohil caught her hand before she could present the blade and twisted her wrist to an awkward angle, pressing the edge against her own throat.

He could feel his hand grow hot with power where he gripped hers. Magic strove against magic as the elements of fire and air contested. His fingers glowed crimson at the edge, but a zephyr of cold wind swept about the pair, cooling the fire of his grip in frosty defiance. People in the room pulled back, but no one left. Those looking on were mesmerized by the perverse expectation of looming death.

"Push or pull, either way cuts your own throat," he warned the girl.

"What if I stab?" she replied through gritted teeth.

Tohil chanced a glance downward and found a dagger pressed against his stomach.

"I'd still cut your throat," he warned.

"A stomach wound is a slow way to die. Release my arm."

"I'd still get to watch you die first." He looked into her cold eyes and ordered, "Drop your blades."

Neither yielded. Neither moved. Tohil increased his focus and numinous smoke leaked out between his fingers. Yet the girl's power did not falter. The breath of the patrons began to show in frosty clouds that were swept into the preternatural breeze that roiled about the pair. The winds grew in force until men caught their caps and the women in the room had to grab at their flailing dresses for the sake of modesty.

"Of all the foolishness!" a man gruffly interrupted the stand-off. "Why all this talk of killing? Where's the profit in it?" The interloper had been sitting with her at the table. He was a man of medium build, slim but muscular. His dark face was tattooed with lines of script.

Those who could read these marks of shame would readily identify him as a criminal of Zimbolay.

"My honor—" she began, but her companion cut her off. "Your honor suffers no bruise from a small bump in a crowded room, Captain." He placed a hand upon her knife arm. "It is nothing, really."

"I am not afraid to die," she insisted above the eerie moaning of the wind. "Fight me!"

Tohil looked into her icy blue eyes and saw the truth of her words.

"Verily, you are not afraid to die," he whispered to her and he let go of her hand. With the conflicting connection broken, the wind died and Tohil's hand was left smoldering with the merest wisps of smoke.

"Draw your sword and fight!" she demanded.

"No."

"Then I shall kill you as you stand!"

"Ummm, if you murder a city guardsman before a hundred witnesses," her companion warned, "It would make trading in Taux rather difficult for your people, would it not?"

Tohil saw the change in her face and she lowered her blades. Frustration played across her features as she looked away.

"You are right, of course." She sheathed her weapons. "I cannot place my honor ahead of the good of my people."

A collective sigh of relief went through the crowd. She returned to her seat without another glance at him. Here was a mystery that piqued Tohil's interest. A Farian in the company of an outcast rogue? That smacked of trouble the like of which Taux did not need. It seemed that the other men at the table were not with the captain. By their attire and attitude, they were simple freemen workers only seated there by a whim of chance and the crowding of the room.

"Then to make amends, I'll buy the beer," Tohil said as he bumped a man over to seat himself upon the corner of a bench at their table. He took advantage of the gap in the crowd to wave to Timina, one of the servers. She waved back and pulled out one of the big pitchers and began filling it.

"Increase Coin," Tohil said to the Farian's tattooed companion. "Whatever are you doing here beyond the Black Gate? The last I heard, Titus the mason said that he was going to twist your head off if he ever got his big hands around your neck." The question was followed with a subtle wink.

"A fellow's got to make a living," Coin replied with a shrug. He waved a hand at the Farian and smiled as he said, "Captain Hajnalka needed a guide and so I must dare the unjust wrath of my foes to assist her." His eyes slid over to his employer as he added, "I trust that my personal risk will be considered when my payment is given."

"The way I heard it," Tohil corrected, "Titus's wrath is hardly unjust. Wasn't the quarrel something about you and his wife?"

"Tush, nothing but loose talk from wagging tongues," Coin said quickly. "I—"

"So, what business does a Farian captain have beyond the Black Gate?" Tohil cut off Coin's protestations to ask.

"I was hired to transport something very expensive from the city," Hajnalka replied simply. "My letters of transport are duly signed by the Port Authority. As a guardsman, you may examine them."

Tohil waved off the offer. "I leave such things to the harbormaster. No, what I'm wondering is, what 'expensive item' are you going to transport?"

"Indeed it is a mystery," Hajnalka replied. "I merely received a message that Rollin Shear wanted to ship twelve stone of cargo out of the city by midnight tonight."

"Tonight?"

"He was very specific."

"So, you sailed all the way to Taux to pick up less than a quintal of cargo?"

"No," she corrected. "I sailed to Taux for an offer of 10,000 silver coatls worth of uncut emeralds. Whatever mysterious item Rollin wants me to ship is of no concern so long as he makes good on the payment."

"Understandable." Tohil's mind raced. Who would pay such a price to ship an item? Rollin Shear certainly couldn't. Shear was a simple tome mage such as one could find collecting trinkets and rubbish in any district of Taux. There was some small notoriety to the job, but most people looked upon him as more of a rag-picker than a mage. Certainly no one would try and cheat a Farian captain. The middling air race, from the high mountains reaches, was notoriously prickly and wielded both earthly and mystical weapons of great power.

Tohil liked mysteries. The only question was, what string of this one should he tug to unravel it? The guardsman could be subtle when necessity demanded, but events in the city were moving too fast to loiter about.

"Well, first of all," he told the Farian Captain, "You're not going to find Rollin Shear here in the Emerald Serpent."

"What makes you think that?"

"See the fellow over at that table?" Tohil pointed across the room. "The big one in sable with knives in his baldric and a scowl on his ugly mug. See him there?"

"I do."

"That man is the noted duelist Nico Masra. Rollin Shear lost a bet to Nico last week. He's not going to step foot in the Serpent until he has the three golden jaguars to pay off his wager."

"If he can't pay a simple bet," Hajnalka asked with a scowl clouding her smooth brow, "how would he pay us?"

"A good point," Tohil agreed. "But what I was really wondering was why Coin would bring you here and have you waiting to meet Rollin, when Nico was sitting right over there the whole time?"

"I didn't know. . ." Increase began.

"You were drinking right in that corner when Nico told everyone what he'd do if Shear didn't come up with what he owed. I recall, you laughed louder than most."

"I—I simply forgot." Increase Coin gave a weak smile and shrugged. "I'll take the Captain to the Raised Market. Rollin likes to woo young Melyne in the . . ."

"Melyne's is no longer capable of doing her night work and well you know it. Don't lean too heavily upon favors owed, Coin," Tohil warned. "There are limits to my gratitude. Who paid you to mislead this young lady?"

"I would never dare mislead—" Coin held up his hands defensively and looked from Tohil to Hajnalka.

Tohil tapped his fingers impatiently upon the table.

"Really, I wouldn't—"

"You're running out of time," Tohil told him. "I saw Titus the Mason wandering this way. He stopped to toss dice with old Rafael Cantor, but I bet he'll arrive soon. I've seen Titus bend iron spikes with his bare hands. Imagine what he'll do if he gets hold of your—"

"All right! All right! Shear paid me to keep her busy. He's in the Silk Purse. He was to send word when to bring her around back to pick up her cargo."

"See there," Tohil smiled broadly. "I knew you could find the truth—given the proper motivation."

"You didn't really see Titus—" Coin was interrupted by a slamming of the front door and a call of, "Good evening, Titus," from a patron near the entrance.

"Ah, there he is now," Tohil said, but Increase Coin was already off his seat and had ducked into the crowd on his way to the back door.

"Amazing how fast Coin can move when he wants to," Tohil commented.

"So, why was he hired to mislead me?" Hajnalka asked.

"Easiest way to find that out is to go and ask Rollin."

"In a house where people's bodies are sold as though they were a haunch of pork in a meat market?" she replied indignantly. "I would not sully my reputation."

"Well, I do see your quandary." The server interrupted by bringing over a pitcher and several clay mugs glazed with a twining emerald serpent in the blocky style of Taux art.

Timina tossed Tohil the mugs one at a time, which he caught familiarly and set upon the table. Then he flipped her a coin which she snatched from the air with a laugh before placing the pitcher upon the lacquered tabletop. It was obviously a regular game between them.

Tohil poured two drinks and pushed one toward the Farian. He raised his and said, "To the success of your voyage." At that toast she raised her mug and took a drink.

Tohil emptied his in a single tilt and stood up. He pushed the pitcher to the men seated at the table, saying, "Gentlemen, I trust you'll finish this. We have other business this night." The men praised his generosity and eagerly gulped down their drinks to refill their mugs at his expense.

He walked toward the door with Captain Hajnalka hastening to follow.

Once outside he turned directly toward the Silk Purse.

"Where are you going?"

"After Rollin Shear."

"I told you, I cannot enter such a place. It is disgraceful."

"More disgraceful than losing a cargo worth 10,000 silver coatls?" he asked pointedly. "What would your crew say?"

She curled her lip and growled in a peculiar way then she hefted her sheath and fell into step alongside him. They moved down a stone path that led between the Serpent and a sunken Ullamalitzli court. The Purse connected to the Serpent's tail but only opening to the public from the other side of the Silver Circle.

As Tohil pushed open the great door to the brothel, Hajnalka grumbled, "I hope you appreciate the weight this casts upon my honor."

"No more so than my own."

She looked at him questioningly but he strode on through the portal without elaboration.

The common room was a riot of lavish color, but no strains of music welcomed them. Groups huddled in various corners, whispering in a guarded fashion and the silken clad staff of the brothel served the customers drinks and tantalizing delicacies in silence.

An armed brute met them as they came in, but he looked worried when he saw Tohil. "You sure you want to come in here tonight?" he asked quietly. "I don't think the Big Fish would like it so much."

Tohil ignored the warning and told the big man, "We're looking for Rollin Shear."

"In the blue room," the man motioned with a thumb. "But that's where 'she' is."

"Is he being questioned?"

"Naw, he's observing. He got a letter from some big wig in the order. Says he's allowed to watch. Don't know why. He don't say nothin'. Just watches."

"Thanks." Tohil nodded as he walked on toward the indicated room.

Hajnalka kept up with him and whispered as they walked, "What's going on?"

"The Order has an investigator nosing into a local killing."

"Shouldn't the city Sturgeons be investigating local crimes?"

"We were. I was with her until this a few days ago."

"What happened?"

"I was taken off the case."

"Why?"

Tohil stopped and turned to her before they got to the blue painted door.

"I have friends in Taux. Sometimes friends need protection. Besides, the arrogant little martinet was looking in the wrong places. This is my city. I know who's a threat and who isn't."

"So you were caught obstructing the investigation?"

"More like 'guiding' the investigation. There are places in Taux that even a Paladin shouldn't poke her nose into. Dark places that'll get you killed in a very messy fashion. We can't let that happen to an Inquisitor from the Order. It would start a damned holy war."

"But she caught you 'guiding'," she prompted.

"And chewed about two feet off the Big Fish's tail about it. So I was relieved of duty and now she's wallowing about following up leads on every lord and petty thug in the city. She'll be searching for years at this rate."

"Ah, I'll be surprised if she's happy to see you tonight."

"Well, if she sees me and pulls one of those knives she wears," he warned her, "you'd best get as far from me as you can."

"Can't we get Shear some other way?"

"It's after eleven. Your contract is for midnight. Is there time for another way?"

She shrugged and admitted, "Nothing comes to mind."

Tohil pushed open the blue door. At the end of the room stood a table under a halo of yellow lamplight. It was strewn with scrolls and piled scraps of paper notes. The slim woman who paced behind it ignored Tohil and Hajnalka's entrance. She was focused upon the masked woman who was sitting upon a single chair before her.

The pacing woman fingered one of the wicked knives that made up her necklace as she demanded, "So then, you expect me to believe that you knew nothing of the killing until after the fact?"

"How could I?" the masked woman replied.

"I ask the questions here," the Inquisitor said.

"Your pardon, Paladin, I shall rephrase." The woman sat up straight and looked directly at her questioner. "I have more than a dozen witnesses proving I was otherwise engaged when the murder happened. Yet you claim that I had some hand in the plotting of it.

"Since I am not to ask questions, I shall not ask you, 'what evidence you have that might incriminate me?' or 'Where are the witnesses who accuse me?' I shall simply say that you are mistaken in your speculations."

Tohil ignored the testimony. He was off the case. He nodded to Hajnalka and walked over to where he spotted Rollin Shear sitting in a chair along the wall not five steps away. Shear stood quietly when he saw them coming and waved back toward the common room with a nervous gesture.

"What are you doing here?" exploded from Shear's mouth the moment the door closed behind them.

"Looking for you, of course," Hajnalka replied.

"That idiot, Increase Coin, was supposed to keep you in the Serpent until I called for you! You're not supposed to be wandering around the streets!"

"Coin was—distracted," Tohil told him. "Wouldn't it have been easier to meet with the captain at the Serpent? I know this job has been whispered on many lips over the ending days of the festival, yet Coin was the man you chose for such an important job?"

"No," Shear barked, "Lareo choose him much to my chagrin, but…"

Shear trailed off as he cast a dark look at Tohil.

"You!" he hissed.

Tohil raised his hands, "I protect the city, but whatever the case, you are running out of time."

Rollin frowned, but nodded. "Indeed, there has been too little time! It's all right, then, as it has seemed to work out. You're here and it's almost the appointed hour anyway. Guardsman, you take the Captain around to the alleyway in back of the Purse. There will be a sedan chair waiting. We'll deliver the cargo in a few minutes. Don't be distracted by anything that may go on. My men will take you and the cargo to the docks. Then you push off. The contract says that you are off by Midnight. You must be away from the docks by that hour or you don't get paid!"

"Then your cargo had better be ready soon," Hajnalka warned.

"It will be!" Shear sputtered. "Just go!"

Tohil turned and headed for the exit as Shear went back through the blue door. Several of the girls gave the big guardsman tentative greetings as he passed or dared a wave from across the room as he was leaving.

"You have friends here," Hajnalka noted.

"I have friends all over the city," Tohil replied in a cavalier manner. He gave the smiling guard at the door a grin and a hearty clap upon the shoulder as they left.

"It is good to have friends when you go places," Hajnalka commented somewhat wistfully. "To know people."

"Don't you have friends?"

"The Farian are a people apart. We travel across the face of the world. We do not abide upon it. There is scarcely a time when I will see the same port twice in a year, much less the same people." Tohil saw that her wide, blue eyes were damp with moisture. "The Farian do not have friends."

"Mayhap not, if that is the way of your people." Tohil wondered how young the Farian Captain really was. She would seem to be perhaps a very tall child of fourteen, yet in human years, she might very well have seen a century pass. "But whether you come back in a month or in a year, you have a friend in Taux."

"I—I thank you, Guardsman. I scarce deserve the honor." The words caught, just a little, as they came out. "You understand that we Farian put the interests of our own people above all others.

"Tush," Tohil brushed off her concern and offered his hand. "I know an honorable person when I meet one."

Hajnalka took the hand and shook it somewhat tentatively.

"Now come my friend," Tohil told her. "Let's sort out what's going on, eh?"

They went around to the lamp-lit half-alley where the Serpent and Purse met. It was mostly clear of revelers although there were still scattered groups churning in the streets even at the late hour.

Tohil loved the Festival of a Thousand Blossoms. It was when the city of Taux shined its brightest. Feuds were set aside and blood rivalries took a back seat to horticultural abundance. And the women! Every female citizen of the city donned her finest, most festive ensemble and enticing masks of delicate make and subtle hue were *de rigueur*. It was a magical time of wondrous scents and flowing silks, a heady week of mystery and magic when beauty and romance were the sole focus of the entire city. No cataclysm, nor forces either natural or mystic, could distract the wild revels of the population. He was sorry to see it pass with the evening of the last day.

"Ah, and here's our transport," Tohil commented as a sedan chair arrived. It was carried by four Jai-Ruk bearers and escorted by a shifty-eyed Lowl guard who snarled at Tohil and Hajnalka.

"What are you two doing loitering about here?" The alley blushed with a burst of heat as the Lowl demanded, "Move on!"

Hajnalka reached for her sword, but Tohil stepped forward and replied coolly, "Perhaps your eyesight is as feeble as your brain, that you don't know a Sturgeon when he stands before you."

"No one said anything about the authorities," the Lowl snarled to the bearers. "Do we kill him or leave him be?" The bearers just shrugged.

"You keep your place, dog-man," Hajnalka ordered. Tohil winced when she said it. Few things were so insulting to Lowl as being called a 'dog-man'. "Unless you want to spoil this whole deal by getting yourself killed."

The Lowl leapt from his perch and rushed them with a roaring bound, but both Tohil and Hajnalka had their swords out before he was within range. The attacker hesitated facing the pair, trying to figure out how to kill one without getting spitted by the other.

His quandary was interrupted by a great hue and cry from inside the Silk Purse. There was the sound of breakage, bellowing orders, and fighting. A back door slammed open and the moonlit alleyway was bathed in lamplight as four men hauled out a long roll of carpet.

"Here's your cargo, Captain," one of the men yelled as they heaved it into the vehicle's open side. "Get moving!" When the roll of carpet hit the floor of the sedan chair, it gave off a muffled roar of vitriolic cursing.

"The hell it is!" Tohil knew it was a kidnapping immediately. Though who would dare pull off a kidnapping with a Paladin of the Order in the building he had no idea.

Tohil suddenly found himself alone facing a wall of armed enemies. The Lowl gave a guttural laugh, deep in its hairy throat as men and Jai-Ruks drew weapons.

"Stop!" Hajnalka ordered and waved them back with her sword. She turned to Tohil and told him, "The bond has already been made, my friend, this is my cargo."

"And you cannot decline it on moral grounds?"

"The offer was accepted by those above me. It is not within my power to break that bond."

"My position also does not allow me to stand down," Tohil warned.

"It is disgraceful to fight with a friend," Hajnalka replied, "but I cannot refuse this cargo." The pair faced each other in the glow of the Ghost Moon and lamp light, hesitating to join into the battle. "I told you that the Farian must put the interests of our own people before all others."

"That does make it difficult to have friends."

"Enough talk!" The Lowl leaped to the attack with a roaring bound and a bloom of heat.

Tohil shifted off the line of attack and fended the blow with a brush of his blade. As he recovered, he slashed his edge across his attacker's throat.

As the Lowl gagged out its life upon the ground, Tohil asked simply, "Next?"

Hajnalka waved the others back.

"As a friend, I can offer you nothing but a fair fight and an honorable death." Hajnalka unclasped her cloak and tossed it into the wagon.

"I've had other friends offer less," Tohil mused with a shrug.

She advanced in good fashion with her hand low and her point high. Her blade was slightly longer than Tohil's for he favored the crippling power of the edge over the more delicate point. The edge was messier. In street fighting, there was nothing like a good gaping wound to scare off gangs of ruffians.

Her attack was well schooled. She executed a bounding thrust and the alleyway was swept with a rolling breeze at her coming. His reply was to block and plant his boot upon her lead toes. Even as her brow clouded in the realization of her entrapment, the guardsman drove his substantial weight forward, ramming her leading knee with his own. Her pinioned boot pulled free as she tumbled. She did a back roll and came to her feet, only to have her right leg buckle under her weight.

She faced him, her sword presented but not able to rise.

"That ankle's only sprained—if you're lucky." He told her. "I usually hear them when they break." .

"Kill him!" one of the men shouted at the hesitating crew.

"As though you could!" a voice scoffed from down the alleyway. Increase Coin wandered into the lamplight with deliberate slowness. He had a halberd upon each shoulder and came up behind Tohil.

"Keep him busy here while we get away!" one of the men shouted to Coin.

Coin gave a shrug of one shoulder as he tossed a halberd to Tohil. He caught the polearm with one hand and sheathed his sword with the other in an almost single motion.

"What kept you?" he asked Coin.

"You know I really do have issues with Titus the Mason, right?" Coin demanded. "And besides, I'm getting tired of bailing you out like a swamped ship."

"Two nights ago was not bailing me out, no matter what you say," Tohil finished with a laugh.

"Yes, well, if you'd killed more of those filthy cultists, maybe my legs wouldn't be so tired."

"I'll try to do better tonight," Tohil replied dryly. "Just to give you a rest." Without signal or command the two brought their halberds into attack position.

The group of kidnappers looked warily from their swords to the halberds facing them.

"We can take them!" someone encouraged.

"The first two men to attack will certainly be skewered before they're within sword range." Coin cautioned them.

"And I'll bet the axe head of a halberd will split even a Jai-Ruk from shoulder to belt." Tohil gave his weapon a quick spin displaying how blindingly fast the polearm could go from a thrusting weapon to a massive chopper.

"They can't get us all!" someone insisted.

"I'll bet we can!" Tohil said with a laugh.

The kidnappers spread out to try and take advantage of their numbers, but the small alley just wasn't wide enough to let any of them get out of reach of the pair of threatening halberds.

"Stop!" an outraged voice screeched. "Are you all mad?" Rollin Shear hustled out of the building with his arms flapping in consternation. "Twelve o'clock is the deadline and you're all dawdling about brawling in an alleyway?"

Tohil bounded to Shear's side and pulled the halberd's haft across the mage's throat. "All right, let's unroll that rug and see what mischief you lads are up to!"

"That's what I've been trying to find out all evening, until you took over that is," Coin interjected.

"No! Listen guardsman, we took her by surprise. We'll never be able to do it again."

"Took who by surprise?"

"The Lady Evynhoe."

"You're kidnapping a Paladin of the Order?" The audacity amazed even Tohil and he pulled the pole tighter. "Their armies will rend Taux from cellar to steeple!"

"No, we're under orders," Shear choked out, "from the High Marshall!"

Tohil eased pressure on the man's throat, but didn't let him loose. "You have proof?"

"Of course," the smaller man drew a letter from one of the many pouches and satchels he carried and passed it to Tohil. "She was ordered back to the citadel but the obstinate vixen has refused to go. This letter is from the High Marshall demanding that she be sent back by whatever force is necessary if she hasn't completed her investigation by this evening. Further, it demands that she be out of Taux by Midnight tonight."

"But why would he end the investigation?" Tohil murmured as he examined the letter, but he was certain the mystical seal was uncounterfeitable.

"The Red Pillars obviously convinced him it was no longer relevant," Shear told him. The mage held up a large, leather purse and hefted it before Hajnalka and Tohil. "How else do such governmental quarrels come to an amicable finish?"

A battery of cursing came from the roll of carpet upon the floor of the sedan chair.

"Of course! Once the threat was removed, and whatever weight it carried against the Black Gate, the Pillars no longer had a need of an Inquisitor poking around their business here," Tohil said with a laugh as he closed the letter. "Then Captain Hajnalka has a cargo to deliver, and I shall se it done." He gave Coin back the halberd and walked over to offer Hajnalka a hand.

"Let's go!" He hoisted her into the sedan chair and followed her in.

The trip to the Harbor was slowed only by drunken clutches of revilers who were clinging to the Eight Queens, the last night of the Festival of a Thousand Blossoms. These spread as Coin walked threateningly before the vehicle with his halberd but they called curses after it for interrupting their evening.

"How did you become involved in this?" Tohil asked Rollin.

"My mastery of the arts, of course," Shear replied indignantly. "They needed someone who could call for Captain Hajnalka's services. How many people in Taux can put out a call for a Farian freighter?"

"Some years ago," Hajnalka explained, "Master Shear collected up a trinket of mine to add to his collection. Possession of that item gives him the ability to speak to me in my dreams when he wishes."

"Truth be in the connections," Shear said smugly. "My rivals may be powerful, but they must have the right artifacts to work with. No talent will suffice without the proper tools."

"And that's why you collect trinkets and bits of junk," Tohil said with a nod of understanding.

"Yes, of course." Shear looked as though he wanted to continue to dissertate about his art, but Tohil simply turned to Hajnalka and said, "I'm sorry about the ankle."

"It will heal." She shrugged. "I am sorry I attacked you. It shall remain a stain upon my honor."

"You've lived a very sheltered life, haven't you?"

"This is my first venture as a full Captain, if that is what you are asking," she admitted.

"I guessed. You must see that there are times when duty places people at cross purposes. Doing your duty is no stain upon your honor. Friendship inherently requires a certain amount of forgiveness."

"I shall remember that."

The evening seemed to get even darker as the cart rolled to a stop. Tohil realized that it was because of a vague bulk that was blocking the moonlight. A huge, shadowy form was moored to the seldom used air tower that rose above the docks.

"You didn't say that you were the captain of an *airship!*" he said in wonder.

"*The Solyom* is a sky ship," she said with a shrug. "And my father made me her captain. Our people fade from the world and I must learn quickly."

Several tall figures slid down ropes dangling from the airship. Their frost-colored hair shone in the moonlight and the polished silver and steel of many weapons glittered about them. The Farian sailors were an eerie, threatening sight.

Hajnalka barked orders to them in their own language and they bound up the carpet and called for it to be hauled up to the ship.

"Oh, I'd pay to see her delivered just like that before the Marshall." Tohil smiled as he watched the prisoner hauled up, "You'd best not let her out until you're well on your way. She's going to be madder than a wet hornet."

"We have a sturdy cell for her," Hajnalka assured him.

"Give her this," Shear handed Hajnalka the letter from the Master of her order. "And now that she is officially out of Taux, I am empowered to deliver your pay." He handed her the pouch he'd shown them earlier. "If anyone knew I'd been carrying emeralds . . ." He gave a shudder. "Well, my part in this is done."

"Not quite," Tohil told him. "You'd best make sure you're more prompt about paying Increase Coin than you've been with Niko Masra.

"Coin's pay?" Rollin laughed nervously. "Well, you yourself told me he'd been distracted and didn't finish the job so I—" he hesitated.

"You what?"

"I sent one of my men over to pay Nico off with the money I was going to pay Coin with—"

"You what!" Coin roared.

"Nothing to fear," Rollin assured him calmly, "I'll just—" He suddenly wheeled and sprinted off into the maze of darkened streets along the wharf.

"You filthy weasel!" Coin yelled after him and ran down the dim streets in pursuit.

The other Farians climbed up the ropes with inhuman alacrity and the sky-ship came to life in a sparkling of running lamps and the hum of blue-fired elemental engines of arcane power. Hajnalka reached out and took Tohil's hand. "Goodbye, friend Tohil. Perhaps we'll share another adventure the next time I visit Taux."

He grasped the offered hand, but also gave her a clap upon the back with his other hand before saying, "Sometime again, Captain. Sometime again."

Illustration by Janet Aulisio

NOTHING GOES UNPAID

By Lynn Flewelling

*T*hird Day: *The Night of Secrets*

*L*urching up in his narrow bed, Shay hastily dried his face on the dingy sheet. Angel of Death, all Taux called him. Beautiful Death. Cold Shay. Thank the Saints there was no one here to see him now.

Just twenty-three, Shay Gatewell was already one of the most feared and fearless Duelists in the city, one who brazenly tied no ribbon on the hilt of his sword. There were precious few people left in the world whom he loved, and fewer still for whom he'd weep, if only in his dreams. And in the days since the monstrous events in the Silk Purse salon, his dreams had grown worse than ever. He hadn't been able to bring himself to go to his mother's brothel since the morning after the priest of the Jaguar cult had imprisoned members of Shay's brothel family in the stone walls of the salon: the courtesans Lin and Ingritrude, Hammil the doorkeeper, and—unluckily arriving in the middle of things—his old sword master Xavier Crane, who'd been as close to a father as Shay had ever had.

Shay wiped at his eye again, hating himself for his weakness. Through the cracked panes of the bare window, he could see that it was just shy of dawn—far too early for Bal to be awake. But he didn't hear any snoring from the next room.

Did I cry out? His throat felt suspiciously raw.

Sure enough, Balthazar, barefoot and wrapped in his dressing gown, pushed the door open and crossed the spare, cheerless room to sit on the end of Shay's bed.

"Another bad one." Bal didn't bother making it a question.

Apart from his family, Shay would have killed anyone who got this close to him when he was unarmed. Bal was a special case; the only real friend he had left.

Shay finger-combed his long brown hair back from his face. "Yeah."

"Same as ever?"

"Yeah." Shay threw back the bedclothes and rose to pull on his trousers.

"Damnation, if you get any thinner you're going to disappear," Bal observed, frowning. "An undead priestess seeking Paladin or no undead priestess seeking Paladin, we're going to your mother's for breakfast. It's been too long since you've seen her."

"No."

"Yes!" Apart from Mama Serene, Bal was the only one who could use that steely tone with him and live to tell the tale.

It was the third day of Festival—The Night of Secrets—but it was still too early to see Eldaryns gleefully throwing fireballs into the Harbor, or see Kin wrestling in the ball court. The sky was overcast and Shay heard a rumble of thunder in the distance, but no rain fell yet so perhaps the air and earth themselves struck a truce after yesterdays scattered showers.

The Silk Purse was quiet, as it had been since the meddling Paladin had taken up her unwelcome residence there on bequest from the Red Pillars. Business at the brothel had definitely suffered, a not so subtle blow perhaps struck against his mother who herself was one of that Order.

Bal said nothing as Shay walked past the front door, which led into the salon, and around to the back half-alley and kitchen door. At this hour only the cooks were awake. Ala greeted Shay and Balthazar warmly.

"Your mother's taking breakfast in her chamber. I'll send the boy up with a tray for you."

"Where's her high and mightiness?" asked Bal.

"Lady Evynhoe? Asleep in the red room at the front of the house."

"Thanks."

Shay and Bal took off their boots and went up the back stair.

The air on the business level of the brothel smelled comfortingly of powder, perfume, and sex. Mama Serene's gilt-and-velvet appointed suite of rooms was at the back of the house, with a view of the rooftop gardens that abutted the Emerald Serpent. Shay scratched softly at the door and a moment later she opened it wrapped in silk and lace. With a displeased look she grabbed them both and pulled them into her chamber. She and Shay shared the same beautiful sultry eyes and olive skin, but the early morning light was less kind to her these days. Her eyelids were red at the edges as if she'd been weeping.

"What are you doing here?" she whispered, standing on tiptoe to embrace her son, and then Bal. "The Paladin has the word out for you, you know!"

"I've heard, Mother, but Bal dragged me here all the same."

"Talk to him, Mama," Bal said as they sat down at the table by the open garden door. "He can hardly sleep or eat since . . ."

"So I see." Mama covered Shay's hand with her own and tears glittered in her eyes. "Xavier wouldn't want you to mourn him like this, my love."

"I'll stop when he and the others walk free under the sun again." Shay turned his hand to twine his cold fingers in her warm ones.

"You look a little peaked yourself, Mama," said Bal. "Isn't that wretched woman done yet?"

"She shows no sign of it." Serene sighed. "The Festival business is ruined for this year, and she put a price on your head. But there's another matter on my mind. In fact, it's a lucky thing you're here. I want you to find Dethocrates and ask him to meet me at the Gold Monkey chocolate house this afternoon. Melyne may be in a bit of trouble."

"Trouble?" Shay's heart fell. Melyne had been among the survivors who'd left the Purse after the attack, too scared to remain.

"Yes, one of her customers was found dead in a room that she rented. I'm worried for her and her daughter."

"Do you want us to go with Dethoc?"

"No, I'd rather you keep out of sight. Dethocrates can handle it. Besides, it's the Night of Secrets, my dear. I hope you two will be otherwise occupied."

Shay gave her a humorless smile. "Bal certainly will be."

As the sun rose on the Night of Secrets the air was always filled with music, laughter, and the fragrance of lotus flowers. The winding streets of the Black Gate district were packed with masked revelers, making it easy for Shay to glide through the throng in his wolf mask. He spotted the big Jai-Ruk near the Black Gate and tilted his mask up to show his face. The boy who'd been walking with Dethocrates took one look at Shay and bolted, but Dethocrates stayed, hands well away from the hilt of his sword.

"It's not every day that I find myself in the presence of an Angel. I hope you're not here on commission?"

"No. The Madame of the Silk Purse has requested your presence at a chocolate house nearby. I was told to mention certain…obligations."

The thief nodded. "At the very least, I owe her a conversation. Lead on, Cold Shay."

As they fell into step Shay picked up the aroma of freshly turned earth from the Jai-Ruk and was impressed, as always, with the calm that emanated from the fellow. Dethoc was bulkier, but they both knew who'd come out the winner in a duel.

Out of the blue, Dethoc asked, "Shay, when you were a stripling, were you ever dared to visit the Ghost Towers?"

The banality of the question surprised Shay. People seldom made small talk with him. "Yes."

Dethocrates waited then pressed, "Did you go?"

"No."

Dethocrates laughed. "I suppose your mother would have sent Xavier Crane after you to drag you home by the heels."

Shay clenched his teeth and shot the man a cold look, but the earth grubbing wretch missed it.

"It's been a while since I've spoken to him," Dethocrates went on obliviously. "By the Saints, he's a good man. Is he still a favorite of you mother?"

"He was until a few days ago, when a necromancer sucked him into the walls of the brothel," Shay gritted out.

This time the Jai-Ruk felt the stab of heat and anger that flashed between them, or perhaps he noticed how the Angel of Death's hand stole to the rapier at his side; the unmistakable wet mud stink of fear filled the air as the earth elemental recoiled, much to Shay's satisfaction. "I'm sorry to hear that! I—"

"Forget it."

They continued on to the chocolate house in uneasy silence. Inside, Shay spotted Mama Serene at a corner table. He stood a moment, debating whether to join them, then shrugged and went outside. He stood a moment, willing his blood to cool; the thief had meant no harm.

Cold Shay once again, he lost himself in the crowd, restless but not knowing exactly what he wanted. The day passed around him, stifling heat replaced by rain, then a calm respite, and finally a deluge that blocked the slow rise of the Ghost Moon for an hour. When it finally ended the hour was late, but from the deepening shadows of evening the Festival's notorious copulations on this night burst into full bloom with a cacophony of moans of ecstasy and laughter echoing amid rooftops and windows.

At last he found himself at the Ullamalitzli ball court. Masked children, cast out of pleasure seeking parent's homes and wreathed in flowers were playing tag there, leaving the dark alleys and bedchambers to the lovers. Shay and Bal had done the same when they were that age, and Bal had punched anyone who called Shay "whore's get." Xavier had taught Shay and Bal their deadly craft there, right up until the day Shay had used those skills to kill his natural father and the Angel of Death was born.

Father Slayer, a voice hissed near his left shoulder. Shay glanced that way in time to see one of the myriad carvings on the alley wall writhe itself into a new position of agony. Since childhood the figures in the stones had spoken to him and never in pleasantries. Why he could hear them when no one else could seemed to remained a mystery.

Killer, killer, killer another voice tittered to his right and he looked across at the opposite wall to see two carved stone serpents devouring a man in a feathered head dress. Who will you kill this night? the doomed figure chuckled, disappearing into the serpent's maw.

It was never good when the pictures on the stones moved and spoke directly to Shay. Bad luck always seemed to follow.

"There he is. That's the bastard!" someone shouted and Shay turned just in time to narrowly miss being grabbed by a hulking Jai-Ruk in a wild boar mask that fittingly accentuated his natural features.

Two others were with him; both masked and armed with clubs. Shay sprang back and faced them, rapier drawn and leveled at Boar Face's heart. "What do you want with me?"

"You killed my twin, the Duelist Cathnoc." The boar ripped off his mask and pointed to his tattooed face. "Does this help you remember, or has the Angel of Death lost track of his kills?"

"Oh yes." Shay had killed Cathnoc two days earlier, near the docks. "I gave the appropriate salute and he agreed to the duel before witnesses. It was legal."

"Tell me who hired you, then?" the furious Jai-Ruk demanded. The angry stink of parched earth billowed around Shay.

He gave the fellow a thin smile. A large part of what his customers paid for was discretion. "Run along and enjoy the Festival. You've got no charge against me and I don't feel like killing you at the moment." His voice dropped to a husky growl. "Go on, before I change my mind."

The Jai-Ruk gave him a poisonous look, but knew better than to try and jump Shay in the midst of the onlookers who'd gathered around them. No doubt some fear was involved, as well. Shay Gatewell was hard to outnumber. The Jai-Ruks stomped off into the crowd, leaving behind that parched earth smell. The onlookers turned away, no doubt disappointed not to see Beautiful Death in action. Disgusted, Shay made his way back toward the Emerald Serpent, hoping to meet Bal there, if his friend had done enough rutting for one evening.

He was nearly there when the boy he'd seen a dozen times running messages around the Silver Circle approached warily. "Sir?" the lad said from what he probably thought was a safe distance. "Sir, I have a message for you."

"Well?" Shay demanded impatiently. "Come here so you don't yell it to the whole street."

The boy sidled up to him and whispered "Dethoc says for you to meet him on Waynside Bridge."

Dethoc again? By all the hells, this seemed to be the night for Jai-Ruks. "When?"

"Soon as you can, sir." And with that, the boy melted into the surrounding crowd with admirable ease.

Shay was less than pleased to find no sign of Dethoc on the bridge when he arrived. The lanterns swung on their poles set in the stonework, casting crazy shadows. He was tempted to leave, but curiosity got the better of him and he paced the deserted bridge twice before he caught sight of a hulking shape coming toward him.

Dethoc threw back his hood and came to a halt well out of arm's reach. "I have something you might want."

"Really?" Shay sized him up, gauging whether the Jai-Ruk had his hand on his hilt beneath his cloak. When Dethoc opened it, however, it was only to toss Shay something that glittered in the light of one of the bridge lanterns: a carved golden bracelet, heavy and strangely cold in his long fingers.

Shay raised a sarcastic eyebrow. "A lover's gift? I had no idea."

Dethoc regarded him levelly, with no scent of fear. "That's what put your friends into the walls of the Silk Purse."

Shay's fingers tightened around the bracelet. "Why are you giving this to me?"

"For your mother's sake. This thing's caused enough suffering, and if it's going to be safe with anyone, it's you. Maybe you'll even find a use for it."

"And?"

"And what?"

"What do you want in return?" Shay snapped.

Dethoc smiled, showing his tusks. "I might need a favor from an angel one day."

"So this puts me in your debt?"

Dethoc shrugged. "One good turn deserves another, that's all. Deal?"

Coldness emanated from the bracelet, tingling with power. The carvings on the bridge stones whispered to him, but he couldn't make out the words. Shay spat in his free hand and held it out. "Deal."

Dethoc spat and stepped closer to shake with him. "Fair festival to you, and good luck."

Shay pulled his hand away and strode off in the other direction, heart pounding with excitement he hadn't been about to show Dethoc. All that stood between him and releasing Xavier and the others was the wretched Paladin. The fingers of his sword hand itched, though he knew better than to pick that fight with a woman no blade could touch.

He found Bal asleep in their rooms, snoring in the embrace of three dark Zimbolay beauties. Lanky, handsome, and charming, Bal never came home alone unless he chose to. Clothing and masks littered the floor. Shay kicked the end of the bed, startling them all awake.

"Get dressed in the other room, my darlings," Balthazar told the women and they hurried out, grabbing up clothing as they went. Bal sat up and yawned at Shay. "What's up, besides you?"

Shay showed him the bracelet. "This put Xavier and the others into the walls, and according to Dethoc, it should get them out."

That got Bal out of bed. "By the Saints, how?" he asked as he hurried into last night's clothes and buckled on his rapier.

"That's what we're going to find out."

The stars clocked midnight by the time they reached the Silk Purse. No light showed at the windows of the brothel, upstairs or down. Hoping the Paladin was a heavy sleeper, Shay let them in the front door with his key.

A night lamp guttered on a stand, casting erratic shadow figures across the walls. The painted stone showed no sign of their prisoners but his mother had shown him the next morning where Xavier, Hammil and the girls had been sucked in. She'd marked each place with an X.

Shay slid the golden bracelet onto his wrist and walked to the wall where Xavier was entombed. Pressing his hand to the X there, he whispered, "Xavier Crane, come out!"

Nothing happened. The bracelet hung cold and inert against his skin. There was no tingle of magic. Slipping it off, he pressed the bracelet to the wall. "Come out!"

Nothing.

"Suppose Dethoc was having you on?" Bal whispered.

"To what end?" Shay hissed back. The Jai-Ruk was anything but stupid. He tried again in several places about the room, but nothing happened. Nothing at all.

Just then they heard the faint squeak of a door opening. He knew every sound in this building: it was door to the red room. It was followed by the whisper of stealthy footsteps coming their way.

Kill the bitch and be done with it.

How could he hear the stones from here?

He and Bal were out the door and around the corner before they heard a woman shouting, "Shay Gatewell, come back here. I command you!"

"Meet the Serpent," Shay whispered. Bal bolted one way and Shay the opposite one, burrowing into the malodorous streets and alleyways of his home ground as fireworks burst under the Blood Moon marking the end of the torrid night. The stones around him remained silent.

It was a risk, showing up at the Emerald Serpent with the Paladin's price on his head, but there was only one person Shay trusted to know what he needed to know and keep his mouth shut afterward: Lareo.

Bal met him in the shadows of the alley beside the tavern. "Stay here. I'll go in," he whispered, pulling up the hood of his cloak.

Shay nodded and went to a half-shuttered window to watch.

Lareo was in his usual corner by the bar, perched on a stool among his boxes of oddities and treasures. When Shay and Bal were just lads they'd slip round to the tavern and beg to see the then much younger Eldaryn's latest treasures. Now Bal towered over most of the patrons as he made his way through the tavern crowd and pushed past the small crowd of customers surrounding Lareo. Bending down, he spoke in the little man's ear. Lareo said something to his admirers and then left the tavern with Bal. The pair slipped into the alley across the Silver Circle to join Shay.

"Young Master Gatewell, fair festival to you!" Lareo said, red eyes shining. "It's been a while."

"It has. I need your opinion on something." Shay held out his left wrist and showed Lareo the bracelet.

"Well now. Well now," the Eldaryn muttered, adjusting his spectacles and looking closely at it. "Very pretty, but cursed, if what I've heard is true. I wouldn't be wearing it if I were you." Shay slipped it off and held it out to him, but Lareo folded his arms. "What exactly do you need from me?"

"The person I got it from intimated that it could release the trapped souls at the Purse. I need to know how it works."

Lareo snorted. "How should I know, boy? It didn't come from me."

"But there is someone who could tell me. Someone I think you know how to get to. I need to see the Weaver."

The little man shook his head. "No good can come from that Wizard. Let things rest as they are."

Shay went down on one knee, putting him eye to eye with the Eldaryn. "If it was your family trapped alive, would you?"

Lareo held his gaze for a long moment and a searing flash of heat passed between them. Shay stayed still as a stone, giving no sign of pain and at last the old fire born threw up his hands. "Who am I to tell the Angel of Death what to do, eh? Balthazar, are you with him on this?"

The tall man nodded. "Always. They're my friends, too."

"Be it on your heads, then," said Lareo, absently pushing his spectacles up his short nose. "That bracelet belonged to the Jaguar Cult priest who wreaked havoc at the Purse, and released the Bloody Lady."

"That much I know," Shay told him.

"Well, did you know that Zhada dispatched her this very night? Last I knew he was recovering at the Purse, tended by your sister."

Shay was annoyed with his distractions that day and hadn't heard about the Lowl. "So how does this thing work?"

"I can get you to the Weaver. But just you, Shay. Come back on the evening of Elemental Day."

"Elemental Day! Why must I wait two days?" Shay resisted the urge to grasp the little man by the shoulders and shake him.

"Hold on! Why does he have to go alone?" Bal demanded.

"Because the Weaver does not like visitors," Lareo told him firmly. "Especially those with no purpose, trust me."

"It's all right, Bal," Shay told him. "But why can't I go now?"

Lareo shrugged. "These things take time when arranging a meeting, my boy, and you have to find an appropriate gift in the meantime. You don't want to arrive empty handed or the Weaver will set a price you won't like. Come back at sundown on Elemental Day, ready to go. Oh, and you'll want a lantern, for all the help it will do you."

"What kind of 'gift' are you supposed to find for this Weaver?" Bal muttered as they made their way back to their shabby rooms.

"Don't worry," Shay said grimly. "I have something I'm sure the Wizard will like."

The Sixth Day of Festival—Elemental Day—dragged long for Shay. He'd spent two long days in the dark, each second whittling away at his already frayed nerves. Thunderstorms played in the east, but the city was spared, and as the sun set he left his hole just inside the Gate wall and moved toward the Serpent.

Stepping next door to the tavern, he found Lareo waiting for him in the alley. Flowers were strewn everywhere, sending up crushed fragrance underfoot.

"It's arranged," the Eldaryn assured him. "Did you find a suitable gift?"

"Oh, I think so." Shay shifted the long parcel he had strapped across his back. "Now how do I get there?"

"You'll find the entrance to the Weaver's lair under a loose paving stone by the great pillar on the left hand side, this end of the Baymourn bridge. Find the stone, follow the long stair down, and look for my marks on the floor of the cavern. If they're still there, they'll help you find your way in and out again quickly if—"

"If what?"

"If negotiations don't go well."

Shay snorted and reached for the heavy purse of gold at his belt.

Lareo looked insulted. "Help Xavier and the others if you can. Good night and good luck!" With that he turned and leapt sprite-like back into the tavern.

Shay set off for the bridge, listening to the sounds of the night. The most raucous part of the festival was over. Most of the revelers were spent, along with their money. All but the most incorrigible were asleep in their beds.

A scream rang out in the distance. A dog howled. An owl hooted mournfully as it glided in front of him, a struggling rat gripped in its cruel talons. *Not an auspicious start*, Shay thought, with a wry smile. At least the carvings on the stone walls had nothing to say on the matter this time.

Mist rose from the bay and wreathed the bridge in layers of undulating white. It formed in droplets on Shay's hair and bejeweled the shoulders of his coat. He went to the pillar Lareo had indicated and found the loose stone easily enough. Underneath were steep, damp, seemingly endless stairs leading down to the treacherous caverns that ran below the harbor and—according to Lareo—the Star Tower itself.

He lit the lantern Lareo had suggested and was soon glad of the advice. Down and down and down he went, every moment expecting to lose his footing, but reluctant to touch the glistening rough stone walls to steady himself.

Still further down, and the air grew thick with the stink of slime and the sea. He could already feel the oppression of water bearing down on him, fighting his own internal fire, driving a chill thorough him. The lantern's flame inside grew dimmer and smaller as he went and he muttered a curse at his namesake Saint.

Down and down and still down he went, while his skin grew cold and his joints ached and his head began to feel like it was stuffed with seaweed. The breath was tight in his chest when he finally reached the bottom. Rough ledge stretched away before him, though the lantern was too weak to help him guess the size or shape of the cavern.

Look for the marks, Lareo had warned him. They'll save you a good deal of time.

Casting around with the lantern, Shay finally discovered a trail of faint scratches wending off into the dark. Without them he might have wandered in the echoing darkness until he died.

There was no sense of time underground, only the wet and the chill and the suffocating knowledge that stone and sea lay overhead rather than the free sky. Shay struggled on for who knew how long before he saw a faint hint of light ahead of him. He increased his pace, coming at last to the opening of a large vaulted chamber filled with an eerie glow and unhealthy vapors. Far off, beside a glowing pool, stood the Weaver, intently waving a hand across the loom that hung in the air in front of—him? It? He unbuckled his baldric and propped his sheathed rapier against the stone wall, then entered the vault.

As he came closer, he could hear the Weaver humming a shapeless tune. The figure was dressed in a tattered, mildew-stained black-and-gold robe, with a deep hood hiding his face. Pale, wizened hands moved over the warp and woof of the fabric on the loom, sending a shuttle back and forth without actually touching it. Shay couldn't make out a pattern, as most of the cloth was wrapped around the lower roller, but it appeared to be very fine cloth. He wondered with an inward shudder what exactly those shining strands were made from. Other tapestries hung just outside the circle of light. Shay wanted very much to see what they depicted.

"Ah, here you are," said Weaver, turning his way. "The infamous Shay Gatewell. Named for the Saint of suffering, deceit, and lust. I smell the first two on you, but not the last. How curious."

Shay stood silent, not rising to the bait.

"Hmmm. The Eldaryn said you have a favor to ask," the Weaver continued. "Did he tell you there is always a price?

"He did, and this is my token." Shay pulled the long parcel free and unwrapped it to reveal the rapier concealed there. Rusty smears and smudges marred the mirror sheen of the steel blade. He held it out on upraised palms.

The Weaver grasped it by the hilt and turned it this way and that, studying it in the sickly glow of the pool. A snuffling sound came from the depths of the hood. "Your natural father's blood stains this, no?" He let out a dusty chuckle that sent a stab of ice up Shay's spine, and then let the blade fall with a clatter. "A token, you say? What for, exactly?"

"My soul."

The Weaver tilted his head, as if regarding him intently from the depths of the hood and Shay thought he caught the glimmer of a pale eye.

Another deathly chill ran through Shay, driving out what felt like the last of his native fire. His knees gave out and he found himself kneeling at the Weaver's feet. Was this what it felt like to be soulless? He'd been accused of it for years.

"And what is so precious to you that you would barter your stained and tattered soul for it?" the Weaver asked with another eerie chuckle.

"I have a question that needs answering," Shay gasped.

"Only that? How very intriguing. Ask away."

Shay considered his request very carefully as he took the golden bracelet from his pocket and held it up. "Tell me how to use this bracelet to free Xavier Crane and three others—alive—from the walls of the Silk Purse."

"Oh, well done!" the Weaver murmured mockingly as he leaned closer. "How appropriate your token is; a blade stained with the blood of the father you killed, to free the father you knew."

Shay started and the Wizard chuckled again, brushing his fingers over the finished cloth on the roller. "Oh yes, I know the tale. But what of these 'others'?"

"Three friends—they're family to me."

"And you thought to trick me with your oh so carefully worded question, did you?"

"I have no intention of tricking you. You allowed me one question and that—"

The Weaver stepped forward and grasped Shay by the hair, then dragged him to the edge of the pool with inexorable strength. "You aspire to deal in souls, do you?"

"Only my own!" Shay gasped as the Weaver yanked him further forward and shoved Shay's face down to within inches of the surface of the vile pool. Shay had no choice but to put his hands down to steady himself. Wrist deep in that pool, he nearly vomited as the water energy mingled with that of the sea crushing down on him from above. He focused desperately on the pain in his knuckles where he still grasped the bracelet.

The Weaver shook him like a rat. "Look deep, Shay Gatewell. See your future home."

Tormented faces surfaced like greedy fish, mouthing their agony up at him. Shay was so deathly cold now he could not imagine ever being warm again.

The Weaver pulled him back to the loom and let him fall on the greasy stone. "My price for what you ask is much higher than one pathetic young Duelist's soul."

"Anything," Shay growled, staring straight into the blackness of that hood.

"Good. You want to save four lives. You owe me three souls besides yours."

"I'll bring you three tonight. I have duels awaiting—"

"Not so fast. I want three particular souls. My choice, not yours."

Another wave of sickness gripped Shay as the faces of the precious few people he loved rose unbidden in his mind.

The Weaver let out an unpleasant sound. "My choice, young Shay."

"Who?"

"Not yet. I will claim your soul and the others when it pleases me to do so, not before. But take them I will—or rather, you will. You shall be my stalking bitch for as long as I require it." He kicked the stained rapier back to Shay. "Your service will be our collateral against the loan I make you tonight. I require the down payment of one soul against the three tonight, and for that I will answer your question."

"Who?" Shay whispered again, aghast at what he'd put in motion.

"As it happens, I require the soul of an infant that has not yet suckled at its mother's breast. And not some whore's get, abandoned on a midnight dung heap. A wanted child. A loved child. You may choose—this time."

"That's not a duel, it's murder!"

"That's right. Three murders. I'm seasoning your soul, you see. I want it black and crisp before I take it. This is the first step. Either you accept my terms, or the bargain's off." He paused. "They are suffering, you know: your beloved Xavier Crane and the others." The Weaver walked slowly back to his loom and stroked the shining threads as yet unwoven. "They are suffering worse than those you see in my pool. Imagine trying to breath with your ribs locked in stone. Imagine your tongue dry as mortar and your limbs crushed in the dirty grasp of elemental earth."

Oppressed as he was by water right now, Shay could imagine it all too easily.

"They should die, but they can't," the Weaver continued. "They'll be there like that—driven mad by their own voiceless screams—for all time . . . Unless you master that bracelet's magic. Tell me, Shay Gatewell, what will your dreams be like now?"

"I'll do it!" The words slipped over Shay's numbed tongue and chill lips before he could take them back.

"I thought you might." The Weaver plucked a long stray thread from the edge of the loom, then went to the pool and dipped it in the water four times. "Come here and hold out your right hand."

Shay staggered to him and the Weaver held up the dripping thread. "This is a loan, Shay Gatewell. Four souls in the thread to free your friends, to be repaid in kind at my command." He bound the wet thread tightly around Shay's wrist. It bit into his flesh like an assassin's garrote, and then sank below the skin, leaving a faint white scar in its place.

"Whose souls?" Shay said, staring down at the new line on his skin with dismay.

"Perhaps a pirate. Perhaps an innocent young virgin. There might even be someone you know in there now. And it's absolutely too late for you to complain. You just concentrate on the souls you'll provide to me." The Weaver reached out and traced a ragged nail down Shay's cheek four times, drawing blood. "This will be our tally board, one mark gone for each soul you take."

"And then you take mine?"

"So hasty! No, you will live your wretched life until I'm ready for you. But as I said, I require the soul of an innocent—before dawn breaks."

Shay stepped back unsteadily, knowing he'd been damned the moment he entered this cavern. "So be it. Now answer my question!"

The Weaver held out a wizened hand and Shay gave him the bracelet.

The Wizard rubbed his fingers over it for a moment, then handed it back. "Place the bracelet on your right wrist, just where the scar is, and invoke the Jaguar god Xolotl. Then touch the wall four times, giving the souls I just leant you to Itzli, the god of sacrifice."

Despite the horror of his situation, Shay's heart suddenly felt half a groat lighter. "Thank you, great Wizard. But how shall I deliver the soul to you?"

The Weaver pointed to the stained rapier. "Each of the three you owe must be killed with this blade, and the souls will fly to me. Use it for no other purpose. And do not try and fool me with some stranger's essence. I assure you, I will know the difference. Now get out."

Shay hastily retreated the way he'd come, pausing only to buckle on his other rapier and take up the flickering lantern. The cursed rapier weighed heavy in his hand, burning his fingers like ice. He cut a strip from his coat and bound it around the hilt, which helped just a little.

The journey out of the cavern was worse than the one in. Already exhausted, he fainted more than once and dreamed of killing Shayla, his mother, Bal…After a while he couldn't tell waking from dream; it was all one interwoven nightmare.

The stairs, when he finally reached them, might as well have been a mountain, and here fainting meant falling, as he soon discovered. The lantern was quickly lost; he clawed his way up in darkness.

Somehow he reached the top and heaved up the stone trapdoor, then gasped. The morning star was bright on the eastern horizon. He had less than two hours to accomplish his first task.

Or am I only dreaming the sky, while I lie dying somewhere below? With no choice but to trust his eyes, he set out for the house of the midwife who serviced the girls at the Silk Purse.

Discarded festival masks were scattered everywhere and he scooped up one at random; it was made of red and gold leather, with a long nose and sneering mouth.

Perhaps the Weaver had foreseen what Shay would do, or the luck of his dark Saint was with him; the midwife's husband sleepily directed Shay to a nearby house where she was overseeing a birth.

Shay made his way into a neighborhood of hovels and followed the sound a woman keening. At a small wooden shack he peered in between the shutters of the only window and saw a pregnant woman on a pallet in front of the fire, skirt rucked up and face contorted with sweat and pain. A white-haired woman knelt between her legs, urging her on. Shay's belly tightened as the ordeal went on and on and the morning star climbed inexorably into the brightening indigo vault of the sky.

At last the pauper's brat slid out in a rush of blood and muck. Shay threw the shutters open and climbed into the room. The young woman had fainted, but the midwife screamed enough for both of them before Shay silenced her with a blow. The squalling brat lay on the rags between its mother's splayed legs, helpless and bloody.

Shay stood over it, the cursed rapier in hand, and a wave of horror swept over him. He tore off the mask and wiped at his eyes with the back of his hand. A cracked mirror hung over the hearth; a murderer glared back at him, with four parallel scratches on his cheek.

For you, my friends and curse the Saints if you ever find out what I did.

The murder was simply done, easier than skewering an apple. Unnatural white fire rippled up the blade and Shay felt burning pain circle his right wrist, as if the hidden thread was cutting off his hand. Biting back a snarl of fear, Shay pulled the blade free and ran.

Another day passed into night as he lay beneath his cloak amid the upper gardens on the stadium's east end. Exhaustion like nothing he'd ever felt blanketed him and yet he dreamed fitful visions of blood and the wailing of babes. When he woke, the Blood Moon was up, the Ghost slipping south along the horizon and marking the turn of the day and the passing of the Festival for another year.

Shakily, he made his way back home, and Bal was waiting for him in the alleyway next to the Purse. Candlelight showed at every window.

"Thank the Saints!" he whispered, gripping Shay by the shoulders. "I was beginning to think you weren't coming back."

Shay shook off his friend's hands. "I'm here now."

"Did you learn what you needed to?"

"Oh, yes. Why is the house lit up?"

Bal chuckled softly. "You're not going to believe what I saw tonight! Just before midnight Rollin Shear kidnapped the Paladin and rolled her up in a carpet. Soon after, she was taken away by a bunch of sailors. Tohil the Sturgeon even helped, along with Coin."

Shay let out a choked laugh; more of the Weaver's work? Or his capricious Saint? "That certainly makes our job easier."

The main salon was crowded with courtesans in their night clothes and wine was being passed.

"Shay!" Pretty Will exclaimed, coming to embrace him.

Shay fended him off. "Everyone out of the Purse, now!"

Mama Serene swept down the stairs, khol and turquoise lidded eyes wide with surprise. "What are you talking about, Shay? We've had a tremendous commotion here tonight and I'm trying to get everyone settled."

"If they value their lives, they'll settle somewhere else," he gritted out. He felt unclean, unworthy of the smiles and questioning looks.

She paused, reading his face, then said, "Everyone, get out. Girls and boys, go across to the Emerald Serpent."

"What about upstairs?" he asked as the others hurried out the front door.

"I'll fetch them." She disappeared upstairs again, and a moment later the most unlikely collection of people came down: the maskmaker and a blind woman with long blue-green hair; Zhada the Lowl and his lover, both looking a bit worse for wear but happy; his pale twin, Shayla in her Hospitallers robe, and behind her, most unlikely of all, the Duelist Savino, half naked, oiled and jeweled like a whore.

Shay's disbelief must have been obvious, because Savino winked and said airly, "I'm here every first and fifth night if you're interested, darling."

"Not likely. Just get out," Shay snapped.

"Shay?" Shayla paused, giving him a worried look. Fair as he was dark, her cheeks were flushed, her golden curls escaping her headscarf. "What happened to your face?"

"I'll tell you later. Please, Shayla, help get the others away from here and make sure they don't come back until I've called them."

Shayla nodded and went out with the others.

Finally only Bal and Mama Serene were left.

"Bal, take Mama to the Serpent and keep everyone there until I come for you."

"Shay, what's all this about?" his mother demanded.

"You'll see, soon enough. Please, Mother. Go!"

Alone finally, Shay made a quick search of the house, and then the kitchen, making sure Ala and her scullions were gone. Returning to the salon, he took the bracelet from his pocket and slipped it around his right wrist, over the scar. First he went to the section of wall where Ingritrude was. "Xolotl, Jaguar god of old, I respectfully entreat you to release the people from these walls. Itzli, I offer you a soul in return to keep the balance."

A great shudder seized him, and the Weaver's icy hand seemed to squeeze his heart. White fire burst under his palm, burning his skin and scorching the wall under his hand. The painted plaster rippled, took on a woman's shape, and Ingritrude literally fell out of the wall and collapsed.

He knelt beside her and patted her cheek. "Ingritrude, wake up. You have to go."

Her eyelids fluttered for an instant, then her eyes fixed and he heard the death rattle in her throat. "No!" he hissed, pressing a finger to the pulse point in her neck. She was dead.

"You bastard," he growled. "You lying bastard of a wizard." Then the wretched truth struck him; he had specified that the people come out of the wall alive. He'd extracted no promise that they would stay that way.

Hoping against hope, he went to the X that marked Hammil and touched the wall. The white fire blazed again, searing his palm. Hammil appeared and fell to his knees, chest heaving. "Shay" he gasped out. "What happened? What's wrong with Ingritrude?"

"No time. Go, please. The others are at the Serpent."

Hammil stumbled out in a daze.

"One dead. One alive," Shay muttered as he approached the mark where tiny Lin was. "Even odds."

The white fire burned worse than ever this time, raising blisters the size of gold jaguar coins that burst and oozed. Lin fell from the wall into Shay's arms like a wilted flower. Her face was bloodless but she was breathing at least. Wracked with pain and nearly at the end of his strength, he carried her outside to find Bal keeping watch. He took Lin in his arms and Shay staggered back inside. One dead. Two living. One to go.

Please, Shay implored whatever Saints would listen. Blood and blister fluid dripped down his wrist as he pressed his burned hand to the wall. His fingers were bumpy and swollen as a toad's back.

"One more soul," he murmured. "Xolotl, Jaguar god of old—" The pain was overwhelming now, making it hard to remember the words. "I respectfully entreat you to—to release Xavier Crane from these walls. Itzli, I offer you a soul in return to keep the balance."

Pain ripped up his arm and blackness took him.

Shay came to with his head in someone's lap and his hand cased in fire, or so it felt. Leaning over him, Xavier Crane looked ten years older than he had a week ago, but he was smiling and his hand was steady around Shay's wrist. "Hold still, lad."

Shayla leaned into view. "A moment, brother," she murmured, finishing wrapping a bandage around his hand and wrist. The familiar scent of salve calmed him a little.

"There, now." She and Xavier helped him sit up and he saw his mother and Bal in the doorway.

Shay embraced Xavier, gripping the back of his old friend's jacket with his good hand. "Thank the Saints!"

"It wasn't the Saints who put me in the stone, or pulled me out again," Xavier said, holding him tight. "Thank you, lad. Thank you! Bal has told us most of it. You're a damn fool, and a brave one."

The words ravaged his bartered soul; if they only knew the truth. He summoned a shaky smile. "I had a good teacher."

Despite Shayla's skill as a healer, Shay's hand healed slowly. His fingers and palm were shiny and tight with scar tissue, and she warned that his fingers might never be as supple as they had been. He told no one, not even Bal, about the bargain he's struck or that the sound of an infant's cry curdled his stomach. He told no one that his secrets hung between him and Xavier, making every kind word from the man burn a little more of his heart.

The weeks passed and his hand healed. He took to wearing a fine kidskin glove, though Bal chided him for his vanity. The fact was that Shay couldn't stand the sight of the scars and what they represented. The three scratches on his cheek had healed to faint white scars that often itched. Of the fourth scratch, there was no sign. The Weaver's tally board, indeed.

He was tossing on his narrow bed one night when pain in his wrist woke him. It was the thread buried in his flesh, exerting its foul influence again. He sat up, holding his hand to his chest, and saw a tall dark shape standing in the corner of his room furthest from the moonlit window.

"It's time, my stalking bitch," an all too familiar voice whispered.

"How did you get in here?" Shay whispered, so as not to wake Bal in the next room.

"I'm not here. Are you ready to make me a payment? I shall set you an easy task this time."

"Who?"

"Just a whore of your choice—from the Silk Purse."

"They're my—" Shay pressed his lips tight around the word Family.

An oppressive thrumming filled the air, and the scar around his wrist throbbed. The Weaver's voice tickled in his ear insidiously as a swamp mosquito. "How is your dear mentor?"

Without a word, Shay rose and pulled back the loose floorboard that hid the bloody rapier.

Two souls to go.

AUTHORS

Lynn Flewelling grew up in northern Maine, United States, and has since lived on both coasts and traveled around the world, all experiences that are reflected in her writing. She has worked as a teacher, a house painter, a necropsy technician, and a free-lance editor and journalist. She has been married to Douglas Flewelling since 1981, and has two sons. She currently lives in Redlands, California, where she continues to write, and offers lectures and creative writing workshops at the University of Redlands. Her first Nightrunner novel, *Luck in the Shadows*, was a Locus Magazine Editor's Pick for Best First Novel and a finalist for the Compton Crook Award. Her novels *Traitor's Moon* (2000) and *Hidden Warrior* (2004) were both finalists for the Spectrum Award. Her novels are currently published in 13 countries, and in 2005, the first volume of the Japanese language version of *Luck in the Shadows* was published.

Todd Lockwood's illustration work has appeared on NY Times best-selling novels, magazines, video games, collectible card games, and fantasy role-playing games. It has been honored with multiple appearances in Spectrum and the Communication Arts Illustration Annual, and with numerous industry awards. Always known for the narrative power of his paintings, Todd now turns his hand to writing, and is working on a novel to be published by DAW Books at a date still to be determined. You may view his art at his website, http://www.toddlockwood.com.

Juliet E. McKenna is a British fantasy author. She studied Greek and Roman history and literature at St Hilda's College, Oxford. McKenna has written three series of books, *The Tales of Einarinn*, *The Aldabreshin Compass* and *The Chronicles of the Lescari Revolution*, as well as many short stories and articles. She is currently working on a new series, *The Hadrumal Crisis*.

Michael Tousignant is a part-time college student, part-time library clerk living in Monroe County, Michigan. He occasionally tries his hand at writing, and is holding off on trying to be clever in his biography until after he's had a few more stories published. Michael is also the super hero Iron Fist… oops, I guess I shouldn't have said that…

Martha Wells is the author of fourteen SF/F novels, including *The Element of Fire*, *The Wizard Hunters*, *Wheel of the Infinite*, *City of Bones*, and the Nebula-nominated *The Death of the Necromancer*. Most recent are *The Cloud Roads* (2011) and *The Serpent Sea* (2012) published by Night Shade Books. Forthcoming novels are *The Siren Depths* (December 2012, Night Shade) and a YA fantasy *Emilie and the Hollow World* (Strange Chemistry, May 2013) She has short stories in *Realms of Fantasy*, *Black Gate*, *Lone Star Stories*, and *Elemental*, and essays in *Farscape Forever*, *Mapping the World of Harry Potter*, and *Chicks Unravel Time*. She also has two *Stargate Atlantis* novels *Reliquary* and *Entanglement*. Her books have been published in seven languages.

Julie E. Czerneda, Canadian author and editor, has transformed her love and knowledge of biology into science fiction novels (published by DAW Books NY) and short stories that have received international acclaim, multiple awards, and best-selling status. Her latest works include the Aurora-nominated *Tesseracts Fifteen: A Case of Quite Curious Tales*, co-edited with Susan MacGregor, and *Rift in the Sky*, latest installment in her SF series, The Clan Chronicles. Coming March 2013 to bookstores everywhere is Book One of her new Night's Edge series, Julie's debut (and really fat) fantasy novel, *A Turn of Light*. There are toads. Writing for *Tales* has been a wonderful experience. For more about Julie's work, please visit www.czerneda.com.

Scott Taylor is a horrible writer. When 'they' say you make it because you never give up, not because of overall talent, they are talking about Scott. In fact, he wasn't even supposed to appear in this anthology but was forced to activate his Microsoft Word program when other signed authors dropped out at the last minute. He currently runs the micro-publishing house Art of the Genre and produces art inspired 1980s throw-back novels like *The Burning City*, *The Gun Kingdoms*, and *The Cursed Legion*. Obviously, he also has a penchant for sticking 'the' at the beginning of all his titles.

Rob Mancebo helped build an orphanage in Mexico, stood watch on the cold war era border in Europe, put-down riots, toured in Ireland, installed and repaired all sorts of security hardware, delivered classified material, chased down thieves, and has helped the authorities put many very bad people in jail. He's read slush and edited books, sold guns and been a range officer. He currently assists the sick and injured in an urgent care facility and in his spare time writes the fantasy and adventure stories which have been featured in numerous magazines and anthologies.

Dave Gross is a writer and recovering editor. He's the author of the Radovan & the Count novels, including *Prince of Wolves*, *Master of Devils*, *Queen of Thorns*, *King of Chaos*, and the upcoming *Lord of Runes*. His other novels include works set in the Forgotten Realms and the Iron Kingdoms. His short fiction includes stories in *Shotguns vs. Cthulhu*, *By Faerie Light*, and the upcoming *Shattered Shields*. He lives in Alberta, Canada, with his fabulous wife and their tolerable critters.

Elaine Cunningham is a *New York Times* bestselling fantasy author whose publications include over 20 novels and three dozen short stories. Most of her novels are set in licensed worlds such as the Forgotten Realms, Star Wars, EverQuest, and Pathfinder Tales. *Shadows in the Starlight*, the second book in her urban fantasy series Changeling Detective, was included in the 2008 *Kirkus* list of 10 Best Sci-Fi Novels. Her short fiction explores most of fantasy's sub genres, from Arthurian fiction to sword & sorcery to cyberpunk. Folklore and mythology provide inspiration for many of her tales; "The Fairest Flower" grew from Mabinogion seed. For more information, please visit Elaine's author website, www.elainecunningham.com.

Howard V. Tayler is the award-winning creator of the webcomic *Schlock Mercenary*. He worked as a volunteer missionary for the LDS Church, then graduated from Brigham Young University. Schlock Mercenary has been nominated multiple times and won the Web Cartoonists' Choice Awards in two different categories. Schlock has also been nominated four times for a Hugo Award. Tayler spends time regularly during the week drawing at a local comic book and gaming store, as well as producing a weekly writing tips podcast called *Writing Excuses* with fellow authors Brandon Sanderson, Dan Wells, Mary

Robinette Kowal, and producer Jordan Sanderson. The podcast has been nominated for a Hugo Award in 2011, 2012 and has won in 2013.

Dan Wells is best known as the author of *I Am Not a Serial Killer*, a horror novel published in the United States by Tor Books. It has been released in the United Kingdom, Australia, Germany, and Taiwan. He also is one of the four authors (including Mary Robinette Kowal, Brandon Sanderson, and Howard Tayler) who contribute to the podcast *Writing Excuses*.

In 2011, Wells was nominated for the John W. Campbell Award for Best New Writer. His novella, *The Butcher of Khardov*, received a nomination for the Hugo Award for Best Novella in 2014.

CHARACTER DESCRIPTIONS

© JANET AULISIO 2013.

ZHADA

Zhada is a Lowl at ease with his dual nature. He honors the divine power that blended superior canine senses with Humankind's abilities to walk upright and hold weapons and tools. Following in his father and grandfather's footsteps, he's quietly determined to be a trail-blazer; to rise in Taux society through his own merits and honorably-earned wealth until no one can gainsay his right to marry the Human woman he loves.

Bold when action is called for, he generally prefers to achieve his aims through negotiation and co-operation. Only a fool would assume his usual calm manner indicates a coward though. Physically strong and a skilled swordsman as well as a capable hunter, he sees no reason to yield to bullies or threats. He won't stand to see his more vulnerable kinfolk abused or exploited either, especially by deceitful tome mages offering 'cures' to turn Lowl fully Human. On the other side of that coin, he has no patience with those Lowl who boast of their bestial nature, denying their own Humanity.

With elemental fire woven into Lowl nature, he can use a little low magic for everyday cantrips. He is very wary of high wizardry's far more perilous powers.

CENOTE

Before coming to Taux to live as a humble maskmaker's assist, her face ever-masked, Cenote had been a powerful Wizard. She'd lived in the Star Tower, her task and talent to use water as a lens to watch for danger as well as wonders. Her magic let her touch the Afterglow and use its power. She was a teacher, a lover, one among many and safe.

Until the day came when she saw too much and too clearly. When disaster struck Taux, only Cenote saw the face behind it. Only she cried out in warning. And when the time came for that evil to rise again, its first act was to blind her forever.

Cut off from the Afterglow, no longer a Wizard, believed dead and lost by her kin, Cenote has found a way to keep her watch. Through the eyes of friends, through her own water magic, and, most of all, through her heart. She will find her nemesis. She will refuse its evil any foothold or gain. Regardless of the cost, ever in secret, she will fight where other Wizards cannot. Within the Black Gate.

TORRENT

Torrent is a Corsair, the sea-going, very Human-looking peoples attuned to a low affinity for elemental water. She has thick, wavy dark hair and dark eyes, and a heart-shaped face. Her hair is usually contained in some way, either in a bandana or tied back in a pony with the same bandana. Not tall—about 5'4", but with a lithe, athletic

build and fluid, cat-like grace. She ordinarily wears breeches, soft, calf-high leather boots, a shirt with loose sleeves (allowing for ease of movement) and a leather vest or sleeveless doublet. She wears her sword on her left hip.

Torrent has a quick temper, but is introspective and wary. She thinks and acts quickly, occasionally with unfortunate haste. She has the rare ability to manipulate water in small volumes, in various ways. Most notably, she can attune herself to the flow of liquids in a person or animal she has touched and cause cramps; heart palpitations; blinding migraines; a sudden need or inability to eliminate body wastes; sweats; or spontaneous orgasm—or failure of same. She used some—but not all—of those abilities in the past at different times, in different ways, in order to keep herself fed and safe. She used to run scams with Savino, and isn't above cheating people out of money.

She has been a Jill-of-many-trades, none of them crafts, unless slicing people with a deadly, slender curved sword is a craft. She's not a duelist, and would never willingly enter into a duel herself. She doesn't like rules. She was most comfortable as a hired sword on the ships of various merchant fleets, where she was also an adept sailor, but has found herself stranded in Taux.

DETHOCRATES

Most citizens of Taux don't think of Jai-Ruk as unobtrusive; they think of them as dull, or brutish. This is how Dethocrates prefers things, as underestimation makes his job easier. Dethocrates – or Dethoc, or Deth, or occasionally 'Thock' – spends his evenings earning money in illegal pursuits, mainly burglary, smuggling, or swindling. He's rarely the mastermind behind a scheme, but he's able to find a way to pull it off.

© JANETAULISIO 2013.

As an archer, Dethoc prefers to be methodical on the job; he likes to find a secluded 'perch' from which he can keep an eye on things, and when the 'perfect shot' appears, to strike.   Of course, in a city like Taux, there are few perfect shots, and Dethoc spends much of his time improvising when a plan falls apart.

Dethocrates sailed into Taux a decade ago, and immediately made his home within the busy streets of the Black Gate. He's fairly quiet about his earlier life; he'll mention on occasion an Aspara who taught him archery, and when drunk enough he'll hurl curses at the Wounded Land, but apart from that, he keeps his past in the past, and considers Taux to be the only place that matters.

SAVINO EMANTRA

Born in the mountain passes of Mistfin, Savino Emantra is a Korys, a product of low affinity for elemental air. This makes him both long-lived and a man of constant movement, be it from lover, city, or job. At his core, his is a charlatan, a man who understands all that he isn't, and yet strives to be so much better than he is, even if it is a grand deception.

His greatest fear is that at some point his house of cards will come crumbling down around him, but to this point he's managed to keep himself just above water, and his time in Taux has been both lucrative and dangerous, a combination that keeps him occupied enough to stay in the city as his wanderlust is always pressing him to move on.

Handsome to a fault, and trained to be a stage actor, he uses these skills to his advantage on any number of scheme he devises to gain money in a way that requires the least effort or reflection of an actual honest day's work. Toiling away at the same thing every day is anathema to Savino, and he's always looking for the next score, the next conquest, and the next move.

TOHIL

Tohil is a man of the Opal Gates, and relocated to Taux where his skill at hunting other men and work with a blade earned him the blue overcoat of a Sturgeon, the mercenary police arm of the city. Having spent years patrolling the streets, he was eventually drawn to the Black Gate, where he found friends among the people there.

One of the few Sturgeons who will venture inside the Black Gate alone, he is a known frequenter of the Silk Purse where the greatest percentage of his weekly pay goes without question.

Heavily tattooed with raised 'scar' markings, his face and arms have become an unforgettable site to behold, and his dark skin marks him as a foreigner even among the immigrants of the city. Still, although he may appear fierce, inside his large chest beats the heart of a man ready to defend the city he has come to love with his life.

JELITH

Jelith was born in the kin city of Madrean, far to the north among along the fringes of Gariny. There, when he came of age he was cast out by his Kin Sire, as all young male Kin are, to fend for themselves in the wild. Instead of staying in the mountain passes, he drifted south through Lowl lands and eventually settled in Taux.

He was small in stature and always preferred stories and scholarly pursuits to anything else, and so not considered to have much potential by his pride. But as he grew older, he became highly skilled at shaping stone. He knew this skill might have secured him a place inside his pride, perhaps even with a mate, but he decided not to return to his people or his Thane. He has journeyed through various cities, supporting himself as a stonemason, while looking for scholars and centers of learning where he could feed his growing passion for knowledge of the past.

The mystery of Taux drew him to the city, where he met his Jai-Ruk partner Kryranen. Together, the duo has made a name for themselves as experience pot hunters inside the Black Gate.

SHAY

© JANET AULISIO 2013.

Is a twenty-four year old master duelist, aka Long Shay, Cold Shay, the Dark Angel of Death, and—to those who raised him— Cricket. Named at birth for St. Shay because of his dark-eyed beauty and circumstances of his birth, Shay and his first born twin sister Shayla are the children of Mama Serene, madam of the Silk Purse, and Esmer Serata, second in command of the Taux Razor Duelist Guild.

Shay is a stunning beauty, inspiring all the lust, deceit, and suffering of his namesake saint. Tall and slender, with soft, dark brown hair, dark brown eyes, smooth tanned skin the color of milk-slaked coffee, and the face of a stern young angel, Shay draws the eye of man and woman alike, and many unwanted advances. But Shay's heart is cold, and the chip on his shoulder is the size of the Gate itself.

Shay's heart is scarred and closed. He grew up petted and spoiled by his mother's people (some of whom still embarrass him by calling him by his childhood nickname, Cricket), and considered them as older brothers and sisters. Most he meets, given his looks and upbringing, assume he's a randy sex god, but the truth is, he's sealed that part of himself off. The only two people he is truly open with are his mother, whom he adores and resents in equal measure, and his twin, whom he worships almost to the point of incest. Both mother and sister despair of him and the path he's chosen.

ATZI

A woman of Tolmic blood, Atzi came to Taux with her husband who sought solid work in the home of their ancestors. She begged him not to come to the place, but he insisted. Once in the city, the couple settled down and managed a decent life, one that even provided them with a daughter.

When Atzi's daughter was lost to the darkness of the city, it drove both her and her husband to abandon all else to find her, but when her husband didn't return one night either Atzi's only choice of companions was madness or alcohol. She chose the latter and her life has been a blur ever since.

TIMAR DHARN

The youngest member of the prominent Dharn Merchant House, Timar is a man of medicine and a devotee to Saint Shera. Knowing he would never inherit his family's business interests, Timar joined the Hospitaler's Guild at an early age, and was encouraged to do so by his father to 'get him away from the home.'

Once his devotion of Saint Shera became clear, he learned her binding and healing magic and move to the abandoned Hospitaler's Clinic inside the Black Gate. There, along with the help of fellow Hospitaler Shayla Gatewell, he became a man of great import as the locals desperately needed those with his skills.

His life would change forever two years ago when his eldest brother was lost at sea and his next oldest brother died in a duel on the bridges of Taux. A month later his father, already in failing health, passed and left all of the Dharn fortune to his sole remaining heir, as well as a coveted seat on the Red Pillar Council. Since that time, Timar has been trying to juggle both his worlds, but that seems much harder than he'd ever suspected.

KALOMIR BOUCHTAT

Kalomir Bouchtat is the famed seven-deathed lich lord of the Nightmare Army. He is a fallen Aspara tome mage who raised an army of the dead in the Black Sands and pillaged most of the Nublar Empire before finally fading into oblivion with his once proud army.

Unknown to the world, he was 'cursed' with a holy blade that allows him to live only if he destroys creatures of undeath. The blade is called Tezcatlecuhtli, the slayer of death, and was said to be the most powerful artifact of the ancient Tolimic Empire.

© JANET AULISIO 2013.

Now Kalomir is forced to live a life that opposes everything he's every believed, while always searching for a way to free himself from the magic of the holy sword.

JONTHREL COLLISH

Jonthrel is a man of distant Zimbolay, a tome-mage and collector of trinkets and old grudges. He has recently come to Taux in an attempt to settle and old debt and found that the Vash family was eager to use his services with magic.

He has spent the better part of his years discovering the secrets of Afterglow essence and material links in items, his specialty designing long distance attacks un unaware foes. Although mercenary in nature, he has a strong

© JANET AULISIO 2013.

sense of self and understands that the world is a place where one leaves his mark, sometimes irrevocably.

What his days in Taux will mean now that he is here, or how long they will last is unknown, but he is anxious to see what secrets the ancient city holds beyond the whispering of its dark stone.

THE CITY OF TAUX

TAUX

1. SERPENT WALL DISTRICT, 2. THE BLACK GATE DISTRICT,
3. GOLD JAGUAR DISTRICT, 4. SMOKE DRAGON DISTRICT
5. TURQUOISE TURTLE DISTRICT, 6. HARBOR DISTRICT,
7. HAUNTED TEMPLE DISTRICT, 8. STAR TOWER

JAL 13

THE CITY OF TAUX

*F*ormerly the Tolimic City of Taux, this stand alone metropolis rests at the tip of the Free Coast and once served as a way station between a dozen large nations all over the northern Halo Ocean. More than half a century before the current date, during the final days of the *Five Year War* that banished all the old gods from the world, the population of the city was destroyed by a necromantic surge of energy. The tale of that destruction is as follows:

> *Near a century ago in the Nameless Realms timeline a council of Moon Priests and a coven of Tome-Mages theorized that like the Afterglow Sea that resides beyond the Elemental Plane of Water, there should be another plane of existence behind each of the known Elemental Planes [Fire, Water, Earth, Air, Positive Radiance, and Negative Shadow]. Because Taux sat so close to the 'Ebon Swamp' which is known to bubble up with Negative Elemental energy, they decided to dedicate a portion of their resources to discovering this 'other plane' from the secret subterranean conduits in Taux. Years passed, and the two Orders built a series of tunnels beneath the surface of Taux that could be used as a kind of elemental broadcasting station. Then, on a night corresponding with the closest proximity of the Negative Elemental Plane to the planetary sphere, they broke into a huge magical ceremony that would 'ping' beyond the Negative Elemental Plane, hoping to find another source of raw magical power there. The theory was that some reverb would come back that proved its existence and they could use that for further contact. Nine hours after the magical ping, just as the city woke in the predawn gloom for work, a nightmare scream struck the city with an apocalyptic wave. Every living thing within a hundred miles was obliterated; all souls flash-burned into the stone of the landscape around it. Since that day the city and surrounding lands have been quiet, but the souls still remember, now trapped forever in the walls of their cursed city...*

Today, Taux is once again a thriving port city, although instead of Tolimic Humans, it is populated from many cultures all over the Halo and beyond, each trying to make a profit on the mass of cargo that moves through the free city without taxation. Although still haunted by the spirits of the past, the current inhabitants try to quiet the stone and live with strange whispers at night or the sounds of cries from rooms no one is currently in.

City Size: Population: 60,000+ [15% are non-Human]

Districts:

Black Gate District: The Ullamalitzli Stadium that once housed 75,000 fans and is now home to perhaps 7,000 squatters who have built tenements in the stadium proper.

Gold Jaguar District: The high class district cut by the prestigious Ruby Lane. Here is where the very wealthy of Taux live and play in the former homes of the greatest nobility the Tolimic every possessed.

Turquoise Tortoise District: A middle to upper class merchant district of the city and home to the Grand Bazaar of Taux.

Harbor District: The port, docks, and wharfs of Taux. Here is the lifeblood of the city, the place where all cultures meet as ships from the entire Halo Ocean trade cargo for shipment all over the world.

The Haunted Temple District [Ghost Towers]: This little populated district is the home to the poor of Taux. With no place else to go, the destitute gather among the screaming stones of the former Tolimic Temple District.

Serpent Wall District: Situated against the outer wall of the city, and thus wrapping it in a large crescent, this outer district is home to the mass of the middle to lower working class of Taux.

Ebon Fields District: Located outside the main wall of the city, this tangled group of farmland is the only true source of local food Taux possesses. Farmer and cattle-folk work to stave off incursion from the Ebon Swamp as they cling to a meager existence among the lowland marshes that now serve as livestock fields and in some areas rice patties.

The Smoke Dragon District: This district is the home of the base production elements of Taux with some industry having sprung up to use cheap raw materials taken from incoming trade ships and turning them into more expensive trade goods to be shipped out. It is also the home of the Sturgeon Keep, where the mercenary army of the city is housed.

RACES

*A*ll races in the world are bound to an elemental spark, that binding element influencing their nature and depending on your affinity [subtle/medium/high] you can also have the power to wield that element in some form. This affinity doesn't necessarily mean an Eldaryn [High Fire] can set a street aflame with a twitch of his nose, but if he's a Tome-Mage Pyromancer his spark's power would be additionally lethal. Examples of elemental manifestation might be that Aspara [High Air] seem to having a phantom breeze blow through their hair when they're thinking hard, or when a Human [Subtle Fire] gets mad the temperature around him goes up a couple of degrees.

Writers gathered together to tell a tale of a single race born into the world, the Byrin, that all races, once touched by the elemental link to the gods, evolved from as they slowly formed to the will of the element of their deity. In this fashion, all the sentient races of the world developed.

Aspara: [High Affinity Air] 6 to 6½ feet in height. These are rather ethereal looking Humans with a personality that can change as quickly as the breeze. The opposite of the Kin in most ways, the Aspara are known to be flighty, pulled in various directions, and hard to negotiate long-term contracts with. They live free lives, rarely settling down for more than a few years at a time, and tend to shun most other races in an almost xenophobic way. In the Opal Gates, Hilani Plains, or Zimbolay, the Aspara are a chocolate-skinned and ebon-haired with sapphire blue eyes. They are a mystical people who travel the savannah and disappear from the site of Humans when pressed. They are immortal creatures, age never touching them, and so they have no need for haste unless provoked. As they are inherently detached, marriage is almost unheard of among their people, and children are scarce because mothers hate being tied down to their offspring for any length of time. Some in the world see the Aspara as inherently uncaring, but that isn't the case. They can be both passionate and heartfelt if the mood strikes them, and are capable of beautiful crafts that might take decades to finish, assuming the items the craft can be carried with them as they travel.

Farian: [Medium Affinity Air] 6 to 6½ feet height. Often thought to be the product of Aspara and Korys mating, the Farian race is an incredibly long-lived and secretive one. They tend to stay removed from society much like their Aspara cousins, but instead of living in the windswept plains of the world, they are people of the high mountain. In the heights of the world, the Farians dwell among the cliffs and snow as close to the heavens as they can reach. These air-born are sky sailors, builders of winged craft, and tethers of the mighty wind. They are fair-skinned and blond-haired with eyes as blue as the open sky. They live at such heights that most Humans can't climb to their lofty eyries. Farians tend to be more 'settled' than Aspara and congregate seasonally for trade and ritual feasts before heading back to solo dwellings along the cliffs.

Korys: [Subtle Affinity Air] 6 feet. Unmistakable from Humans, the Korys are often flighty, rarely bound to a single local, and yet possess an increased lifespan that's keeps them looking young for up to three hundred years. They are very few in number, mostly because they don't congregate as a unified race, instead flitting away with the wind and often having progeny with Humans or Corsairs rather than seek out other Korys who they typically find impossible to deal with because they can never agree on any one thing for long.

Kin: [High Affinity Earth] 4½ to 5 feet height. They are a hard race, intractable and fierce, but are also master builders and shape stone with deft hands. Sometimes this race lives within mountains, but their greatest creations come from shaping cities from stone on the surface, molding it in the passing of years. This unique connection with the earth

plays out in the nature of the Kin's coloring. Whatever natural stone they are around 'bleeds' into the Kin's pigmentation, and like a Flamingo turns pink eating pink shrimp, the Kin take on the aspect of the stone in which they live. In this fashion they marbleize, sometimes looking to have metallic veins running through the rich tones of their flesh.

They are small in stature compared to Humanity, averaging no more than five feet in height. This smaller size helps them navigate natural passages in the earth, and it is often whispered among other races that Kin can actually pass through stone, although this is unproven. The Kin also have very limited eyesight, and direct sunlight is a constant irritation. In standard daylight they wear masks or eyeshades. Under the ground, the Kin can go without any light and use echolocation to sense where they are, large ears helping to capture the sound of their incessant clicking when they travel.

No Kin have hair anywhere on their bodies, but Female Kin are known to decorate their heads with specially cultivated moss, fungus, or grass to make a kind of hair-like crown.

Jai-Ruk: [Medium Affinity Earth] 6 to 7 foot in height. They are something like the civilization's definition of brutes, tan-skinned, dark haired, and yet more muscular and square-jawed than most Humans would look. They also have slightly enlarged lower canine teeth that might just peak out of their lips on occasion. Again, otherwise they are pretty close to Humans in appearance. Jai-Ruks are large, sometimes standing as tall as seven feet, and broad at the shoulder. They are heavily muscled, but not so much it distorts their body shape, as their true strength comes from their association with the Earth. Their skin tends toward grey hues, and their hair is usually dark although some have been known to have coppery hair and their eyes are deep brown and flecked with gold or silver.

Loam: [Subtle Affinity Earth: 6 feet in height. Some say that the Loam are the product of Human and Jai-Ruk mating, but that is unproven. It is more likely that rogue bands of Humanity that settled far in the mountains or grew tied to the earth as farmers shed their fire spark for that of a subtle earth affinity. However, there are known to be more Loam in the nation of Aflyr than any other, and it boards on the Broken Land, a nation populated almost exclusively by Jai-Ruks and their Delver servants. Whatever the case, Loam are a sturdy hill folk, a people bound to the earth and steadfast in its defense.

Delver: [Subtle Affinity Earth]: This cursed race was once Human-like as well, but was corrupted by Arcxas, the God of Night. They have become a harsh barbaric race, sloped at the neck, and beast-like in their face. They live in loose bands away from most civilizations until they are roused by a leader who seeks plunder among local populations of other races.

Eldaryn: [High Affinity Fire] 3 ½ to 4 feet. This small race is bound to the pure fire and always has red hair sometimes touched with blue on the tips. As they age, and they age quickly, their hair can turn to yellow, orange, and sometimes copper, especially with facial hair. They are known as tricksters, merchants, and sometimes pyromancers, and they are considered attractive little fellows by most other races. They live fast lives, and have a standard lifespan of no

more than 60 years at the most, with the bulk living less than 50. The fire of this race burns so bright that when angry they can be extremely dangerous, especially if they are in possession of 'Eldaryn Powder'. This explosive has been harnessed by the race in what they sometimes call 'Dragon Wands'. It is basically a flintlock pistol without the need of hammer or flint. Eldaryn can ignite the power simply by using their spark which makes the weapon completely attuned to them. It has been said that properly trained Lowl, and sometimes even Humans, are capable of setting off Dragon Wands, but this is unproven. Males are known for loving to have coppery-colored mustaches which they take great pride in, and females are notorious flirts who are said to have the ability to shape-shift for limited amounts of time. Many are the tales of Humans seduced by a lovely female of their own race only to awake the next morning in bed with a diminutive female Eldaryn.

Lowl: [Medium Affinity Fire] 6½ feet in height. These 'Dog-headed' Humans are one of the most 'odd' of races of the Nameless Realms next to the reptilian Candon. The Lowl can be quick to anger, and use their element to their advantage as it can fuel a powerful strength common to the species. They are known to be valuable mercenaries, and have a highly attuned sense of smell and a keen sense of hearing. In their own communities, they tend to run in tribal packs, but in Human society, they adapt quickly and are more respected in common company than Jai-Ruks.

Human: [Subtle Affinity Fire] Much like we are Humanity in our own world, save that they have a simple affinity with fire which manifests as increased temperature when they are excited in some fashion. By far the largest contingent of the Nameless Realms population, the Human race consists of more than 60% of all sentient souls in the world. Their patron of creation has long been the Sun, and although old world deities no longer hold power in the Taux and much of the rest of the world, Humanity's spark is still tied to the rising and falling of the sun.

Wizard: [High Affinity Water] Usually above 6 and a half feet in height. Human-like in most cases, although bound completely to the plane of water, they tend to 'flow' as they move about, having long hair and wearing clothing that resembles the ocean waves [mostly robes]. They are high sorcerers, their elemental plane bound closely to the Afterglow Sea of magic where they draw their power. Tall and proud, this race is sometimes considered dour, often harsh, and certainly foreboding, but like the depth of their element, there is more below the surface than can ever be perceived. They tend toward dark hair, sometimes touched with green or even more rarely violet, and their eyes are like polished emeralds. Their skin is pale *like a pristine cloud unless* they are emotional when violet and blue washes along cheekbones, or sets into the tips of their fingers. Power flows through them, not from the water that is inherently theirs, but instead from the connection that water brings pure raw energy of the Afterglow. For this reason and powerful connection, the race of High Water are referred to as Wizards.

Wizards are more artists than sorcerers, the true power inside them tied to their ability to visualize and 'paint' pictures with the *Afterglow* energy they siphon through the plane of water and into the mundane world. Certainly, there is no doubt they are powerful, but to master what they do takes countless years of exercise and dedication to their craft. Like a master of oil painting, there are too few Michelangelos or Da Vincis in the world, and so too is it with Wizards.

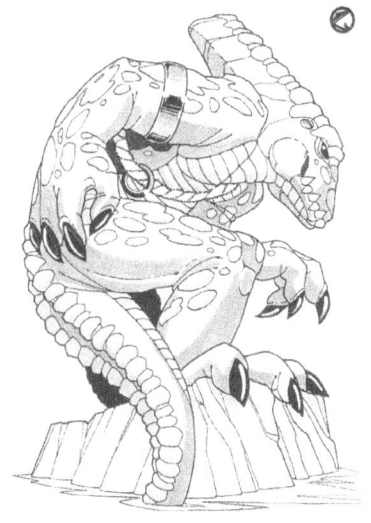

Candon: [Medium Affinity Water] 5+ foot tall 'Lizardmen' with Alien-like heads, scales, and all that. They have long ago moved into swamps, marshes, and secluded rivers where their medium water affinity makes them hard to pursue or fight. They don't hold a dedicated connection with *Afterglow*, having never studied it like Wizards, but sometimes shaman in the culture to have a way with magic not seen in other races.

Corsair: [Subtle Affinity Water] Roughly 6 feet in height. These are standard 'water humans'. Corsairs wouldn't be picked out from a crowd of Humans, although they do sometimes become lesser tome mages, and thus have power that isn't seen in most races. They are bound to the sea, most never leaving the coasts, and make fine sailors.

RELIGION

There are six 'High Saints' that comprise the worshipped pantheon of the Taux settlers from the New Kingdoms across the Shining Sea to the west and over the full Halo Ocean to Dragmarsh in the east. Their power and influence has all but overwhelmed the ancient temples of the previous inhabitants who had elemental gods like sun, moon, stars, sky, etc…

All of these Saints were actual living people in the Realms and were raised to the level of 'sainthood' by the will of world cultures desperately looking for something to follow in the wake of the Five Year War and the banishment of the Old Gods from the world.

Saint Siegfried the Brave, Patron of Knights, Warriors, and the Just. Siegfried was a fabled Knight of Gariny who renounced his claim to the Ducal Throne of the nation so that he could pursue a life of unencumbered justice against all evil that still walked the world once the Five Year War ended. His deeds quickly became legend, and soon, people were praying to him for guidance which elevated him to the role of saint.

Saint Erik of the Thousand Faces, Parton of Rogues, Charlatans, and Gamblers. Erik was the leader of the rebel armies that allied against the tyranny of his brother Gorwin, King of Thalonia, as he tried to take over the globe under a single unified banner. He was a known thief and womanizer, many saying he stole his first crown in the Old Kingdoms by committing regicide. Still, when the world needed a hero, he answered the call before he was finally killed during the Battle of the Realms Gate that helped seal the world off from the Old Gods. However, some whispered that he hadn't died, but once again taken on a new form, and so the rumors of his rise from the ashes helped him gain sainthood.

Saint Shera of the Happy Hall, Parton of Hearth and Home, Travelers, and Lovers. Shera is the counterbalance to Erik, and many say the two were lovers before the Five Year War, and even more tell tales that Erik came back from the dead to find his love once more. One thing is clear, Shera was once the owner of the infamous Emerald Serpent Inn that lies at the heart of the Black Gate in Taux and was one of the first to enter the city after its fateful apocalypse. Her service was legendary, and it is said she was instrumental in the final victory of the Five Year War.

Saint Amanda of Virgins, Parton of Nobility, Good, Healers, and Radiant Light. Sister to Erik and Gorwin, she was the only relation that could claim the throne of the new World Empire once the two brothers were lost in the Battle of the Realms Gate. She was the first World Empress, and was beyond reproach as she never took a husband and was known as the Virgin Empress until the day of her assent into the ranks of sainthood.

Saint Shay of the Dark Beauty, Parton of Lust, Deceit, and Suffering. Birthed from the fabled Burning City, Saint Shay was once a Human woman like any other, but after confinement in that cursed otherworld she emerged something entirely different. Taking up the mantel of suffering that swept the world in the aftermath of the first great plagues once the Old Gods were lost, Shay plied her dark talents to any who would listen until word of her power spread over the world and she took on the form of a saint of darkness.

Saint Colin of the Flaming Blade, Patron of Warriors, Doom, and Battle. Many are the tales of Saint Colin, some say that he is the son of Saint Erik, and that he followed his love into the Burning City of his own volition, only to return again as an avenging blade of destruction. He is also claimed by the Jai-Ruk's of the both the Wounded and Broken Land as a patron of battle, and their legends tell that he is one of their race, a friend to the elemental earth, and that his power comes from the heart of their people. Whatever the truth, it is known he is a consort of the Saint Shay, and that the two are said to be seen in the aftermath of great wars or terrible disasters, either as collectors of souls or specters feeding off the flesh of the dead.

MAGIC

Magic in the Nameless Realms, and therefore in Taux can be a confusing thing. In essence, there are two distinct kinds of magic in the world, Faith-Born Miracles delivered by the Old Gods or even the new Saints which is sometimes 'perceived' magic and certainly far from potent, and Afterglow magic, which is the more functional type employed by Wizards and to a lesser degree Tome-Mages.

Faith-Born Miracles: These are gifts and blessings of the Gods and Saints. They manifest inside people of faith, typically priests, prophets, or hospitalers, and produce effects that might sway the outcome of a game of chance, heal minor injury, or ease the suffering of a troubled mind. They are rarely dramatic, and should be perceived as a very passive type of magic.

Afterglow Magic: There are six known Elemental Planes, a dozen Para-Elemental Planes, and of course the Planar Archipelago where the Old Gods dwell, but none of these directly accounts for magic in its purest form. Long ago, Wizards, being of the High Water, found that if they delved deeply enough into their element, they could piece the membrane of the Elemental Plane of Water and connect another yet unknown plane of existence, something they called the Afterglow Sea. This veritable ocean of raw energy was a place where they slowly learned to draw power from, shaping the 'magic' of its essence like an artist moves paint on a canvas Afterglow, therefore, has nothing to do with Elemental Water, it simply exists on the far side of that plane. Because of this, only Wizards have direct access to it, all other races too far removed from the connection needed to penetrate the Elemental membrane. This Afterglow magic is hard to control, and deadly in the extreme, but as a master artist can make masterworks with a brush, so can a Wizard wield terrible power with his will. Wizards don't need spell-books or such simple trappings to play with Afterglow, but there are others who have learned to siphon Afterglow and store it, typically in items or foci, for later use. These magical practitioners are called Tome Mages and they can manipulate Afterglow with elaborate storage foci and intricate spell formulas. To a Wizard, such people are simple charlatans, but to the general populace they are powerful and dedicated individuals who are to be taken seriously. Also, it has been documented by Tome Mages that Afterglow can often 'bleed' into this world through the elemental connection of all things. In this fashion, common items can sometimes 'become' magical foci just because of the situations in which they are used. This effect is called 'imprinting', and many fabled magical relics are known to exist simply from this connection and not from the forging of Wizards.

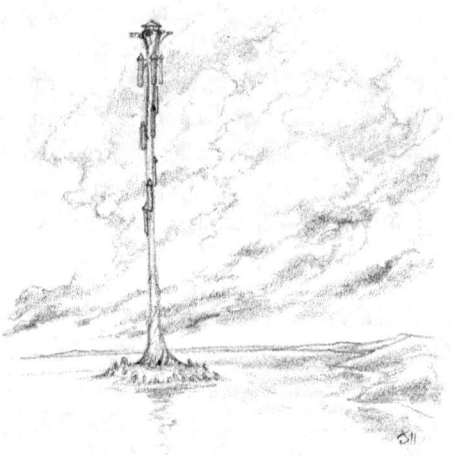

The Star Tower: The race of Wizards is a breed apart, and even though a coven of them [known as the Order of Towers] are housed within the harbor of Taux, they're secluded on a magnificent 'Star Tower' that dominates a central harbor of the city, and looks much like a larger version of Rapunzel's tower, the middle becoming precariously thin while the top houses seven massive towers that hang off the central spire. People of Taux often see the top of this structure shrouded in mist, and that mist is known to populate the city streets on nights when the Ghost and Blood Moons are full. It is said that the water magic of the Star Tower keeps the harbor clean and fresh, as well as the city's canals. One thing that is certain, however, is that any boat approaching the tower is turned away by a mysterious tide, and even the strongest rowers will break their backs before coming within a hundred yards of the circular reefs that ring it... unless the Wizards wish them to make landfall.

GLOSSARY

Baymourn Bridge: Ancient and normally non-utilized dueling bridge that connects the city to the Sun Arm of the southwest breakwater island in the bay.

Champurrado: A thick, hot drink made with milk, masa harina, chocolate, and anise, usually served in colorfully glazed cups.

Coins: Silver Coatl is the most common coin in the city, followed by standard coppers and then the Gold Jaguar [and that reflects the wealth of the Gold Jaguar District, as well as the Gold Jaguar Ulama Ball team, which is to say the wealthy aren't always the most imaginative people]

Death's Kiss: A crimson flower that grows deep in the Black Swamp and is deadly beyond measure if distilled and consumed by that intelligent races of the world. They are so deadly, in fact, that rumor has it that while still on the vine, the flowers can emit dark magic that will strike a living soul dead an arm's length from the blossom.

Ebon Swamp: Also called the 'Black Swamp', this is the massive corrupted delta that surrounds the city of Taux which eventually gives way to uncharted rainforest to the east and the Lowl plains to the north.

Golden Jaguar District: The highest class district in the city of Taux.

Gold Monkey: The highest class eatery in the Black Gate, situated just across Circle Street from the Emerald Serpent.

Hairyfist Spider: Tarantula-like spiders that frequent the dark friezes of the cities walls and often prey on birds.

Hospitaler's Guild: A league of physicians and petty healing priests mostly dedicated to Saint Amanda, although all faiths are welcome as healers inside the various guild halls and clinics.

Haunted Temple District: Also known as the 'Ghost Quarters', 'Pauper's Quarter' and 'Ghost Towers', this is a section of the city where the most downtrodden live. It is located on the western side of the city.

Moon Isle: This is the twin island to the Sun Isle, also called the Moon Arm, and it shields the eastern side of the city harbor.

Nightmen Guild: The thieves' guild of Taux

Razor Duelist Guild: The renowned duelist's guild in the city. Although open dueling is illegal, this guild moonlights as a secondary police force and also hires out as a mercenary force for the wealthy of the city.

Red Pillar: A ruling council of mostly secret, wealthy, and powerful men and women who control the government of Taux. They few of the council who let the city known their position walk around with crimson scarves about their neck, the most notable of these being Tlacolotl Vash.

Ruby Lane: The great road that leads through the Golden Jaguar District and ends at the gates of the Black Gate District.

Sepak Ball: A game much like real world Hacky Sack

Serpent's Head: A game much like modern badminton, with a feathered cock and open palms.

The Shining Sea: The great reach of the sea stretching out from the sheltered bay of Taux, and is part of the larger Halo Ocean.

Sons of the Moon: A local street gang that has been growing in power and has territory in Haunted Temple District.

Smoke Dragon District: The industrial quarter of the city where the bulk of the workforce goes each day via canal barges.

The Silver Circle: The main oval street that runs the full circumference of the Black Gate's inner floor.

Sun Isle: This is the old ceremonial island that is often referred to as an 'arm' as it shields the western side of the harbor.

Tolimic Empire: The fallen and cursed society that created Taux and was destroyed by the dark magic apocalypse.

Ullamalitzli: A Tolimic game set between two, four man, teams, that utilizes a heavy rubber ball called a Ulama. The purpose is to get the ball inside an open stone hole set high in a kind of goal on each side of a sunken field of play. Notable professional teams within the city include the Black Gate Snakes and the Gold Jaguar Jaguars [coached by Gamemaster Ixchel a Human female].

Waynside Bridge: Ancient and normally unused bridge that connects the city to the Moon's Arm island that surrounds half of the bay. Beneath this bridge, Jai-Ruk longshoremen sleep in hammocks to avoid fees from local dives while still staying close to their work.

Whispering Shoals: The shoreline of the Moon Isle that surrounds northeast section of the bay, also known for its Jai-Ruk squatters and breakwater that often gets valuable flotsam from the deep ocean.

Zimbolay: A city the lies far across the ocean to the south of Taux and resides among the fabled cities of the Opal Gates. Zimbolay is not the largest of these coastal city-states, Ulandm holding that honor, but it is known for producing the most tome mages in the southern hemisphere.

Cast of Characters

Balthazar Della Nova: Male Human dueling partner of Shay Gatewell of the Silk Purse, Balthazar is often the calm rational voice of reason to the brazen young Shay, although technically only two years his elder.

Esmeralda Serata: A young female Human duelist and former noble, she has attained the silver badge of a 2nd degree duelist in the Razor's Guild of Taux and is always looking to learn new techniques with the blade.

Emil Lacosta & Mariella: Emil is a Human tome mage practitioner and maker of potions from the dark coasts of Zimbolay who has taken Mariella, as seventeen year-old Human female, as his apprentice in all matters of magical elixirs, including his trademark love potions.

Fynn & Analyse: Eldaryn street performers and petty rogues with a trained monkey inside the Black Gate.

Increase Coin: Male of Zimbolay, Human with various scars about his deeply black face. He is a bodyguard, and sometimes cutpurse who is often employed as a guide to the Black Gate by outsiders with plenty of coin.

Oswald Burgunzi: One of the three richest men in Taux, and fat beyond measure. His family is only pressed for full mercantile control by the Vash and Dharn clans respectively, although the Dharn family's power is waning after several recent deaths including that of their patriarch.

Quilan: The tavernkeeper at the Emerald Serpent

Shayla Gatewell: Twin to Shay Gatewell and daughter to Mama Serene of the Silk Purse, Shayla is a Human female and devout worshiper of Saint Amanda as well as a practiced surgeon and member of the Hospitaler's Guild.

Serene Gatewell: Known as 'Mama Serene' this Human woman is the madam of the infamous Silk Purse, the finest brothel in the Black Gate, and arguably all of Taux. She is also one of the Red Pillars, a secret ruling council of twelve that makes most of the decisions concerning the running of the city of Taux.

Tlacolotl Vash: The patriarch of the wealthiest family on Taux, the Vash Clan. His family employees commonly wear black livery while 'off duty' and black and gold when serving the family in public.

Xavier Craine: A Human and former duelist of the Ebontra Cross style, he is now the sole teacher of the craft of swordplay inside the Black Gate District.

www.ingramcontent.com/pod-product-compliance
Lightning Source LLC
Chambersburg PA
CBHW071104250626
47159CB00002B/590